Stories of the
Napoleonic Age

Stories of the Napoleonic Age

Uncle Bernac
★
The Great Shadow
★
and Three Short Stories

Sir Arthur Conan Doyle

LEONAUR

Stories of the Napoleonic Age
Uncle Bernac, The Great Shadow and Three Short Stories
by Sir Arthur Conan Doyle

Leonaur is an imprint of Oakpast Ltd

Material original to this edition and
presentation of text in this form
copyright © 2009 Oakpast Ltd

ISBN: 978-1-84677-788-2 (hardcover)
ISBN: 978-1-84677-787-5 (softcover)

http://www.leonaur.com

Publisher's Notes

The views expressed in this book are not necessarily
those of the publisher.

Contents

Uncle Bernac	7
The Great Shadow	169
Three Short Stories	279
A Foreign Office Romance	281
A Straggler of '15	292
The "Slapping Sal"	307
My Napoleonic Library	319

Uncle Bernac

CHAPTER 1

The Coast of France

I dare say that I had already read my uncle's letter a hundred times, and I am sure that I knew it by heart. None the less I took it out of my pocket, and, sitting on the side of the lugger, I went over it again with as much attention as if it were for the first time. It was written in a prim, angular hand, such as one might expect from a man who had begun life as a village attorney, and it was addressed to Louis de Laval, to the care of William Hargreaves, of the Green Man in Ashford, Kent. The landlord had many a hogshead of untaxed French brandy from the Normandy coast, and the letter had found its way by the same hands.

My Dear Nephew Louis,' said the letter, *now that your father is dead, and that you are alone in the world, I am sure that you will not wish to carry on the feud which has existed between the two halves of the family. At the time of the troubles your father was drawn towards the side of the King, and I towards that of the people, and it ended, as you know, by his having to fly from the country, and by my becoming the possessor of the estates of Grosbois. No doubt it is very hard that you should find yourself in a different position to your ancestors, but I am sure that you would rather that the land should be held by a Bernac than by a stranger. From the brother of your mother you will at least always meet with sympathy and consideration.*

And now I have some advice for you. You know that I have always been a Republican, but it has become evident to me that there is no use in fighting against fate, and that Napoleon's power is far too great to be shaken. This being so, I have tried to serve him, for it is well to howl when you are among wolves. I have been able to do so much for him that he has become my very good friend, so that I may ask him what I like in return. He is now, as you are probably aware, with the army at Boulogne, within a few miles of Grosbois. If you will come over at once he will certainly forget the hostility of your father in consideration of the services of your uncle. It is true that your name is still proscribed, but my influence with the Emperor will set that matter right. Come to me, then, come at once, and come with confidence.

Your uncle

C. Bernac

So much for the letter, but it was the outside which had puzzled me most. A seal of red wax had been affixed at either end, and my uncle had apparently used his thumb as a signet. One could see the little rippling edges of a coarse skin imprinted upon the wax. And then above one of the seals there was written in English the two words, 'Don't come.' It was hastily scrawled, and whether by a man or a woman it was impossible to say; but there it stared me in the face, that sinister addition to an invitation.

'Don't come!' Had it been added by this unknown uncle of mine on account of some sudden change in his plans? Surely that was inconceivable, for why in that case should he send the invitation at all? Or was it placed there by some one else who wished to warn me from accepting this offer of hospitality? The letter was in French. The warning was in English. Could it have been added in England? But the seals were unbroken, and how could any one in England know what were the contents of the letter?

And then, as I sat there with the big sail humming like a shell above my head and the green water hissing beside me, I thought over all that I had heard of this uncle of mine. My father, the descendant of one of the proudest and oldest families in France, had chosen beauty and virtue rather than rank in his wife. Never for an hour had she given him cause to regret it; but this lawyer brother of hers had, as I understood, offended my father by his slavish obsequiousness in days of prosperity and his venomous enmity in the days of trouble. He had hounded on the peasants until my family had been compelled to fly from the country, and had afterwards aided Robespierre in his worst excesses, receiving as a reward the castle and estate of Grosbois, which was our own. At the fall of Robespierre he had succeeded in conciliating Barras, and through every successive change he still managed to gain a fresh tenure of the property. Now it appeared from his letter that the new Emperor of France had also taken his part, though why he should befriend a man with such a history, and what service my Republican uncle could possibly render to him, were matters upon which I could form no opinion.

And now you will ask me, no doubt, why I should accept the invitation of such a man—a man whom my father had always stigmatised as a usurper and a traitor. It is easier to speak of it now than then, but the fact was that we of the new generation felt it very irksome and difficult to carry on the bitter quarrels of the last. To the older *emigres* the clock of time seemed to have stopped in the year 1792, and they remained for ever with the loves and the hatreds of that era fixed indelibly upon their souls. They had been burned into them by the fiery furnace through which they had passed. But we, who had grown up upon a strange soil, understood that the world had moved, and that new issues had arisen. We were inclined to forget these feuds of the last generation. France to us was no longer the murderous land of the *sans-culotte* and the guillotine basket; it was rather the glorious queen of war, attacked by all and conquering all, but still so hard pressed that her scattered sons could hear her call to arms for ever sounding in their ears. It was that call more than my uncle's letter which was taking me over the waters of the Channel.

For long my heart had been with my country in her struggle, and yet while my father lived I had never dared to say so; for to him, who had served under Conde and fought at Quiberon, it would have seemed the blackest treason. But after his death there was no reason why I should not return to the land of my birth, and my desire was the stronger because Eugenie—the same Eugenie who has been thirty years my wife—was of the same way of thinking as myself. Her parents were a branch of the de Choiseuls, and their prejudices were even stronger than those of my father. Little did they think what was passing in the minds of their children. Many a time when they were mourning a French victory in the parlour we were both capering with joy in the garden. There was a little window, all choked round with laurel bushes, in the corner of the bare brick house, and there we used to meet at night, the dearer to each other from our difference with all who surrounded us. I would tell her my ambitions; she would strengthen them by her enthusiasm. And so all was ready when the time came.

But there was another reason besides the death of my father and the receipt of this letter from my uncle. Ashford was becoming too hot to hold me. I will say this for the English, that they were very generous hosts to the French emigrants. There was not one of us who did not carry away a kindly remembrance of the land and its people. But in every country there are overbearing, swaggering folk, and even in quiet, sleepy Ashford we were plagued by them. There was one young Kentish squire, Farley was his name, who had earned a reputation in the town as a bully and a roisterer. He could not meet one of us without uttering insults not merely against the present French Government, which might have been excusable in an English patriot, but against France itself and all Frenchmen. Often we were forced to be deaf in his presence, but at last his conduct became so intolerable that I determined to teach him a lesson. There were several of us in the coffee-room at the Green Man one evening, and he, full of wine and malice, was heaping insults upon the French, his eyes creeping round to me every moment to see how I was taking it. 'Now, Monsieur de Laval,' he cried, putting his rude hand upon my shoulder, 'here is a toast for you to drink. This is to the arm of Nelson which strikes down the French.' He stood leering at me to see if I would drink it. 'Well, sir,' said I, 'I will drink your toast if you will drink mine in return.' 'Come on, then!' said he. So we drank. 'Now, monsieur, let us have your toast,' said he. 'Fill your glass, then,' said I. 'It is full now.' 'Well, then, here's to the cannon-ball which carried off that arm!' In an instant I had a glass of port wine running down my face, and within an hour a meeting had been arranged. I shot him through the shoulder, and that night, when I came to the little window, Eugenie plucked off some of the laurel leaves and stuck them in my hair.

There were no legal proceedings about the duel, but it made my position a little difficult in the town, and it will explain, with other things, why I had no hesitation in accepting my unknown uncle's invitation, in spite of the singular addition which I found upon the cover. If he had indeed sufficient influence with the Emperor to remove the proscription which was attached to our name, then the only barrier which shut me off from my country would be demolished.

You must picture me all this time as sitting upon the side of the lugger and turning my prospects and my position over in my head. My reverie was interrupted by the heavy hand of the English skipper dropping abruptly upon my arm.

'Now then, master,' said he, it's time you were stepping into the dingy.'

I do not inherit the politics of the aristocrats, but I have never lost their sense of personal dignity. I gently pushed away his polluting hand, and I remarked that we were still a long way from the shore.

'Well, you can do as you please,' said he roughly; 'I'm going no nearer, so you can take your choice of getting into the dingy or of swimming for it.'

It was in vain that I pleaded that he had been paid his price. I did not add that that price meant that the watch which had belonged to three generations of de Lavals was now lying in the shop of a Dover goldsmith.

'Little enough, too!' he cried harshly. 'Down sail, Jim, and bring her to! Now, master, you can step over the side, or you can come back to Dover, but I don't take the Vixen a cable's length nearer to Ambleteuse Beef with this gale coming up from the sou'-west.'

'In that case I shall go,' said I.

'You can lay your life on that!' he answered, and laughed in so irritating a fashion that I half turned upon him with the intention of chastising him. One is very helpless with these fellows, however, for a serious affair is of course out of the question, while if one uses a cane upon them they have a vile habit of striking with their hands, which gives them an advantage. The Marquis de Chamfort told me that, when he first settled in Sutton at the time of the emigration, he lost a tooth when reproving an unruly peasant. I made the best of a necessity, therefore, and, shrugging my shoulders, I passed over the side of the lugger into the little boat. My bundle was dropped in after me—conceive to yourself the heir of all the de Lavals travelling with a single bundle for his baggage!—and two seamen pushed her off, pulling with long slow strokes towards the low-lying shore.

There was certainly every promise of a wild night, for the dark cloud which had rolled up over the setting sun was now frayed and ragged at the edges, extending a good third of the way across the heavens. It had split low down near the horizon, and the crimson glare of the sunset beat through the gap, so that there was the appearance of fire with a monstrous reek of smoke. A red dancing belt of light lay across the broad slate-coloured ocean, and in the centre of it the little black craft was wallowing and tumbling. The two seamen kept looking up at the heavens, and then over their shoulders at the land, and I feared every moment that they would put back before the gale burst. I was filled with apprehension every time when the end of their pull turned their faces skyward, and it was to draw their attention away from the storm-drift that I asked them what the lights were which had begun to twinkle through the dusk both to the right and to the left of us.

'That's Boulogne to the north, and Etaples upon the south,' said one of the seamen civilly.

Boulogne! Etaples! How the words came back to me! It was to Boulogne that in my boyhood we had gone down for the summer bathing. Could I not remember as a little lad trotting along by my father's side as he paced the beach, and wondering why every fisherman's cap flew off at our approach? And as to Etaples, it was thence that we had fled for England, when the folks came raving to the pier-head as we passed, and I joined my thin voice to my father's as he shrieked back at them, for a stone had broken my mother's knee, and we were all frenzied with our fear and our hatred. And here they were, these places of my childhood, twinkling to the north and south of me, while there, in the darkness between them, and only ten miles off at the furthest, lay my own castle, my own land of Grosbois, where the men of my blood had lived and died long before some of us had gone across with Duke William to conquer the proud island over the water. How I strained my eager eyes through the darkness as I thought that the distant black keep of our fortalice might even now be visible!

'Yes, sir,' said the seaman, ''tis a fine stretch of lonesome coast, and many is the cock of your hackle that I have helped ashore there.'

'What do you take me for, then?' I asked.

'Well, 'tis no business of mine, sir,' he answered. 'There are some trades that had best not even be spoken about.'

'You think that I am a conspirator?'

'Well, master, since you have put a name to it. Lor' love you, sir, we're used to it.'

'I give you my word that I am none.'

'An escaped prisoner, then?'

'No, nor that either.'

The man leaned upon his oar, and I could see in the gloom that his face was thrust forward, and that it was wrinkled with suspicion.

'If you're one of Boney's spies—' he cried.

'I! A spy!' The tone of my voice was enough to convince him.

'Well,' said he,' I'm darned if I know what you are. But if you'd been a spy I'd ha' had no hand in landing you, whatever the skipper might say.'

'Mind you, I've no word to say against Boney,' said the other seaman, speaking in a very thick rumbling voice. 'He's been a rare good friend to the poor mariner.'

It surprised me to hear him speak so, for the virulence of feeling against the new French Emperor in England exceeded all belief, and high and low were united in their hatred of him; but the sailor soon gave me a clue to his politics.

'If the poor mariner can run in his little bit of coffee and sugar, and run out his silk and his brandy, he has Boney to thank for it,' said he. 'The merchants have had their spell, and now it's the turn of the poor mariner.'

I remembered then that Buonaparte was personally very popular amongst the smugglers, as well he might be, seeing that he had made over into their hands all the trade of the Channel. The seaman continued to pull with his left hand, but he pointed with his right over the slate-coloured dancing waters.

'There's Boney himself,' said he.

You who live in a quieter age cannot conceive the thrill which these simple words sent through me. It was but ten years since we had first heard of this man with the curious Italian name—think of it, ten years, the time that it takes for a private to become a non-commissioned officer, or a clerk to win a fifty-pound advance in his salary. He had sprung in an instant out of nothing into everything. One month people were asking who he was, the next he had broken out in the north of Italy like the plague; Venice and Genoa withered at the touch of this swarthy ill-nourished boy. He cowed the soldiers in the field, and he outwitted the statesmen in the council chamber. With a frenzy of energy he rushed to the east, and then, while men were still marvelling at the way in which he had converted Egypt into a French department, he was back again in Italy and had beaten Austria for the second time to the earth. He travelled as quickly as the rumour of his coming; and where he came there were new victories, new combinations, the crackling of old systems and the blurring of ancient lines of frontier. Holland, Savoy, Switzerland—they were become mere names upon the map. France was eating into Europe in every direction. They had made him Emperor, this beardless artillery officer, and without an effort he had crushed down those Republicans before whom the oldest king and the proudest nobility of Europe had been helpless. So it came about that we, who watched him dart from place to place like the shuttle of destiny, and who heard his name always in connection with some new achievement and some new success, had come at last to look upon him as something more than human, something monstrous, overshadowing France and menacing Europe. His giant presence loomed over the continent, and so deep was the impression which his fame had made in my mind that, when the English sailor pointed confidently over the darkening waters, and cried 'There's Boney!' I looked up for the instant with a foolish expectation of seeing some gigantic figure, some elemental creature, dark, inchoate, and threatening, brooding over the waters of the Channel. Even now, after the long gap of years and the knowledge of his downfall, that great man casts his spell upon you, but all that you read and all that you hear cannot give you an idea of what his name meant in the days when he was at the summit of his career.

What actually met my eye was very different from this childish expectation of mine. To the north there was a long low cape, the name of which has now escaped me. In the evening light it had been of the same greyish green tint as the other headlands; but now, as the darkness fell, it gradually broke into a dull glow, like a cooling iron. On that wild night, seen and lost with the heave and sweep of the boat, this lurid streak carried with it a vague but sinister suggestion. The red line splitting the darkness might have been a giant half-forged sword-blade with its point towards England.

'What is it, then?' I asked.

'Just what I say, master,' said he. 'It's one of Boney's armies, with Boney himself in the middle of it as like as not. Them is their camp fires, and you'll see a dozen such between this and Ostend. He's audacious enough to come across, is little Boney, if he could dowse Lord Nelson's other eye; but there's no chance for him until then, and well he knows it.'

'How can Lord Nelson know what he is doing?' I asked.

The man pointed out over my shoulder into the darkness, and far on the horizon I perceived three little twinkling lights.

'Watch dog,' said he, in his husky voice.

'Andromeda. Forty-four,' added his companion.

I have often thought of them since, the long glow upon the land, and the three little lights upon the sea, standing for so much, for the two great rivals face to face, for the power of the land and the power of the water, for the centuries-old battle, which may last for centuries to come. And yet, Frenchman as I am, do I not know that the struggle is already decided?—for it lies between the childless nation and that which has a lusty young brood springing up around her. If France falls she dies, but if England falls how many nations are there who will carry her speech, her traditions and her blood on into the history of the future?

The land had been looming darker, and the thudding of waves upon the sand sounded louder every instant upon my ears. I could already see the quick dancing gleam of the surf in front of me. Suddenly, as I peered through the deepening shadow, a long dark boat shot out from it, like a trout from under a stone, making straight in our direction.

'A guard boat!' cried one of the seamen.

'Bill, boy, we're done!' said the other, and began to stuff something into his sea boot.

But the boat swerved at the sight of us, like a shying horse, and was off in another direction as fast as eight frantic oars could drive her. The seamen stared after her and wiped their brows. 'Her conscience don't seem much easier than our own,' said one of them. 'I made sure it was the preventives.'

'Looks to me as if you weren't the only queer cargo on the coast tonight, mister,' remarked his comrade. 'What could she be?'

'Cursed if I know what she was. I rammed a cake of good Trinidad tobacco into my boot when I saw her. I've seen the inside of a French prison before now. Give way, Bill, and have it over.'

A minute later, with a low grating sound, we ran aground upon a gravelly leach. My bundle was thrown ashore, I stepped after it, and a seaman pushed the prow off again, springing in as his comrade backed her into deep water. Already the glow in the west had vanished, the storm-cloud was half up the heavens, and a thick blackness had gathered over the ocean. As I turned to watch the vanishing boat a keen wet blast flapped in my face, and the air was filled with the high piping of the wind and with the deep thunder of the sea.

And thus it was that, on a wild evening in the early spring of the year 1805, I, Louis de Laval, being in the twenty-first year of my age, returned, after an exile of thirteen years, to the country of which my family had for many centuries been the ornament and support. She had treated us badly, this country; she had repaid our services by insult, exile, and confiscation. But all that was forgotten as I, the only de Laval of the new generation, dropped upon my knees upon her sacred soil, and, with the strong smell of the seaweed in my nostrils, pressed my lips upon the wet and pringling gravel.

CHAPTER 2

The Salt-Marsh

When a man has reached his mature age he can rest at that point of vantage, and cast his eyes back at the long road along which he has travelled, lying with its gleams of sunshine and its stretches of shadow in the valley behind him. He knows then its whence and its whither, and the twists and bends which were so full of promise or of menace as he approached them lie exposed and open to his gaze. So plain is it all that he can scarce remember how dark it may have seemed to him, or how long he once hesitated at the cross roads. Thus when he tries to recall each stage of the journey he does so with the knowledge of its end, and can no longer make it clear, even to himself, how it may have seemed to him at the time. And yet, in spite of the strain of years, and the many passages which have befallen me since, there is no time of my life which comes back so very clearly as that gusty evening, and to this day I cannot feel the briny wholesome whiff of the seaweed without being carried back, with that intimate feeling of reality which only the sense of smell can confer, to the wet shingle of the French beach.

When I had risen from my knees, the first thing that I did was to put my purse into the inner pocket of my coat. I had taken it out in order to give a gold piece to the sailor who had handed me ashore, though I have little doubt that the fellow was both wealthier and of more assured prospects than myself. I had actually drawn out a silver half-crown, but I could not bring myself to offer it to him, and so ended by giving a tenth part of my whole fortune to a stranger. The other nine sovereigns I put very carefully away, and then, sitting down upon a flat rock just above high water mark, I turned it all over in my mind and weighed what I should do. Already I was cold and hungry, with the wind lashing my face and the spray smarting in my eyes, but at least I was no longer living upon the charity of the enemies of my country, and the thought set my heart dancing within me. But the castle, as well as I could remember, was a good ten miles off. To go there now was to arrive at an unseemly hour, unkempt and weather-stained, before this uncle whom I had never seen. My sensitive pride conjured up a picture of the scornful faces of his servants as they looked out upon this bedraggled wanderer from England slinking back to the castle which should have been his own. No, I must seek shelter for the night, and then at my leisure, with as fair a show of appearances as possible, I must present myself before my relative. Where then could I find a refuge from the storm?

You will ask me, doubtless, why I did not make for Etaples or Boulogne. I answer that it was for the same reason which forced me to land secretly upon that forbidding coast. The name of de Laval still headed the list of the proscribed, for my father had been a famous and energetic leader of the small but influential body of men who had remained true at all costs to the old order of things. Do not think that, because I was of another way of thinking, I despised those who had given up so much for their principles. There is a curious saint-like trait in our natures which draws us most strongly towards that which involves the greatest sacrifice, and I have sometimes thought that if the conditions had been less onerous the Bourbons might have had fewer, or at least less noble, followers. The French nobles had been more faithful to them than the English to the Stuarts, for Cromwell had no luxurious court or rich appointments which he could hold out to those who would desert the royal cause. No words can exaggerate the self-abnegation of those men. I have seen a supper party under my father's roof where our guests were two fencing-masters, three professors of language, one ornamental gardener, and one translator of books, who held his hand in the front of his coat to conceal a rent in the lapel. But these eight men were of the highest nobility of France, who might have had what they chose to ask if they would only consent to forget the past, and to throw themselves heartily into the new order of things. But the humble, and what is sadder the incapable, monarch of Hartwell still held the allegiance of those old Montmorencies, Rohans, and Choiseuls, who, having shared the greatness of his family, were determined also to stand by it in its ruin. The dark chambers of that exiled monarch were furnished with something better than the tapestry of Gobelins or the china of Sevres. Across the gulf which separates my old age from theirs I can still see those ill-clad, grave-mannered men, and I raise my hat to the noblest group of nobles that our history can show.

To visit a coast-town, therefore, before I had seen my uncle, or learnt whether my return had been sanctioned, would be simply to deliver myself into the hands of the *gens d'armes,* who were ever on the look-out for strangers from England. To go before the new Emperor was one thing and to be dragged before him another. On the whole, it seemed to me that my best course was to wander inland, in the hope of finding some empty barn or out-house, where I could pass the night unseen and undisturbed. Then in the morning I should consider how it was best for me to approach my uncle Bernac, and through him the new master of France.

The wind had freshened meanwhile into a gale, and it was so dark upon the seaward side that I could only catch the white flash of a leaping wave here and there in the blackness. Of the lugger which had brought me from Dover I could see no sign. On the land side of me there seemed, as far as I could make it out, to be a line of low hills, but when I came to traverse them I found that the dim light had exaggerated their size, and that they were mere scattered sand-dunes, mottled with patches of bramble. Over these I toiled with my bundle slung over my shoulder, plodding heavily through the loose sand, and tripping over the creepers, but forgetting my wet clothes and my numb hands as I recalled the many hardships and adventures which my ancestors had undergone. It amused me to think that the day might come when my own descendants might fortify themselves by the recollection of that which was happening to me, for in a great family like ours the individual is always subordinate to the race.

It seemed to me that I should never get to the end of the sand-dunes, but when at last I did come off them I heartily wished that I was back upon them again; for the sea in that part comes by some creek up the back of the beach, forming at low tide a great desolate salt-marsh, which must be a forlorn place even in the daytime, but upon such a night as that it was a most dreary wilderness. At first it was but a softness of the ground, causing me to slip as I walked, but soon the mud was over my ankles and half-way up to my knees, so that each foot gave a loud flop as I raised it, and a dull splash as I set it down again. I would willingly have made my way out, even if I had to return to the sand-dunes, but in trying to pick my path I had lost all my bearings, and the air was so full of the sounds of the storm that the sea seemed to be on every side of me. I had heard of how one may steer oneself by observation of the stars, but my quiet English life had not taught me how such things were done, and had I known I could scarcely have profited by it, since the few stars which were visible peeped out here and there in the rifts of the flying storm-clouds. I wandered on then, wet and weary, trusting to fortune, but always blundering deeper and deeper into this horrible bog, until I began to think that my first night in France was destined also to be my last, and that the heir of the de Lavals was destined to perish of cold and misery in the depths of this obscene morass.

I must have toiled for many miles in this dreary fashion, sometimes coming upon shallower mud and sometimes upon deeper, but never making my way on to the dry, when I perceived through the gloom something which turned my heart even heavier than it had been before. This was a curious clump of some whitish shrub—cotton-grass of a flowering variety—which glimmered suddenly before me in the darkness. Now, an hour earlier I had passed just such a square-headed, whitish clump; so that I was confirmed in the opinion which I had already begun to form, that I was wandering in a circle. To make it certain I stooped down, striking a momentary flash from my tinder-box, and there sure enough was my own old track very clearly marked in the brown mud in front of me. At this confirmation of my worst fears I threw my eyes up to heaven in my despair, and there I saw something which for the first time gave me a clue in the uncertainty which surrounded me.

It was nothing else than a glimpse of the moon between two flowing clouds. This in itself might have been of small avail to me, but over its white face was marked a long thin V, which shot swiftly across like a shaftless arrow. It was a flock of wild ducks, and its flight was in the same direction as that towards which my face was turned. Now, I had observed in Kent how all these creatures come further inland when there is rough weather breaking, so I made no doubt that their course indicated the path which would lead me away from the sea. I struggled on, therefore, taking every precaution to walk in a straight line, above all being very careful to make a stride of equal length with either leg, until at last, after half an hour or so, my perseverance was rewarded by the welcome sight of a little yellow light, as from a cottage window, glimmering through the darkness. Ah, how it shone through my eyes and down into my heart, glowing and twinkling there, that little golden speck, which meant food, and rest, and life itself to the wanderer! I blundered towards it through the mud and the slush as fast as my weary legs would bear me. I was too cold and miserable to refuse any shelter, and I had no doubt that for the sake of one of my gold pieces the fisherman or peasant who lived in this strange situation would shut his eyes to whatever might be suspicious in my presence or appearance.

As I approached it became more and more wonderful to me that any one should live there at all, for the bog grew worse rather than better, and in the occasional gleams of moonshine I could make out that the water lay in glimmering pools all round the low dark cottage from which the light was breaking. I could see now that it shone through a small square window. As I approached the gleam was suddenly obscured, and there in a yellow frame appeared the round black outline of a man's head peering out into the darkness. A second time it appeared before I reached the cottage, and there was something in the stealthy manner in which it peeped and whisked away, and peeped once more, which filled me with surprise, and with a certain vague apprehension.

So cautious were the movements of this sentinel, and so singular the position of his watch-house, that I determined, in spite of my misery, to see something more of him before I trusted myself to the shelter of his roof. And, indeed, the amount of shelter which I might hope for was not very great, for as I drew softly nearer I could see that the light from within was beating through at several points, and that the whole cottage was in the most crazy state of disrepair. For a moment I paused, thinking that even the salt-marsh might perhaps be a safer resting-place for the night than the headquarters of some desperate smuggler, for such I conjectured that this lonely dwelling must be. The scud, however, had covered the moon once more, and the darkness was so pitchy black that I felt that I might reconnoitre a little more closely without fear of discovery. Walking on tiptoe I approached the little window and looked in.

What I saw reassured me vastly. A small wood fire was crackling in one of those old-fashioned country grates, and beside it was seated a strikingly handsome young man, who was reading earnestly out of a fat little book. He had an oval, olive-tinted face, with long black hair, ungathered in a queue, and there was something of the poet or of the artist in his whole appearance. The sight of that refined face, and of the warm yellow firelight which beat upon it, was a very cheering one to a cold and famished traveller. I stood for an instant gazing at him, and noticing the way in which his full and somewhat loose-fitting lower lip quivered continually, as if he were repeating to himself that which he was reading. I was still looking at him when he put his book down upon the table and approached the window. Catching a glimpse of my figure in the darkness he called out something which I could not hear, and waved his hand in a gesture of welcome. An instant later the door flew open, and there was his thin tall figure standing upon the threshold, with his skirts flapping in the wind.

'My dear friends,' he cried, peering out into the gloom with his hand over his eyes to screen them from the salt-laden wind and driving sand, 'I had given you up. I thought that you were never coming. I've been waiting for two hours.'

For answer I stepped out in front of him, so that the light fell upon my face.

'I am afraid, sir—' said I.

But I had no time to finish my sentence. He struck at me with both hands like an angry cat, and, springing back into the room, he slammed the door with a crash in my face.

The swiftness of his movements and the malignity of his gesture were in such singular contrast with his appearance that I was struck speechless with surprise. But as I stood there with the door in front of me I was a witness to something which filled me with even greater astonishment.

I have already said that the cottage was in the last stage of disrepair. Amidst the many seams and cracks through which the light was breaking there was one along the whole of the hinge side of the door, which gave me from where I was standing a view of the further end of the room, at which the fire was burning. As I gazed then I saw this man reappear in front of the fire, fumbling furiously with both his hands in his bosom, and then with a spring he disappeared up the chimney, so that I could only see his shoes and half of his black calves as he stood upon the brickwork at the side of the grate. In an instant he was down again and back at the door.

'Who are you?' he cried, in a voice which seemed to me to be thrilling with some strong emotion.

'I am a traveller, and have lost my way.' There was a pause as if he were thinking what course he should pursue.

'You will find little here to tempt you to stay,' said he at last.

'I am weary and spent, sir; and surely you will not refuse me shelter. I have been wandering for hours in the salt-marsh.'

'Did you meet anyone there?' he asked eagerly.

'No.'

'Stand back a little from the door. This is a wild place, and the times are troublous. A man must take some precautions.'

I took a few steps back, and he then opened the door sufficiently to allow his head to come through. He said nothing, but he looked at me for a long time in a very searching manner.

'What is your name?'

'Louis Laval,' said I, thinking that it might sound less dangerous in this plebeian form.

'Whither are you going?'

'I wish to reach some shelter.'

'You are from England?'

'I am from the coast.'

He shook his head slowly to show me how little my replies had satisfied him.

'You cannot come in here,' said he.

'But surely—'

'No, no, it is impossible.'

'Show me then how to find my way out of the marsh.'

'It is easy enough. If you go a few hundred paces in that direction you will perceive the lights of a village. You are already almost free of the marsh.'

He stepped a pace or two from the door in order to point the way for me, and then turned upon his heel. I had already taken a stride or two away from him and his inhospitable hut, when he suddenly called after me.

'Come, Monsieur Laval,' said he, with quite a different ring in his voice; 'I really cannot permit you to leave me upon so tempestuous a night. A warm by my fire and a glass of brandy will hearten you upon your way.'

You may think that I did not feel disposed to contradict him, though I could make nothing of this sudden and welcome change in his manner.

'I am much obliged to you, sir,' said I.

And I followed him into the hut.

CHAPTER 3

The Ruined Cottage

It was delightful to see the glow and twinkle of the fire and to escape from the wet wind and the numbing cold, but my curiosity had already risen so high about this lonely man and his singular dwelling that my thoughts ran rather upon that than upon my personal comfort. There was his remarkable appearance, the fact that he should be awaiting company within that miserable ruin in the heart of the morass at so sinister an hour, and finally the inexplicable incident of the chimney, all of which excited my imagination. It was beyond my comprehension why he should at one moment charge me sternly to continue my journey, and then, in almost the same breath, invite me most cordially to seek the shelter of his hut. On all these points I was keenly on the alert for an explanation. Yet I endeavoured to conceal my feelings, and to assume the air of a man who finds everything quite natural about him, and who is much too absorbed in his own personal wants to have a thought to spare upon anything outside himself.

A glance at the inside of the cottage, as I entered, confirmed me in the conjecture which the appearance of the outside had already given rise to, that it was not used for human residence, and that this man was only here for a rendezvous. Prolonged moisture had peeled the plaster in flakes from the walls, and had covered the stones with blotches and rosettes of lichen. The whole place was rotten and scaling like a leper. The single large room was unfurnished save for a crazy table, three wooden boxes, which might be used as seats, and a great pile of decayed fishing-net in the corner. The splinters of a fourth box, with a hand-axe, which leaned against the wall, showed how the wood for the fire had been gathered. But it was to the table that my gaze was chiefly drawn, for there, beside the lamp and the book, lay an open basket, from which projected the knuckle-end of a ham, the corner of a loaf of bread, and the black neck of a bottle.

If my host had been suspicious and cold at our first meeting he was now atoning for his inhospitality by an overdone cordiality even harder for me to explain. With many lamentations over my mud-stained and sodden condition, he drew a box close to the blaze and cut me off a corner of the bread and ham. I could not help observing, however, that though his loose under-lipped mouth was wreathed with smiles, his beautiful dark eyes were continually running over me and my attire, asking and re-asking what my business might be.

'As for myself,' said he, with an air of false candour, 'you will very well understand that in these days a worthy merchant must do the best he can to get his wares, and if the Emperor, God save him, sees fit in his wisdom to put an end to open trade, one must come to such places as these to get into touch with those who bring across the coffee and the tobacco. I promise you that in the Tuileries itself there is no difficulty about getting either one or the other, and the Emperor drinks his ten cups a day of the real Mocha without asking questions, though he must know that it is not grown within the confines of France. The vegetable kingdom still remains one of the few which Napoleon has not yet conquered, and, if it were not for traders, who are at some risk and inconvenience, it is hard to say what we should do for our supplies. I suppose, sir, that you are not yourself either in the seafaring or in the trading line?'

I contented myself by answering that I was not, by which reticence I could see that I only excited his curiosity the more. As to his account of himself, I read a lie in those tell-tale eyes all the time that he was talking. As I looked at him now in the full light of the lamp and the fire, I could see that he was even more good-looking than I had at first thought, but with a type of beauty which has never been to my taste. His features were so refined as to be almost effeminate, and so regular that they would have been perfect if it had not been for that ill-fitting, slabbing mouth. It was a clever, and yet it was a weak face, full of a sort of fickle enthusiasm and feeble impulsiveness. I felt that the more I knew him the less reason I should probably find either to like him or to fear him, and in my first conclusion I was right, although I had occasion to change my views upon the second.

'You will forgive me, Monsieur Laval, if I was a little cold at first,' said he. 'Since the Emperor has been upon the coast the place swarms with police agents, so that a trader must look to his own interests. You will allow that my fears of you were not unnatural, since neither your dress nor your appearance were such as one would expect to meet with in such a place and at such a time.'

It was on my lips to return the remark, but I refrained.

'I can assure you,' said I, 'that I am merely a traveller who have lost my way. Now that I am refreshed and rested I will not encroach further upon your hospitality, except to ask you to point out the way to the nearest village.'

'Tut; you had best stay where you are, for the night grows wilder every instant.' As he spoke there came a whoop and scream of wind in the chimney, as if the old place were coming down about our ears. He walked across to the window and looked very earnestly out of it, just as I had seen him do upon my first approach. 'The fact is, Monsieur Laval,' said he, looking round at me with his false-air of good fellowship, 'you may be of some good service to me if you will wait here for half an hour or so.'

'How so?' I asked, wavering between my distrust and my curiosity.

'Well, to be frank with you'—and never did a man look less frank as he spoke—'I am waiting here for some of those people with whom I do business; but in some way they have not come yet, and I am inclined to take a walk round the marsh on the chance of finding them, if they have lost their way. On the other hand, it would be exceedingly awkward for me if they were to come here in my absence and imagine that I am gone. I should take it as a favour, then, if you would remain here for half an hour or so, that you may tell them how matters stand if I should chance to miss them.'

The request seemed reasonable enough, and yet there was that same oblique glance which told me that it was false. Still, I could not see what harm could come to me by complying with his request, and certainly I could not have devised any arrangement which would give me such an opportunity of satisfying my curiosity. What was in that wide stone chimney, and why had he clambered up there upon the sight of me? My adventure would be inconclusive indeed if I did not settle that point before I went on with my journey.

'Well,' said he, snatching up his black broad-brimmed hat and running very briskly to the door, 'I am sure that you will not refuse me my request, and I must delay no longer or I shall never get my business finished.' He closed the door hurriedly behind him, and I heard the splashing of his foot-steps until they were lost in the howling of the gale.

And so the mysterious cottage was mine to ransack if I could pluck its secrets from it. I lifted the book which had been left upon the table. It was Rousseau's *Social Contract*—excellent literature, but hardly what one would expect a trader to carry with him whilst awaiting an appointment with smugglers. On the fly-leaf was written 'Lucien Lesage,' and beneath it, in a woman's hand, 'Lucien, from Sibylle.' Lesage, then, was the name of my good-looking but sinister acquaintance. It only remained for me now to discover what it was which he had concealed up the chimney. I listened intently, and as there was no sound from without save the cry of the storm, I stepped on to the edge of the grate as I had seen him do, and sprang up by the side of the fire.

It was a very broad, old-fashioned cottage chimney, so that standing on one side I was not inconvenienced either by the heat or by the smoke, and the bright glare from below showed me in an instant that for which I sought. There was a recess at the back, caused by the fall or removal of one of the stones, and in this was lying a small bundle. There could not be the least doubt that it was this which the fellow had striven so frantically

31

to conceal upon the first alarm of the approach of a stranger. I took it down and held it to the light. It was a small square of yellow glazed cloth tied round with white tape. Upon my opening it a number of letters appeared, and a single large paper folded up. The addresses upon the letters took my breath away. The first that I glanced at was to Citizen Talleyrand. The others were in the Republican style addressed to Citizen Fouche, to Citizen Soult, to Citizen MacDonald, to Citizen Berthier, and so on through the whole list of famous names in war and in diplomacy who were the pillars of the new Empire. What in the world could this pretended merchant of coffee have to write to all these great notables about? The other paper would explain, no doubt. I laid the letters upon the shelf and I unfolded the paper which had been enclosed with them. It did not take more than the opening sentence to convince me that the salt-marsh outside might prove to be a very much safer place than this accursed cottage.

These were the words which met my eyes:

> Fellow-citizens of France. The deed of today has proved that, even in the midst of his troops, a tyrant is unable to escape the vengeance of an outraged people. The committee of three, acting temporarily for the Republic, has awarded to Buonaparte the same fate which has already befallen Louis Capet. In avenging the outrage of the 18th Brumaire—

So far I had got when my heart sprang suddenly into my mouth and the paper fluttered down from my fingers. A grip of iron had closed suddenly round each of my ankles, and there in the light of the fire I saw two hands which, even in that terrified glance, I perceived to be covered with black hair and of an enormous size.

'So, my friend,' cried a thundering voice, 'this time, at least, we have been too many for you.'

Chapter 4

Men of the Night

I had little time given me to realise the extraordinary and humiliating position in which I found myself, for I was lifted up by my ankles, as if I were a fowl pulled off a perch, and jerked roughly down into the room, my back striking upon the stone floor with a thud which shook the breath from my body.

'Don't kill him yet, Toussac,' said a soft voice. 'Let us make sure who he is first.'

I felt the pressure of a thumb upon my chin and of fingers upon my throat, and my head was slowly forced round until the strain became unbearable.

'Quarter of an inch does it and no mark,' said the thunderous voice. 'You can trust my old turn.'

'Don't, Toussac; don't!' said the same gentle voice which had spoken first. 'I saw you do it once before, and the horrible snick that it made haunted me for a long time. To think that the sacred flame of life can be so readily snuffed out by that great material finger and thumb! Mind can indeed conquer matter, but the fighting must not be at close quarters.'

My neck was so twisted that I could not see any of these people who were discussing my fate. I could only lie and listen.

'The fact remains, my dear Charles, that the fellow has our all-important secret, and that it is our lives or his.

'I recognised in the voice which was now speaking that of the man of the cottage.

'We owe it to ourselves to put it out of his power to harm us. Let him sit up, Toussac, for there is no possibility of his escaping.'

Some irresistible force at the back of my neck dragged me instantly into a sitting position, and so for the first time I was able to look round me in a dazed fashion, and to see these men into whose hands I had fallen. That they were murderers in the past and had murderous plans for the future I already gathered from what I had heard and seen. I understood also that in the heart of that lonely marsh I was absolutely in their power. None the less, I remembered the name that I bore, and I concealed as far as I could the sickening terror which lay at my heart.

There were three of them in the room, my former acquaintance and two new comers. Lesage stood by the table, with his fat brown book in his hand, looking at me with a composed face, but with that humorous questioning twinkle in his eyes which a master chess-player might assume when he had left his opponent without a move. On the top of the box beside him sat a very ascetic-faced, yellow, hollow-eyed man of fifty, with prim lips and a shrunken skin, which hung loosely over the long jerking tendons under his prominent chin. He was dressed in snuff-coloured clothes, and his legs under his knee-breeches were of a ludicrous thinness. He shook his head at me with an air of sad wisdom, and I could read little comfort in his inhuman grey eyes. But it was the man called Toussac who alarmed me most. He was a colossus; bulky rather than tall, but misshapen from his excess of muscle. His huge legs were crooked like those of a great ape; and, indeed, there was something animal about his whole appearance, something for he was bearded up to his eyes, and it was a paw rather than a hand which still clutched me by the collar. As to his expression, he was too thatched with hair to show one, but his large black eyes looked with a sinister questioning from me to the others. If they were the judge and jury, it was clear who was to be executioner.

'Whence did he come? What is his business? How came he to know the hiding-place?' asked the thin man.

'When he first came I mistook him for you in the darkness,' Lesage answered. 'You will acknowledge that it was not a night on which one would expect to meet many people in the salt-marsh. On discovering my mistake I shut the door and concealed the papers in the chimney. I had forgotten that he might see me do this through that crack by the hinges, but when I went out again, to show him his way and so get rid of him, my eye caught the gap, and I at once realised that he had seen my action, and that it must have aroused his curiosity to such an extent that it would be quite certain that he would think and speak of it. I called him back into the hut, therefore, in order that I might have time to consider what I had best do with him.'

'*Sapristi!* a couple of cuts of that wood-axe, and a bed in the softest corner of the marsh, would have settled the business at once,' said the fellow by my side.

'Quite true, my good Toussac; but it is not usual to lead off with your ace of trumps. A little delicacy—a little finesse—'

'Let us hear what you did then?'

'It was my first object to learn whether this man Laval—'

'What did you say his name was?' cried the thin man.

'His name, according to his account, is Laval. My first object then was to find out whether he had in truth seen me conceal the papers or not. It was an important question for us, and, as things have turned out, more important still for him. I made my little plan, therefore. I waited until I saw you approach, and I then left him alone in the hut. I watched through the window and saw him fly to the hiding-place. We then entered, and I asked you, Toussac, to be good enough to lift him down—and there he lies.'

The young fellow looked proudly round for the applause of his comrades, and the thin man clapped his hands softly together, looking very hard at me while he did so.

'My dear Lesage,' said he, 'you have certainly excelled yourself. When our new republic looks for its minister of police we shall know where to find him. I confess that when, after guiding Toussac to this shelter, I followed you in and perceived a gentleman's legs projecting from the fireplace, even my wits, which are usually none of the slowest, hardly grasped the situation. Toussac, however, grasped the legs. He is always practical, the good Toussac.'

'Enough words!' growled the hairy creature beside me. 'It is because we have talked instead of acting that this Buonaparte has a crown upon his head or a head upon his shoulders. Let us have done with the fellow and come to business.'

The refined features of Lesage made me look towards him as to a possible protector, but his large dark eyes were as cold and hard as jet as he looked back at me.

'What Toussac says is right,' said he. 'We imperil our own safety if he goes with our secret.'

'The devil take our own safety!' cried Toussac. 'What has that to do with the matter? We imperil the success of our plans—that is of more importance.'

'The two things go together,' replied Lesage. 'There is no doubt that Rule 13 of our confederation defines exactly what should be done in such a case. Any responsibility must rest with the passers of Rule 13.'

My heart had turned cold when this man with his poet's face supported the savage at my side. But my hopes were raised again when the thin man, who had said little hitherto, though he had continued to stare at me very intently, began now to show some signs of alarm at the bloodthirsty proposals of his comrades.

'My dear Lucien,' said he, in a soothing voice, laying his hand upon the young man's arm, 'we philosophers and reasoners must have a respect for human life. The tabernacle is not to be lightly violated. We have frequently agreed that if it were not for the excesses of Marat—'

'I have every respect for your opinion, Charles,' the other interrupted. 'You will allow that I have always been a willing and obedient disciple. But I again say that our personal safety is involved, and that, as far as I see, there is no middle course. No one could be more averse from cruelty than I am, but you were present with me some months ago when Toussac silenced the man from Bow Street, and certainly it was done with such dexterity that the process was probably more painful to the spectators than to the victim. He could not have been aware of the horrible sound which announced his own dissolution. If you and I had constancy enough to endure this—and if I remember right it was chiefly at your instigation that the deed was done—then surely on this more vital occasion—'

'No, no, Toussac, stop!' cried the thin man, his voice rising from its soft tones to a perfect scream as the giant's hairy hand gripped me by the chin once more. 'I appeal to you, Lucien, upon practical as well as upon moral grounds, not to let this deed be done. Consider that if things should go against us this will cut us off from all hopes of mercy. Consider also—'

This argument seemed for a moment to stagger the younger man, whose olive complexion had turned a shade greyer.

'There will be no hope for us in any case, Charles,' said he. 'We have no choice but to obey Rule 13.'

'Some latitude is allowed to us. We are ourselves upon the inner committee.'

'But it takes a quorum to change a rule, and we have no powers to do it.' His pendulous lip was quivering, but there was no softening in his eyes. Slowly under the pressure of those cruel fingers my chin began to sweep round to my shoulder, and I commended my soul to the Virgin and to Saint Ignatius, who has always been the especial patron of my family. But this man Charles, who had already befriended me, darted forwards and began to tear at Toussac's hands with a vehemence which was very different from his former philosophic calm.

'You *shall* not kill him!' he cried angrily.

'Who are you, to set your wills up against mine? Let him go, Toussac! Take your thumb from his chin! I won't have it done, I tell you!' Then, as he saw by the inflexible faces of his companions that blustering would not help him, he turned suddenly to tones of entreaty. 'See, now! I'll make you a promise!' said he. 'Listen to me, Lucien! Let me examine him! If he is a police spy he shall die! You may have him then, Toussac. But if he is only a harmless traveller, who has blundered in here by an evil chance, and who has been led by a foolish curiosity to inquire into our business, then you will leave him to me.'

You will observe that from the beginning of this affair I had never once opened my mouth, nor said a word in my defence, which made me mightily pleased with myself afterwards, though my silence came rather from pride than from courage. To lose life and self-respect together was more than I could face. But now, at this appeal from my advocate, I turned my eyes from the monster who held me to the other who condemned me. The brutality of the one alarmed me less than the self-interested attitude of the other, for a man is never so dangerous as when he is afraid, and of all judges the judge who has cause to fear you is the most inflexible.

My life depended upon the answer which was to come to the appeal of my champion. Lesage tapped his fingers upon his teeth, and smiled indulgently at the earnestness of his companion.

'Rule 13! Rule 13!' he kept repeating, in that exasperating voice of his.

'I will take all responsibility.'

'I'll tell you what, mister,' said Toussac, in his savage voice. 'There's another rule besides Rule 13, and that's the one that says that if any man shelters an offender he shall be treated as if he was himself guilty of the offence.'

This attack did not shake the serenity of my champion in the least.

'You are an excellent man of action, Toussac,' said he calmly; 'but when it comes to choosing the right course, you must leave it to wiser heads than your own.'

His air of tranquil superiority seemed to daunt the fierce creature who held me. He shrugged his huge shoulders in silent dissent.

'As to you, Lucien,' my friend continued, 'I am surprised, considering the position to which you aspire in my family, that you should for an instant stand in the way of any wish which I may express. If you have grasped the true principles of liberty, and if you are privileged to be one of the small band who have never despaired of the republic, to whom is it that you owe it?'

'Yes, yes, Charles; I acknowledge what you say,' the young man answered, with much agitation. 'I am sure that I should be the last to oppose any wish which you might express, but in this case I fear lest your tenderness of heart may be leading you astray. By all means ask him any questions that you like; but it seems to me that there can be only one end to the matter.'

So I thought also; for, with the full secret of these desperate men in my possession, what hope was there that they would ever suffer me to leave the hut alive? And yet, so sweet is human life, and so dear a respite, be it ever so short a one, that when that murderous hand was taken from my chin I heard a sudden chiming of little bells, and the lamp blazed up into a strange fantastic blur. It was but for a moment, and then my mind was clear again, and I was looking up at the strange gaunt face of my examiner.

'Whence have you come?' he asked.

'From England.'

'But you are French?'

'Yes.'

'When did you arrive?'

'Tonight.'

'How?'

'In a lugger from Dover.'

'The fellow is speaking the truth,' growled Toussac. 'Yes, I'll say that for him, that he is speaking the truth. We saw the lugger, and someone was landed from it just after the boat that brought me over pushed off.'

I remembered that boat, which had been the first thing which I had seen upon the coast of France. How little I had thought what it would mean to me!

And now my advocate began asking questions—vague, useless questions—in a slow, hesitating fashion which set Toussac grumbling. This cross-examination appeared to me to be a useless farce; and yet there was a certain eagerness and intensity in my questioner's manner which gave me the assurance that he had some end in view. Was it merely that he wished to gain time? Time for what? And then, suddenly, with that quick perception which comes upon those whose nerves are strained by an extremity of danger, I became convinced that he really was awaiting something—that he was tense with expectation. I read it upon his drawn face, upon his sidelong head with his ear scooped into his hand, above all in his twitching, restless eyes. He expected an interruption, and he was talking, talking, talking, in order to gain time for it. I was as sure of it as if he had whispered his secret in my ear, and down in my numb, cold heart a warm little spring of hope began to bubble and run.

But Toussac had chafed at all this word-fencing, and now with an oath he broke in upon our dialogue.

'I have had enough of this!' he cried. 'It is not for child's play of this sort that I risked my head in coming over here. Have we nothing better to talk about than this fellow? Do you suppose I came from London to listen to your fine phrases? Have done with it, I say, and get to business.'

'Very good,' said my champion. 'There's an excellent little cupboard here which makes as fine a prison as one could wish for. Let us put him in here, and pass on to business. We can deal with him when we have finished.'

'And have him overhear all that we say,' said Lesage.

'I don't know what the devil has come over you,' cried Toussac, turning suspicious eyes upon my protector. 'I never knew you squeamish before, and certainly you were not backward in the affair of the man from Bow Street. This fellow has our secret, and he must either die, or we shall see him at our trial. What is the sense of arranging a plot, and then at the last moment turning a man loose who will ruin us all? Let us snap his neck and have done with it.'

The great hairy hands were stretched towards me again, but Lesage had sprung suddenly to his feet. His face had turned very white, and he stood listening with his forefinger up and his head slanted. It was a long, thin, delicate hand, and it was quivering like a leaf in the wind.

'I heard something,' he whispered.

'And I,' said the older man.

'What was it?'

'Silence. Listen!'

For a minute or more we all stayed with straining ears while the wind still whimpered in the chimney or rattled the crazy window.

'It was nothing,' said Lesage at last, with a nervous laugh. 'The storm makes curious sounds sometimes.'

'I heard nothing,' said Toussac.

'Hush!' cried the other. 'There it is again!'

A clear rising cry floated high above the wailing of the storm; a wild, musical cry, beginning on a low note, and thrilling swiftly up to a keen, sharp-edged howl.

'A hound!'

'They are following us!'

Lesage dashed to the fireplace, and I saw him thrust his papers into the blaze and grind them down with his heel.

Toussac seized the wood-axe which leaned against the wall. The thin man dragged the pile of decayed netting from the corner, and opened a small wooden screen, which shut off a low recess.

'In here,' he whispered, 'quick!'

And then, as I scrambled into my refuge, I heard him say to the others that I would be safe there, and that they could lay their hands upon me when they wished.

Chapter 5

The Law

The cupboard—for it was little more—into which I had been hurried was low and narrow, and I felt in the darkness that it was heaped with peculiar round wickerwork baskets, the nature of which I could by no means imagine, although I discovered afterwards that they were lobster traps. The only light which entered was through the cracks of the old broken door, but these were so wide and numerous that I could see the whole of the room which I had just quitted. Sick and faint, with the shadow of death still clouding my wits, I was none the less fascinated by the scene which lay before me.

My thin friend, with the same prim composure upon his emaciated face, had seated himself again upon the box. With his hands clasped round one of his knees he was rocking slowly backwards and forwards; and I noticed, in the lamplight, that his jaw muscles were contracting rhythmically, like the gills of a fish. Beside him stood Lesage, his white face glistening with moisture and his loose lip quivering with fear. Every now and then he would make a vigorous attempt to compose his features, but after each rally a fresh wave of terror would sweep everything before it, and set him shaking once more. As to Toussac, he stood before the fire, a magnificent figure, with the axe held down by his leg, and his head thrown back in defiance, so that his great black beard bristled straight out in front of him. He said not a word, but every fibre of his body was braced for a struggle. Then, as the howl of the hound rose louder and clearer from the marsh outside, he ran forward and threw open the door.

'No, no, keep the dog out!' cried Lesage in an agony of apprehension.

'You fool, our only chance is to kill it.'

'But it is in leash.'

'If it is in leash nothing can save us. But if, as I think, it is running free, then we may escape yet.'

Lesage cowered up against the table, with his agonised eyes fixed upon the blue-black square of the door. The man who had befriended me still swayed his body about with a singular half-smile upon his face. His skinny hand was twitching at the frill of his shirt, and I conjectured that he held some weapon concealed there. Toussac stood between them and the open door, and, much as I feared and loathed him, I could not take my eyes from his gallant figure. As to myself, I was so much occupied by the singular drama before me, and by the impending fate of those three men of the cottage, that all thought of my own fortunes had passed completely out of my mind. On this mean stage a terrible all-absorbing drama was being played, and I, crouching in a squalid recess, was to be the sole spectator of it. I could but hold my breath and wait and watch.

And suddenly I became conscious that they could all three see something which was invisible to me. I read it from their tense faces and their staring eyes. Toussac swung his axe over his shoulder and poised himself for a blow. Lesage cowered away and put one hand between his eyes and the open door. The other ceased swinging his spindle legs and sat like a little brown image upon the edge of his box. There was a moist pattering of feet, a yellow streak shot through the doorway, and Toussac lashed at it as I have seen an English cricketer strike at a ball. His aim was true, for he buried the head of the hatchet in the creature's throat, but the force of his blow shattered his weapon, and the weight of the hound carried him backwards on to the floor. Over they rolled and over, the hairy man and the hairy dog, growling and worrying in a bestial combat. He was fumbling at the animal's throat, and I could not see what he was doing, until it gave a sudden sharp yelp of pain, and there was a rending sound like the tearing of canvas. The man staggered up with his hands dripping, and the tawny mass with the blotch of crimson lay motionless upon the floor.

'Now!' cried Toussac in a voice of thunder, 'now!' and he rushed from the hut.

Lesage had shrunk away into the corner in a frenzy of fear whilst Toussac had been killing the hound, but now he raised his agonised face, which was as wet as if he had dipped it into a basin.

'Yes, yes,' he cried; 'we must fly, Charles. The hound has left the police behind, and we may still escape.'

But the other, with the same imperturbable face, motionless save for the rhythm of his jaw muscles, walked quietly over and closed the door upon the inside.

'I think, friend Lucien,' said he in his quiet voice, 'that you had best stay where you are.'

Lesage looked at him with amazement gradually replacing terror upon his pallid features.

'But you do not understand, Charles,' he cried.

'Oh, yes, I think I do,' said the other, smiling.

'They may be here in a few minutes. The hound has slipped its leash, you see, and has left them behind in the marsh; but they are sure to come here, for there is no other cottage but this.'

'They are sure to come here.'

'Well, then, let us fly. In the darkness we may yet escape.'

'No; we shall stay where we are.'

'Madman, you may sacrifice your own life, but not mine. Stay if you wish, but for my part I am going.'

He ran towards the door with a foolish, helpless flapping of his hands, but the other sprang in front of him with so determined a gesture of authority that the younger man staggered back from it as from a blow.

'You fool!' said his companion. 'You poor miserable dupe!'

Lesage's mouth opened, and he stood staring with his knees bent and his spread-fingered hands up, the most hideous picture of fear that I have ever seen.

'You, Charles, you!' he stammered, hawking up each word.

'Yes, me,' said the other, smiling grimly.

'A police agent all the time! You who were the very soul of our society! You who were in our inmost council! You who led us on! Oh, Charles, you have not the heart! I think I hear them coming, Charles. Let me pass; I beg and implore you to let me pass.'

The granite face shook slowly from side to side.

'But why me? Why not Toussac?'

'If the dog had crippled Toussac, why then I might have had you both. But friend Toussac is rather vigorous for a thin little fellow like me. No, no, my good Lucien, you are destined to be the trophy of my bow and my spear, and you must reconcile yourself to the fact.'

Lesage slapped his forehead as if to assure himself that he was not dreaming.

'A police agent!' he repeated, 'Charles a police agent!'

'I thought it would surprise you.'

'But you were the most republican of us all. We were none of us advanced enough for you. How often have we gathered round you, Charles, to listen to your philosophy! And there is Sibylle, too! Don't tell me that Sibylle was a police spy also. But you are joking, Charles. Say that you are joking!'

The man relaxed his grim features, and his eyes puckered with amusement.

'Your astonishment is very flattering,' said he. 'I confess that I thought that I played my part rather cleverly. It is not my fault that these bunglers unleashed their hound, but at least I shall have the credit of having made a single-handed capture of one very desperate and dangerous conspirator.' He smiled drily at this description of his prisoner. 'The Emperor knows how to reward his friends,' he added, 'and also how to punish his enemies.'

All this time he had held his hand in his bosom, and now he drew it out so far as to show the brass gleam of a pistol butt.

'It is no use,' said he, in answer to some look in the other's eye. 'You stay in the hut, alive or dead.'

Lesage put his hands to his face and began to cry with loud, helpless sobbings.

'Why, you have been worse than any of us, Charles,' he moaned. 'It was you who told Toussac to kill the man from Bow

45

Street, and it was you also who set fire to the house in the Rue Basse de la Rampart. And now you turn on us!'

'I did that because I wished to be the one to throw light upon it all—and at the proper moment.'

'That is very fine, Charles, but what will be thought about that when I make it all public in my own defence? How can you explain all that to your Emperor? There is still time to prevent my telling all that I know about you.'

'Well, really, I think that you are right, my friend,' said the other, drawing out his pistol and cocking it. 'Perhaps I *did* go a little beyond my instructions in one or two points, and, as you very properly remark, there is still time to set it right. It is a matter of detail whether I give you up living or give you up dead, and I think that, on the whole, it had better be dead.'

It had been horrible to see Toussac tear the throat out of the hound, but it had not made my flesh creep as it crept now. Pity was mingled with my disgust for this unfortunate young man, who had been fitted by Nature for the life of a retired student or of a dreaming poet, but who had been dragged by stronger wills than his own into a part which no child could be more incapable of playing. I forgave him the trick by which he had caught me and the selfish fears to which he had been willing to sacrifice me. He had flung himself down upon the ground, and floundered about in a convulsion of terror, whilst his terrible little companion, with his cynical smile, stood over him with his pistol in his hand. He played with the helpless panting coward as a cat might with a mouse; but I read in his inexorable eyes that it was no jest, and his finger seemed to be already tightening upon his trigger. Full of horror at so cold-blooded a murder, I pushed open my crazy cupboard, and had rushed out to plead for the victim, when there came a buzz of voices and a clanking of steel from without. With a stentorian shout of 'In the name of the Emperor!' a single violent wrench tore the door of the hut from its hinges.

It was still blowing hard, and through the open doorway I could see a thick cluster of mounted men, with plumes slanted and mantles flapping, the rain shining upon their shoulders. At the side the light from the hut struck upon the heads of two beautiful horses, and upon the heavy red-toupeed busbies of the hussars who stood at their heads. In the doorway stood another hussar—a man of high rank, as could be seen from the richness of his dress and the distinction of his bearing. He was booted to the knees, with a uniform of light blue and silver, which his tall, slim, light-cavalry figure suited to a marvel. I could not but admire the way in which he carried himself, for he never deigned to draw the sword which shone at his side, but he stood in the doorway glancing round the blood-bespattered hut, and staring at its occupants with a very cool and alert expression. He had a handsome face, pale and clear-cut, with a bristling moustache, which cut across the brass chin-chain of his busby.

'Well,' said he, 'well?'

The older man had put his pistol back into the breast of his brown coat.

'This is Lucien Lesage,' said he.

The hussar looked with disgust at the prostrate figure upon the floor.

'A pretty conspirator!' said he. 'Get up, you grovelling hound! Here, Gerard, take charge of him and bring him into camp.'

A younger officer with two troopers at his heels came clanking in to the hut, and the wretched creature, half swooning, was dragged out into the darkness.

'Where is the other—the man called Toussac?'

'He killed the hound and escaped. Lesage would have got away also had I not prevented him. If you had kept the dog in leash we should have had them both, but as it is, Colonel Lasalle, I think that you may congratulate me.' He held out his hand as he spoke, but the other turned abruptly on his heel.

'You hear that, General Savary?' said he, looking out of the door. 'Toussac has escaped.'

A tall, dark young man appeared within the circle of light cast by the lamp. The agitation of his handsome swarthy face showed the effect which the news had upon him.

'Where is he then?'

'It is a quarter of an hour since he got away.'

'But he is the only dangerous man of them all. The Emperor will be furious. In which direction did he fly?'

'It must have been inland.'

'But who is this?' asked General Savary, pointing at me. 'I understood from your information that there were only two besides yourself, Monsieur—.'

'I had rather no names were mentioned,' said the other abruptly.

'I can well understand that,' General Savary answered with a sneer.

'I would have told you that the cottage was the rendezvous, but it was not decided upon until the last moment. I gave you the means of tracking Toussac, but you let the hound slip. I certainly think that you will have to answer to the Emperor for the way in which you have managed the business.'

'That, sir, is our affair,' said General Savary sternly. 'In the meantime you have not told us who this person is.'

It seemed useless for me to conceal my identity, since I had a letter in my pocket which would reveal it.

'My name is Louis de Laval,' said I proudly.

I may confess that I think we had exaggerated our own importance over in England. We had thought that all France was wondering whether we should return, whereas in the quick march of events France had really almost forgotten our existence. This young General Savary was not in the least impressed by my aristocratic name, but he jotted it down in his notebook.

'Monsieur de Laval has nothing whatever to do with the matter,' said the spy. 'He has blundered into it entirely by chance, and I will answer for his safe keeping in case he should be wanted.'

'He will certainly be wanted,' said General Savary. 'In the meantime I need every trooper that I have for the chase, so, if you make yourself personally responsible, and bring him to the camp when needed, I see no objection to his remaining in your keeping. I shall send to you if I require him.'

'He will be at the Emperor's orders.'

'Are there any papers in the cottage?'

'They have been burned.'

'That is unfortunate.'

'But I have duplicates.'

'Excellent! Come, Lasalle, every minute counts, and there is nothing to be done here. Let the men scatter, and we may still ride him down.'

The two tall soldiers clanked out of the cottage without taking any further notice of my companion, and I heard the sharp stern order and the jingling of metal as the troopers sprang back into their saddles once more. An instant later they were off, and I listened to the dull beat of their hoofs dying rapidly into a confused murmur. My little snuff-coloured champion went to the door of the hut and peered after them through the darkness. Then he came back and looked me up and down, with his usual dry sardonic smile.

'Well, young man,' said he, 'we have played some pretty *tableaux vivants* for your amusement, and you can thank me for that nice seat in the front row of the parterre.'

'I am under a very deep obligation to you, sir,' I answered, struggling between my gratitude and my aversion. 'I hardly know how to thank you.'

He looked at me with a singular expression in his ironical eyes.

'You will have the opportunity for thanking me later,' said he. 'In the meantime, as you say that you are a stranger upon our coast, and as I am responsible for your safe keeping, you cannot do better than follow me, and I will take you to a place where you may sleep in safety.'

CHAPTER 6

The Secret Passage

The fire had already smouldered down, and my companion blew out the lamp, so that we had not taken ten paces before we had lost sight of the ill-omened cottage, in which I had received so singular a welcome upon my home-coming. The wind had softened down, but a fine rain, cold and clammy, came drifting up from the sea. Had I been left to myself I should have found myself as much at a loss as I had been when I first landed; but my companion walked with a brisk and assured step, so that it was evident that he guided himself by landmarks which were invisible to me. For my part, wet and miserable, with my forlorn bundle under my arm, and my nerves all jangled by my terrible experiences, I trudged in silence by his side, turning over in my mind all that had occurred to me. Young as I was, I had heard much political discussion amongst my elders in England, and the state of affairs in France was perfectly familiar to me. I was aware that the recent elevation of Buonaparte to the throne had enraged the small but formidable section of Jacobins and extreme Republicans, who saw that all their efforts to abolish a kingdom had only ended in transforming it into an empire. It was, indeed, a pitiable result of their frenzied strivings that a crown with eight *fleurs-de-lis* should be changed into a higher crown surmounted by a cross and ball. On the other hand, the followers of the Bourbons, in whose company I had spent my youth, were equally disappointed at the manner in which the mass of the French people hailed this final step in the return from chaos to order. Contradictory as were their motives, the more violent spirits of both parties were united in their hatred to Napoleon, and in their fierce determination to get rid of him by any means. Hence a series of conspiracies, most of them with their base in England; and hence also a large use of spies and informers upon the part of Fouche and of Savary, upon whom the responsibility of the safety of the Emperor lay. A strange chance had landed me upon the French coast at the very same time as a murderous conspirator, and had afterwards enabled me to see the weapons with which the police contrived to thwart and outwit him and his associates. When I looked back upon my series of adventures, my wanderings in the salt-marsh, my entrance into the cottage, my discovery of the papers, my capture by the conspirators, the long period of suspense with Toussac's dreadful thumb upon my chin, and finally the moving scenes which I had witnessed—the killing of the hound, the capture of Lesage, and the arrival of the soldiers—I could not wonder that my nerves were overwrought, and that I surprised myself in little convulsive gestures, like those of a frightened child.

The chief thought which now filled my mind was what my relations were with this dangerous man who walked by my side. His conduct and bearing had filled me with abhorrence. I had seen the depth of cunning with which he had duped and betrayed his companions, and I had read in his lean smiling face the cold deliberate cruelty of his nature, as he stood, pistol in hand, over the whimpering coward whom he had outwitted. Yet I could not deny that when, through my own foolish curiosity, I had placed myself in a most hopeless position, it was he who had braved the wrath of the formidable Toussac in order to extricate me. It was evident also that he might have made his achievement more striking by delivering up two prisoners instead of one to the troopers. It is true that I was not a conspirator, but I might have found it difficult to prove it. So inconsistent did such conduct seem in this little yellow flint-stone of a man that, after walking a mile or two in silence, I asked him suddenly what the meaning of it might be.

I heard a dry chuckle in the darkness, as if he were amused by the abruptness and directness of my question.

'You are a most amusing person, Monsieur—Monsieur—let me see, what did you say your name was?'

'De Laval.'

'Ah, quite so, Monsieur de Laval. You have the impetuosity and the ingenuousness of youth. You want to know what is up a chimney, you jump up the chimney. You want to know the reason of a thing, and you blurt out a question. I have been in the habit of living among people who keep their thoughts to themselves, and I find you very refreshing.'

'Whatever the motives of your conduct, there is no doubt that you saved my life,' said I. 'I am much obliged to you for your intercession.' It is the most difficult thing in the world to express gratitude to a person who fills you with abhorrence, and I fear that my halting speech was another instance of that ingenuousness of which he accused me.

'I can do without your thanks,' said he coldly. 'You are perfectly right when you think that if it had suited my purpose I should have let you perish, and I am perfectly right when I think that if it were not that you are under an obligation you would fail to see my hand if I stretched it out to you just as that overgrown puppy Lasalle did. It is very honourable, he thinks, to serve the Emperor upon the field of battle, and to risk life in his behalf, but when it comes to living amidst danger as I have done, consorting with desperate men, and knowing well that the least slip would mean death, why then one is beneath the notice of a fine clean-handed gentleman. Why,' he continued in a burst of bitter passion, 'I have dared more, and endured more, with Toussac and a few of his kidney for comrades, than this Lasalle has done in all the childish cavalry charges that ever he undertook. As to service, all his Marshals put together have not rendered the Emperor as pressing a service as I have done. But I daresay it does not strike you in that light, Monsieur—Monsieur—'

'De Laval.'

'Quite so—it is curious how that name escapes me. I daresay you take the same view as Colonel Lasalle?'

'It is not a question upon which I can offer an opinion,' said I. 'I only know that I owe my life to your intercession.'

I do not know what reply he might have made to this evasion, but at that moment we heard a couple of pistol shots and a distant shouting from far away in the darkness. We stopped for a few minutes, but all was silent once more.

'They must have caught sight of Toussac,' said my companion. 'I am afraid that he is too strong and too cunning to be taken by them. I do not know what impression he left upon you, but I can tell you that you will go far to meet a more dangerous man.'

I answered that I would go far to avoid meeting one, unless I had the means of defending myself, and my companion's dry chuckle showed that he appreciated my feelings.

'Yet he is an absolutely honest man, which is no very common thing in these days,' said he. 'He is one of those who, at the outbreak of the Revolution, embraced it with the whole strength of his simple nature. He believed what the writers and the speakers told him, and he was convinced that, after a little disturbance and a few necessary executions, France was to become a heaven upon earth, the centre of peace and comfort and brotherly love. A good many people got those fine ideas into their heads, but the heads have mostly dropped into the sawdust-basket by this time. Toussac was true to them, and when instead of peace he found war, instead of comfort a grinding poverty, and instead of equality an Empire, it drove him mad. He became the fierce creature you see, with the one idea of devoting his huge body and giant's strength to the destruction of those who had interfered with his ideal. He is fearless, persevering, and implacable. I have no doubt at all that he will kill me for the part that I have played tonight.'

It was in the calmest voice that my companion uttered the remark, and it made me understand that it was no boast when he said there was more courage needed to carry on his unsavoury trade than to play the part of a *beau sabreur* like Lasalle. He paused a little, and then went on as if speaking to himself.

'Yes,' said he, 'I missed my chance. I certainly ought to have shot him when he was struggling with the hound. But if I had only wounded him he would have torn me into bits like an over-boiled pullet, so perhaps it is as well as it is.'

We had left the salt-marsh behind us, and for some time I had felt the soft springy turf of the downland beneath my feet, and our path had risen and dipped over the curves of the low coast hills. In spite of the darkness my companion walked with great assurance, never hesitating for an instant, and keeping up a stiff pace which was welcome to me in my sodden and benumbed condition. I had been so young when I left my native place that it is doubtful whether, even in daylight, I should have recognised the countryside, but now in the darkness, half stupefied by my adventures, I could not form the least idea as to where we were or what we were making for. A certain recklessness had taken possession of me, and I cared little where I went as long as I could gain the rest and shelter of which I stood in need.

I do not know how long we had walked; I only know that I had dozed and woke and dozed again whilst still automatically keeping pace with my comrade, when I was at last aroused by his coming to a dead stop. The rain had ceased, and although the moon was still obscured, the heavens had cleared somewhat, and I could see for a little distance in every direction. A huge white basin gaped in front of us, and I made out that it was a deserted chalk quarry, with brambles and ferns growing thickly all round the edges. My companion, after a stealthy glance round to make sure that no one was observing us, picked his way amongst the scattered clumps of bushes until he reached the wall of chalk. This he skirted for some distance, squeezing between the cliff and the brambles until he came at last to a spot where all further progress appeared to be impossible.

'Can you see a light behind us?' asked my companion.

I turned round and looked carefully in every direction, but was unable to see one.

'Never mind,' said he. 'You go first, and I will follow.'

In some way during the instant that my back had been turned he had swung aside or plucked out the tangle of bush which had barred our way. When I turned there was a square dark opening in the white glimmering wall in front of us.

'It is small at the entrance, but it grows larger further in,' said he.

I hesitated for an instant. Whither was it that this strange man

54

was leading me? Did he live in a cave like a wild beast, or was this some trap into which he was luring me? The moon shone out at the instant, and in its silver light this black, silent porthole looked inexpressibly cheerless and menacing.

'You have gone rather far to turn back, my good friend,' said my companion. 'You must either trust me altogether or not trust me at all.'

'I am at your disposal.'

'Pass in then, and I shall follow.'

I crept into the narrow passage, which was so low that I had to crawl down it upon my hands and knees. Craning my neck round, I could see the black angular silhouette of my companion as he came after me. He paused at the entrance, and then, with a rustling of branches and snapping of twigs, the faint light was suddenly shut off from outside, and we were left in pitchy darkness. I heard the scraping of his knees as he crawled up behind me.

'Go on until you come to a step down,' said he. 'We shall have more room there, and we can strike a light.'

The ceiling was so low that by arching my back I could easily strike it, and my elbows touched the wall upon either side. In those days I was slim and lithe, however, so that I found no difficulty in making my way onwards until, at the end of a hundred paces, or it may have been a hundred and fifty, I felt with my hands that there was a dip in front of me. Down this I clambered, and was instantly conscious from the purer air that I was in some larger cavity. I heard the snapping of my companion's flint, and the red glow of the tinder paper leaped suddenly into the clear yellow flame of the taper. At first I could only see that stern, emaciated face, like some grotesque carving in walnut wood, with the ceaseless fishlike vibration of the muscles of his jaw. The light beat full upon it, and it stood strangely out with a dim halo round it in the darkness. Then he raised the taper and swept it slowly round at arm's length so as to illuminate the place in which we stood.

I found that we were in a subterranean tunnel, which appeared to extend into the bowels of the earth. It was so high that I could stand erect with ease, and the old lichen-blotched stones which lined the walls told of its great age. At the spot where we stood the ceiling had fallen in and the original passage been blocked, but a cutting had been made from this point through the chalk to form the narrow burrow along which we had come. This cutting appeared to be quite recent, for a mound of debris and some trenching tools were still lying in the passage. My companion, taper in hand, started off down the tunnel, and I followed at his heels, stepping over the great stones which had fallen from the roof or the walls, and now obstructed the path.

'Well,' said he, grinning at me over his shoulder, 'have you ever seen anything like this in England?'

'Never,' I answered.

'These are the precautions and devices which men adopted in rough days long ago. Now that rough days have come again, they are very useful to those who know of such places.'

'Whither does it lead, then?' I asked.

'To this,' said he, stopping before an old wooden door, powerfully clamped with iron. He fumbled with the metal-work, keeping himself between me and it, so that I could not see what he was doing. There was a sharp snick, and the door revolved slowly upon its hinges. Within there was a steep flight of time-worn steps leading upwards. He motioned me on, and closed the door behind us. At the head of the stair there was a second wooden gate, which he opened in a similar manner.

I had been dazed before ever I came into the chalk pit, but now, at this succession of incidents, I began to rub my eyes and ask myself whether this was young Louis de Laval, late of Ashford, in Kent, or whether it was some dream of the adventures of a hero of Pigault Lebrun. These massive moss-grown arches and mighty iron-clamped doors were, indeed, like the dim shadowy background of a vision; but the guttering taper, my sodden bundle, and all the sordid details of my disarranged toilet assured me only too clearly of their reality. Above all, the swift, brisk, business-like manner of my companion, and his occasional abrupt remarks, brought my fancies back to the ground once more. He held the door open for me now, and closed it again when I had passed through.

We found ourselves in a long vaulted corridor, with a stone-flagged floor, and a dim oil lamp burning at the further end. Two iron-barred windows showed that we had come above the earth's surface once more. Down this corridor we passed, and then through several passages and up a short winding stair. At the head of it was an open door, which led into a small but comfortable bedroom.

'I presume that this will satisfy your wants for tonight,' said he.

I asked for nothing better than to throw myself down, damp clothes and all, upon that snowy coverlet; but for the instant my curiosity overcame my fatigue.

'I am much indebted to you, sir,' said I. 'Perhaps you will add to your favours by letting me know where I am.'

'You are in my house, and that must suffice you for tonight. In the morning we shall go further into the matter.' He rang a small bell, and a gaunt shock-headed country man-servant came running at the call.

'Your mistress has retired, I suppose?'

'Yes, sir, a good two hours ago.'

'Very good. I shall call you myself in the morning.' He closed my door, and the echo of his steps seemed hardly to have died from my ears before I had sunk into that deep and dreamless sleep which only youth and fatigue can give.

Chapter 7

The Owner of Grosbois

My host was as good as his word, for, when a noise in my room awoke me in the morning, it was to find him standing by the side of my bed, so composed in his features and so drab in his attire, that it was hard to associate him with the stirring scenes of yesterday and with the repulsive part which he had played in them. Now in the fresh morning sunlight he presented rather the appearance of a pedantic schoolmaster, an impression which was increased by the masterful, and yet benevolent, smile with which he regarded me. In spite of his smile, I was more conscious than ever that my whole soul shrank from him, and that I should not be at my ease until I had broken this companionship which had been so involuntarily formed. He carried a heap of clothes over one arm, which he threw upon a chair at the bottom of my bed.

'I gather from the little that you told me last night,' said he, 'that your wardrobe is at present somewhat scanty. I fear that your inches are greater than those of anyone in my household, but I have brought a few things here amongst which you may find something to fit you. Here, too, are the razors, the soap, and the powder-box. I will return in half an hour, when your toilet will doubtless be completed.'

I found that my own clothes, with a little brushing, were as good as ever, but I availed myself of his offer to the extent of a ruffled shirt and a black satin cravat. I had finished dressing and was looking out of the window of my room, which opened on to a blank wall, when my host returned. He looked me all over with a keenly scrutinising eye, and appeared to be satisfied with what he saw.

'That will do! That will do very well indeed!' said he, nodding a critical head. 'In these times a slight indication of travel or hard work upon a costume is more fashionable than the foppishness of the Incroyable. I have heard ladies remark that it was in better taste. Now, sir, if you will kindly follow me.'

His solicitude about my dress filled me with surprise, but this was soon forgotten in the shock which was awaiting me. For as we passed down the passage and into a large hall which seemed strangely familiar to me, there was a full-length portrait of my father standing right in front of me. I stood staring with a gasp of astonishment, and turned to see the cold grey eyes of my companion fixed upon me with a humorous glitter.

'You seem surprised, Monsieur de Laval,' said he.

'For God's sake,' said I, 'do not trifle with me any further! Who are you, and what is this place to which you have taken me?'

For answer he broke into one of his dry chuckles, and, laying his skinny brown hand upon my wrist, he led me into a large apartment. In the centre was a table, tastefully laid, and beyond it in a low chair a young lady was seated, with a book in her hand. She rose as we entered, and I saw that she was tall and slender, with a dark face, pronounced features, and black eyes of extraordinary brilliancy. Even in that one glance it struck me that the expression with which she regarded me was by no means a friendly one.

'Sibylle,' said my host, and his words took the breath from my lips, 'this is your cousin from England, Louis de Laval. This, my dear nephew, is my only daughter, Sibylle Bernac.'

'Then you—'

'I am your mother's brother, Charles Bernac.'

'You are my Uncle Bernac!' I stammered at him like an idiot. 'But why did you not tell me so?' I cried.

'I was not sorry to have a chance of quietly observing what his English education had done for my nephew. It might also have been harder for me to stand your friend if my comrades had any reason to think that I was personally interested in you. But you will permit me now to welcome you heartily to France, and to express my regret if your reception has been a rough one. I am sure that Sibylle will help me to atone for it.' He smiled archly at his daughter, who continued to regard me with a stony face.

I looked round me, and gradually the spacious room, with the weapons upon the wall, and the deer's heads, came dimly back to my memory. That view through the oriel window, too, with the clump of oaks in the sloping park, and the sea in the distance beyond, I had certainly seen it before. It was true then, and I was in our own castle of Grosbois, and this dreadful man in the snuff-coloured coat, this sinister plotter with the death's-head face, was the man whom I had heard my poor father curse so often, the man who had ousted him from his own property and installed himself in his place. And yet I could not forget that it was he also who, at some risk to himself, had saved me the night before, and my soul was again torn between my gratitude and my repulsion.

We had seated ourselves at the table, and as we ate, this newly-found uncle of mine continued to explain all those points which I had failed to understand.

'I suspected that it was you the instant that I set eyes upon you,' said he. 'I am old enough to remember your father when he was a young gallant, and you are his very double—though I may say, without flattery, that where there is a difference it is in your favour. And yet he had the name of being one of the handsomest men betwixt Rouen and the sea. You must bear in mind that I was expecting you, and that there are not so many young aristocrats of your age wandering about along the coast. I was surprised when you did not recognise where you were last night. Had you never heard of the secret passage of Grosbois?'

It came vaguely back to me that in my childhood I had heard of this underground tunnel, but that the roof had fallen in and rendered it useless.

'Precisely,' said my uncle. 'When the castle passed into my hands, one of the very first things which I did was to cut a new opening at the end of it, for I foresaw that in these troublesome times it might be of use to me; indeed, had it been in repair it might have made the escape of your mother and father a very much easier affair.'

His words recalled all that I had heard and all that I could remember of those dreadful days when we, the Lords of the country side, had been chased across it as if we had been wolves, with the howling mob still clustering at the pier-head to shake their fists and hurl their stones at us. I remembered, too, that it was this very man who was speaking to me who had thrown oil upon the flames in those days, and whose fortunes had been founded upon our ruin. As I looked across at him I found that his keen grey eyes were fixed upon me, and I could see that he had read the thoughts in my mind.

'We must let bygones be bygones,' said he. 'Those are quarrels of the last generation, and Sibylle and you represent a new one.'

My cousin had not said one word or taken any notice of my presence, but at this joining of our names she glanced at me with the same hostile expression which I had already remarked.

'Come, Sibylle,' said her father, 'you can assure your cousin Louis that, so far as you are concerned, any family misunderstanding is at an end.'

'It is very well for us to talk in that way, father,' she answered. 'It is not your picture that hangs in the hall, or your coat-of-arms that I see upon the wall. We hold the castle and the land, but it is for the heir of the de Lavals to tell *us* if he is satisfied with this.' Her dark scornful eyes were fixed upon me as she waited for my reply, but her father hastened to intervene.

'This is not a very hospitable tone in which to greet your cousin,' said he harshly. 'It has so chanced that Louis' heritage has fallen to us, but it is not for us to remind him of the fact.'

'He needs no reminding,' said she.

'You do me an injustice,' I cried, for the evident and malignant scorn of this girl galled me to the quick. 'It is true that I cannot forget that this castle and these grounds belonged to my ancestors—I should be a clod indeed if I *could* forget it—but if you think that I harbour any bitterness, you are mistaken. For my own part, I ask nothing better than to open up a career for myself with my own sword.'

'And never was there a time when it could be more easily and more brilliantly done,' cried my uncle. 'There are great things about to happen in the world, and if you are at the Emperor's court you will be in the middle of them. I understand that you are content to serve him?'

'I wish to serve my country.'

'By serving the Emperor you do so, for without him the country becomes chaos.'

'From all we hear it is not a very easy service,' said my cousin. 'I should have thought that you would have been very much more comfortable in England—and then you would have been so much safer also.'

Everything which the girl said seemed to be meant as an insult to me, and yet I could not imagine how I had ever offended her. Never had I met a woman for whom I conceived so hearty and rapid a dislike. I could see that her remarks were as offensive to her father as they were to me, for he looked at her with eyes which were as angry as her own.

'Your cousin is a brave man, and that is more than can be said for someone else that I could mention,' said he.

'For whom?' she asked.

'Never mind!' he snapped, and, jumping up with the air of a man who is afraid that his rage may master him, and that he may say more than he wished, he ran from the room.

She seemed startled by this retort of his, and rose as if she would follow him. Then she tossed her head and laughed incredulously.

'I suppose that you have never met your uncle before?' said she, after a few minutes of embarrassed silence.

'Never,' answered I.

'Well, what do you think of him now you *have* met him?'

Such a question from a daughter about her father filled me with a certain vague horror. I felt that he must be even a worse man than I had taken him for if he had so completely forfeited the loyalty of his own nearest and dearest.

'Your silence is a sufficient answer,' said she, as I hesitated for a reply. 'I do not know how you came to meet him last night, or what passed between you, for we do not share each other's confidences. I think, however, that you have read him aright. Now

I have something to ask you. You had a letter from him inviting you to leave England and to come here, had you not?'

'Yes, I had.'

'Did you observe nothing on the outside?'

I thought of those two sinister words which had puzzled me so much.

'What! it was you who warned me not to come?'

'Yes, it was I. I had no other means of doing it.'

'But why did you do it?'

'Because I did not wish you to come here.'

'Did you think that I would harm you?'

She sat silent for a few seconds like one who is afraid of saying too much. When her answer came it was a very unexpected one:

'I was afraid that you would be harmed.'

'You think that I am in danger here?'

'I am sure of it.'

'You advise me to leave?'

'Without losing an instant.'

'From whom is the danger then?'

Again she hesitated, and then, with a reckless motion like one who throws prudence to the winds, she turned upon me.

'It is from my father,' said she.

'But why should he harm me?'

'That is for your sagacity to discover.'

'But I assure you, mademoiselle, that in this matter you misjudge him,' said I. 'As it happens, he interfered to save my life last night.'

'To save your life! From whom?'

'From two conspirators whose plans I had chanced to discover.'

'Conspirators!' She looked at me in surprise.

'They would have killed me if he had not intervened.'

'It is not his interest that you should be harmed yet awhile. He had reasons for wishing you to come to Castle Grosbois. But I have been very frank with you, and I wish you to be equally so with me. Does it happen—does it happen that during your youth in England you have ever—you have ever had an affair of the heart?'

Everything which this cousin of mine said appeared to me to be stranger than the last, and this question, coming at the end of so serious a conversation, was the strangest of all. But frankness begets frankness, and I did not hesitate.

'I have left the very best and truest girl in the world behind me in England,' said I. 'Eugenie is her name, Eugenie de Choiseul, the niece of the old Duke.'

My reply seemed to give my cousin great satisfaction. Her large dark eyes shone with pleasure.

'You are very attached?' she asked.

'I shall never be happy until I see her.'

'And you would not give her up?'

'God forbid!'

'Not for the Castle of Grosbois?'

'Not even for that.'

My cousin held out her hand to me with a charmingly frank impulsiveness.

'You will forgive me for my rudeness,' said she. 'I see that we are to be allies and not enemies.'

And our hands were still clasped when her father re-entered the room.

Chapter 8

Cousin Sibylle

I could see in my uncle's grim face as he looked at us the keenest satisfaction contending with surprise at this sign of our sudden reconciliation. All trace of his recent anger seemed to have left him as he addressed his daughter, but in spite of his altered tone I noticed that her eyes looked defiance and distrust.

'I have some papers of importance to look over,' said he. 'For an hour or so I shall be engaged. I can guess that Louis would like to see the old place once again, and I am sure that he could not have a better guide than you, Sibylle, if you will take him over it.'

She raised no objection, and for my part I was overjoyed at the proposal, as it gave me an opportunity of learning more of this singular cousin of mine, who had told me so much and yet seemed to know so much more. What was the meaning of this obscure warning which she had given me against her father, and why was she so frankly anxious to know about my love affairs? These were the two questions which pressed for an answer. So out we went together into the sweet coast-land air, the sweeter for the gale of the night before, and we walked through the old yew-lined paths, and out into the park, and so round the castle, looking up at the gables, the grey pinnacles, the oak-mullioned windows, the ancient wing with its crenulated walls and its *meurtriere* windows, the modern with its pleasant veranda and veil of honeysuckle. And as she showed me each fresh little detail, with a particularity which made me understand how dear the place had become to her, she would still keep offering her apologies for the fact that she should be the hostess and I the visitor.

'It is not against you but against ourselves that I was bitter,' said she, 'for are we not the cuckoos who have taken a strange nest and driven out those who built it? It makes me blush to think that my father should invite you to your own house.'

'Perhaps we had been rooted here too long,' I answered. 'Perhaps it is for our own good that we are driven out to carve our own fortunes, as I intend to do.'

'You say that you are going to the Emperor?'

'Yes.'

'You know that he is in camp near here?'

'So I have heard.'

'But your family is still proscribed?'

'I have done him no harm. I will go boldly to him and ask him to admit me into his service.'

'Well,' said she, 'there are some who call him a usurper, and wish him all evil; but for my own part I have never heard of anything that he has said and done which was not great and noble. But I had expected that you would be quite an Englishman, Cousin Louis, and come over here with your pockets full of Pitt's guineas and your heart of treason.'

'I have met nothing but hospitality from the English,' I answered; 'but my heart has always been French.'

'But your father fought against us at Quiberon.'

'Let each generation settle its own quarrels,' said I. 'I am quite of your father's opinion about that.'

'Do not judge my father by his words, but by his deeds,' said she, with a warning finger upraised; 'and, above all, Cousin Louis, unless you wish to have my life upon your conscience, never let him suspect that I have said a word to set you on your guard.'

'Your life!' I gasped.

'Oh, yes, he would not stick at that!' she cried. 'He killed my mother. I do not say that he slaughtered her, but I mean that his cold brutality broke her gentle heart. Now perhaps you begin to understand why I can talk of him in this fashion.'

As she spoke I could see the secret broodings of years, the bitter resentments crushed down in her silent soul, rising suddenly to flush her dark cheeks and to gleam in her splendid eyes.

I realised at that moment that in that tall slim figure there dwelt an unconquerable spirit.

'You must think that I speak very freely to you, since I have only known you a few hours, Cousin Louis,' said she.

'To whom should you speak freely if not to your own relative?'

'It is true; and yet I never expected that I should be on such terms with you. I looked forward to your coming with dread and sorrow. No doubt I showed something of my feelings when my father brought you in.'

'Indeed you did,' I answered. 'I feared that my presence was unwelcome to you.'

'Most unwelcome, both for your own sake and for mine,' said she. 'For your sake because I suspected, as I have told you, that my father's intentions might be unfriendly. For mine—'

'Why for yours?' I asked in surprise, for she had stopped in embarrassment.

'You have told me that your heart is another's. I may tell you that my hand is also promised, and that my love has gone with it.'

'May all happiness attend it!' said I. 'But why should this make my coming unwelcome?'

'That thick English air has dimmed your wits, cousin,' said she, shaking her stately head at me. 'But I can speak freely now that I know that this plan would be as hateful to you as to me. You must know, then, that if my father could have married us he would have united all claims to the succession of Grosbois. Then, come what might—Bourbon or Buonaparte—nothing could shake his position.'

I thought of the solicitude which he had shown over my toilet in the morning, his anxiety that I should make a favourable impression, his displeasure when she had been cold to me, and the smile upon his face when he had seen us hand in hand.

'I believe you are right!' I cried.

'Right! Of course I am right! Look at him watching us now.'

We were walking on the edge of the dried moat, and as I looked up there, sure enough, was the little yellow face toned towards us in the angle of one of the windows. Seeing that I was watching him, he rose and waved his hand merrily.

'Now you know why he saved your life—since you say that he saved it,' said she. 'It would suit his plans best that you should marry his daughter, and so he wished you to live. But when once he understands that that is impossible, why then, my poor Cousin Louis, his only way of guarding against the return of the de Lavals must lie in ensuring that there are none to return.'

It was those words of hers, coupled with that furtive yellow face still lurking at the window, which made me realise the imminence of my danger. No one in France had any reason to take an interest in me. If I were to pass away there was no one who could make inquiry—I was absolutely in his power. My memory told me what a ruthless and dangerous man it was with whom I had to deal.

'But,' said I, 'he must have known that your affections were already engaged.'

'He did,' she answered; 'it was that which made me most uneasy of all. I was afraid for you and afraid for myself, but, most of all, I was afraid for Lucien. No man can stand in the way of his plans.'

'Lucien! 'The name was like a lightning flash upon a dark night. I had heard of the vagaries of a woman's love, but was it possible that this spirited woman loved that poor creature whom I had seen grovelling last night in a frenzy of fear? But now I remembered also where I had seen the name Sibylle. It was upon the fly-leaf of his book. 'Lucien, from Sibylle,' was the inscription. I recalled also that my uncle had said something to him about his aspirations.

'Lucien is hot-headed, and easily carried away,' said she. 'My father has seen a great deal of him lately. They sit for hours in his room, and Lucien will say nothing of what passes between them. I fear that there is something going forward which may lead to evil. Lucien is a student rather than a man of the world, but he has strong opinions about politics.'

I was at my wit's ends what to do, whether to be silent, or to tell her of the terrible position in which her lover was placed; but, even as I hesitated, she, with the quick intuition of a woman, read the doubts which were in my mind.

'You know something of him,' she cried. 'I understood that he had gone to Paris. For God's sake tell me what you know about him!'

'His name is Lesage?'

'Yes, yes. Lucien Lesage.'

'I have—I have seen him,' I stammered.

'You have seen him! And you only arrived in France last night. Where did you see him? What has happened to him?' She gripped me by the wrist in her anxiety.

It was cruel to tell her, and yet it seemed more cruel still to keep silent. I looked round in my bewilderment, and there was my uncle himself coming along over the close-cropped green lawn. By his side, with a merry clashing of steel and jingling of spurs, there walked a handsome young hussar—the same to whom the charge of the prisoner had been committed upon the night before. Sibylle never hesitated for an instant, but, with a set face and blazing eyes, she swept towards them.

'Father,' said she, 'what have you done with Lucien?'

I saw his impassive face wince for a moment before the passionate hatred and contempt which he read in her eyes.

'We will discuss this at some future time,' said he.

'I will know here and now,' she cried. 'What have you done with Lucien?'

'Gentlemen,' said he, turning to the young hussar and me, 'I am sorry that we should intrude our little domestic differences upon your attention. You will, I am sure, make allowances, lieutenant, when I tell you that your prisoner of last night was a very dear friend of my daughter's. Such family considerations do not prevent me from doing my duty to the Emperor, but they make that duty more painful than it would otherwise be.'

'You have my sympathy, mademoiselle,' said the young hussar.

It was to him that my cousin had now turned.

'Do I understand that you took him prisoner?' she asked.

'It was unfortunately my duty.'

'From you I will get the truth. Whither did you take him?'

'To the Emperor's camp.'

'And why?'

'Ah, mademoiselle, it is not for me to go into politics. My duties are but to wield a sword, and sit a horse, and obey my orders. Both these gentlemen will be my witnesses that I received my instructions from Colonel Lasalle.'

'But on what charge was he arrested?'

'Tut, tut, child, we have had enough of this!' said my uncle harshly. 'If you insist upon knowing I will tell you once and for all, that Monsieur Lucien Lesage has been seized for being concerned in a plot against the life of the Emperor, and that it was my privilege to denounce the would-be assassin.'

'To denounce him!' cried the girl. 'I know that it was you who set him on, who encouraged him, who held him to it whenever he tried to draw back. Oh, you villain! you villain! What have I over done, what sin of my ancestors am I expiating, that I should be compelled to call such a man Father?'

My uncle shrugged his shoulders as if to say that it was useless to argue with a woman's tantrums. The hussar and I made as if we would stroll away, for it was embarrassing to stand listening to such words, but in her fury she called to us to stop and be witnesses against him. Never have I seen such a recklessness of passion as blazed in her dry wide-opened eyes.

'You have deceived others, but you have never deceived me,' she cried. 'I know you as your own conscience knows you. You may murder me, as you murdered my mother before me, but you can never frighten me into being your accomplice. You proclaimed yourself a Republican that you might creep into a house and estate which do not belong to you. And now you try to make a friend of Buonaparte by betraying your old associates, who still trust in you. And you have sent Lucien to his death! But I know your plans, and my Cousin Louis knows them also, and I can assure you that there is just as much chance of his agreeing to them as there is of my doing so. I'd rather lie in my grave than be the wife of any man but Lucien.'

'If you had seen the pitiful poltroon that he proved himself you would not say so,' said my uncle coolly. 'You are not yourself at present, but when you return to your right mind you will be ashamed of having made this public exposure of your weakness. And now, lieutenant, you have something to say.'

'My message was to you, Monsieur de Laval,' said the young hussar, turning his back contemptuously upon my uncle. 'The Emperor has sent me to bring you to him at once at the camp at Boulogne.'

My heart leapt at the thought of escaping from my uncle.

'I ask nothing better,' I cried.

'A horse and an escort are waiting at the gates.'

'I am ready to start at this instant.'

'Nay, there can be no such very great hurry,' said my uncle. 'Surely you will wait for luncheon, Lieutenant Gerard.'

'The Emperor's commissions, sir, are not carried out in such a manner,' said the young hussar sternly. 'I have already wasted too much time. We must be upon our way in five minutes.'

My uncle placed his hand upon my arm and led me slowly towards the gateway, through which my cousin Sibylle had already passed.

'There is one matter that I wish to speak to you about before you go. Since my time is so short you will forgive me if I introduce it without preamble. You have seen your cousin Sibylle, and though her behaviour this morning is such as to prejudice you against her, yet I can assure you that she is a very amiable girl. She spoke just now as if she had mentioned the plan which I had conceived to you. I confess to you that I cannot imagine anything more convenient than that we should unite in order to settle once for all every question as to which branch of the family shall hold the estates.'

'Unfortunately,' said I, 'there are objections.'

'And pray what are they?'

'The fact that my cousin's hand, as I have just learned, is promised to another.'

'That need not hinder us,' said he, with a sour smile; 'I will undertake that he never claims the promise.'

'I fear that I have the English idea of marriage, that it should go by love and not by convenience. But in any case your scheme is out of the question, for my own affections are pledged to a young lady in England.'

He looked wickedly at me out of the corners of his grey eyes.

'Think well what you are doing, Louis,' said he, in a sibilant whisper which was as menacing as a serpent's hiss. 'You are deranging my plans, and that is not done with impunity.'

'It is not a matter in which I have any choice.'

He gripped me by the sleeve, and waved his hand round as Satan may have done when he showed the kingdoms and principalities. 'Look at the park,' he cried, 'the fields, the woods. Look at the old castle in which your fathers have lived for eight hundred years. You have but to say the word and it is all yours once more.'

There flashed up into my memory the little red-brick house at Ashford, and Eugenie's sweet pale face looking over the laurel bushes which grew by the window.

'It is impossible!' said I.

There must have been something in my manner which made him comprehend that it really was so, for his face darkened with anger, and his persuasion changed in an instant to menace.

'If I had known this they might have done what they wished with you last night,' said he, 'I would never have put out a finger to save you.'

'I am glad to hear you say so,' I answered, 'for it makes it easier for me to say that I wish to go my own way, and to have nothing more to do with you. What you have just said frees me from the bond of gratitude which held me back.'

'I have no doubt that you would like to have nothing more to do with me,' he cried. 'You will wish it more heartily still before you finish. Very well, sir, go your own way and I will go mine, and we shall see who comes out the best in the end.'

A group of hussars were standing by their horses' heads in the gateway. In a few minutes I had packed my scanty possessions, and I was hastening with them down the corridor when a chill struck suddenly through my heart at the thought of my cousin Sibylle. How could I leave her alone with this grim companion in the old castle? Had she not herself told me that her very life might be at stake? I had stopped in my perplexity, and suddenly there was a patter of feet, and there she was running towards me.

'Good-bye, Cousin Louis,' she cried, with outstretched hands.

'I was thinking of you,' said I; 'your father and I have had an explanation and a quarrel.'

'Thank God!' she cried. 'Your only chance was to get away from him. But beware, for he will do you an injury if he can!'

'He may do his worst; but how can I leave you here in his power?'

'Have no fears about me. He has more reason to avoid me than I him. But they are calling for you, Cousin Louis. Good-bye, and God be with you!'

CHAPTER 9

The Camp of Boulogne

My uncle was still standing at the castle gateway, the very
picture of a usurper, with our own old coat-of-arms of the bend
argent and the three blue martlets engraved upon the stones at
either side of him. He gave me no sign of greeting as I mounted the large grey horse which was awaiting me, but he looked
thoughtfully at me from under his down-drawn brows, and his
jaw muscles still throbbed with that stealthy rhythmical movement. I read a cold and settled malice in his set yellow face and
his stern eyes. For my own part I sprang readily enough into the
saddle, for the man's presence had, from the first, been loathsome
to me, and I was right glad to be able to turn my back upon him.
And so, with a stern quick order from the lieutenant and a jingle
and clatter from the troopers, we were off upon our journey. As
I glanced back at the black keep of Grosbois, and at the sinister
figure who stood looking after us from beside the gateway, I saw
from over his head a white handkerchief gleam for an instant in
a last greeting from one of the gloomy *meurtriere* windows, and
again a chill ran through me as I thought of the fearless girl and
of the hands in which we were leaving her.

But sorrow clears from the mind of youth like the tarnish
of breath upon glass, and who could carry a heavy heart upon
so light-footed a horse and through so sweet an air? The white
glimmering road wound over the downs with the sea far upon
the left, and between lay that great salt-marsh which had been
the scene of our adventures. I could even see, as I fancied, a
dull black spot in the distance to mark the position of that ter-

rible cottage. Far away the little clusters of houses showed the positions of Etaples, Ambleterre, and the other fishing villages, whilst I could see that the point which had seemed last night to glow like a half-forged red-hot sword-blade was now white as a snow-field with the camp of a great army. Far, far away, a little dim cloud upon the water stood for the land where I had spent my days—the pleasant, homely land which will always rank next to my own in my affections.

And now I turned my attention from the downs and the sea to the hussars who rode beside me, forming, as I could perceive, a guard rather than an escort. Save for the patrol last night, they were the first of the famous soldiers of Napoleon whom I had ever seen, and it was with admiration and curiosity that I looked upon men who had won a world-wide reputation for their discipline and their gallantry. Their appearance was by no means gorgeous, and their dress and equipment was much more modest than that of the East Kent Yeomanry, which rode every Saturday through Ashford; but the stained tunics, the worn leathers, and the rough hardy horses gave them a very workmanlike appearance. They were small, light, brown-faced fellows, heavily whiskered and moustached, many of them wearing ear-rings in their ears. It surprised me that even the youngest and most boyish-looking of them should be so bristling with hair, until, upon a second look, I perceived that his whiskers were formed of lumps of black wax stuck on to the sides of his face. The tall young lieutenant noticed the astonishment with which I gazed at his boyish trooper.

'Yes, yes,' said he, 'they are artificial, sure enough; but what can you expect from a lad of seventeen? On the other hand, we cannot spoil the appearance of the regiment upon parade by having a girl's cheeks in the ranks.'

'It melts terribly in this warm weather, lieutenant,' said the hussar, joining in the conversation with the freedom which was one of the characteristics of Napoleon's troops.

'Well, well, Caspar, in a year or two you will dispense with them.'

'Who knows? Perhaps he will have dispensed with his head

also by that time,' said a corporal in front, and they all laughed together in a manner which in England would have meant a court-martial. This seemed to me to be one of the survivals of the Revolution, that officer and private were left, upon a very familiar footing, which was increased, no doubt, by the freedom with which the Emperor would chat with his old soldiers, and the liberties which he would allow them to take with him. It was no uncommon thing for a shower of chaff to come from the ranks directed at their own commanding officers, and I am sorry to say, also, that it was no very unusual thing for a shower of bullets to come also. Unpopular officers were continually assassinated by their own men; at the battle of Montebello it is well known that every officer, with the exception of one lieutenant belonging to the 24th demi-brigade, was shot down from behind. But this was a relic of the bad times, and, as the Emperor gained more complete control, a better feeling was established. The history of our army at that time proved, at any rate, that the highest efficiency could be maintained without the flogging which was still used in the Prussian and the English service, and it was shown, for the first time, that great bodies of men could be induced to act from a sense of duty and a love of country, without hope of reward or fear of punishment. When a French general could suffer his division to straggle as they would over the face of the country, with the certainty that they would concentrate upon the day of battle, he proved that he had soldiers who were worthy of his trust.

One thing had struck me as curious about these hussars—that they pronounced French with the utmost difficulty. I remarked it to the lieutenant as he rode by my side, and I asked him from what foreign country his men were recruited, since I could perceive that they were not Frenchmen.

'My faith, you must not let them hear you say so,' said he, 'for they would answer you as like as not by a thrust from their sabres. We are the premier regiment of the French cavalry, the First Hussars of Bercheny, and, though it is true that our men are all recruited in Alsace, and few of them can speak anything but German, they are as good Frenchmen as Kleber or Kellermann, who came from the same parts. Our men are all picked, and our officers,' he added, pulling at his light moustache, 'are the finest in the service.'

The swaggering vanity of the fellow amused me, for he cocked his busby, swung the blue dolman which hung from his shoulder, sat his horse, and clattered his scabbard in a manner which told of his boyish delight and pride in himself and his regiment. As I looked at his lithe figure and his fearless bearing, I could quite imagine that he did himself no more than justice, while his frank smile and his merry blue eyes assured me that he would prove a good comrade. He had himself been taking observations of me, for he suddenly placed his hand upon my knee as we rode side by side.

'I trust that the Emperor is not displeased with you,' said he, with a very grave face.

'I cannot think that he can be so,' I answered, 'for I have come from England to put my services at his disposal.'

'When the report was presented last night, and he heard of your presence in that den of thieves, he was very anxious that you should be brought to him. Perhaps it is that he wishes you to be guide to us in England. No doubt you know your way all over the island.'

The hussar's idea of an island seemed to be limited to the little patches which lie off the Norman or Breton coast. I tried to explain to him that this was a great country, not much smaller than France.

'Well, well,' said he, 'we shall know all about it presently, for we are going to conquer it. They say in the camp that we shall probably enter London either next Wednesday evening or else on the Thursday morning. We are to have a week for plundering the town, and then one army corps is to take possession of Scotland and another of Ireland.'

His serene confidence made me smile. 'But how do you know you can do all this?' I asked.

'Oh!' said he, 'the Emperor has arranged it.'

'But they have an army, and they are well prepared. They are brave men and they will fight.'

77

'There would be no use their doing that, for the Emperor is going over himself,' said he; and in the simple answer I understood for the first time the absolute trust and confidence which these soldiers had in their leader. Their feeling for him was fanaticism, and its strength was religion, and never did Mahomet nerve the arms of his believers and strengthen them against pain and death more absolutely than this little grey-coated idol did to those who worshipped him. If he had chosen—and he was more than once upon the point of it—to assert that he was indeed above humanity he would have found millions to grant his claim. You who have heard of him as a stout gentleman in a straw hat, as he was in his later days, may find it hard to understand it, but if you had seen his mangled soldiers still with their dying breath crying out to him, and turning their livid faces towards him as he passed, you would have realised the hold which he had over the minds of men.

'You have been over there?' asked the lieutenant presently, jerking his thumb towards the distant cloud upon the water.

'Yes, I have spent my life there.'

'But why did you stay there when there was such good fighting to be had in the French service?'

'My father was driven out of the country as an aristocrat. It was only after his death that I could offer my sword to the Emperor.'

'You have missed a great deal, but I have no doubt that we shall still have plenty of fine wars. And you think that the English will offer us battle?'

'I have no doubt of it.'

'We feared that when they understood that it was the Emperor in person who had come they would throw down their arms. I have heard that there are some fine women over there.'

'The women are beautiful.'

He said nothing, but for some time he squared his shoulders and puffed out his chest, curling up the ends of his little yellow moustache.

'But they will escape in boats,' he muttered at last; and I could see that he had still that picture of a little island in his imagination. 'If they could but see us they might remain. It has been said of the Hussars of Bercheny that they can set a whole population running, the women towards us, the men away. We are, as you have no doubt observed, a very fine body of men, and the officers are the pick of the service, though the seniors are hardly up to the same standard as the rest of us.'

With all his self-confidence, this officer did not seem to me to be more than my own age, so I asked him whether he had seen any service. His moustache bristled with indignation at my question, and he looked me up and down with a severe eye.

'I have had the good fortune to be present at nine battles, sir, and at more than forty skirmishes,' said he. 'I have also fought a considerable number of duels, and I can assure you that I am always ready to meet anyone—even a civilian—who may wish to put me to the proof.'

I assured him that he was very fortunate to be so young and yet to have seen so much, upon which his ill-temper vanished as quickly as it came, and he explained that he had served in the Hohenlinden campaign under Moreau, as well as in Napoleon's passage of the Alps, and the campaign of Marengo.

'When you have been with the army for a little time the name of Etienne Gerard will not be so unfamiliar to you,' said he. 'I believe that I may claim to be the hero of one or two little stories which the soldiers love to tell about their camp fires. You will hear of my duel with the six fencing masters, and you will be told how, single-handed, I charged the Austrian Hussars of Graz and brought their silver kettledrum back upon the crupper of my mare. I can assure you that it was not by accident that I was present last night, but it was because Colonel Lasalle was very anxious to be sure of any prisoners whom he might make. As it turned out, however, I only had the one poor chicken-hearted creature, whom I handed over to the provost-marshal.'

'And the other—Toussac?'

'Ah, he seems to have been a man of another breed. I could have asked nothing better than to have had him at my sword-point. But he has escaped. They caught sight of him and fired a pistol or two, but he knew the bog too well, and they could not follow him.'

'And what will be done to your prisoner?' I asked.

Lieutenant Gerard shrugged his shoulders.

'I am very sorry for Mademoiselle your cousin,' said he, 'but a fine girl should not love such a man when there are so many gallant soldiers upon the country side. I hear that the Emperor is weary of these endless plottings, and that an example will be made of him.'

Whilst the young hussar and I had been talking we had been cantering down the broad white road, until we were now quite close to the camp, which we could see lying in its arrangement of regiments and brigades beneath us. Our approach lay over the high ground, so that we could see down into this canvas city, with its interminable lines of picketed horses, its parks of artillery, and its swarms of soldiers. In the centre was a clear space, with one very large tent and a cluster of low wooden houses in the middle of it, with the tricolour banner waving above them.

'That is the Emperor's quarters, and the smaller tent there is the headquarters of General Ney, who commands this corps. You understand that this is only one of several armies dotted along from Dunkirk in the north to this, which is the most southerly. The Emperor goes from one to the other, inspecting each in its turn, but this is the main body, and contains most of the picked troops, so that it is we who see most of him, especially now that the Empress and the Court have come to Pont de Briques. He is in there at the present moment,' he added in a hushed voice, pointing to the great white tent in the centre.

The road into the camp ran through a considerable plain, which was covered by bodies of cavalry and infantry engaged upon their drill. We had heard so much in England about Napoleon's troops, and their feats had appeared so extraordinary, that my imagination had prepared me for men of very striking appearance. As a matter of fact, the ordinary infantry of the line, in their blue coats and white breeches and gaiters, were quite little fellows, and even their high brass-covered hats and red plumes could not make them very imposing.

In spite of their size, however, they were tough and wiry, and after their eighteen months in camp they were trained to the highest pitch of perfection. The ranks were full of veterans, and all the under-officers had seen much service, while the generals in command have never been equalled in ability, so that it was no mean foe which lay with its menacing eyes fixed upon the distant cliffs of England. If Pitt had not been able to place the first navy in the world between the two shores the history of Europe might be very different today.

Lieutenant Gerard, seeing the interest with which I gazed at the manoeuvring troops, was good enough to satisfy my curiosity about such of them as approached the road along which we were journeying.

'Those fellows on the black horses with the great blue rugs upon their croups are the Cuirassiers,' said he. 'They are so heavy that they cannot raise more than a trot, so when they charge we manage that there shall be a brigade of chasseurs or hussars behind them to follow up the advantage.'

'Who is the civilian who is inspecting them?' I asked.

'That is not a civilian, but it is General St. Cyr, who is one of those whom they called the Spartans of the Rhine. They were of opinion that simplicity of life and of dress were part of a good soldier, and so they would wear no uniform beyond a simple blue riding coat, such as you see. St. Cyr is an excellent officer, but he is not popular, for he seldom speaks to anyone, and he sometimes shuts himself up for days on end in his tent, where he plays upon his violin. I think myself that a soldier is none the worse because he enjoys a glass of good wine, or has a smart jacket and a few Brandenburgs across his chest. For my part I do both, and yet those who know me would tell you that it has not harmed my soldiering. You see this infantry upon the left?'

'The men with the yellow facings?'

'Precisely. Those are Oudinot's famous grenadiers. And the other grenadiers, with the red shoulder-knots and the fur hats strapped above their knapsacks, are the Imperial Guard, the successors of the old Consular Guard who won Marengo for us. Eighteen hundred of them got the cross of honour after the battle. There is the 57th of the line, which has been named "The Terrible," and there is the 7th Light Infantry, who come from the Pyrenees, and who are well known to be the best marchers and the greatest rascals in the army. The light cavalry in green are the Horse Chasseurs of the Guard, sometimes called the Guides, who are said to be the Emperor's favourite troops, although he makes a great mistake if he prefers them to the Hussars of Bercheny. The other cavalry with the green pelisses are also chasseurs, but I cannot tell from here what regiment they are. Their colonel handles them admirably. They are moving to a flank in open column of half-squadrons and then wheeling into line to charge. We could not do it better ourselves. And now, Monsieur de Laval, here we are at the gates of the Camp of Boulogne, and it is my duty to take you straight to the Emperor's quarters.'

CHAPTER 10

The Ante-Room

The camp of Boulogne contained at that time one hundred and fifty thousand infantry, with fifty thousand cavalry, so that its population was second only to Paris among the cities of France. It was divided into four sections, the right camp, the left camp, the camp of Wimereux, and the camp of Ambleteuse, the whole being about a mile in depth, and extending along the seashore for a length of about seven miles. On the land side it was open, but on the sea side it was fringed by powerful batteries containing mortars and cannon of a size never seen before. These batteries were placed along the edges of the high cliffs, and their lofty position increased their range, and enabled them to drop their missiles upon the decks of the English ships.

It was a pretty sight to ride through the camp, for the men had been there for more than a year, and had done all that was possible to decorate and ornament their tents. Most of them had little gardens in front or around them, and the sun-burned fellows might be seen as we passed kneeling in their shirt-sleeves with their spuds and their watering-cans in the midst of their flower-beds. Others sat in the sunshine at the openings of the tents tying up their queues, pipe-claying their belts, and polishing their arms, hardly bestowing a glance upon us as we passed, for patrols of cavalry were coming and going in every direction. The endless lines were formed into streets, with their names printed up upon boards. Thus we had passed through the Rue d'Arcola, the Rue de Kleber, the Rue d'Egypte, and the Rue d'Artillerie Volante, before we found ourselves in the great central square in which the headquarters of the army were situated.

The Emperor at this time used to sleep at a village called Pont de Briques, some four miles inland, but his days were spent at the camp, and his continual councils of war were held there. Here also were his ministers, and the generals of the army corps which were scattered up and down the coast came thither to make their reports and to receive their orders. For these consultations a plain wooden house had been constructed containing one very large room and three small ones. The pavilion which we had observed from the Downs served as an ante-chamber to the house, in which those who sought audience with the Emperor might assemble. It was at the door of this, where a strong guard of grenadiers announced Napoleon's presence, that my guardian sprang down from his horse and signed to me to follow his example. An officer of the guard took our names and returned to us accompanied by General Duroc, a thin, hard, dry man of forty, with a formal manner and a suspicious eye.

'Is this Monsieur Louis de Laval?' he asked, with a stiff smile. I bowed.

'The Emperor is very anxious to see you. You are no longer needed, Lieutenant.'

'I am personally responsible for bringing him safely, General.'

'Very good. You may come in, if you prefer it!' And he passed us into the huge tent, which was unfurnished, save for a row of wooden benches round the sides. A number of men in naval and military uniforms were seated upon these, and numerous groups were standing about chatting in subdued tones. At the far end was a door which led into the Imperial council chamber. Now and then I saw some man in official dress walk up to this door, scratch gently upon it with his nail, and then, as it instantly opened, slip discreetly through, closing it softly behind him. Over the whole assembly there hung an air of the Court rather than of the camp, an atmosphere of awe and of reverence which was the more impressive when it affected these bluff soldiers and sailors. The Emperor had seemed to me to be formidable in the distance, but I found him even more overwhelming now that he was close at hand.

'You need have no fears, Monsieur de Laval,' said my companion. 'You are going to have a good reception.'

'How do you know that?'

'From General Duroc's manner. In these cursed Courts, if the Emperor smiles upon you everyone smiles, down to that flunkey in the red velvet coat yonder. But if the Emperor frowns, why, you have only to look at the face of the man who washes the Imperial plates, and you will see the frown reflected upon it. And the worst of it is that, if you are a plain-witted man, you may never find out what earned you either the frown or the smile. That is why I had rather wear the shoulder-straps of a lieutenant, and be at the side of my squadron, with a good horse between my knees and my sabre clanking against my stirrup-iron, than have Monsieur Talleyrand's grand hotel in the Rue Saint Florentin, and his hundred thousand *livres* of income.'

I was still wondering whether the hussar could be right, and if the smile with which Duroc had greeted me could mean that the Emperor's intentions towards me were friendly, when a very tall and handsome young man, in a brilliant uniform, came towards me. In spite of the change in his dress, I recognised him at once as the General Savary who had commanded the expedition of the night before.

'Well, Monsieur de Laval,' said he, shaking hands with me very pleasantly, 'you have heard, no doubt, that this fellow Toussac has escaped us. He was really the only one whom we were anxious to seize, for the other is evidently a mere dupe and dreamer. But we shall have him yet, and between ourselves we shall keep a very strict guard upon the Emperor's person until we do, for Master Toussac is not a man to be despised.'

I seemed to feel his great rough thumb upon my chin as I answered that I thought he was a very dangerous man indeed.

'The Emperor will see you presently,' said Savary. 'He is very busy this morning, but he bade me say that you should have an audience.' He smiled and passed on.

'Assuredly you are getting on,' whispered Gerard. 'There are a good many men here who would risk something to have Savary address them as he addressed you. The Emperor is certainly going to do something for you. But attention, friend, for here is Monsieur de Talleyrand himself coming towards us.'

A singular-looking person was shuffling in our direction. He was a man about fifty years of age, largely made about the shoulders and chest, but stooping a good deal, and limping heavily in one leg. He walked slowly, leaning upon a silver-headed stick, and his sober suit of black, with silk stockings of the same hue, looked strangely staid among the brilliant uniforms which surrounded him. But in spite of his plain dress there was an expression of great authority upon his shrewd face, and every one drew back with bows and salutes as he moved across the tent.

'Monsieur Louis de Laval?' said he, as he stopped in front of me, and his cold grey eyes played over me from head to heel.

I bowed, and with some coldness, for I shared the dislike which my father used to profess for this unfrocked priest and perjured politician; but his manner was so polished and engaging that it was hard to hold out against it.

'I knew your cousin de Rohan very well indeed,' said he. 'We were two rascals together when the world was not quite so serious as it is at present. I believe that you are related to the Cardinal de Montmorency de Laval, who is also an old friend of mine. I understand that you are about to offer your services to the Emperor?'

'I have come from England for that purpose, sir.'

'And met with some little adventure immediately upon your arrival, as I understand. I have heard the story of the worthy police agent, the two Jacobins, and the lonely hut. Well, you have seen the danger to which the Emperor is exposed, and it may make you the more zealous in his service. Where is your uncle, Monsieur Bernac?'

'He is at the Castle of Grosbois.'

'Do you know him well?'

'I had not seen him until yesterday.'

'He is a very useful servant of the Emperor, but—but—' he inclined his head downward to my ear, 'some more congenial service will be found for you, Monsieur de Laval,' and so, with a bow, he whisked round, and tapped his way across the tent again.

'Why, my friend, you are certainly destined for something great,' said the hussar lieutenant. 'Monsieur de Talleyrand does not waste his smiles and his bows, I promise you. He knows which way the wind blows before he flies his kite, and I foresee that I shall be asking for your interest to get me my captaincy in this English campaign. Ah, the council of war is at an end.'

As he spoke the inner door at the end of the great tent opened, and a small knot of men came through dressed in the dark blue coats, with trimmings of gold oak-leaves, which marked the marshals of the Empire. They were, all but one, men who had hardly reached their middle age, and who, in any other army, might have been considered fortunate if they had gained the command of a regiment; but the continuous wars and the open system by which rules of seniority yielded to merit had opened up a rapid career to a successful soldier. Each carried his curved cocked hat under his arm, and now, leaning upon their sword-hilts, they fell into a little circle and chatted eagerly among themselves.

'You are a man of family, are you not?' asked my hussar.

'I am of the same blood as the de Rohans and the Montmorencies.'

'So I had understood. Well, then, you will understand that there have been some changes in this country when I tell you that those men, who, under the Emperor, are the greatest in the country have been the one a waiter, the next a wine smuggler, the next a cooper of barrels, and the next a house painter. Those are the trades which gave us Murat, Massena, Ney, and Lannes.'

Aristocrat as I was, no names had ever thrilled me as those did, and I eagerly asked him to point me out each of these famous soldiers.

'Oh, there are many famous soldiers in the room,' said he. 'Besides,' he added, twisting his moustache, 'there may be junior officers here who have it in them to rise higher than any of them. But there is Ney to the right.'

I saw a man with close-cropped red hair and a large square-jowled face, such as I have seen upon an English prize-fighter.

'We call him Peter the Red, and sometimes the Red Lion, in the army,' said my companion. 'He is said to be the bravest man in the army, though I cannot admit that he is braver than some other people whom I could mention. Still he is undoubtedly a very good leader.'

'And the general next him?' I asked. 'Why does he carry his head all upon one side?'

'That is General Lannes, and he carries his head upon his left shoulder because he was shot through the neck at the siege of St. Jean d'Acre. He is a Gascon, like myself, and I fear that he gives some ground to those who accuse my countrymen of being a little talkative and quarrelsome. But monsieur smiles?'

'You are mistaken.'

'I thought that perhaps something which I had said might have amused monsieur. I thought that possibly he meant that Gascons really were quarrelsome, instead of being, as I contend, the mildest race in France—an opinion which I am always ready to uphold in any way which may be suggested. But, as I say, Lannes is a very valiant man, though, occasionally, perhaps, a trifle hot-headed. The next man is Auguereau.'

I looked with interest upon the hero of Castiglione, who had taken command upon the one occasion when Napoleon's heart and spirit had failed him. He was a man, I should judge, who would shine rather in war than in peace, for, with his long goat's face and his brandy nose, he looked, in spite of his golden oak-leaves, just such a long-legged, vulgar, swaggering, foul-mouthed old soldier as every barrack-room can show. He was an older man than the others, and his sudden promotion had come too late for him to change. He was always the Corporal of the Prussian Guard under the hat of the French Marshal.

'Yes, yes; he is a rough fellow,' said Gerard, in answer to my remark. 'He is one of those whom the Emperor had to warn that he wished them to be soldiers only with the army. He and Rapp and Lefebvre, with their big boots and their clanking sabres, were too much for the Empress's drawing-room at the Tuileries. There is Vandamme also, the dark man with the heavy face. Heaven help the English village that he finds his quarters in! It was he who got into trouble because he broke the jaw of a Westphalian priest who could not find him a second bottle of Tokay.'

'And that is Murat, I suppose?'

'Yes; that is Murat with the black whiskers and the red, thick lips, and the brown of Egypt upon his face. He is the man for me! My word, when you have seen him raving in front of a brigade of light cavalry, with his plumes tossing and his sabre flashing, you would not wish to see anything finer. I have known a square of grenadiers break and scatter at the very sight of him. In Egypt the Emperor kept away from him, for the Arabs would not look at the little General when this fine horseman and swordsman was before them. In my opinion Lasalle is the better light cavalry officer, but there is no one whom the men will follow as they do Murat.'

'And who is the stern-looking man, leaning on the Oriental sword?'

'Oh, that is Soult! He is the most obstinate man in the world. He argues with the Emperor. The handsome man beside him is Junot, and Bernadotte is leaning against the tent-pole.'

I looked with interest at the extraordinary face of this adventurer, who, after starting with a musket and a knapsack in the ranks, was not contented with the baton of a marshal, but passed on afterwards to grasp the sceptre of a king. And it might be said of him that, unlike his fellows, he gained his throne in spite of Napoleon rather than by his aid. Any man who looked at his singular pronounced features, the swarthiness of which proclaimed his half Spanish origin, must have read in his flashing black eyes and in that huge aggressive nose that he was reserved for a strange destiny. Of all the fierce and masterful men who surrounded the Emperor there was none with greater gifts, and none, also, whose ambitions he more distrusted, than those of Jules Bernadotte.

And yet, fierce and masterful as these men were, having, as Augereau boasted, fear neither of God nor of the devil, there was something which thrilled or cowed them in the pale smile or black frown of the little man who ruled them. For, as I watched them, there suddenly came over the assembly a start and hush such as you see in a boys' school when the master enters unexpectedly, and there near the open doors of his headquarters stood the master himself. Even without that sudden silence, and the scramble to their feet of those upon the benches, I felt that I should have known instantly that he was present. There was a pale luminosity about his ivory face which drew the eye towards it, and though his dress might be the plainest of a hundred, his appearance would be the first which one would notice. There he was, with his little plump, heavy-shouldered figure, his green coat with the red collar and cuffs, his white, well-formed legs, his sword with the gilt hilt and the tortoise-shell scabbard. His head was uncovered, showing his thin hair of a ruddy chestnut colour. Under one arm was the flat cocked hat with the two-penny tricolour rosette, which was already reproduced in his pictures. In his right hand he held a little riding switch with a metal head. He walked slowly forward, his face immutable, his eyes fixed steadily before him, measured, inexorable, the very personification of Destiny.

'Admiral Bruix!'

I do not know if that voice thrilled through every one as it did through me. Never had I heard anything more harsh, more menacing, more sinister. From under his puckered brows his light-blue eyes glanced swiftly round with a sweep like a sabre.

'I am here, Sire!' A dark, grizzled, middle-aged man, in a naval uniform, had advanced from the throng. Napoleon took three quick little steps towards him in so menacing a fashion, that I saw the weather-stained cheeks of the sailor turn a shade paler, and he gave a helpless glance round him, as if for assistance.

'How comes it, Admiral Bruix,' cried the Emperor, in the same terrible rasping voice, 'that you did not obey my commands last night?'

'I could see that a westerly gale was coming up, Sire. I knew that—,' he could hardly speak for his agitation, 'I knew that if the ships went out with this lee shore—'

'What right have you to judge, sir?' cried the Emperor, in a cold fury of indignation. 'Do you conceive that your judgment is to be placed against mine?'

'In matters of navigation, Sire.'

'In no matters whatsoever.'

'But the tempest, Sire! Did it not prove me to be in the right?'

'What! You still dare to bandy words with me?'

'When I have justice on my side.'

There was a hush amidst all the great audience; such a heavy silence as comes only when many are waiting, and all with bated breath. The Emperor's face was terrible. His cheeks were of a greenish, livid tint, and there was a singular rotary movement of the muscles of his forehead. It was the countenance of an epileptic. He raised the whip to his shoulder, and took a step towards the admiral.

'You insolent rascal!' he hissed. It was the Italian word *coglione* which he used, and I observed that as his feelings overcame him his French became more and more that of a foreigner.

For a moment he seemed to be about to slash the sailor across the face with his whip. The latter took a step back, and clapped his hand to his sword.

'Have a care, Sire,' said he.

For a few instants the tension was terrible. Then Napoleon brought the whip down with a sharp crack against his own thigh.

'Vice-Admiral Magon,' he cried, 'you will in future receive all orders connected with the fleet. Admiral Bruix, you will leave Boulogne in twenty-four hours and withdraw to Holland. Where is Lieutenant Gerard, of the Hussars of Bercheny?'

My companion's gauntlet sprang to his busby.

'I ordered you to bring Monsieur Louis de Laval from the castle of Grosbois.'

'He is here, Sire.'

'Good! You may retire.'

The lieutenant saluted, whisked round upon his heel, and clattered away, whilst the Emperor's blue eyes were turned upon me. I had often heard the phrase of eyes looking through you, but that piercing gaze did really give one the feeling that it penetrated to one's inmost thoughts. But the sternness had all melted out of it, and I read a great gentleness and kindness in their expression.

'You have come to serve me, Monsieur de Laval?'

'Yes, Sire.'

'You have been some time in making up your mind.'

'I was not my own master, Sire.'

'Your father was an aristocrat?'

'Yes, Sire.'

'And a supporter of the Bourbons?'

'Yes, Sire.'

'You will find that in France now there are no aristocrats and no Jacobins; but that we are all Frenchmen working for the glory of our country. Have you seen Louis de Bourbon?'

'I have seen him once, Sire?'

'An insignificant-looking man, is he not?'

'No, Sire, I thought him a fine-looking man.'

For a moment I saw a hard gleam of resentment in those changing blue eyes. Then he put out his hand and pinched one of my ears.

'Monsieur de Laval was not born to be a courtier,' said he. 'Well, well, Louis de Bourbon will find that he cannot gain a throne by writing proclamations in London and signing them Louis. For my part, I found the crown of France lying upon the ground, and I lifted it upon my sword-point.'

'You have lifted France with your sword also, Sire,' said Talleyrand, who stood at his elbow.

Napoleon looked at his famous minister, and I seemed to read suspicion in his eyes. Then he turned to his secretary.

'I leave Monsieur de Laval in your hands, de Meneval,' said he. 'I desire to see him in the council chamber after the inspection of the artillery.'

CHAPTER 11

The Secretary

Emperor, generals, and officials all streamed away to the review, leaving me with a gentle-looking, large-eyed man in a black suit with very white cambric ruffles, who introduced himself to me as Monsieur de Meneval, private secretary to His Majesty.

'We must get some food, Monsieur de Laval,' said he. 'It is always well, if you have anything to do with the Emperor, to get your food whenever you have the chance. It may be many hours before he takes a meal, and if you are in his presence you have to fast also. I assure you that I have nearly fainted from hunger and from thirst.'

'But how does the Emperor manage himself?' I asked. This Monsieur de Meneval had such a kindly human appearance that I already felt much at my ease with him.

'Oh, he, he is a man of iron, Monsieur de Laval. We must not set our watches by his. I have known him work for eighteen hours on end and take nothing but a cup or two of coffee. He wears everybody out around him. Even the soldiers cannot keep up with him. I assure you that I look upon it as the very highest honour to have charge of his papers, but there are times when it is very trying all the same. Sometimes it is eleven o'clock at night, Monsieur de Laval, and I am writing to his dictation with my head aching for want of sleep. It is dreadful work, for he dictates as quickly as he can talk, and he never repeats anything. "Now, Meneval," says he suddenly, "we shall stop here and have a good night's rest." And then, just as I am congratulating myself, he adds, "and we shall continue with the dictation at three to-morrow morning." That is what he means by a good night's rest.'

'But has he no hours for his meals, Monsieur de Meneval?' I asked, as I accompanied the unhappy secretary out of the tent.

'Oh, yes, he has hours, but he will not observe them. You see that it is already long after dinner time, but he has gone to this review. After the review something else will probably take up his attention, and then something else, until suddenly in the evening it will occur to him that he has had no dinner. "My dinner, Constant, this instant!" he will cry, and poor Constant has to see that it is there.'

'But it must be unfit to eat by that time,' said I.

The secretary laughed in the discreet way of a man who has always been obliged to control his emotions.

'This is the Imperial kitchen,' said he, indicating a large tent just outside the headquarters. 'Here is Borel, the second cook, at the door. How many pullets today, Borel?'

'Ah, Monsieur de Meneval, it is heartrending,' cried the cook. 'Behold them!' and, drawing back the flap of the entrance, he showed us seven dishes, each of them containing a cold fowl. 'The eighth is now on the fire and done to a turn, but I hear that His Majesty has started for the review, so we must put on a ninth.'

'That is how it is managed,' said my companion, as we turned from the tent. 'I have known twenty-three fowls got ready for him before he asked for his meal. That day he called for his dinner at eleven at night. He cares little what he eats or drinks, but he will not be kept waiting. Half a bottle of Chambertin, a red mullet, or a pullet a la Marengo satisfy every need, but it is unwise to put pastry or cream upon the table, because he is as likely as not to eat it before the fowl. Ah, that is a curious sight, is it not?'

I had halted with an exclamation of astonishment. A groom was cantering a very beautiful Arab horse down one of the lanes between the tents. As it passed, a grenadier who was standing with a small pig under his arm hurled it down under the feet of the horse. The pig squealed vigorously and scuttled away, but the horse cantered on without changing its step.

'What does that mean?' I asked.

'That is Jardin, the head groom, breaking in a charger for the Emperor's use. They are first trained by having a cannon fired in their ears, then they are struck suddenly by heavy objects, and finally they have the test of the pig being thrown under their feet. The Emperor has not a very firm seat, and he very often loses himself in a reverie when be is riding, so it might not be very safe if the horse were not well trained. Do you see that young man asleep at the door of a tent?'

'Yes, I see him.'

'You would not think that he is at the present moment serving the Emperor?'

'It seems a very easy service.'

'I wish all our services were as easy, Monsieur de Laval. That is Joseph Linden, whose foot is the exact size of the Emperor's. He wears his new boots and shoes for three days before they are given to his master. You can see by the gold buckles that he has a pair on at the present moment. Ah, Monsieur de Caulaincourt, will you not join us at dinner in my tent?'

A tall, handsome man, very elegantly dressed, came across and greeted us. 'It is rare to find you at rest, Monsieur de Meneval. I have no very light task myself as head of the household, but I think I have more leisure than you. Have we time for dinner before the Emperor returns?'

'Yes, yes; here is the tent, and everything ready. We can see when the Emperor returns, and be in the room before he can reach it. This is camp fare, Monsieur de Laval, but no doubt you will excuse it.'

For my own part I had an excellent appetite for the cutlets and the salad, but what I relished above all was to hear the talk of my companions, for I was full of curiosity as to everything which concerned this singular man, whose genius had elevated him so rapidly to the highest position in the world. The head of his household discussed him with an extraordinary frankness.

'What do they say of him in England, Monsieur de Laval?' he asked.

'Nothing very good.'

'So I have gathered from their papers. They drive the Emperor frantic, and yet he will insist upon reading them. I am willing to lay a wager that the very first thing which he does when he enters London will be to send cavalry detachments to the various newspaper offices, and to endeavour to seize the editors.'

'And the next?'

'The next,' said he, laughing, 'will be to issue a long proclamation to prove that we have conquered England entirely for the good of the English, and very much against our own inclinations. And then, perhaps, the Emperor will allow the English to understand that, if they absolutely demand a Protestant for a ruler, it is possible that there are a few little points in which he differs from Holy Church.'

'Too bad! Too bad!' cried de Meneval, looking amused and yet rather frightened at his companion's audacity. 'No doubt for state reasons the Emperor had to tamper a little with Mahomedanism, and I daresay he would attend this Church of St. Paul's as readily as he did the Mosque at Cairo; but it would not do for a ruler to be a bigot. After all, the Emperor has to think for all.'

'He thinks too much,' said Caulaincourt, gravely. 'He thinks so much that other people in France are getting out of the way of thinking at all. You know what I mean, de Meneval, for you have seen it as much as I have.'

'Yes, yes,' answered the secretary. 'He certainly does not encourage originality among those who surround him. I have heard him say many a time that he desired nothing but mediocrity, which was a poor compliment, it must be confessed, to us who have the honour of serving him.'

'A clever man at his Court shows his cleverness best by pretending to be dull,' said Caulaincourt, with some bitterness.

'And yet there are many famous characters there,' I remarked.

'If so, it is only by concealing their characters that they remain there. His ministers are clerks, his generals are superior aides-de-camp. They are all agents. You have this wonderful man in the middle, and all around you have so many mirrors which reflect different sides of him. In one you see him as a financier, and you call it Lebrun. In another you have him as a *gendarme*, and you name it Savary or Fouche. In yet another he figures as a diplomatist, and is called Talleyrand. You see different figures, but it is really the same man. There is a Monsieur de Caulaincourt, for example, who arranges the household; but he cannot dismiss a servant without permission. It is still always the Emperor. And he plays upon us. We must confess, de Meneval, that he plays upon us. In nothing else do I see so clearly his wonderful cleverness. He will not let us be too friendly lest we combine. He has set his Marshals against each other until there are hardly two of them on speaking terms. Look how Davoust hates Bernadotte, or Lannes and Bessieres, or Ney and Massena. It is all they can do to keep their sabres in they sheaths when they meet. And then he knows our weak points. Savary's thirst for money, Cambaceres's vanity, Duroc's bluntness, Berthier's foolishness, Maret's insipidity, Talleyrand's mania for speculation, they are all so many tools in his hand. I do not know what my own greatest weakness may be, but I am sure that he does, and that he uses his knowledge.'

'But how he must work!' I exclaimed.

'Ah, you may say so,' said de Meneval. 'What energy! Eighteen hours out of twenty-four for weeks on end. He has presided over the Legislative Council until they were fainting at their desks. As to me, he will be the death of me, just as he wore out de Bourrienne; but I will die at my post without a murmur, for if he is hard upon us he is hard upon himself also.'

'He was the man for France,' said de Caulaincourt. 'He is the very genius of system and of order, and of discipline. When one renumbers the chaos in which our poor country found itself after the Revolution, when no one would be governed and everyone wanted to govern someone else, you will understand that only Napoleon could have saved us. We were all longing for something fixed to secure ourselves to, and then we came upon this iron pillar of a man. And what a man he was in those days, Monsieur de Laval! You see him now when he has got all that he can want. He is good-humoured and easy. But at that time he had got nothing, but coveted everything. His glance frightened women. He walked the streets like a wolf. People looked after him as he passed. His face was quite different—it was craggy, hollow-cheeked, with an oblique menacing gaze, and the jaws of a pike. Oh, yes, this little Lieutenant Buonaparte from the

Military School of Brienne was a singular figure. "There is a man," said I, when I saw him, "who will sit upon a throne or kneel upon a scaffold." And now look at him!'

'And that is ten years ago,' I exclaimed.

'Only ten years, and they have brought him from a barrack-room to the Tuileries. But he was born for it. You could not keep him down. De Bourrienne told me that when he was a little fellow at Brienne he had the grand Imperial manner, and would praise or blame, glare or smile, exactly as he does now. Have you seen his mother, Monsieur de Laval? She is a tragedy queen, tall, stern, reserved, silent. There is the spring from which he flowed.'

I could see in the gentle, spaniel-eyes of the secretary that he was disturbed by the frankness of de Caulaincourt's remarks.

'You can tell that we do not live under a very terrible tyranny, Monsieur de Laval,' said he, 'or we should hardly venture to discuss our ruler so frankly. The fact is that we have said nothing which he would not have listened to with pleasure and perhaps with approval. He has his little frailties, or he would not be human, but take his qualities as a ruler and I would ask you if there has ever been a man who has justified the choice of a nation so completely. He works harder than any of his subjects. He is a general beloved by his soldiers. He is a master beloved by his servants. He never has a holiday, and he is always ready for his work. There is not under the roof of the Tuileries a more abstemious eater or drinker. He educated his brothers at his own expense when he was a very poor man, and he has caused even his most distant relatives to share in his prosperity. In a word, he is economical, hard-working, and temperate. We read in the London papers about this Prince of Wales, Monsieur de Laval, and I do not think that he comes very well out of the comparison.'

I thought of the long record of Brighton scandals, London scandals, Newmarket scandals, and I had to leave George undefended.

'As I understand it,' said I, 'it is not the Emperor's private life, but his public ambition, that the English attack.'

'The fact is,' said de Caulaincourt, 'that the Emperor knows, and we all know, that there is not room enough in the world for both France and England. One or other must be supreme. If England were once crushed we could then lay the foundations of a permanent peace. Italy is ours. Austria we can crush again as we have crushed her before. Germany is divided. Russia can expand to the south and east. America we can take at our leisure, finding our pretext in Louisiana or in Canada. There is a world empire waiting for us, and there is the only thing that stops us.' He pointed out through the opening of the tent at the broad blue Channel.

Far away, like snow-white gulls in the distance, were the sails of the blockading fleet. I thought again of what I had seen the night before—the lights of the ships upon the sea and the glow of the camp upon the shore. The powers of the land and of the ocean were face to face whilst a waiting world stood round to see what would come of it.

CHAPTER 12

The Man of Action

De Meneval's tent had been pitched in such a way that he could overlook the Royal headquarters, but whether it was that we were too absorbed in the interest of our conversation, or that the Emperor had used the other entrance in returning from the review, we were suddenly startled by the appearance of a captain dressed in the green jacket of the Chasseurs of the Guard, who had come to say that Napoleon was waiting for his secretary. Poor de Meneval's face turned as white as his beautiful ruffles as he sprang to his feet, hardly able to speak for agitation.

'I should have been there!' he gasped. 'Oh, what a misfortune! Monsieur de Caulaincourt, you must excuse me! Where is my hat and my sword? Come, Monsieur de Laval, not an instant is to be lost!'

I could judge from the terror of de Meneval, as well as from the scene which I had witnessed with Admiral Bruix, what the influence was which the Emperor exercised over those who were around him. They were never at their ease, always upon the brink of a catastrophe, encouraged one day only to be rudely rebuffed the next, bullied in public and slighted in private, and yet, in spite of it all, the singular fact remains that they loved him and served him as no monarch has been loved and served.

'Perhaps I had best stay here,' said I, when we had come to the ante-chamber, which was still crowded with people.

'No, no, I am responsible for you. You must come with me. Oh, I trust he is not offended with me! How could he have got in without my seeing him?'

My frightened companion scratched at the door, which was opened instantly by Rousten the Mameluke, who guarded it within. The room into which we passed was of considerable size, but was furnished with extreme simplicity. It was papered of a silver-grey colour, with a sky-blue ceiling, in the centre of which was the Imperial eagle in gold, holding a thunderbolt. In spite of the warm weather, a large fire was burning at one side, and the air was heavy with heat and the aromatic smell of aloes. In the middle of the room was a large oval table covered with green cloth and littered with a number of letters and papers. A raised writing-desk was at one side of the table, and behind it in a green morocco chair with curved arms there sat the Emperor. A number of officials were standing round the walls, but he took no notice of them. In his hand he had a small penknife, with which he whittled the wooden knob at the end of his chair. He glanced up as we entered, and shook his head coldly at de Meneval.

'I have had to wait for you, Monsieur de Meneval,' said he. 'I cannot remember that I ever waited for my late secretary de Bourrienne. That is enough! No excuses! Take this report which I have written in your absence, and make a copy of it.'

Poor de Meneval took the paper with a shaking hand, and carried it to the little side table which was reserved for his use. Napoleon rose and paced slowly up and down the room with his hands behind his back, and his big round head stooping a little forwards. It was certainly as well that he had a secretary, for I observed that in writing this single document he had spattered the whole place with ink, and it was obvious that he had twice used his white kerseymere knee-breeches as a pen-wiper. As for me, I stood quietly beside Rousten at the door, and he took not the slightest notice of my presence.

'Well,' he cried presently, 'is it ready, de Meneval? We have something more to do.'

The secretary half turned in his chair, and his face was more agitated than ever.

'If it please you, Sire——' he stammered.

'Well, well, what is the matter now?'

'If it please you, Sire, I find some little difficulty in reading what you have written.'

'Tut, tut, sir. You see what the report is about.'

'Yes, Sire, it is about forage for the cavalry horses.'

Napoleon smiled, and the action made his face look quite boyish.

'You remind me of Cambaceres, de Meneval. When I wrote him an account of the battle of Marengo, he thought that my letter was a rough plan of the engagement. It is incredible how much difficulty you appear to have in reading what I write. This document has nothing to do with cavalry horses, but it contains the instructions to Admiral Villeneuve as to the concentration of his fleet so as to obtain command of the Channel. Give it to me and I will read it to you.'

He snatched the paper up in the quick impulsive way which was characteristic of him. But after a long fierce stare he crumpled it up and hurled it under the table.

'I will dictate it to you,' said he; and, pacing up and down the long room, he poured forth a torrent of words, which poor de Meneval, his face shining with his exertions, strove hard to put upon paper. As he grew excited by his own ideas, Napoleon's voice became shriller, his step faster, and he seized his right cuff in the fingers of the same hand, and twisted his right arm in the singular epileptic gesture which was peculiar to him. But his thoughts and plans were so admirably clear that even I, who knew nothing of the matter, could readily follow them, while above all I was impressed by the marvellous grasp of fact which enabled him to speak with confidence, not only of the line-of-battle ships, but of the frigates, sloops, and brigs at Ferrol, Rochefort, Cadiz, Carthagena, and Brest, with the exact strength of each in men and in guns; while the names and force of the English vessels were equally at his fingers' ends. Such familiarity would have been remarkable in a naval officer, but when I thought that this question of the ships was only one out of fifty with which this man had to deal, I began to realise the immense grasp of that capacious mind. He did not appear to be paying the least attention to me, but it seems that he was really watching me closely, for he turned upon me when he had finished his dictation.

'You appear to be surprised, Monsieur de Laval, that I should be able to transact my naval business without having my minister of marine at my elbow; but it is one of my rules to know and to do things for myself. Perhaps if these good Bourbons had had the same habit they would not now be living amidst the fogs of England.'

'One must have your Majesty's memory in order to do it,' I observed.

'It is the result of system,' said he. 'It is as if I had drawers in my brain, so that when I opened one I could close the others. It is seldom that I fail to find what I want there. I have a poor memory for names or dates, but an excellent one for facts or faces. There is a good deal to bear in mind, Monsieur de Laval. For example, I have, as you have seen, my one little drawer full of the ships upon the sea. I have another which contains all the harbours and forts of France. As an example, I may tell you that when my minister of war was reading me a report of all the coast defences, I was able to point out to him that he had omitted two guns in a battery near Ostend. In yet another of my brain-drawers I have the regiments of France. Is that drawer in order, Marshal Berthier?'

A clean-shaven man, who had stood biting his nails in the window, bowed at the Emperor's question.

'I am sometimes tempted to believe, Sire, that you know the name of every man in the ranks,' said he.

'I think that I know most of my old Egyptian grumblers,' said he. 'And then, Monsieur de Laval, there is another drawer for canals, bridges, roads, manufactures, and every detail of internal administration. The law, finance, Italy, the Colonies, Holland, all these things demand drawers of their own. In these days, Monsieur de Laval, France asks something more of its ruler than that he should carry eight yards of ermine with dignity, or ride after a stag in the forest of Fontainebleau.'

I thought of the helpless, gentle, pompous Louis whom my father had once taken me to visit, and I understood that France, after her convulsions and her sufferings, did indeed require another and a stronger head.

'Do you not think so, Monsieur de Laval?' asked the Emperor. He had halted for a moment by the fire, and was grinding his dainty gold-buckled shoe into one of the burning logs.

'You have come to a very wise decision,' said he when I had answered his question. 'But you have always been of this way of thinking, have you not? Is it not true that you once defended me when some young Englishman was drinking toasts to my downfall at an inn in this village in which you lived?'

I remembered the incident, although I could not imagine how it had reached his ears.

'Why should you have done this?'

'I did it on impulse, Sire.'

'On impulse!' he cried, in a tone of contempt. 'I do not know what people mean when they say that they do things upon impulse. In Charenton things are doubtless done upon impulse, but not amongst sane people. Why should you risk your life over there in defending me when at the time you had nothing to hope for from me?'

'It was because I felt that you stood for France, Sire.'

During this conversation he had still walked up and down the room, twisting his right arm about, and occasionally looking at one or other of us with his eyeglass, for his sight was so weak that he always needed a single glass indoors and binoculars outside. Sometimes he stopped and helped himself to great pinches of snuff from a tortoise-shell box, but I observed that none of it ever reached his nose, for he dropped it all from between his fingers on to his waistcoat and the floor. My answer seemed to please him, for he suddenly seized my ear and pulled it with considerable violence.

'You are quite right, my friend,' said he. 'I stand for France just as Frederic the Second stood for Prussia. I will make her the great Power of the world, so that every monarch in Europe will find it necessary to keep a palace in Paris, and they will all come to hold the train at the coronation of my descendants—' a spasm of pain passed suddenly over his face. 'My God! for whom am I building? Who will be my descendants?' I heard him mutter, and he passed his hand over his forehead.

'Do they seem frightened in England about my approaching invasion?' he asked suddenly. 'Have you heard them express fears lest I get across the Channel?'

I was forced in truth to say that the only fears which I had ever heard expressed were lest he should not get across.

'The soldiers are very jealous that the sailors should always have the honour,' said I.

'But they have a very small army.'

'Nearly every man is a volunteer, Sire.'

'Pooh, conscripts!' he cried, and made a motion with his hands as if to sweep them from before him. I will land with a hundred thousand men in Kent or in Sussex. I will fight a great battle which I will win with a loss of ten thousand men. On the third day I shall be in London. I will seize the statesmen, the bankers, the merchants, the newspaper men. I will impose an indemnity of a hundred millions of their pounds. I will favour the poor at the expense of the rich, and so I shall have a party. I will detach Scotland and Ireland by giving them constitutions which will put them in a superior condition to England. Thus I will sow dissensions everywhere. Then as a price for leaving the island I will claim their fleet and their colonies. In this way I shall secure the command of the world to France for at least a century to come.'

In this short sketch I could perceive the quality which I have since heard remarked in Napoleon, that his mind could both conceive a large scheme, and at the same time evolve those practical details which would seem to bring it within the bounds of possibility. One instant it would be a wild dream of overrunning the East. The next it was a schedule of the ships, the ports, the stores, the troops, which would be needed to turn dream into fact. He gripped the heart of a question with the same decision which made him strike straight for an enemy's capital. The soul of a poet, and the mind of a man of business of the first order, that is the combination which may make a man dangerous to the world.

I think that it may have been his purpose—for he never did anything without a purpose—to give me an object-lesson of his own capacity for governing, with the idea, perhaps, that I might in turn influence others of the Emigres by what I told them. At any rate he left me there to stand and to watch the curious succession of points upon which he had to give an opinion during a few hours. Nothing seemed to be either too large or too small for that extraordinary mind. At one instant it was the arrangements for the winter cantonments of two hundred thousand men, at the next he was discussing with de Caulaincourt the curtailing of the expenses of the household, and the possibility of suppressing some of the carriages.

'It is my desire to be economical at home so as to make a good show abroad,' said he. 'For myself, when I had the honour to be a sub-lieutenant I found that I could live very well upon 1,200 *francs* a year, and it would be no hardship to me to go back to it. This extravagance of the palace must be stopped. For example, I see upon your accounts that 155 cups of coffee are drunk a day, which with sugar at 4 *francs* and coffee at 5 *francs* a pound come to 20 *sous* a cup. It would be better to make an allowance for coffee. The stable bills are also too high. At the present price of fodder seven or eight *francs* a week should be enough for each horse in a stable of two hundred. I will not have any waste at the Tuileries.'

Thus within a few minutes he would pass from a question of milliards to a question of *sous*, and from the management of a empire to that of a stable. From time to time I could observe that he threw a little oblique glance at me as if to ask what I thought of it all, and at the time I wondered very much why my approval should be of any consequence to him. But now, when I look back and see that my following his fortunes brought over so many others of the young nobility, I understand that he saw very much further than I did.

'Well, Monsieur de Laval,' said he suddenly, 'you have seen something of my methods. Are you prepared to enter my service?'

'Assuredly, Sire,' I answered.

'I can be a very hard master when I like,' said he smiling. 'You were there when I spoke to Admiral Bruix. We have all our duty to do, and discipline is as necessary in the highest as in the lowest ranks. But anger with me never rises above here,' and he drew his hand across his throat. 'I never permit it to cloud my brain. Dr. Corvisart here would tell you that I have the slowest pulse of all his patients.'

'And that you are the fastest eater, Sire,' said a large-faced, benevolent-looking person who had been whispering to Marshal Berthier.

'Ohe, you rascal, you rake that up against me, do you? The Doctor will not forgive me because I tell him when I am unwell that I had rather die of the disease than of the remedies. If I eat too fast it is the fault of the State, which does not allow me more than a few minutes for my meals. Which reminds me that it must be rather after my dinner hour, Constant?'

'It is four hours after it, Sire.'

'Serve it up then at once.'

'Yes, Sire. Monsieur Isabey is outside, Sire, with his dolls.'

'Ah, we shall see them at once. Show him in.'

A man entered who had evidently just arrived from a long journey. Under his arm he carried a large flat wickerwork basket.

'It is two days since I sent for you, Monsieur Isabey.'

'The courier arrived yesterday, Sire. I have been travelling from Paris ever since.'

'Have you the models there?'

'Yes, Sire.'

'Then you may lay them out on that table.'

I could not at first imagine what it meant when I saw, upon Isabey opening his basket, that it was crammed with little puppets about a foot high, all of them dressed in the most gorgeous silk and velvet costumes, with trimmings of ermine and hangings of gold lace. But presently, as the designer took them out one by one and placed them on the table, I understood that the Emperor, with his extraordinary passion for detail and for directly controlling everything in his Court, had had these dolls dressed in order to judge the effect of the gorgeous costumes which had been ordered for his grand functionaries upon State occasions.

'What is this?' he asked, holding up a little lady in hunting costume of amaranth and gold with a toque and plume of white feathers.

'That is for the Empress's hunt, Sire.'

'You should have the waist rather lower,' said Napoleon, who had very definite opinions about ladies' dresses. 'These cursed fashions seem to be the only thing in my dominions which I cannot regulate. My tailor, Duchesne, takes three inches from my coat-tails, and all the armies and fleets of France cannot prevent him. Who is this?'

He had picked up a very gorgeous figure in a green coat.

'That is the grand master of the hunt, Sire.'

'Then it is you, Berthier. How do you like your new costume? And this in red?'

'That is the Arch-Chancellor.'

'And the violet?'

'That is the Grand Chamberlain.'

The Emperor was as much amused as a child with a new toy. He formed little groups of the figures upon the table, so that he might have an idea of how the dignitaries would look when they chatted together. Then he threw them all back into the basket.

'Very good,' said he. 'You and David have done your work very well, Isabey. You will submit these designs to the Court outfitters and have an estimate for the expense. You may tell Lenormand that if she ventures to send in such an account as the last which she sent to the Empress she shall see the inside of Vincennes. You would not think it right, Monsieur de Laval, to spend twenty-five thousand *francs* upon a single dress, even though it were for Mademoiselle Eugenie de Choiseul.'

Was there anything which this wizard of a man did not know? What could my love affairs be to him amidst the clash of armies and the struggles of nations? When I looked at him, half in amazement and half in fear, that pleasant boyish smile lit up his pale face, and his plump little hand rested for an instant upon my shoulder. His eyes were of a bright blue when he was amused, though they would turn dark when he was thoughtful, and steel-grey in moments of excitement.

'You were surprised when I told you a little while ago about your encounter with the Englishman in the village inn. You are still more surprised now when I tell you about a certain young lady. You must certainly have thought that I was very badly served by my agents in England if I did not know such important details as these.'

'I cannot conceive, Sire, why such trifles should be reported to you, or why you should for one instant remember them.'

'You are certainly a very modest young man, and I hope you will not lose that charming quality when you have been for a little time at my Court. So you think that your own private affairs are of no importance to me?'

'I do not know why they should be, Sire.'

'What is the name of your great-uncle?'

'He is the Cardinal de Laval de Montmorency.'

'Precisely. And where is he?'

'He is in Germany.'

'Quite so—in Germany, and not at Notre Dame, where I should have placed him. Who is your first cousin?'

'The Duke de Rohan.'

'And where is he?'

'In London.'

'Yes, in London, and not at the Tuileries, where he might have had what he liked for the asking. I wonder if I were to fall whether I should have followers as faithful as those of the Bourbons. Would the men that I have made go into exile and refuse all offers until I should return? Come here, Berthier!' he took his favourite by the ear with the caressing gesture which was peculiar to him. 'Could I count upon you, you rascal—eh?'

'I do not understand you, Sire.' Our conversation had been carried on in a voice which had made it inaudible to the other people in the room, but now they were all listening to what Berthier had to say.

'If I were driven out, would you go into exile also?'

'No, Sire.'

'*Diable!* At least you are frank.'

'I could not go into exile, Sire.'

'And why?'

'Because I should be dead, Sire.'

Napoleon began to laugh.

'And there are some who say that our Berthier is dull-witted,' said he. 'Well, I think I am pretty sure of you, Berthier, for although I am fond of you for reasons of my own I do not think that you would be of much value to anyone else. Now I could not say that of you, Monsieur Talleyrand. You would change very quickly to a new master as you have changed from an old one. You have a genius, you know, for adapting yourself.'

There was nothing which the Emperor loved more than to suddenly produce little scenes of this sort which made everybody very uncomfortable, for no one could tell what awkward or compromising question he was going to put to them next. At present, however, they all forgot their own fears of what might come in their interest at the reply which the famous diplomatist might make to a suggestion which everybody knew to be so true. He stood, leaning upon his black ebony stick, with his bulky shoulders stooping forward, and an amused smile upon his face, as if the most innocent of compliments had been addressed to him. One of his few titles to respect is that he always met Napoleon upon equal terms, and never condescended to fawn upon him or to flatter him.

'You think I should desert you, Sire, if your enemies offered me more than you have given me?'

'I am perfectly sure that you would.'

'Well, really I cannot answer for myself, Sire, until the offer has been made. But it will have to be a very large one. You see, apart from my very nice hotel in the Rue St. Florentin, and the two hundred thousand or so which you are pleased to allow me, there is my position as the first minister in Europe. Really, Sire, unless they put me on the throne I cannot see how I can better my position.'

'No, I think I have you pretty safe,' said Napoleon, looking hard at him with thoughtful eyes. 'By the way, Talleyrand, you must either marry Madame Grand or get rid of her, for I cannot have a scandal about the Court.'

I was astounded to hear so delicate and personal a matter discussed in this public way, but this also was characteristic of the rule of this extraordinary man, who proclaimed that he looked upon delicacy and good taste as two of the fetters with which mediocrity attempted to cripple genius. There was no question of private life, from the choosing of a wife to the discarding of a mistress, that this young conqueror of thirty-six did not claim the right of discussing and of finally settling. Talleyrand broke once more into his benevolent but inscrutable smile.

'I suppose that it is from early association, Sire,' said he, 'but my instincts are to avoid marriage.'

Napoleon began to laugh.

'I forget sometimes that it is really the Bishop of Autun to whom I am speaking,' said he. 'I think that perhaps I have interest enough with the Pope to ask him, in return for any little attention which we gave him at the Coronation, to show you some leniency in this matter. She is a clever woman, this Madame Grand. I have observed that she listens with attention.'

Talleyrand shrugged his rounded shoulders. 'Intellect in a woman is not always an advantage, Sire. A clever woman compromises her husband. A stupid woman only compromises herself.'

'The cleverest woman,' said Napoleon, 'is the woman who is clever enough to conceal her cleverness. The women in France have always been a danger, for they are cleverer than the men. They cannot understand that it is their hearts and not their heads that we want. When they have had influence upon a monarch, they have invariably ruined his career. Look at Henry the Fourth and Louis the Fourteenth. They are all ideologists, dreamers, sentimentalists, full of emotion and energy, but without logic or foresight. Look at that accursed Madame de Stael! Look at the Salons of the Quartier St. Germain! Their eternal clack, clack, clack give me more trouble than the fleet of England. Why cannot they look after their babies and their needlework? I suppose you think that these are very dreadful opinions, Monsieur de Laval?'

It was not an easy question to answer, so I was silent.

'You have not at your age become a practical man,' said the Emperor. 'You will understand then. I dare say that I thought as you do at the time when the stupid Parisians were saying what a misalliance the widow of the famous General de Beauharnais was making by marrying the unknown Buonaparte. It was a beautiful dream! There are nine inns in a single day's journey between Milan and Mantua, and I wrote a letter to my wife from each of them. Nine letters in a day—but one becomes disillusioned, monsieur. One learns to accept things as they are.'

I could not but think what a beautiful young man he must have been before he had learned to accept things as they are. The glamour, the romance—what a bald dead thing is life without it! His own face had clouded over as if that old life had perhaps had a charm which the Emperor's crown had never given. It may be that those nine letters written in one day at wayside inns had brought him more true joy than all the treaties by which he had torn provinces from his neighbours. But the sentiment passed from his face, and he came back in his sudden concise fashion to my own affairs.

'Eugenie de Choiseul is the niece of the Duc de Choiseul, is she not?' he asked.

'Yes, Sire.'

'You are affianced!'

'Yes, Sire.'

He shook his head impatiently.

'If you wish to advance yourself in my Court, Monsieur de Laval,' said he,' you must commit such matters to my care. Is it likely that I can look with indifference upon a marriage between emigres—an alliance between my enemies?'

'But she shares my opinions, Sire.'

'*Ta, ta, ta,* at her age one has no opinions. She has the *emigre* blood in her veins, and it will come out. Your marriage shall be my care, Monsieur de Laval. And I wish you to come to the Pont de Briques that you may be presented to the Empress. What is it, Constant?'

'There is a lady outside who desires to see your Majesty. Shall I tell her to come later?'

'A lady!' cried the Emperor smiling. 'We do not see many faces in the camp which have not a moustache upon them. Who is she? What does she want?'

'Her name, Sire, is Mademoiselle Sibylle Bernac.'

'What!' cried Napoleon. 'It must be the daughter of old Bernac of Grosbois. By the way, Monsieur de Laval, he is your uncle upon your mother's side, is he not?'

I may have flushed with shame as I acknowledged it, for the Emperor read my feelings.

'Well, well, he has not a very savoury trade, it is true, and yet I can assure you that it is one which is very necessary to me. By the way, this uncle of yours, as I understand, holds the estates which should have descended to you, does he not?'

'Yes, Sire.'

His blue eyes flashed suspicion at me.

'I trust that you are not joining my service merely in the hope of having them restored to you.'

'No, Sire. It is my ambition to make a career for myself.'

'It is a prouder thing,' said the Emperor, 'to found a family than merely to perpetuate one. I could not restore your estates, Monsieur de Laval, for things have come to such a pitch in France that if one once begins restorations the affair is endless. It would shake all public confidence. I have no more devoted adherents than the men who hold land which does not belong to them. As long as they serve me, as your uncle serves me, the land must remain with them. But what can this young lady require of me? Show her in, Constant!'

An instant later my cousin Sibylle was conducted into the room. Her face was pale and set, but her large dark eyes were filled with resolution, and she carried herself like a princess.

'Well, mademoiselle, why do you come here? What is it that you want?' asked the Emperor in the brusque manner which he adopted to women, even if he were wooing them.

Sibylle glanced round, and as our eyes met for an instant I felt that my presence had renewed her courage. She looked bravely at the Emperor as she answered him.

'I come, Sire, to implore a favour of you.'

'Your father's daughter has certainly claims upon me, mademoiselle. What is it that you wish?'

'I do not ask it in my father's name, but in my own. I implore you, Sire, to spare the life of Monsieur Lucien Lesage, who was arrested yesterday upon a charge of treason. He is a student, Sire—a mere dreamer who has lived away from the world and has been made a tool by designing men.'

'A dreamer!' cried the Emperor harshly. 'They are the most dangerous of all.' He took a bundle of notes from his table and glanced them over. 'I presume that he is fortunate enough to be your lover, mademoiselle?'

Sibylle's pale face flushed, and she looked down before the Emperor's keen sardonic glance.

'I have his examination here. He does not come well out of it. I confess that from what I see of the young man's character I should not say that he is worthy of your love.'

'I implore you to spare him, Sire.'

'What you ask is impossible, mademoiselle. I have been conspired against from two sides—by the Bourbons and by the Jacobins. Hitherto I have been too long-suffering, and they have been encouraged by my patience. Since Cadoudal and the Duc d'Enghien died the Bourbons have been quiet. Now I must teach the same lesson to these others.'

I was astonished and am still astonished at the passion with which my brave and pure cousin loved this cowardly and low-minded man, though it is but in accordance with that strange law which draws the extremes of nature together. As she heard the Emperor's stern reply the last sign of colour faded from her pale face, and her eyes were dimmed with despairing tears, which gleamed upon her white cheeks like dew upon the petals of a lily.

'For God's sake, Sire! For the love of your mother spare him!' she cried, falling upon her knees at the Emperor's feet. 'I will answer for him that he never offends you again.'

'Tut, tut!' cried Napoleon angrily, turning upon his heel and walking impatiently up and down the room. 'I cannot grant you what you ask, mademoiselle. When I say so once it is finished.

I cannot have my decisions in high matters of State affected by the intrusion of women. The Jacobins have been dangerous of late, and an example must be made or we shall have the Faubourg St. Antoine upon our hands once more.'

The Emperors set face and firm manner showed it was hopeless, and yet my cousin persevered as no one but a woman who pleads for her lover would have dared to do.

'He is harmless, Sire.'

'His death will frighten others.'

'Spare him and I will answer for his loyalty.'

'What you ask is impossible.'

Constant and I raised her from the ground.

'That is right, Monsieur de Laval,' said the Emperor. 'This interview can lead to nothing. Remove your cousin from the room!'

But she had again turned to him with a face which showed that even now all hope had not been abandoned.

'Sire,' she cried. 'You say that an example must be made. There is Toussac—!'

'Ah, if I could lay my hands upon Toussac!'

'He is the dangerous man. It was he and my father who led Lucien on. If an example must be made it should be an example of the guilty rather than of the innocent.'

'They are both guilty. And, besides, we have our hands upon the one but not upon the other.'

'But if I could find him?'

Napoleon thought for a moment.

'If you do,' said he, 'Lesage will be forgiven!'

'But I cannot do it in a day.'

'How long do you ask?'

'A week at the least.'

'Then he has a respite of a week. If you can find Toussac in the time, Lesage will be pardoned. If not he will die upon the eighth day. It is enough. Monsieur de Laval, remove your cousin, for I have matters of more importance to attend to. I shall expect you one evening at the Pont de Briques, when you are ready to be presented to the Empress.'

CHAPTER 13

The Man of Dreams

When I had escorted my cousin Sibylle from the presence of the Emperor, I was surprised to find the same young hussar officer waiting outside who had commanded the guard which had brought me to the camp.

'Well, mademoiselle, what luck?' he asked excitedly, clanking towards us.

For answer Sibylle shook her head.

'Ah, I feared as much, for the Emperor is a terrible man. It was brave, indeed, of you to attempt it. I had rather charge an unshaken square upon a spent horse than ask him for anything. But my heart is heavy, mademoiselle, that you should have been unsuccessful.' His boyish blue eyes filled with tears and his fair moustache drooped in such a deplorable fashion, that I could have laughed had the matter been less serious.

'Lieutenant Gerard chanced to meet me, and escorted me through the camp,' said my cousin. 'He has been kind enough to give me sympathy in my trouble.'

'And so do I, Sibylle,' I cried; 'you carried yourself like an angel, and it is a lucky man who is blessed with your love. I trust that he may be worthy of it.'

She turned cold and proud in an instant when anyone threw a doubt upon this wretched lover of hers.

'I know him as neither the Emperor nor you can do,' said she. 'He has the heart and soul of a poet, and he is too high-minded to suspect the intrigues to which he has fallen a victim. But as to Toussac, I should have no pity upon him, for I know him to be a murderer five times over, and I know also that there will be no peace in France until he has been taken. Cousin Louis, will you help me to do it?'

The lieutenant had been tugging at his moustache and looking me up and down with a jealous eye.

'Surely, mademoiselle, you will permit me to help you?' he cried in a piteous voice.

'I may need you both,' said she. 'I will come to you if I do. Now I will ask you to ride with me to the edge of the camp and there to leave me.'

She had a quick imperative way which came charmingly from those sweet womanly lips. The grey horse upon which I had come to the camp was waiting beside that of the hussar, so we were soon in the saddle. When we were clear of the huts my cousin turned to us. 'I had rather go alone now,' said she. 'It is understood, then, that I can rely upon you.'

'Entirely,' said I.

'To the death,' cried Gerard.

'It is everything to me to have two brave men at my back,' said she, and so, with a smile, gave her horse its head and cantered off over the downland in the direction of Grosbois.

For my part I remained in thought for some time, wondering what plan she could have in her head by which she hoped to get upon the track of Toussac. A woman's wit, spurred by the danger of her lover, might perhaps succeed where Fouche and Savary had failed. When at last I turned my horse I found my young hussar still staring after the distant rider.

'My faith! There is the woman for you, Etienne!' he kept repeating. 'What an eye! What a smile! What a rider! And she is not afraid of the Emperor. Oh, Etienne, here is the woman who is worthy of you!'

These were the little sentences which he kept muttering to himself until she vanished over the hill, when he became conscious at last of my presence.

'You are mademoiselle's cousin?' he asked. 'You are joined with me in doing something for her. I do not yet know what it is, but I am perfectly ready to do it.'

'It is to capture Toussac.'

'Excellent!'

'In order to save the life of her lover.'

There was a struggle in the face of the young hussar, but his more generous nature won.

'*Sapristi!* I will do even that if it will make her the happier!' he cried, and he shook the hand which I extended towards him. 'The Hussars of Bercheny are quartered over yonder, where you see the lines of picketed horses. If you will send for Lieutenant Etienne Gerard you will find a sure blade always at your disposal. Let me hear from you then, and the sooner the better!' He shook his bridle and was off, with youth and gallantry in every line of him, from his red toupee and flowing dolman to the spur which twinkled on his heel.

But for four long days no word came from my cousin as to her quest, nor did I hear from this grim uncle of mine at the Castle of Grosbois. For myself I had gone into the town of Boulogne and had hired such a room as my thin purse could afford over the shop of a baker named Vidal, next to the Church of St. Augustin, in the Rue des Vents. Only last year I went back there under that strange impulse which leads the old to tread once more with dragging feet the same spots which have sounded to the crisp tread of their youth. The room is still there, the very pictures and the plaster head of Jean Bart which used to stand upon the side table. As I stood with my back to the narrow window, I had around me every smallest detail upon which my young eyes had looked; nor was I conscious that my own heart and feelings had undergone much change. And yet there, in the little round glass which faced me, was the long drawn, weary face of an aged man, and out of the window, when I turned, were the bare and lonely downs which had been peopled by that mighty host of a hundred and fifty thousand men. To think that the Grand Army should have vanished away like a shredding cloud upon a windy day, and yet that every sordid detail of a bourgeois lodging should remain unchanged! Truly, if man is not humble it is not for want of having his lesson taught to him by Nature.

My first care after I had chosen my room was to send to Grosbois for that poor little bundle which I had carried ashore with me that squally night from the English lugger. My next was to use the credit which my favourable reception by the Emperor and his assurance of employment had given me in order to obtain such a wardrobe as would enable me to appear without discredit among the richly dressed courtiers and soldiers who surrounded him. It was well known that it was his whim that he should himself be the only plainly-dressed man in the company, and that in the most luxurious times of the Bourbons there was never a period when fine linen and a brave coat were more necessary for a man who would keep in favour. A new court and a young empire cannot afford to take anything for granted.

It was upon the morning of the fifth day that I received a message from Duroc, who was the head of the household, that I was to attend the Emperor at the headquarters in the camp, and that a seat in one of the Imperial carriages would be at my disposal that I might proceed with the Court to Pont de Briques, there to be present at the reception of the Empress. When I arrived I was shown at once through the large entrance tent, and admitted by Constant into the room beyond, where the Emperor stood with his back to the fire, kicking his heels against the grate. Talleyrand and Berthier were in attendance, and de Meneval, the secretary, sat at the writing-table.

'Ah, Monsieur de Laval,' said the Emperor with a friendly nod. 'Have you heard anything yet of your charming cousin?'

'Nothing, Sire,' I answered.

'I fear that her efforts will be in vain. I wish her every success, for we have no reason at all to fear this miserable poet, while the other is formidable. All the same, an example of some sort must be made.'

The darkness was drawing in, and Constant had appeared with a taper to light the candles, but the Emperor ordered him out.

'I like the twilight,' said he. 'No doubt, Monsieur de Laval, after your long residence in England you find yourself also most at home in a dim light. I think that the brains of these people must be as dense as their fogs, to judge by the nonsense which they write in their accursed papers.' With one of those convulsive gestures which accompanied his sudden outbursts of passion he seized a sheaf of late London papers from the table, and ground them into the fire with his heel. 'An editor!' he cried in the guttural rasping voice which I had heard when I first met him. 'What is he? A dirty man with a pen in a back office. And he will talk like one of the great Powers of Europe. I have had enough of this freedom of the Press. There are some who would like to see it established in Paris. You are among them, Talleyrand. For my part I see no need for any paper at all except the *Moniteur* by which the Government may make known its decisions to the people.'

'I am of opinion, Sire,' said the minister, 'that it is better to have open foes than secret ones, and that it is less dangerous to shed ink than blood. What matter if your enemies have leave to rave in a few Paris papers, as long as you are at the head of five hundred thousand armed men?'

'Ta, ta, ta!' cried the Emperor impatiently. 'You speak as if I had received my crown from my father the late king. But even if I had, it would be intolerable, this government by newspaper. The Bourbons allowed themselves to be criticised, and where are they now? Had they used their Swiss Guards as I did the Grenadiers upon the eighteenth Brumaire what would have become of their precious National Assembly? There was a time when a bayonet in the stomach of Mirabeau might have settled the whole matter. Later it took the heads of a king and queen and the blood of a hundred thousand people.'

He sat down, and stretched his plump, white-clad legs towards the fire. Through the blackened shreds of the English papers the red glow beat upwards upon the beautiful, pallid, sphinx-like face—the face of a poet, of a philosopher—of anything rather than of a ruthless and ambitious soldier. I have heard folk remark that no two portraits of the Emperor are alike, and the fault does not lie with the artists but with the fact that every varying mood made him a different man. But in his prime, before his features became heavy, I, who have seen sixty years of mankind, can say that in repose I have never looked upon a more beautiful face.

'You have no dreams and no illusions, Talleyrand,' said he. 'You are always practical, cold, and cynical. But with me, when I am in the twilight, as now, or when I hear the sound of the sea, my imagination begins to work. It is the same when I hear some music—especially music which repeats itself again and again like some pieces of Passaniello. They have a strange effect upon me, and I begin to Ossianise. I get large ideas and great aspirations. It is at such times that my mind always turns to the East, that swarming ant-heap of the human race, where alone it is possible to be very great. I renew my dreams of '98. I think of the possibility of drilling and arming these vast masses of men, and of precipitating them upon Europe. Had I conquered Syria I should have done this, and the fate of the world was really decided at the siege of Acre. With Egypt at my feet I already pictured myself approaching India, mounted upon an elephant, and holding in my hand a new version of the Koran which I had myself composed. I have been born too late. To be accepted as a world's conqueror one must claim to be divine. Alexander declared himself to be the son of Jupiter, and no one questioned it. But the world has grown old, and has lost its enthusiasms. What would happen if I were to make the same claim? Monsieur de Talleyrand would smile behind his hand, and the Parisians would write little lampoons upon the walls.'

He did not appear to be addressing us, but rather to be expressing his thoughts aloud, while allowing them to run to the most fantastic and extravagant lengths. This it was which he called Ossianising, because it recalled to him the wild vague dreams of the Gaelic Ossian, whose poems had always had a fascination for him. De Meneval has told me that for an hour at a time he has sometimes talked in this strain of the most intimate thoughts and aspirations of his heart, while his courtiers have stood round in silence waiting for the instant when he would return once more to his practical and incisive self.

'The great ruler,' said he, 'must have the power of religion behind him as well as the power of the sword. It is more important to command the souls than the bodies of men. The Sultan, for example, is the head of the faith as well as of the army. So were some of the Roman Emperors. My position must be incomplete until this is accomplished. At the present instant there are thirty departments in France where the Pope is more powerful than I am. It is only by universal dominion that peace can be assured in the world. When there is only one authority in Europe, seated at Paris, and when all the kings are so many lieutenants who hold their crowns from the central power of France, it is then that the reign of peace will be established. Many powers of equal strength must always lead to struggles until one becomes predominant. Her central position, her wealth and her history, all mark France out as being the power which will control and regulate the others. Germany is divided. Russia is barbarous. England is insular. France only remains.'

I began to understand as I listened to him that my friends in England had not been so far wrong when they had declared that as long as he lived—this little thirty-six year old artilleryman—there could not possibly be any peace in the world. He drank some coffee which Constant had placed upon the small round table at his elbow. Then he leaned back in his chair once more, still staring moodily at the red glow of the fire, with his chin sunk upon his chest.

'In those days,' said he, 'the kings of Europe will walk behind the Emperor of France in order to hold up his train at his coronation. Each of them will have to maintain a palace in Paris, and the city will stretch as far as Versailles. These are the plans which I have made for Paris if she will show herself to be worthy of them. But I have no love for them, these Parisians, and they have none for me, for they cannot forget that I turned my guns upon them once before, and they know that I am ready to do so again. I have made them admire me and fear me, but I have never made them like me. Look what I have done for them. Where are the treasures of Genoa, the pictures and statues of Venice and of the Vatican? They are in the Louvre. The spoils of my victories have gone to decorate her. But they must always be changing, always chattering. They wave their hats at me now, but they would soon be waving their fists if I did not give them something to talk over and to wonder at. When other things are quiet, I have the dome of the Invalides regilded to keep their thoughts from mischief. Louis XIV. gave them wars. Louis XV. gave them the gallantries and scandals of his Court. Louis XVI. gave them nothing, so they cut off his head. It was you who helped to bring him to the scaffold, Talleyrand.'

'No, Sire, I was always a moderate.'

'At least, you did not regret his death.'

'The less so, since it has made room for you, Sire.'

'Nothing could have held me down, Talleyrand. I was born to reach the highest. It has always been the same with me. I remember when we were arranging the Treaty of Campo Formio—I a young general under thirty—there was a high vacant throne with the Imperial arms in the Commissioner's tent. I instantly sprang up the steps, and threw myself down upon it. I could not endure to think that there was anything above myself. And all the time I knew in my heart all that was going to happen to me. Even in the days when my brother Lucien and I lived in a little room upon a few *francs* a week, I knew perfectly well that the day would come when I should stand where I am now. And yet I had no prospects and no reason for any great hopes. I was not clever at school. I was only the forty-second out of fifty-eight. At mathematics I had perhaps some ability, but at nothing else. The truth is that I was always dreaming when the others were working. There was nothing to encourage my ambition, for the only thing which I inherited from my father was a weak stomach. Once, when I was very young, I went up to Paris with my father and my sister Caroline. We were in the Rue Richelieu, and we saw the king pass in his carriage. Who would have thought that the little boy from Corsica, who took his hat off and stared, was destined to be the next monarch of France? And yet even then I felt as if that carriage ought to belong to me. What is it, Constant?'

The discreet valet bent down and whispered something to the Emperor.

'Ah, of course,' said he. 'It was an appointment. I had forgotten it. Is she there?'

'Yes, Sire.'

'In the side room?'

'Yes, Sire.'

Talleyrand and Berthier exchanged glances, and the minister began to move towards the door.

'No, no, you can remain here,' said the Emperor. 'Light the lamps, Constant, and have the carriages ready in half-an-hour. Look over this draft of a letter to the Emperor of Austria, and let me have your observations upon it, Talleyrand. De Meneval, there is a lengthy report here as to the new dockyard at Brest. Extract what is essential from it, and leave it upon my desk at five o'clock to-morrow morning. Berthier, I will have the whole army into the boats at seven. We will see if they can embark within three hours. Monsieur de Laval, you will wait here until we start for Pont de Briques.' So with a crisp order to each of us, he walked with little swift steps across the room, and I saw his square green back and white legs framed for an instant in the doorway. There was the flutter of a pink skirt beyond, and then the curtains closed behind him.

Berthier stood biting his nails, while Talleyrand looked at him with a slight raising of his bushy eyebrows. De Meneval with a rueful face was turning over the great bundle of papers which had to be copied by morning. Constant, with a noiseless tread, was lighting the candles upon the sconces round the room.

'Which is it?' I heard the minister whisper.

'The girl from the Imperial Opera,' said Berthier.

'Is the little Spanish lady out of favour then?'

'No, I think not. She was here yesterday.'

'And the other, the Countess?'

'She has a cottage at Ambleteuse?'

'But we must have no scandal about the Court,' said Talleyrand, with a sour smile, recalling the moral sentiments with which the Emperor had reproved him. 'And now, Monsieur de Laval,' he added, drawing me aside, 'I very much wish to hear from you about the Bourbon party in England. You must have heard their views. Do they imagine that they have any chance of success?'

And so for ten minutes he plied me with questions, which

showed me clearly that the Emperor had read him aright, and that he was determined, come what might, to be upon the side which won. We were still talking when Constant entered hurriedly, with a look of anxiety and perplexity which I could not have imagined upon so smooth and imperturbable a face.

'Good Heavens, Monsieur Talleyrand,' he cried, clasping and unclasping his hands. 'Such a misfortune! Who could have expected it?'

'What is it, then, Constant?'

'Oh, Monsieur, I dare not intrude upon the Emperor. And yet—And yet—The Empress is outside, and she is coming in.'

CHAPTER 14

Josephine

At this unexpected announcement Talleyrand and Berthier looked at each other in silence, and for once the trained features of the great diplomatist, who lived behind a mask, betrayed the fact that he was still capable of emotion. The spasm which passed over them was caused, however, rather by mischievous amusement than by consternation, while Berthier—who had an honest affection for both Napoleon and Josephine—ran frantically to the door as if to bar the Empress from entering. Constant rushed towards the curtains which screened the Emperor's room, and then, losing courage, although he was known to be a stout-hearted man, he came running back to Talleyrand for advice. It was too late now, however, for Rousten the Mameluke had opened the door, and two ladies had entered the room. The first was tall and graceful, with a smiling face, and an affable though dignified manner. She was dressed in a black velvet cloak with white lace at the neck and sleeves, and she wore a black hat with a curling white feather. Her companion was shorter, with a countenance which would have been plain had it not been for the alert expression and large dark eyes, which gave it charm and character. A small black terrier dog had followed them in, but the first lady turned and handed the thin steel chain with which she led it to the Mameluke attendant.

'You had better keep Fortune outside, Rousten,' said she, in a peculiarly sweet musical voice. 'The Emperor is not very fond of dogs, and if we intrude upon his quarters we cannot do less than consult his tastes. Good evening, Monsieur de Talleyrand!

Madame de Remusat and I have driven all along the cliffs, and we have stopped as we passed to know if the Emperor is coming to Pont de Briques. But perhaps he has already started. I had expected to find him here.'

'His Imperial Majesty was here a short time ago,' said Talleyrand, bowing and rubbing his hands.

'I hold my *salon*—such a *salon* as Pont de Briques is capable of—this evening, and the Emperor promised me that he would set his work aside for once, and favour us with his presence. I wish we could persuade him to work less, Monsieur de Talleyrand. He has a frame of iron, but he cannot continue in this way. These nervous attacks come more frequently upon him. He will insist upon doing everything, everything himself. It is noble, but it is to be a martyr. I have no doubt that at the present moment—but you have not yet told me where he is, Monsieur de Talleyrand.'

'We expect him every instant, your Majesty.'

'In that case we shall sit down and await his return. Ah, Monsieur de Meneval, how I pity you when I see you among all those papers! I was desolate when Monsieur de Bourrienne deserted the Emperor, but you have more than taken his place. Come up to the fire, Madame de Remusat! Yes, yes, I insist upon it, for I know that you must be cold. Constant, come and put the rug under Madame de Remusat's feet.'

It was by little acts of thoughtfulness and kindness like this that the Empress so endeared herself that she had really no enemies in France, even among those who were most bitterly opposed to her husband. Whether as the consort of the first man in Europe, or as the lonely divorced woman eating her heart out at Malmaison, she was always praised and beloved by those who knew her. Of all the sacrifices which the Emperor ever made to his ambition that of his wife was the one which cost him the greatest struggle and the keenest regret.

Now as she sat before the fire in the same chair which had so recently been occupied by the Emperor, I had an opportunity of studying this person, whose strange fate had raised her from being the daughter of a lieutenant of artillery to the first position among the women of Europe. She was six years older than Napoleon, and on this occasion, when I saw her first, she was in her forty-second year; but at a little distance or in a discreet light, it was no courtier's flattery to say that she might very well have passed for thirty. Her tall, elegant figure was girlish in its supple slimness, and she had an easy and natural grace in every movement, which she inherited with her tropical West Indian blood. Her features were delicate, and I have heard that in her youth she was strikingly beautiful; but, like most Creole women, she had become *passee* in early middle age. She had made a brave fight, however—with art as her ally—against the attacks of time, and her success had been such that when she sat aloof upon a dais or drove past in a procession, she might still pass as a lovely woman. In a small room, however, or in a good light, the crude pinks and whites with which she had concealed her sallow cheeks became painfully harsh and artificial. Her own natural beauty, however, still lingered in that last refuge of beauty—the eyes, which were large, dark, and sympathetic. Her mouth, too, was small and amiable, and her most frequent expression was a smile, which seldom broadened into a laugh, as she had her own reasons for preferring that her teeth should not be seen. As to her bearing, it was so dignified, that if this little West Indian had come straight from the loins of Charlemagne, it could not have been improved upon. Her walk, her glance, the sweep of her dress, the wave of her hand—they had all the happiest mixture of the sweetness of a woman and the condescension of a queen. I watched her with admiration as she leaned forward, picking little pieces of aromatic aloes wood out of the basket and throwing them on to the fire.

'Napoleon likes the smell of burning aloes,' said she. 'There was never anyone who had such a nose as he, for he can detect things which are quite hidden from me.'

'The Emperor has an excellent nose for many things,' said Talleyrand. 'The State contractors have found that out to their cost.'

'Oh, it is dreadful when he comes to examine accounts—dreadful, Monsieur de Talleyrand! Nothing escapes him. He will make no allowances. Everything must be exact. But who is this young gentleman, Monsieur de Talleyrand? I do not think that he has been presented to me.'

The minister explained in a few words that I had been received into the Emperor's personal service, and Josephine congratulated me upon it with the most kindly sympathy.

'It eases my mind so to know that he has brave and loyal men round him. Ever since that dreadful affair of the infernal machine I have always been uneasy if he is away from me. He is really safest in time of war, for it is only then that he is away from the assassins who hate him. And now I understand that a new Jacobin plot has only just been discovered.'

'This is the same Monsieur de Laval who was there when the conspirator was taken,' said Talleyrand.

The Empress overwhelmed me with questions, hardly waiting for the answers in her anxiety.

'But this dreadful man Toussac has not been taken yet,' she cried. 'Have I not heard that a young lady is endeavouring to do what has baffled the secret police, and that the freedom of her lover is to be the reward of her success?'

'She is my cousin, your Imperial Majesty. Mademoiselle Sibylle Bernac is her name.'

'You have only been in France a few days, Monsieur de Laval,' said Josephine, smiling, 'but it seems to me that all the affairs of the Empire are already revolving round you. You must bring this pretty cousin of yours—the Emperor said that she is pretty—to Court with you, and present her to me. Madame de Remusat, you will take a note of the name.'

The Empress had stooped again to the basket of aloes wood which stood beside the fireplace. Suddenly I saw her stare hard at something, and then, with a little cry of surprise, she stooped and lifted an object from the carpet. It was the Emperor's soft flat beaver with the little tricolour cockade. Josephine sprang up, and looked from the hat in her hand to the imperturbable face of the minister.

'How is this, Monsieur de Talleyrand,' she cried, and the dark eyes began to shine with anger and suspicion. 'You said to me that the Emperor was out, and here is his hat!'

'Pardon me, your Imperial Majesty, I did not say that he was out.'

'What did you say then?'

'I said that he left the room a short time before.'

'You are endeavouring to conceal something from me,' she cried, with the quick instinct of a woman.

'I assure you that I tell you all I know.'

The Empress's eyes darted from face to face.

'Marshal Berthier,' she cried, 'I insist upon your telling me this instant where the Emperor is, and what he is doing.'

The slow-witted soldier stammered and twisted his cocked hat about.

'I know no more than Monsieur de Talleyrand does,' said he; 'the Emperor left us some time ago.'

'By which door?'

Poor Berthier was more confused than ever.

'Really, your Imperial Majesty, I cannot undertake to say by which door it was that the Emperor quitted the apartment.'

Josephine's eyes flashed round at me, and my heart shrunk within me as I thought that she was about to ask me that same dreadful question. But I had just time to breathe one prayer to the good Saint Ignatius, who has always been gracious to our family, and the danger passed.

'Come, Madame de Remusat,' said she. 'If these gentlemen will not tell us we shall very soon find out for ourselves.'

She swept with great dignity towards the curtained door, followed at the distance of a few yards by her waiting lady, whose frightened face and lagging, unwilling steps showed that she perfectly appreciated the situation. Indeed, the Emperor's open infidelities, and the public scenes to which they gave rise, were so notorious, that even in Ashford they had reached our ears. Napoleon's self-confidence and his contempt of the world had the effect of making him careless as to what was thought or said of him, while Josephine, when she was carried away by jealousy, lost all the dignity and restraint which usually marked her conduct; so between them they gave some embarrassing moments to those who were about them. Talleyrand turned away with his fingers over his lips, while Berthier, in an agony of apprehension, continued to double up and to twist the cocked hat which he held between his hands. Only Constant, the faithful valet, ventured to intervene between his mistress and the fatal door.

'If your Majesty will resume your seat I shall inform the Emperor that you are here,' said he, with two deprecating hands outstretched.

'Ah, then he *is* there!' she cried furiously. 'I see it all! I understand it all! But I will expose him—I will reproach him with his perfidy! Let me pass, Constant! How dare you stand in my way?'

'Allow me to announce you, your Majesty.'

'I shall announce myself.' With swift undulations of her beautiful figure she darted past the protesting valet, parted the curtains, threw open the door, and vanished into the next room.

She had seemed a creature full of fire and of spirit as, with a flush which broke through the paint upon her cheeks, and with eyes which gleamed with the just anger of an outraged wife, she forced her way into her husband's presence. But she was a woman of change and impulse, full of little squirts of courage and corresponding reactions into cowardice. She had hardly vanished from our sight when there was a harsh roar, like an angry beast, and next instant Josephine came flying into the room again, with the Emperor, inarticulate with passion, raving at her heels. So frightened was she, that she began to run towards the fireplace, upon which Madame de Remusat, who had no wish to form a rearguard upon such an occasion, began running also, and the two of them, like a pair of startled hens, came rustling and fluttering back to the seats which they had left. There they cowered whilst the Emperor, with a convulsed face and a torrent of camp-fire oaths, stamped and raged about the room.

'You, Constant, you!' he shouted; 'is this the way in which you serve me? Have you no sense then—no discretion? Am I never to have any privacy? Must I eternally submit to be spied upon by women? Is everyone else to have liberty, and I only to have none? As to you, Josephine, this finishes it all. I had hesitations before, but now I have none. This brings everything to an end between us.'

We would all, I am sure, have given a good deal to slip from the room—at least, my own embarrassment far exceeded my interest—but the Emperor from his lofty standpoint cared as little about our presence as if we had been so many articles of furniture. In fact, it was one of this strange man's peculiarities that it was just those delicate and personal scenes with which privacy is usually associated that he preferred to have in public, for he knew that his reproaches had an additional sting when they fell upon other ears besides those of his victim. From his wife to his groom there was not one of those who were about him who did not live in dread of being held up to ridicule and infamy before a smiling crowd, whose amusement was only tempered by the reflection that each of them might be the next to endure the same exposure.

As to Josephine, she had taken refuge in a woman's last resource, and was crying bitterly, with her graceful neck stooping towards her knees and her two hands over her face. Madame de Remusat was weeping also, and in every pause of his hoarse scolding—for his voice was very hoarse and raucous when he was angry—there came the soft hissing and clicking of their sobs. Sometimes his fierce taunts would bring some reply from the Empress, some gentle reproof to him for his gallantries, but each remonstrance only excited him to a fresh rush of vituperation. In one of his outbursts he threw his snuff-box with a crash upon the floor as a spoiled child would hurl down its toys.

'Morality!' he cried, 'morality was not made for me, and I was not made for morality. I am a man apart, and I accept nobody's conditions. I tell you always, Josephine, that these are the foolish phrases of mediocre people who wish to fetter the great. They do not apply to me. I will never consent to frame my conduct by the puerile arrangements of society.'

'Have you no feeling then?' sobbed the Empress.

'A great man is not made for feeling. It is for him to decide what he shall do, and then to do it without interference from anyone. It is your place, Josephine, to submit to all my fancies, and you should think it quite natural that I should allow myself some latitude.'

It was a favourite device of the Emperor's, when he was in the wrong upon one point, to turn the conversation round so as to get upon some other one on which he was in the right. Having worked off the first explosion of his passion he now assumed the offensive, for in argument, as in war, his instinct was always to attack.

'I have been looking over Lenormand's accounts, Josephine,' said he. 'Are you aware how many dresses you have had last year? You have had a hundred and forty—no less—and many of them cost as much as twenty-five thousand *livres*. I am told that you have six hundred dresses in your wardrobes, many of which have hardly ever been used. Madame de Remusat knows that what I say is true. She cannot deny it.'

'You like me to dress well, Napoleon.'

'I will not have such monstrous extravagance. I could have two regiments of cuirassiers, or a fleet of frigates, with the money which you squander upon foolish silks and furs. It might turn the fortunes of a campaign. Then again, Josephine, who gave you permission to order that *parure* of diamonds and sapphires from Lefebvre? The bill has been sent to me and I have refused to pay for it. If he applies again, I shall have him marched to prison between a file of grenadiers, and your milliner shall accompany him there.'

The Emperor's fits of anger, although tempestuous, were never very prolonged. The curious convulsive wriggle of one of his arms, which always showed when he was excited, gradually died away, and after looking for some time at the papers of de Meneval—who had written away like an automaton during all this uproar—he came across to the fire with a smile upon his lips, and a brow from which the shadow had departed.

'You have no excuse for extravagance, Josephine,' said he, laying his hand upon her shoulder. 'Diamonds and fine dresses are very necessary to an ugly woman in order to make her attractive, but *you* cannot need them for such a purpose. You had no fine dresses when first I saw you in the Rue Chautereine, and yet there was no woman in the world who ever attracted me so. Why will you vex me, Josephine, and make me say things which seem unkind? Drive back, little one, to Pont de Briques, and see that you do not catch cold.'

'You will come to the salon, Napoleon?' asked the Empress, whose bitterest resentment seemed to vanish in an instant at the first kindly touch from his hand. She still held her handkerchief before her eyes, but it was chiefly, I think, to conceal the effect which her tears had had upon her cheeks.

'Yes, yes, I will come. Our carriages will follow yours. See the ladies into the *berline*, Constant. Have you ordered the embarkation of the troops, Berthier? Come here, Talleyrand, for I wish to describe my views about the future of Spain and Portugal. Monsieur de Laval, you may escort the Empress to Pont de Briques, where I shall see you at the reception.'

CHAPTER 15

The Reception of the Empress

Pont de Briques is but a small village, and this sudden arrival of the Court, which was to remain for some weeks, had crammed it with visitors. It would have been very much simpler to have come to Boulogne, where there were more suitable buildings and better accommodation, but Napoleon had named Pont de Briques, so Pont de Briques it had to be. The word impossible was not permitted amongst those who had to carry out his wishes. So an army of cooks and footmen settled upon the little place, and then there arrived the dignitaries of the new Empire, and then the ladies of the Court, and then their admirers from the camp. The Empress had a chateau for her accommodation. The rest quartered themselves in cottages or where they best might, and waited ardently for the moment which was to take them back to the comforts of Versailles or Fontainebleau.

The Empress had graciously offered me a seat in her berline, and all the way to the village, entirely forgetful apparently of the scene through which she passed, she chatted away, asking me a thousand personal questions about myself and my affairs, for a kindly curiosity in the doings of everyone around her was one of her most marked characteristics. Especially was she interested in Eugenie, and as the subject was one upon which I was equally interested in talking it ended in a rhapsody upon my part, amid little sympathetic ejaculations from the Empress and titterings from Madame de Remusat.

'But you must certainly bring her over to the Court!' cried the kindly woman. 'Such a paragon of beauty and of virtue must not be allowed to waste herself in this English village. Have you spoken about her to the Emperor?'

'I found that he knew all about her, your Majesty.'

'He knows all about everything. Oh, what a man he is! You heard him about those diamonds and sapphires. Lefebvre gave me his word that no one should know of it but ourselves, and that I should pay at my leisure, and yet you see that the Emperor knew. But what did he say, Monsieur de Laval?'

'He said that my marriage should be his affair.'

Josephine shook her head and groaned.

'But this is serious, Monsieur de Laval. He is capable of singling out any one of the ladies of the Court and marrying you to her within a week. It is a subject upon which he will not listen to argument. He has brought about some extraordinary matches in this way. But I will speak to the Emperor before I return to Paris, and I will see what I can arrange for you.'

I was still endeavouring to thank her for her sympathy and kindness when the berline rattled up the drive and pulled up at the entrance to the chateau, where the knot of scarlet footmen and the bearskins of two sentries from the Guards announced the Imperial quarters. The Empress and her lady hurried away to prepare their toilets for the evening, and I was shown at once into the salon, in which the guests had already begun to assemble.

This was a large square room furnished as modestly as the sitting-room of a provincial gentleman would be likely to be. The wall-paper was gloomy, and the furniture was of dark mahogany upholstered in faded blue nankeen, but there were numerous candles in candelabra upon the tables and in sconces upon the walls which gave an air of festivity even to these sombre surroundings. Out of the large central room were several smaller ones in which card-tables had been laid out, and the doorways between had been draped with Oriental chintz. A number of ladies and gentlemen were standing about, the former in the high evening dresses to which the Emperor had given his sanction, the latter about equally divided between the civilians in black court costumes and the soldiers in their uniforms. Bright colours and graceful draperies predominated, for in spite of his lectures about economy the Emperor was very harsh to any lady who did not dress in a manner which would sustain the brilliancy of his Court. The prevailing fashions gave an opening to taste and to display, for the simple classical costumes had died out with the Republic, and Oriental dresses had taken their place as a compliment to the Conqueror of Egypt. Lucretia had changed to Zuleika, and the salons which had reflected the austerity of old Rome had turned suddenly into so many Eastern harems.

On entering the room I had retired into a corner, fearing that I should find none there whom I knew; but someone plucked at my arm, and turning round I found myself looking into the yellow inscrutable face of my uncle Bernac. He seized my unresponsive hand and wrung it with a false cordiality.

'My dear Louis,' said he. 'It was really the hope of meeting you here which brought me over from Grosbois—although you can understand that living so far from Paris I cannot afford to miss such an opportunity of showing myself at Court. Nevertheless I can assure you that it was of you principally that I was thinking. I hear that you have had a splendid reception from the Emperor, and that you have been taken into his personal service. I had spoken to him about you, and I made him fully realise that if he treats you well he is likely to coax some of the other young emigres into his service.'

I was convinced that he was lying, but none the less I had to bow and utter a few words of cold thanks.

'I see that you still bear me some grudge for what passed between us the other day,' said he, 'but really, my dear Louis, you have no occasion to do so. It was your own good which I had chiefly at heart. I am neither a young nor a strong man, Louis, and my profession, as you have seen, is a dangerous one. There is my child, and there is my estate. Who takes one, takes both. Sibylle is a charming girl, and you must not allow yourself to be prejudiced against her by any ill temper which she may have shown towards me. I will confess that she had some reason to be annoyed at the turn which things had taken. But I hope to hear that you have now thought better upon this matter.'

'I have never thought about it at all, and I beg that you will not discuss it,' said I curtly.

He stood in deep thought for a few moments, and then he raised his evil face and his cruel grey eyes to mine.

'Well, well, that is settled then,' said he. 'But you cannot bear me a grudge for having wished you to be my successor. Be reasonable, Louis. You must acknowledge that you would now be six feet deep in the salt-marsh with your neck broken if I had not stood your friend, at some risk to myself. Is that not true?'

'You had your own motive for that,' said I.

'Very likely. But none the less I saved you. Why should you bear me ill will? It is no fault of mine if I hold your estate.'

'It is not on account of that.'

'Why is it then?'

I could have explained that it was because he had betrayed his comrades, because his daughter hated him, because he had ill-used his wife, because my father regarded him as the source of all his troubles—but the salon of the Empress was no place for a family quarrel, so I merely shrugged my shoulders, and was silent.

'Well, I am very sorry,' said he, 'for I had the best of intentions towards you. I could have advanced you, for there are few men in France who exercise more influence. But I have one request to make to you.'

'What is that, sir?'

'I have a number of personal articles, belonging to your father—his sword, his seals, a deskful of letters, some silver plate—such things in short as you would wish to keep in memory of him. I should be glad if you will come to Grosbois—if it is only for one night—and look over these things, choosing what you wish to take away. My conscience will then be clear about them.'

I promised readily that I would do so.

'And when would you come?' he asked eagerly. Something in the tone of his voice aroused my suspicions, and glancing at him I saw exultation in his eyes. I remembered the warning of Sibylle.

'I cannot come until I have learned what my duties with the Emperor are to be. When that is settled I shall come.'

'Very good. Next week perhaps, or the week afterwards. I

shall expect you eagerly, Louis. I rely upon your promise, for a Laval was never known to break one.' With another unanswered squeeze of my hand, he slipped off among the crowd, which was growing denser every instant in the salon.

I was standing in silence thinking over this sinister invitation of my uncle's, when I heard my own name, and, looking up, I saw de Caulaincourt, with his brown handsome face and tall elegant figure, making his way towards me.

'It is your first entrance at Court, is it not, Monsieur de Laval,' said he, in his high-bred cordial manner; 'you should not feel lonely, for there are certainly many friends of your father here who will be overjoyed to make the acquaintance of your father's son. From what de Meneval told me I gather that you know hardly anyone—even by sight.'

'I know the Marshals,' said I; 'I saw them all at the council in the Emperor's tent. There is Ney with the red head. And there is Lefebvre with his singular mouth, and Bernadotte with the beak of a bird of prey.'

'Precisely. And that is Rapp, with the round, bullet head. He is talking to Junot, the handsome dark man with the whiskers. These poor soldiers are very unhappy.'

'Why so?' I asked.

'Because they are all men who have risen from nothing. This society and etiquette terrifies them much more than all the dangers of war. When they can hear their sabres clashing against their big boots they feel at home, but when they have to stand about with their cocked hats under their arms, and have to pick their spurs out of the ladies' trains, and talk about David's picture or Passaniello's opera, it prostrates them. The Emperor will not even permit them to swear, although he has no scruples upon his own account. He tells them to be soldiers with the army, and courtiers with the Court, but the poor fellows cannot help being soldiers all the time. Look at Rapp with his twenty wounds, endeavouring to exchange little delicate drolleries with that young lady. There, you see, he has said something which would have passed very well with a *vivandiere*, but it has made her fly to her mamma, and he is scratching his head, for he cannot imagine how he has offended her.'

'Who is the beautiful woman with the white dress and the tiara of diamonds?' I asked.

'That is Madame Murat, who is the sister of the Emperor. Caroline is beautiful, but she is not as pretty as her sister Marie, whom you see over yonder in the corner. Do you see the tall stately dark-eyed old lady with whom she is talking? That is Napoleon's mother—a wonderful woman, the source of all their strength, shrewd, brave, vigorous, forcing respect from everyone who knows her. She is as careful and as saving as when she was the wife of a small country gentleman in Corsica, and it is no secret that she has little confidence in the permanence of the present state of things, and that she is always laying by for an evil day. The Emperor does not know whether to be amused or exasperated by her precautions. Well, Murat, I suppose we shall see you riding across the Kentish hop-fields before long.'

The famous soldier had paused opposite to us, and shook hands with my companion. His elegant well-knit figure, large fiery eyes, and noble bearing made this innkeeper's boy a man who would have drawn attention and admiration to himself in any assembly in Europe. His mop of curly hair and thick red lips gave that touch of character and individuality to his appearance which redeem a handsome face from insipidity.

'I am told that it is devilish bad country for cavalry—all cut up into hedges and ditches,' said he. 'The roads are good, but the fields are impossible. I hope that we are going soon, Monsieur de Caulaincourt, for our men will all settle down as gardeners if this continues. They are learning more about watering-pots and spuds than about horses and sabres.'

'The army, I hear, is to embark to-morrow.'

'Yes, yes, but you know very well that they will disembark again upon the wrong side of the Channel. Unless Villeneuve scatters the English fleet, nothing can be attempted.'

'Constant tells me that the Emperor was whistling *Malbrook* all the time that he was dressing this morning, and that usually comes before a move.'

'It was very clever of Constant to tell what tune it was which the Emperor was whistling,' said Murat, laughing. 'For my part I do not think that he knows the difference between the *Malbrook* and the *Marseillaise*. Ah, here is the Empress—and how charming she is looking!'

Josephine had entered, with several of her ladies in her train, and the whole assembly rose to do her honour. The Empress was dressed in an evening gown of rose-coloured tulle, spangled with silver stars—an effect which might have seemed meretricious and theatrical in another woman, but which she carried off with great grace and dignity. A little sheaf of diamond wheat-ears rose above her head, and swayed gently as she walked. No one could entertain more charmingly than she, for she moved about among the people with her amiable smile, setting everybody at their ease by her kindly natural manner, and by the conviction which she gave them that she was thoroughly at her ease herself. 'How amiable she is!' I exclaimed. 'Who could help loving her?'

'There is only one family which can resist her,' said de Caulaincourt, glancing round to see that Murat was out of hearing. 'Look at the faces of the Emperor's sisters.'

I was shocked when I followed his direction to see the malignant glances with which these two beautiful women were following the Empress as she walked about the room. They whispered together and tittered maliciously. Then Madame Murat turned to her mother behind her, and the stern old lady tossed her haughty head in derision and contempt.

'They feel that Napoleon is theirs and that they ought to have everything. They cannot bear to think that she is Her Imperial Majesty and they are only Her Highness. They all hate her, Joseph, Lucien—all of them. When they had to carry her train at the coronation they tried to trip her up, and the Emperor had to interfere. Oh yes, they have the real Corsican blood, and they are not very comfortable people to get along with.'

But in spite of the evident hatred of her husband's family, the Empress appeared to be entirely unconcerned and at her ease as she strolled about among the groups of her guests with a kindly glance and a pleasant word for each of them. A tall, soldierly man, brown-faced and moustached, walked beside her, and she occasionally laid her hand with a caressing motion upon his arm.

'That is her son, Eugene de Beauharnais,' said my companion.

'Her son!' I exclaimed, for he seemed to me to be the older of the two.

De Caulaincourt smiled at my surprise.

'You know she married Beauharnais when she was very young—in fact she was hardly sixteen. She has been sitting in her boudoir while her son has been baking in Egypt and Syria, so that they have pretty well bridged over the gap between them. Do you see the tall, handsome, clean-shaven man who has just kissed Josephine's hand. That is Talma the famous actor. He once helped Napoleon at a critical moment of his career, and the Emperor has never forgotten the debt which the Consul contracted. That is really the secret of Talleyrand's power. He lent Napoleon a hundred thousand *francs* before he set out for Egypt, and now, however much he distrusts him, the Emperor cannot forget that old kindness. I have never known him to abandon a friend or to forgive an enemy. If you have once served him well you may do what you like afterwards. There is one of his coachmen who is drunk from morning to night. But he gained the cross at Marengo, and so he is safe.'

De Caulaincourt had moved on to speak with some lady, and I was again left to my own thoughts, which turned upon this extraordinary man, who presented himself at one moment as a hero and at another as a spoiled child, with his nobler and his worse side alternating so rapidly that I had no sooner made up my mind about him than some new revelation would destroy my views and drive me to some fresh conclusion. That he was necessary to France was evident, and that in serving him one was serving one's country. But was it an honour or a penance to serve him? Was he worthy merely of obedience, or might love and esteem be added to it? These were the questions which we found it difficult to answer—and some of us will never have answered them up to the end of time.

The company had now lost all appearance of formality, and even the soldiers seemed to be at their ease. Many had gone into the side rooms, where they had formed tables for whist and for *vingt-et-un*. For my own part I was quite entertained by watching the people, the beautiful women, the handsome men, the bearers of names which had been heard of in no previous generation, but which now rung round the world. Immediately in front of me were Ney, Lannes, and Murat chatting together and laughing with the freedom of the camp. Of the three, two were destined to be executed in cold blood, and the third to die upon the battle-field, but no coming shadow ever cast a gloom upon their cheery, full-blooded lives.

A small, silent, middle-aged man, who looked unhappy and ill at ease, had been leaning against the wall beside me. Seeing that he was as great a stranger as myself, I addressed some observation to him, to which he replied with great good-will, but in the most execrable French.

'You don't happen to understand English?' he asked. 'I've never met one living soul in this country who did.'

'Oh yes, I understand it very well, for I have lived most of my life over yonder. But surely you are not English, sir? I understood that every Englishman in France was under lock and key ever since the breach of the treaty of Amiens.'

'No, I am not English,' he answered, 'I am an American. My name is Robert Fulton, and I have to come to these receptions because it is the only way in which I can keep myself in the memory of the Emperor, who is examining some inventions of mine which will make great changes in naval warfare.'

Having nothing else to do I asked this curious American what his inventions might be, and his replies very soon convinced me that I had to do with a madman. He had some idea of making a ship go against the wind and against the current by means of coal or wood which was to be burned inside of her. There was some other nonsense about floating barrels full of gunpowder which would blow a ship to pieces if she struck against them. I listened to him at the time with an indulgent smile, but now looking back from the point of vantage of my old age I can see that not all the warriors and statesmen in that room—no, not even the Emperor himself—have had as great an effect upon the history of the world as that silent American who looked so drab and so commonplace among the gold-slashed uniforms and the Oriental dresses.

But suddenly our conversation was interrupted by a hush in the room—such a cold, uncomfortable hush as comes over a roomful of happy, romping children when a grave-faced elder comes amongst them. The chatting and the laughter died away. The sound of the rustling cards and of the clicking counters had ceased in the other rooms. Everyone, men and women, had risen to their feet with a constrained expectant expression upon their faces. And there in the doorway were the pale face and the green coat with the red cordon across the white waistcoat.

There was no saying how he might behave upon these occasions. Sometimes he was capable of being the merriest and most talkative of the company, but this was rather in his consular than in his imperial days. On the other hand he might be absolutely ferocious, with an insulting observation for everyone with whom he came in contact. As a rule he was between these two extremes, silent, morose, ill at ease, shooting out curt little remarks which made everyone uncomfortable. There was always a sigh of relief when he would pass from one room into the next.

On this occasion he seemed to have not wholly recovered from the storm of the afternoon, and he looked about him with a brooding eye and a lowering brow. It chanced that I was not very far from the door, and that his glance fell upon me.

'Come here, Monsieur de Laval,' said he. He laid his hand upon my shoulder and turned to a big, gaunt man who had accompanied him into the room. 'Look here, Cambaceres, you simpleton,' said he. 'You always said that the old families would never come back, and that they would settle in England as the Huguenots have done. You see that, as usual, you have miscalculated, for here is the heir of the de Lavals come to offer his services. Monsieur de Laval, you are now my *aide-de-camp*, and I beg you to keep with me wherever I go.'

This was promotion indeed, and yet I had sense enough to know that it was not for my own sweet sake that the Emperor had done it, but in order to encourage others to follow me. My conscience approved what I had done, for no sordid motive and nothing but the love of my country had prompted me; but now, as I walked round behind Napoleon, I felt humiliated and ashamed, like a prisoner led behind the car of his captor.

And soon there was something else to make me ashamed, and that was the conduct of him whose servant I had become. His manners were outrageous. As he had himself said, it was his nature to be always first, and this being so he resented those courtesies and gallantries by which men are accustomed to disguise from women the fact that they are the weaker sex. The Emperor, unlike Louis XIV., felt that even a temporary and conventional attitude of humility towards a woman was too great a condescension from his own absolute supremacy. Chivalry was among those conditions of society which he refused to accept.

To the soldiers he was amiable enough, with a nod and a joke for each of them. To his sisters also he said a few words, though rather in the tone of a drill sergeant to a pair of recruits. It was only when the Empress had joined him that his ill-humour came to a head.

'I wish you would not wear those wisps of pink about your head, Josephine,' said he, pettishly. 'All that women have to think about is how to dress themselves, and yet they cannot even do that with moderation or taste. If I see you again in such a thing I will thrust it in the fire as I did your shawl the other day.'

'You are so hard to please, Napoleon. You like one day what you cannot abide the next. But I will certainly change it if it offends you,' said Josephine, with admirable patience.

The Emperor took a few steps between the people, who had formed a lane for us to pass through. Then he stopped and looked over his shoulder at the Empress.

'How often have I told you, Josephine, that I cannot tolerate fat women.'

'I always bear it in mind, Napoleon.'

'Then why is Madame de Chevreux present?'

'But surely, Napoleon, *madame* is not very fat.'

'She is fatter than she should be. I should prefer not to see her. Who is this?' He had paused before a young lady in a blue dress, whose knees seemed to be giving way under her as the terrible Emperor transfixed her with his searching eyes.

145

'This is Mademoiselle de Bergerot.'

'How old are you?'

'Twenty-three, sire.'

'It is time that you were married. Every woman should be married at twenty-three. How is it that you are not married?'

The poor girl appeared to be incapable of answering, so the Empress gently remarked that it was to the young men that that question should be addressed.

'Oh, that is the difficulty, is it?' said the Emperor. 'We must look about and find a husband for you.' He turned, and to my horror I found his eyes fixed with a questioning gaze upon my face.

'We have to find you a wife also, Monsieur de Laval,' said he. 'Well, well, we shall see—we shall see. What is your name?' to a quiet refined man in black.

'I am Gretry, the musician.'

'Yes, yes, I remember you. I have seen you a hundred times, but I can never recall your name. Who are you?'

'I am Joseph de Chenier.'

'Of course. I have seen your tragedy. I have forgotten the name of it, but it was not good. You have written some other poetry, have you not?'

'Yes, sire. I had your permission to dedicate my last volume to you.'

'Very likely, but I have not had time to read it. It is a pity that we have no poets now in France, for the deeds of the last few years would have given a subject for a Homer or a Virgil. It seems that I can create kingdoms but not poets. Whom do you consider to be the greatest French writer?'

'Racine, sire.'

'Then you are a blockhead, for Corneille was infinitely greater. I have no ear for metre or trivialities of the kind, but I can sympathise with the spirit of poetry, and I am conscious that Corneille is far the greatest of poets. I would have made him my prime minister had he had the good fortune to live in my epoch. It is his intellect which I admire, his knowledge of the human heart, and his profound feeling. Are you writing anything at present?'

'I am writing a tragedy upon Henry IV., sire.'

'It will not do, sir. It is too near the present day, and I will not have politics upon the stage. Write a play about Alexander. What is your name?'

He had pitched upon the same person whom he had already addressed.

'I am still Gretry, the musician,' said he meekly.

The Emperor flushed for an instant at the implied rebuke. He said nothing, however, but passed on to where several ladies were standing together near the door of the card-room.

'Well, *madame*,' said he to the nearest of them, 'I hope you are behaving rather better. When last I heard from Paris your doings were furnishing the Quartier St. Germain with a good deal of amusement and gossip.'

'I beg that your Majesty will explain what you mean,' said she with spirit.

'They had coupled your name with that of Colonel Lasalle.'

'It is a foul calumny, sire.'

'Very possibly, but it is awkward when so many calumnies cluster round one person. You are certainly a most unfortunate lady in that respect. You had a scandal once before with General Rapp's *aide-de-camp*. This must come to an end. What is your name?' he continued, turning to another.

'Mademoiselle de Perigord.'

'Your age?'

'Twenty.'

'You are very thin and your elbows are red. My God, Madame Boismaison, are we never to see anything but this same grey gown and the red turban with the diamond crescent?'

'I have never worn it before, sire?'

'Then you had another the same, for I am weary of the sight of it. Let me never see you in it again. Monsieur de Remusat, I make you a good allowance. Why do you not spend it?'

'I do, sire.'

'I hear that you have been putting down your carriage. I do not give you money to hoard in a bank, but I give it to you that you may keep up a fitting appearance with it. Let me hear that your carriage is back in the coach-house when I return to Paris. Junot, you rascal, I hear that you have been gambling and losing.'

'The most infernal run of luck, sire,' said the soldier, 'I give you my word that the ace fell four times running.'

'*Ta, ta*, you are a child, with no sense of the value of money. How much do you owe?'

'Forty thousand, sire.'

'Well, well, go to Lebrun and see what he can do for you. After all, we were together at Toulon.'

'A thousand thanks, sire.'

'Tut! You and Rapp and Lasalle are the spoiled children of the army. But no more cards, you rascal! I do not like low dresses, Madame Picard. They spoil even pretty women, but in you they are inexcusable. Now, Josephine, I am going to my room, and you can come in half an hour and read me to sleep. I am tired tonight, but I came to your salon, since you desired that I should help you in welcoming and entertaining your guests. You can remain here, Monsieur de Laval, for your presence will not be necessary until I send you my orders.'

And so the door closed behind him, and with a long sigh of relief from everyone, from the Empress to the waiter with the *negus*, the friendly chatter began once more, with the click of the counters and the rustle of the cards just as they had been before he came to help in the entertainment.

CHAPTER 16

The Library of Grosbois

And now, my friends, I am coming to the end of those singular adventures which I encountered upon my arrival in France, adventures which might have been of some interest in themselves had I not introduced the figure of the Emperor, who has eclipsed them all as completely as the sun eclipses the stars. Even now, you see, after all these years, in an old man's memoirs, the Emperor is still true to his traditions, and will not brook any opposition. As I draw his words and his deeds I feel that my own poor story withers before them. And yet if it had not been for that story I should not have had an excuse for describing to you my first and most vivid impressions of him, and so it has served a purpose after all. You must bear with me now while I tell you of our expedition to the Red Mill and of what befell in the library of Grosbois.

Two days had passed away since the reception of the Empress Josephine, and only one remained of the time which had been allowed to my cousin Sibylle in which she might save her lover, and capture the terrible Toussac. For my own part I was not so very anxious that she should save this craven lover of hers, whose handsome face belied the poor spirit within him. And yet this lonely beautiful woman, with the strong will and the loyal heart, had touched my feelings, and I felt that I would help her to anything—even against my own better judgment, if she should desire it. It was then with a mixture of feelings that late in the afternoon I saw her and General Savary enter the little room in which I lodged at Boulogne. One glance at her flushed cheeks and triumphant eyes told me that she was confident in her own success.

'I told you that I would find him, Cousin Louis!' she cried; 'I have come straight to you, because you said that you would help in the taking of him.'

'Mademoiselle insists upon it that I should not use soldiers,' said Savary, shrugging his shoulders.

'No, no, no,' she cried with vehemence. 'It has to be done with discretion, and at the sight of a soldier he would fly to some hiding-place, where you would never be able to follow him. I cannot afford to run a risk. There is too much already at stake.'

'In such an affair three men are as useful as thirty,' said Savary. 'I should not in any case have employed more. You say that you have another friend, Lieutenant—?'

'Lieutenant Gerard of the Hussars of Bercheny.'

'Quite so. There is not a more gallant officer in the Grand Army than Etienne Gerard. The three of us, Monsieur de Laval, should be equal to any adventure.'

'I am at your disposal.'

'Tell us then, mademoiselle, where Toussac is hiding.'

'He is hiding at the Red Mill.'

'But we have searched it, I assure you that he is not there.'

'When did you search it?'

'Two days ago.'

'Then he has come there since. I knew that Jeanne Portal loved him. I have watched her for six days. Last night she stole down to the Red Mill with a basket of wine and fruit. All the morning I have seen her eyes sweeping the country side, and I have read the terror in them whenever she has seen the twinkle of a bayonet. I am as sure that Toussac is in the mill as if I had seen him with my own eyes.'

'In that case there is not an instant to be lost,' cried Savary. 'If he knows of a boat upon the coast he is as likely as not to slip away after dark and make his escape for England. From the Red Mill one can see all the surrounding country, and Mademoiselle is right in thinking that a large body of soldiers would only warn him to escape.'

'What do you propose then?' I asked.

'That you meet us at the south gate of the camp in an hour's time dressed as you are. You might be any gentleman travelling upon the high road. I shall see Gerard, and we shall adopt some suitable disguise. Bring your pistols, for it is with the most desperate man in France we have to do. We shall have a horse at your disposal.'

The setting sun lay dull and red upon the western horizon, and the white chalk cliffs of the French coast had all flushed into pink when I found myself once more at the gate of the Boulogne Camp. There was no sign of my companions, but a tall man, dressed in a blue coat with brass buttons like a small country farmer, was tightening the girth of a magnificent black horse, whilst a little further on a slim young ostler was waiting by the roadside, holding the bridles of two others. It was only when I recognised one of the pair as the horse which I had ridden on my first coming to camp that I answered the smile upon the keen handsome face of the ostler, and saw the swarthy features of Savary under the broad-brimmed hat of the farmer.

'I think that we may travel without fearing to excite suspicion,' said he. 'Crook that straight back of yours a little, Gerard! And now we shall push upon our way, or we may find that we are too late.'

My life has had its share of adventures, and yet, somehow, this ride stands out above the others.

There over the waters I could dimly see the loom of the English coast, with its suggestions of dreamy villages, humming bees, and the pealing of Sunday bells. I thought of the long, white High Street of Ashford, with its red brick houses, and the inn with the great swinging sign. All my life had been spent in these peaceful surroundings, and now, here I was with a spirited horse between my knees, two pistols peeping out of my holsters, and a commission upon which my whole future might depend, to arrest the most redoubtable conspirator in France. No wonder that, looking back over many dangers and many vicissitudes, it is still that evening ride over the short crisp turf of the downs which stands out most clearly in my memory. One becomes *blasé* to adventure, as one becomes *blasé* to all else which the world can give, save only the simple joys of home, and to taste the full relish of such an expedition one must approach it with the hot blood of youth still throbbing in one's veins.

Our route, when we had left the uplands of Boulogne behind us, lay along the skirts of that desolate marsh in which I had wandered, and so inland, through plains of fern and bramble, until the familiar black keep of the Castle of Grosbois rose upon the left. Then, under the guidance of Savary, we struck to the right down a sunken road, and so over the shoulder of a hill until, on a further slope beyond, we saw the old windmill black against the evening sky. Its upper window burned red like a spot of blood in the last rays of the setting sun. Close by the door stood a cart full of grain sacks, with the shafts pointing downwards and the horse grazing at some distance. As we gazed, a woman appeared upon the downs and stared round, with her hand over her eyes.

'See that!' said Savary eagerly. 'He is there sure enough, or why should they be on their guard? Let us take this road which winds round the hill, and they will not see us until we are at the very door.'

'Should we not gallop forward?' I suggested.

'The ground is too cut up. The longer way is the safer. As long as we are upon the road they cannot tell us from any other travellers.'

We walked our horses along the path, therefore, with as unconcerned an air as we could assume; but a sharp exclamation made us glance suddenly round, and there was the woman standing on a hillock by the roadside and gazing down at us with a face that was rigid with suspicion. The sight of the military bearing of my companions changed all her fear into certainties. In an instant she had whipped the shawl from her shoulders, and was waving it frantically over her head. With a hearty curse Savary spurred his horse up the bank and galloped straight for the mill, with Gerard and myself at his heels.

It was only just in time. We were still a hundred paces from the door when a man sprang out from it, and gazed about him, his head whisking this way and that. There could be no mistaking the huge bristling beard, the broad chest, and the rounded shoulders of Toussac. A glance showed him that we would ride him down before he could get away, and he sprang back into the mill, closing the heavy door with a clang behind him.

'The window, Gerard, the window!' cried Savary.

There was a small, square window opening into the basement room of the mill. The young hussar disengaged himself from the saddle and flew through it as the clown goes through the hoops at Franconi's. An instant later he had opened the door for us, with the blood streaming from his face and hands.

'He has fled up the stair,' said he.

'Then we need be in no hurry, since he cannot pass us,' said Savary, as we sprang from our horses. 'You have carried his first line of entrenchments most gallantly, Lieutenant Gerard. I hope you are not hurt?'

'A few scratches, General, nothing more.'

'Get your pistols, then. Where is the miller?'

'Here I am,' said a squat, rough little fellow, appearing in the open doorway. 'What do you mean, you brigands, by entering my mill in this fashion? I am sitting reading my paper and smoking my pipe of coltsfoot, as my custom is about this time of the evening, and suddenly, without a word, a man comes flying through my window, covers me with glass, and opens my door to his friends outside. I've had trouble enough with my one lodger all day without three more of you turning up.'

'You have the conspirator Toussac in your house.'

'Toussac!' cried the miller. 'Nothing of the kind. His name is Maurice, and he is a merchant in silks.'

'He is the man we want. We come in the Emperor's name.'

The miller's jaw dropped as he listened.

'I don't know who he is, but he offered a good price for a bed and I asked no more questions. In these days one cannot expect a certificate of character from every lodger. But, of course, if it is a matter of State, why, it is not for me to interfere. But, to do him justice, he was a quiet gentleman enough until he had that letter just now.'

'What letter? Be careful what you say, you rascal, for your own head may find its way into the sawdust basket.'

'It was a woman who brought it. I can only tell you what I know. He has been talking like a madman ever since. It made my blood run cold to hear him. There's someone whom he swears he will murder. I shall be very glad to see the last of him.'

'Now, gentlemen,' said Savary, drawing his sword, 'we may leave our horses here. There is no window for forty feet, so he cannot escape from us. If you will see that your pistols are primed, we shall soon bring the fellow to terms.'

The stair was a narrow winding one made of wood, which led to a small loft lighted from a slit in the wall.

Some remains of wood and a litter of straw showed that this was where Toussac had spent his day. There was, however, no sign of him now, and it was evident that he had ascended the next flight of steps. We climbed them, only to find our way barred by a heavy door.

'Surrender, Toussac!' cried Savary. 'It is useless to attempt to escape us.

A hoarse laugh sounded from behind the door.

'I am not a man who surrenders. But I will make a bargain with you. I have a small matter of business to do tonight. If you will leave me alone, I will give you my solemn pledge to surrender at the camp to-morrow. I have a little debt that I wish to pay. It is only today that I understood to whom I owed it.'

'What you ask is impossible.'

'It would save you a great deal of trouble.'

'We cannot grant such a request. You must surrender.'

'You'll have some work first.'

'Come, come, you cannot escape us. Put your shoulders against the door! Now, all together?'

There was the hot flash of a pistol from the keyhole, and a bullet smacked against the wall between us. We hurled ourselves against the door. It was massive, but rotten with age. With a splintering and rending it gave way before us. We rushed in, weapons in hand, to find ourselves in an empty room.

'Where the devil has he got to?' cried Savary, glaring round him. 'This is the top room of all. There is nothing above it.'

It was a square empty space with a few corn-bags littered

about. At the further side was an open window, and beside it lay a pistol, still smoking from the discharge. We all rushed across, and, as we craned our heads over, a simultaneous cry of astonishment escaped from us.

The distance to the ground was so great that no one could have survived the fall, but Toussac had taken advantage of the presence of that cart full of grain-sacks, which I have described as having lain close to the mill. This had both shortened the distance and given him an excellent means of breaking the fall. Even so, however, the shock had been tremendous, and as we looked out he was lying panting heavily upon the top of the bags. Hearing our cry, however, he looked up, shook his fist defiantly, and, rolling from the cart, he sprang on to the back of Savary's black horse, and galloped off across the downs, his great beard flying in the wind, untouched by the pistol bullets with which we tried to bring him down.

How we flew down those creaking wooden stairs and out through the open door of the mill! Quick as we were, he had a good start, and by the time Gerard and I were in the saddle he had become a tiny man upon a small horse galloping up the green slope of the opposite hill.

The shades of evening, too, were drawing in, and upon his left was the huge salt-marsh, where we should have found it difficult to follow him. The chances were certainly in his favour. And yet he never swerved from his course, but kept straight on across the downs on a line which took him farther and farther from the sea. Every instant we feared to see him dart away in the morass, but still he held his horse's head against the hill-side. What could he be making for? He never pulled rein and never glanced round, but flew onwards, like a man with a definite goal in view.

Lieutenant Gerard and I were lighter men, and our mounts were as good as his, so that it was not long before we began to gain upon him. If we could only keep him in sight it was certain that we should ride him down; but there was always the danger that he might use his knowledge of the country to throw us off his track. As we sank beneath each hill my heart sank also, to rise again with renewed hope as we caught sight of him once more galloping in front of us.

But at last that which I had feared befell us. We were not more than a couple of hundred paces behind him when we lost all trace of him. He had vanished behind some rolling ground, and we could see nothing of him when we reached the summit.

'There is a road there to the left,' cried Gerard, whose Gascon blood was aflame with excitement.

'On, my friend, on, let us keep to the left!'

'Wait a moment!' I cried. 'There is a bridle-path upon the right, and it is as likely that he took that.'

'Then do you take one and I the other.'

'One moment, I hear the sound of hoofs!'

'Yes, yes, it is his horse!'

A great black horse, which was certainly that of General Savary, had broken out suddenly through a dense tangle of brambles in front of us. The saddle was empty.

'He has found some hiding-place here amongst the brambles,' I cried.

Gerard had already sprung from his horse, and was leading him through the bushes. I followed his example, and in a minute or two we made our way down a winding path into a deep chalk quarry.

'There is no sign of him!' cried Gerard. 'He has escaped us.'

But suddenly I had understood it all. His furious rage which the miller had described to us was caused no doubt by his learning how he came to be betrayed upon the night of his arrival. This sweetheart of his had in some way discovered it, and had let him know. His promise to deliver himself up to-morrow was in order to give him time to have his revenge upon my uncle. And now with one idea in his head he had ridden to this chalk quarry. Of course, it must be the same chalk quarry into which the underground passage of Grosbois opened, and no doubt during his treasonable meetings with my uncle he had learned the secret. Twice I hit upon the wrong spot, but at the third trial I gained the face of the cliff, made my way between it and the bushes, and found the narrow opening, which was hardly visible in the gathering darkness. During our search Savary had overtaken us on foot, so now, leaving our horses in the chalk-pit, my two companions followed me through the narrow entrance tunnel, and on into the larger and older passage beyond. We had no lights, and it was as black as pitch within, so I stumbled forward as best I might, feeling my way by keeping one hand upon the side wall, and tripping occasionally over the stones which were scattered along the path. It had seemed no very great distance when my uncle had led the way with the light, but now, what with the darkness, and what with the uncertainty and the tension of our feelings, it appeared to be a long journey, and Savary's deep voice at my elbow growled out questions as to how many more miles we were to travel in this mole heap.

'Hush!' whispered Gerard. 'I hear someone in front of us.'

We stood listening in breathless silence. Then far away through the darkness I heard the sound of a door creaking upon its hinges.

'On, on!' cried Savary, eagerly. 'The rascal is there, sure enough. This time at least we have got him!'

But for my part I had my fears. I remembered that my uncle had opened the door which led into the castle by some secret catch. This sound which we had heard seemed to show that Toussac had also known how to open it. But suppose that he had closed it behind him. I remembered its size and the iron clampings which bound it together. It was possible that even at the last moment we might find ourselves face to face with an insuperable obstacle. On and on we hurried in the dark, and then suddenly I could have raised a shout of joy, for there in the distance was a yellow glimmer of light, only visible in contrast with the black darkness which lay between. The door was open. In his mad thirst for vengeance Toussac had never given a thought to the pursuers at his heels.

And now we need no longer grope. It was a race along the passage and up the winding stair, through the second door, and into the stone-flagged corridor of the Castle of Grosbois, with the oil-lamp still burning at the end of it. A frightful cry—a long-drawn scream of terror and of pain—rang through it as we entered.

'He is killing him! He is killing him!' cried a voice, and a woman servant rushed madly out into the passage. 'Help, help; he is killing Monsieur Bernac!'

'Where is he?' shouted Savary.

'There! The library! The door with the green curtain!' Again that horrible cry rang out, dying down to a harsh croaking. It ended in a loud, sharp snick, as when one cracks one's joint, but many times louder. I knew only too well what that dreadful sound portended. We rushed together into the room, but the hardened Savary and the dare-devil hussar both recoiled in horror from the sight which met our gaze.

My uncle had been seated writing at his desk, with his back to the door, when his murderer had entered. No doubt it was at the first glance over his shoulder that he had raised the scream when he saw that terrible hairy face coming in upon him, while the second cry may have been when those great hands clutched at his head. He had never risen from his chair—perhaps he had been too paralysed by fear—and he still sat with his back to the door. But what struck the colour from our cheeks was that his head had been turned completely round, so that his horribly distorted purple face looked squarely at us from between his shoulders. Often in my dreams that thin face, with the bulging grey eyes, and the shockingly open mouth, comes to disturb me. Beside him stood Toussac, his face flushed with triumph, and his great arms folded across his chest.

'Well, my friends,' said he, 'you are too late, you see. I have paid my debts after all.'

'Surrender!' cried Savary.

'Shoot away! Shoot away!' he cried, drumming his hands upon his breast. 'You don't suppose I fear your miserable pellets, do you? Oh, you imagine you will take me alive! I'll soon knock that idea out of your heads.'

In an instant he had swung a heavy chair over his head, and was rushing furiously at us. We all fired our pistols into him together, but nothing could stop that thunderbolt of a man. With the blood spurting from his wounds, he lashed madly out with his chair, but his eyesight happily failed him, and his swashing blow came down upon the corner of the table with a crash which broke it into fragments. Then with a mad bellow of rage he sprang upon Savary, tore him down to the ground, and had his hand upon his chin before Gerard and I could seize him by the arms. We were three strong men, but he was as strong as all of us put together, for again and again he shook himself free, and again and again we got our grip upon him once more. But he was losing blood fast. Every instant his huge strength ebbed away. With a supreme effort he staggered to his feet, the three of us hanging on to him like hounds on to a bear. Then, with a shout of rage and despair which thundered through the whole castle, his knees gave way under him, and he fell in a huge inert heap upon the floor, his black beard bristling up towards the ceiling. We all stood panting round, ready to spring upon him if he should move; but it was over. He was dead.

Savary, deadly pale, was leaning with his hand to his side against the table. It was not for nothing that those mighty arms had been thrown round him.

'I feel as if I had been hugged by a bear,' said he. 'Well, there is one dangerous man the less in France, and the Emperor has lost one of his enemies. And yet he was a brave man too!'

'What a soldier he would have made!' said Gerard thoughtfully. 'What a quartermaster for the Hussars of Bercheny! He must have been a very foolish person to set his will against that of the Emperor.'

I had seated myself, sick and dazed, upon the settee, for scenes of bloodshed were new to me then, and this one had been enough to shock the most hardened. Savary gave us all a little cognac from his flask, and then tearing down one of the curtains he laid it over the terrible figure of my Uncle Bernac.

'We can do nothing here,' said he. 'I must get back and report to the Emperor as soon as possible. But all these papers of Bernac's must be seized, for many of them bear upon this and other conspiracies.' As he spoke he gathered together a number of documents which were scattered about the table—among the others a letter which lay before him upon the desk, and which he had apparently just finished at the time of Toussac's irruption.

'Hullo, what's this?' said Savary, glancing over it. 'I fancy that our friend Bernac was a dangerous man also. "My dear Catulle—I beg of you to send me by the very first mail another phial of the same tasteless essence which you sent three years ago. I mean the almond decoction which leaves no traces. I have particular reasons for wanting it in the course of next week, so I implore you not to delay. You may rely upon my interest with the Emperor whenever you have occasion to demand it."'

'Addressed to a chemist in Amiens,' said Savary, turning over the letter. 'A poisoner then, on the top of his other virtues. I wonder for whom this essence of almonds which leaves no trace was intended.'

'I wonder,' said I.

After all, he was my uncle, and he was dead, so why should I say further?

The End

General Savary rode straight to Pont de Briques to report to the Emperor, while Gerard returned with me to my lodgings to share a bottle of wine. I had expected to find my Cousin Sibylle there, but to my surprise there was no sign of her, nor had she left any word to tell us whither she had gone.

It was just after daybreak in the morning when I woke to find an equerry of the Emperor with his hand upon my shoulder.

'The Emperor desires to see you, Monsieur de Laval,' said he.

'Where?'

'At the Pont de Briques.'

I knew that promptitude was the first requisite for those who hoped to advance themselves in his service. In ten minutes I was in the saddle, and in half an hour I was at the chateau. I was conducted upstairs to a room in which were the Emperor and Josephine, she reclining upon a sofa in a charming dressing-gown of pink and lace, he striding about in his energetic fashion, dressed in the curious costume which he assumed before his official hours had begun—a white sleeping suit, red Turkish slippers, and a white bandanna handkerchief tied round his head, the whole giving him the appearance of a West Indian planter. From the strong smell of eau-de-Cologne I judged that he had just come from his bath. He was in the best of humours, and she, as usual, reflected him, so that they were two smiling faces which were turned upon me as I was announced. It was hard to believe that it was this man with the kindly expression and the genial eye who had come like an east wind into the reception-room the other night, and left a trail of wet cheeks and downcast faces wherever he had passed.

'You have made an excellent debut as *aide-de-camp*,' said he; 'Savary has told me all that has occurred, and nothing could have been better arranged. I have not time to think of such things myself, but my wife will sleep more soundly now that she knows that this Toussac is out of the way.'

'Yes, yes, he was a terrible man,' cried the Empress. 'So was that Georges Cadoudal. They were both terrible men.'

'I have my star, Josephine,' said Napoleon, patting her upon the head. 'I see my own career lying before me and I know exactly what I am destined to do. Nothing can harm me until my work is accomplished. The Arabs are believers in Fate, and the Arabs are in the right.'

'Then why should you plan, Napoleon, if everything is to be decided by Fate?'

'Because it is fated that I should plan, you little stupid. Don't you see that that is part of Fate also, that I should have a brain which is capable of planning. I am always building behind a scaffolding, and no one can see what I am building until I have finished. I never look forward for less than two years, and I have been busy all morning, Monsieur de Laval, in planning out the events which will occur in the autumn and winter of 1807. By the way, that good-looking cousin of yours appears to have managed this affair very cleverly. She is a very fine girl to be wasted upon such a creature as the Lucien Lesage who has been screaming for mercy for a week past. Do you not think that it is a great pity?'

I acknowledged that I did.

'It is always so with women—ideologists, dreamers, carried away by whims and imaginings. They are like the Easterns, who cannot conceive that a man is a fine soldier unless he has a formidable presence. I could not get the Egyptians to believe that I was a greater general than Kleber, because he had the body of a porter and the head of a hair-dresser. So it is with this poor creature Lesage, who will be made a hero by women because he has an oval face and the eyes of a calf. Do you imagine that if she were to see him in his true colours it would turn her against him?'

'I am convinced of it, sire. From the little that I have seen of my cousin I am sure that no one could have a greater contempt for cowardice or for meanness.'

'You speak warmly, sir. You are not by chance just a little touched yourself by this fair cousin of yours?'

'Sire, I have already told you—'

'*Ta, ta, ta,* but she is across the water, and many things have happened since then.'

Constant had entered the room.

'He has been admitted, sire.'

'Very good. We shall move into the next room. Josephine, you shall come too, for it is your business rather than mine.'

The room into which we passed was a long, narrow one. There were two windows at one side, but the curtains had been drawn almost across, so that the light was not very good. At the further door was Rousten the Mameluke, and beside him, with arms folded and his face sunk downwards in an attitude of shame and contrition, there was standing the very man of whom we had been talking. He looked up with scared eyes, and started with fear when he saw the Emperor approaching him. Napoleon stood with legs apart and his hands behind his back, and looked at him long and searchingly.

'Well, my fine fellow,' said he at last, 'you have burned your fingers, and I do not fancy that you will come near the fire again. Or do you perhaps think of continuing with politics as a profession?'

'If your Majesty will overlook what I have done,' Lesage stammered, 'I shall faithfully promise you that I will be your most loyal servant until the day of my death.'

'Hum!' said the Emperor, spilling a pinch of snuff over the front of his white jacket. 'There is some sense in what you say, for no one makes so good a servant as the man who has had a thorough fright. But I am a very exacting master.'

'I do not care what you require of me. Everything will be welcome, if you will only give me your forgiveness.'

'For example,' said the Emperor. 'It is one of my whims that when a man enters my service I shall marry him to whom I like. Do you agree to that?'

There was a struggle upon the poet's face, and he clasped and unclasped his hands.

'May I ask, sire—?'

'You may ask nothing.'

'But there are circumstances, sire—'

'There, there, that is enough!' cried the Emperor harshly, turning upon his heel. 'I do not argue, I order. There is a young lady, Mademoiselle de Bergerot, for whom I desire a husband. Will you marry her, or will you return to prison?'

Again there was the struggle in the man's face, and he was silent, twitching and writhing in his indecision.'

'It is enough!' cried the Emperor. 'Rousten, call the guard!'

'No, no, sire, do not send me back to prison.'

'The guard, Rousten!'

'I will do it, sire! I will do it! I will marry whomever you please!'

'You villain!' cried a voice, and there was Sibylle standing in the opening of the curtains at one of the windows. Her face was pale with anger and her eyes shining with scorn; the parting curtains framed her tall, slim figure, which leaned forwards in her fury of passion. She had forgotten the Emperor, the Empress, everything, in her revulsion of feeling against this craven whom she had loved.

'They told me what you were,' she cried. 'I would not believe them, I *could* not believe them—for I did not know that there was upon this earth a thing so contemptible. They said that they would prove it, and I defied them to do so, and now I see you as you are. Thank God that I have found you out in time! And to think that for your sake I have brought about the death of a man who was worth a hundred of you! Oh, I am rightly punished for an unwomanly act. Toussac has had his revenge.'

'Enough!' said the Emperor sternly. 'Constant, lead Mademoiselle Bernac into the next room. As to you, sir, I do not think that I can condemn any lady of my Court to take such a man as a husband. Suffice it that you have been shown in your true colours, and that Mademoiselle Bernac has been cured of a foolish infatuation. Rousten, remove the prisoner!'

'There, Monsieur de Laval,' said the Emperor, when the wretched Lesage had been conducted from the room. 'We have not done such a bad piece of work between the coffee and the breakfast. It was your idea, Josephine, and I give you credit for it. But now, de Laval, I feel that we owe you some recompense for having set the young aristocrats a good example, and for having had a share in this Toussac business. You have certainly acted very well.'

'I ask no recompense, sire,' said I, with an uneasy sense of what was coming.

'It is your modesty that speaks. But I have already decided upon your reward. You shall have such an allowance as will permit you to keep up a proper appearance as my *aide-de-camp*, and I have determined to marry you suitably to one of the ladies-in-waiting of the Empress.' My heart turned to lead within me.

'But, sire,' I stammered, 'this is impossible.'

'Oh, you have no occasion to hesitate. The lady is of excellent family and she is not wanting in personal charm. In a word, the affair is settled, and the marriage takes place upon Thursday.'

'But it is impossible, sire,' I repeated.

'Impossible! When you have been longer in my service, sir, you will understand that that is a word which I do not tolerate. I tell you that it is settled.'

'My love is given to another, sire. It is not possible for me to change.'

'Indeed!' said the Emperor coldly. 'If you persist in such a resolution you cannot expect to retain your place in my household.'

Here was the whole structure which my ambition had planned out crumbling hopelessly about my ears. And yet what was there for me to do?

'It is the bitterest moment of my life, sire,' said I, 'and yet I must be true to the promise which I have given. If I have to be a beggar by the roadside, I shall none the less marry Eugenie de Choiseul or no one.'

The Empress had risen and had approached the window.

'Well, at least, before you make up your mind, Monsieur de

Laval,' said she, 'I should certainly take a look at this lady-in-waiting of mine, whom you refuse with such indignation.'

With a quick rasping of rings she drew back the curtain of the second window. A woman was standing in the recess. She took a step forward into the room, and then—and then with a cry and a spring my arms were round her, and hers round me, and I was standing like a man in a dream, looking down into the sweet laughing eyes of my Eugenie. It was not until I had kissed her and kissed her again upon her lips, her cheeks, her hair, that I could persuade myself that she was indeed really there.

'Let us leave them,' said the voice of the Empress behind me. 'Come, Napoleon. It makes me sad! It reminds me too much of the old days in the Rue Chautereine.'

So there is an end of my little romance, for the Emperor's plans were, as usual, carried out, and we were married upon the Thursday, as he had said. That long and all-powerful arm had plucked her out from the Kentish town, and had brought her across the Channel, in order to make sure of my allegiance, and to strengthen the Court by the presence of a de Choiseul. As to my cousin Sibylle, it shall be written some day how she married the gallant Lieutenant Gerard many years afterwards, when he had become the chief of a brigade, and one of the most noted cavalry leaders in all the armies of France. Some day also I may tell how I came back into my rightful inheritance of Grosbois, which is still darkened to me by the thought of that terrible uncle of mine, and of what happened that night when Toussac stood at bay in the library. But enough of me and of my small fortunes. You have already heard more of them, perhaps, than you care for.

As to the Emperor, some faint shadow of whom I have tried in these pages to raise before you, you have heard from history how, despairing of gaining command of the Channel, and fearing to attempt an invasion which might be cut off from behind, he abandoned the camp of Boulogne. You have heard also how, with this very army which was meant for England, he struck down Austria and Russia in one year, and Prussia in the next. From the day that I entered his service until that on which he sailed forth over the Atlantic, never to return, I have faithfully shared his fortunes, rising with his star and sinking with it also. And yet, as I look back at my old master, I find it very difficult to say if he was a very good man or a very bad one. I only know that he was a very great one, and that the things in which he dealt were also so great that it is impossible to judge him by any ordinary standard. Let him rest silently, then, in his great red tomb at the Invalides, for the workman's work is done, and the mighty hand which moulded France and traced the lines of modern Europe has crumbled into dust. The Fates have used him, and the Fates have thrown him away, but still it lives, the memory of the little man in the grey coat, and still it moves the thoughts and actions of men. Some have written to praise and some to blame, but for my own part I have tried to do neither one nor the other, but only to tell the impression which he made upon me in those far-off days when the Army of England lay at Boulogne, and I came back once more to my Castle of Grosbois.

The Great Shadow

CHAPTER 1

The Night of the Beacons

It is strange to me, Jock Calder of West Inch, to feel that though now, in the very centre of the nineteenth century, I am but five-and-fifty years of age, and though it is only once in a week perhaps that my wife can pluck out a little grey bristle from over my ear, yet I have lived in a time when the thoughts and the ways of men were as different as though it were another planet from this. For when I walk in my fields I can see, down Berwick way, the little fluffs of white smoke which tell me of this strange new hundred-legged beast, with coals for food and a thousand men in its belly, for ever crawling over the border. On a shiny day I can see the glint of the brass work as it takes the curve near Corriemuir; and then, as I look out to sea, there is the same beast again, or a dozen of them maybe, leaving a trail of black in the air and of white in the water, and swimming in the face of the wind as easily as a salmon up the Tweed. Such a sight as that would have struck my good old father speechless with wrath as well as surprise; for he was so stricken with the fear of offending the Creator that he was chary of contradicting Nature, and always held the new thing to be nearly akin to the blasphemous. As long as God made the horse, and a man down Birmingham way the engine, my good old dad would have stuck by the saddle and the spurs.

But he would have been still more surprised had he seen the peace and kindliness which reigns now in the hearts of men, and the talk in the papers and at the meetings that there is to be no more war—save, of course, with blacks and such like.

171

For when he died we had been fighting with scarce a break, save only during two short years, for very nearly a quarter of a century. Think of it, you who live so quietly and peacefully now! Babies who were born in the war grew to be bearded men with babies of their own, and still the war continued. Those who had served and fought in their stalwart prime grew stiff and bent, and yet the ships and the armies were struggling. It was no wonder that folk came at last to look upon it as the natural state, and thought how queer it must seem to be at peace. During that long time we fought the Dutch, we fought the Danes, we fought the Spanish, we fought the Turks, we fought the Americans, we fought the Monte-Videans, until it seemed that in this universal struggle no race was too near of kin, or too far away, to be drawn into the quarrel. But most of all it was the French whom we fought, and the man whom of all others we loathed and feared and admired was the great Captain who ruled them.

It was very well to draw pictures of him, and sing songs about him, and make as though he were an impostor; but I can tell you that the fear of that man hung like a black shadow over all Europe, and that there was a time when the glint of a fire at night upon the coast would set every woman upon her knees and every man gripping for his musket. He had always won: that was the terror of it. The Fates seemed to be behind him. And now we knew that he lay upon the northern coast with a hundred and fifty thousand veterans, and the boats for their passage. But it is an old story, how a third of the grown folk of our country took up arms, and how our little one-eyed, one-armed man crushed their fleet. There was still to be a land of free thinking and free speaking in Europe.

There was a great beacon ready on the hill by Tweedmouth, built up of logs and tar-barrels; and I can well remember how, night after night, I strained my eyes to see if it were ablaze. I was only eight at the time, but it is an age when one takes a grief to heart, and I felt as though the fate of the country hung in some fashion upon me and my vigilance. And then one night as I looked I suddenly saw a little flicker on the beacon hill—a single red tongue of flame in the darkness. I remember how I rubbed my eyes, and pinched myself, and rapped my knuckles against the stone window-sill, to make sure that I was indeed awake. And then the flame shot higher, and I saw the red quivering line upon the water between; and I dashed into the kitchen, screeching to my father that the French had crossed and the Tweedmouth light was aflame. He had been talking to Mr. Mitchell, the law student from Edinburgh; and I can see him now as he knocked his pipe out at the side of the fire, and looked at me from over the top of his horn spectacles.

"Are you sure, Jock?" says he.

"Sure as death!" I gasped.

He reached out his hand for the Bible upon the table, and opened it upon his knee as though he meant to read to us; but he shut it again in silence, and hurried out. We went too, the law student and I, and followed him down to the gate which opens out upon the highway. From there we could see the red light of the big beacon, and the glimmer of a smaller one to the north of us at Ayton. My mother came down with two plaids to keep the chill from us, and we all stood there until morning, speaking little to each other, and that little in a whisper. The road had more folk on it than ever passed along it at night before; for many of the yeomen up our way had enrolled themselves in the Berwick volunteer regiments, and were riding now as fast as hoof could carry them for the muster. Some had a stirrup cup or two before parting, and I cannot forget one who tore past on a huge white horse, brandishing a great rusty sword in the moonlight. They shouted to us as they passed that the North Berwick Law fire was blazing, and that it was thought that the alarm had come from Edinburgh Castle. There were a few who galloped the other way, couriers for Edinburgh, and the laird's son, and Master Clayton, the deputy sheriff, and such like. And among others there was one a fine built, heavy man on a roan horse, who pulled up at our gate and asked some question about the road. He took off his hat to ease himself, and I saw that he had a kindly long-drawn face, and a great high brow that shot away up into tufts of sandy hair.

"I doubt it's a false alarm," said he. "Maybe I'd ha' done well to bide where I was; but now I've come so far, I'll break my fast with the regiment."

He clapped spurs to his horse, and away he went down the brae.

"I ken him weel," said our student, nodding after him. "He's a lawyer in Edinburgh, and a braw hand at the stringin' of verses. Wattie Scott is his name."

None of us had heard of it then; but it was not long before it was the best known name in Scotland, and many a time we thought of how he speered his way of us on the night of the terror.

But early in the morning we had our minds set at ease. It was grey and cold, and my mother had gone up to the house to make a pot of tea for us, when there came a gig down the road with Dr. Horscroft of Ayton in it and his son Jim. The collar of the doctor's brown coat came over his ears, and he looked in a deadly black humour; for Jim, who was but fifteen years of age, had trooped off to Berwick at the first alarm with his father's new fowling piece. All night his dad had chased him, and now there he was, a prisoner, with the barrel of the stolen gun sticking out from behind the seat. He looked as sulky as his father, with his hands thrust into his side-pockets, his brows drawn down, and his lower lip thrusting out.

"It's all a lie!" shouted the doctor as he passed. "There has been no landing, and all the fools in Scotland have been gadding about the roads for nothing."

His son Jim snarled something up at him on this, and his father struck him a blow with his clenched fist on the side of his head, which sent the boy's chin forward upon his breast as though he had been stunned. My father shook his head, for he had a liking for Jim; but we all walked up to the house again, nodding and blinking, and hardly able to keep our eyes open now that we knew that all was safe, but with a thrill of joy at our hearts such as I have only matched once or twice in my lifetime.

Now all this has little enough to do with what I took my pen up to tell about; but when a man has a good memory and little skill, he cannot draw one thought from his mind without a dozen others trailing out behind it. And yet, now that I come to think of it, this had something to do with it after all; for Jim Horscroft had so deadly a quarrel with his father, that he was packed off to the Berwick Academy, and as my father had long wished me to go there, he took advantage of this chance to send me also.

But before I say a word about this school, I shall go back to where I should have begun, and give you a hint as to who I am; for it may be that these words of mine may be read by some folk beyond the border country who never heard of the Calders of West Inch.

It has a brave sound, West Inch, but it is not a fine estate with a braw house upon it, but only a great hard-bitten, wind-swept sheep run, fringing off into links along the sea-shore, where a frugal man might with hard work just pay his rent and have butter instead of treacle on Sundays. In the centre there is a grey-stoned slate-roofed house with a byre behind it, and "1703" scrawled in stonework over the lintel of the door. There for more than a hundred years our folk have lived, until, for all their poverty, they came to take a good place among the people; for in the country parts the old yeoman is often better thought of than the new laird.

There was one queer thing about the house of West Inch. It has been reckoned by engineers and other knowing folk that the boundary line between the two countries ran right through the middle of it, splitting our second-best bedroom into an Eng-lish half and a Scotch half. Now the cot in which I always slept was so placed that my head was to the north of the line and my feet to the south of it. My friends say that if I had chanced to lie the other way my hair might not have been so sandy, nor my mind of so solemn a cast. This I know, that more than once in my life, when my Scotch head could see no way out of a danger, my good thick English legs have come to my help, and carried me clear away. But at school I never heard the end of this, for they would call me "Half-and-half" and "The Great Britain," and sometimes "Union Jack." When there was a battle between the Scotch and English boys, one side would kick my shins and the other cuff my ears, and then they would both stop and laugh as though it were something funny.

At first I was very miserable at the Berwick Academy. Birtwhistle was the first master, and Adams the second, and I had no love for either of them. I was shy and backward by nature, and slow at making a friend either among masters or boys. It was nine miles as the crow flies, and eleven and a half by road, from Berwick to West Inch, and my heart grew heavy at the weary distance that separated me from my mother; for, mark you, a lad of that age pretends that he has no need of his mother's caresses, but ah, how sad he is when he is taken at his word! At last I could stand it no longer, and I determined to run away from the school and make my way home as fast as I might. At the very last moment, however, I had the good fortune to win the praise and admiration of every one, from the headmaster downwards, and to find my school life made very pleasant and easy to me. And all this came of my falling by accident out of a second-floor window.

This was how it happened. One evening I had been kicked by Ned Barton, who was the bully of the school; and this injury coming on the top of all my other grievances, caused my little cup to overflow. I vowed that night, as I buried my tear-stained face beneath the blankets, that the next morning would either find me at West Inch or well on the way to it. Our dormitory was on the second floor, but I was a famous climber, and had a fine head for heights. I used to think little, young as I was, of swinging myself with a rope round my thigh off the West Inch gable, and that stood three-and-fifty feet above the ground. There was not much fear then but that I could make my way out of Birtwhistle's dormitory. I waited a weary while until the coughing and tossing had died away, and there was no sound of wakefulness from the long line of wooden cots; then I very softly rose, slipped on my clothes, took my shoes in my hand, and walked tiptoe to the window. I opened the casement and looked out. Underneath me lay the garden, and close by my hand was the stout branch of a pear tree. An active lad could ask no better ladder. Once in the garden I had but a five-foot wall to get over, and then there was nothing but distance between me and home. I took a firm grip of a branch with one hand, placed my knee upon another one, and was about to swing myself out of the window, when in a moment I was as silent and as still as though I had been turned to stone.

There was a face looking at me from over the coping of the wall. A chill of fear struck to my heart at its whiteness and its stillness. The moon shimmered upon it, and the eyeballs moved slowly from side to side, though I was hid from them behind the screen of the pear tree. Then in a jerky fashion this white face ascended, until the neck, shoulders, waist, and knees of a man became visible. He sat himself down on the top of the wall, and with a great heave he pulled up after him a boy about my own size, who caught his breath from time to time as though to choke down a sob. The man gave him a shake, with a few rough whispered words, and then the two dropped together down into the garden. I was still standing balanced with one foot upon the bough and one upon the casement, not daring to budge for fear of attracting their attention, for I could hear them moving stealthily about in the long shadow of the house. Suddenly, from immediately beneath my feet, I heard a low grating noise and the sharp tinkle of falling glass.

"That's done it," said the man's eager whisper. "There is room for you."

"But the edge is all jagged!" cried the other in a weak quaver.

The fellow burst out into an oath that made my skin pringle.

"In with you, you cub," he snarled, "or—"

I could not see what he did, but there was a short, quick gasp of pain.

"I'll go! I'll go!" cried the little lad.

But I heard no more, for my head suddenly swam, my heel shot off the branch, I gave a dreadful yell, and came down, with my ninety-five pounds of weight, right upon the bent back of the burglar. If you ask me, I can only say that to this day I am not quite certain whether it was an accident or whether I designed it. It may be that while I was thinking of doing it Chance settled the matter for me. The fellow was stooping with his head forward thrusting the boy through a tiny window, when I came down upon him just where the neck joins the spine. He gave a kind of whistling cry, dropped upon his face, and rolled three times over, drumming on the grass with his heels. His little companion flashed off in the moonlight, and was over the wall in a trice. As for me, I sat yelling at the pitch of my lungs and nursing one of my legs, which felt as if a red-hot ring were welded round it.

It was not long, as may be imagined, before the whole household, from the headmaster to the stable boy, were out in the garden with lamps and lanterns. The matter was soon cleared: the man carried off upon a shutter, and I borne in much state and solemnity to a special bedroom, where the small bone of my leg was set by Surgeon Purdie, the younger of the two brothers of that name. As to the robber, it was found that his legs were palsied, and the doctors were of two minds as to whether he would recover the use of them or no; but the Law never gave them a chance of settling the matter, for he was hanged after Carlisle assizes, some six weeks later. It was proved that he was the most desperate rogue in the North of England, for he had done three murders at the least, and there were charges enough against him upon the sheet to have hanged him ten times over.

Well now, I could not pass over my boyhood without telling you about this, which was the most important thing that happened to me. But I will go off upon no more side tracks; for when I think of all that is coming, I can see very well that I shall have more than enough to do before I have finished. For when a man has only his own little private tale to tell, it often takes him all his time; but when he gets mixed up in such great matters as I shall have to speak about, then it is hard on him, if he has not been brought up to it, to get it all set down to his liking. But my memory is as good as ever, thank God, and I shall try to get it all straight before I finish.

It was this business of the burglar that first made a friendship between Jim Horscroft, the doctor's son, and me. He was cock boy of the school from the day he came; for within the hour he had thrown Barton, who had been cock before him, right through the big blackboard in the class-room. Jim always ran to muscle and bone, and even then he was square and tall, short of speech and long in the arm, much given to lounging with his broad back against walls, and his hands deep in his breeches pockets. I can even recall that he had a trick of keeping a straw in the corner of his mouth, just where he used afterwards to hold his pipe. Jim was always the same for good and for bad since first I knew him.

Heavens, how we all looked up to him! We were but young savages, and had a savage's respect for power. There was Tom Carndale of Appleby, who could write alcaics as well as mere pentameters and hexameters, yet nobody would give a snap for Tom; and there was Willie Earnshaw, who had every date, from the killing of Abel, on the tip of his tongue, so that the masters themselves would turn to him if they were in doubt, yet he was but a narrow-chested lad, over long for his breadth; and what did his dates help him when Jack Simons of the lower third chivvied him down the passage with the buckle end of a strap? But you didn't do things like that with Jim Horscroft. What tales we used to whisper about his strength! How he put his fist through the oak-panel of the game-room door; how, when Long Merridew was carrying the ball, he caught up Merridew, ball and all, and ran swiftly past every opponent to the goal. It did not seem fit to us that such a one as he should trouble his head about spondees and dactyls, or care to know who signed the Magna Charta. When he said in open class that King Alfred was the man, we little boys all felt that very likely it was so, and that perhaps Jim knew more about it than the man who wrote the book.

Well, it was this business of the burglar that drew his attention to me; for he patted me on my head, and said that I was a spunky little devil, which blew me out with pride for a week on end. For two years we were close friends, for all the gap that the years had made between us, and though in passion or in want of thought he did many a thing that galled me, yet I loved him like a brother, and wept as much as would have filled an ink bottle when at last he went off to Edinburgh to study his father's profession. Five years after that did I tide at Birtwhistle's, and when

I left had become cock myself, for I was wiry and as tough as whalebone, though I never ran to weight and sinew like my great predecessor. It was in Jubilee Year that I left Birtwhistle's, and then for three years I stayed at home learning the ways of the cattle; but still the ships and the armies were wrestling, and still the great shadow of Bonaparte lay across the country. How could I guess that I too should have a hand in lifting that shadow for ever from our people?

CHAPTER 2

Cousin Edie of Eyemouth

Some years before, when I was still but a lad, there had come over to us upon a five weeks' visit the only daughter of my father's brother. Willie Calder had settled at Eyemouth as a maker of fishing nets, and he had made more out of twine than ever we were like to do out of the whin-bushes and sand-links of West Inch. So his daughter, Edie Calder, came over with a braw red frock and a five shilling bonnet, and a kist full of things that brought my dear mother's eyes out like a partan's. It was wonderful to see her so free with money, and she but a slip of a girl, paying the carrier man all that he asked and a whole twopence over, to which he had no claim. She made no more of drinking ginger-beer than we did of water, and she would have her sugar in her tea and butter with her bread just as if she had been English.

I took no great stock of girls at that time, for it was hard for me to see what they had been made for. There were none of us at Birtwhistle's that thought very much of them; but the smallest laddies seemed to have the most sense, for after they began to grow bigger they were not so sure about it. We little ones were all of one mind: that a creature that couldn't fight and was aye carrying tales, and couldn't so much as shy a stone without flapping its arm like a rag in the wind, was no use for anything. And then the airs that they would put on, as if they were mother and father rolled into one; for ever breaking into a game with "Jimmy, your toe's come through your boot," or "Go home, you dirty boy, and clean yourself," until the very sight of them was weariness.

So when this one came to the steading at West Inch I was not best pleased to see her. I was twelve at the time (it was in the holidays) and she eleven, a thin, tallish girl with black eyes and the queerest ways. She was for ever staring out in front of her with her lips parted, as if she saw something wonderful; but when I came behind her and looked the same way, I could see nothing but the sheep's trough or the midden, or father's breeches hanging on a clothes-line. And then if she saw a lump of heather or bracken, or any common stuff of that sort, she would mope over it, as if it had struck her sick, and cry, "How sweet! how perfect!" just as though it had been a painted picture. She didn't like games, but I used to make her play "tig" and such like; but it was no fun, for I could always catch her in three jumps, and she could never catch me, though she would come with as much rustle and flutter as ten boys would make. When I used to tell her that she was good for nothing, and that her father was a fool to bring her up like that, she would begin to cry, and say that I was a rude boy, and that she would go home that very night, and never forgive me as long as she lived. But in five minutes she had forgot all about it. What was strange was that she liked me a deal better than I did her, and she would never leave me alone; but she was always watching me and running after me, and then saying, "Oh, here you are!" as if it were a surprise.

But soon I found that there was good in her too. She used sometimes to give me pennies, so that once I had four in my pocket all at the same time; but the best part of her was the stories that she could tell. She was sore frightened of frogs, so I would bring one to her, and tell her that I would put it down her neck unless she told a story. That always helped her to begin; but when once she was started it was wonderful how she would carry on. And the things that had happened to her, they were enough to take your breath away. There was a Barbary rover that had been at Eyemouth, and he was coming back in five years in a ship full of gold to make her his wife; and then there was a wandering knight who had been there also, and he had given her a ring which he said he would redeem when the time came. She showed me the ring, which was very like the ones upon my bed curtain; but she said that this one was virgin gold. I asked her what the knight would do if he met the Barbary rover, and she told me that he would sweep his head from his shoulders. What they could all see in her was more than I could think. And then she told me that she had been followed on her way to West Inch by a disguised prince. I asked her how she knew it was a prince, and she said by his disguise. Another day she said that her father was preparing a riddle, and that when it was ready it would be put in the papers, and anyone who guessed it would have half his fortune and his daughter. I said that I was good at riddles, and that she must send it to me when it was ready. She said it would be in the *Berwick Gazette*, and wanted to know what I would do with her when I won her. I said I would sell her by public roup for what she would fetch; but she would tell no more stories that evening, for she was very tetchy about some things.

Jim Horscroft was away when Cousin Edie was with us, but he came back the very week she went; and I mind how surprised I was that he should ask any questions or take any interest in a mere lassie. He asked me if she were pretty; and when I said I hadn't noticed, he laughed and called me a mole, and said my eyes would be opened some day. But very soon he came to be interested in something else, and I never gave Edie another thought until one day she just took my life in her hands and twisted it as I could twist this quill.

That was in 1813, after I had left school, when I was already eighteen years of age, with a good forty hairs on my upper lip and every hope of more. I had changed since I left school, and was not so keen on games as I had been, but found myself instead lying about on the sunny side of the braes, with my own lips parted and my eyes staring just the same as Cousin Edie's used to do. It had satisfied me and filled my whole life that I could run faster and jump higher than my neighbour; but now all that seemed such a little thing, and I yearned, and yearned, and looked up at the big arching sky, and down at the flat blue sea, and felt that there was something wanting, but could never lay my tongue to what that something was. And I became quick of temper too, for my nerves seemed all of a fret, and when my mother would ask me what ailed me, or my father would speak of my turning my hand to work, I would break into such sharp bitter answers as I have often grieved over since. Ah! a man may have more than one wife, and more than one child, and more than one friend; but he can never have but the one mother, so let him cherish her while he may.

One day when I came in from the sheep, there was my father sitting with a letter in his hands, which was a very rare thing with us, except when the factor wrote for the rent. Then as I came nearer to him I saw that he was crying, and I stood staring, for I had always thought that it was not a thing that a man could do. I can see him now, for he had so deep a crease across his brown cheek that no tear could pass it, but must trickle away sideways and so down to his ear, hopping off on to the sheet of paper. My mother sat beside him and stroked his hands like she did the cat's back when she would soothe it.

"Aye, Jeannie," said he, "poor Willie's gone. It's from the law-yer, and it was sudden or they'd ha' sent word of it. Carbuncle, he says, and a flush o' blood to the head."

"Ah! well, his trouble's over," said my mother.

My father rubbed his ears with the tablecloth.

"He's left a' his savings to his lassie," said he, "and by gom if she's not changed from what she promised to be she'll soon gar them flee. You mind what she said of weak tea under this very roof, and it at seven shillings the pound!"

My mother shook her head, and looked up at the flitches of bacon that hung from the ceiling.

"He doesn't say how much, but she'll have enough and to spare, he says. And she's to come and bide with us, for that was his last wish."

"To pay for her keep!" cried my mother sharply. I was sorry that she should have spoken of money at that moment, but then if she had not been sharp we would all have been on the road-side in a twelvemonth.

"Aye, she'll pay, and she's coming this very day. Jock lad, I'll want you to drive to Ayton and meet the evening coach. Your Cousin Edie will be in it, and you can fetch her over to West Inch."

And so off I started at quarter past five with Souter Johnnie, the long-haired fifteen-year-old, and our cart with the new-painted tail-board that we only used on great days. The coach was in just as I came, and I, like a foolish country lad, taking no heed to the years that had passed, was looking about among the folk in the Inn front for a slip of a girl with her petticoats just under her knees. And as I slouched past and craned my neck there came a touch to my elbow, and there was a lady dressed all in black standing by the steps, and I knew that it was my cousin Edie.

I knew it, I say, and yet had she not touched me I might have passed her a score of times and never known it. My word, if Jim Horscroft had asked me then if she were pretty or no, I should have known how to answer him! She was dark, much darker than is common among our border lasses, and yet with such a faint blush of pink breaking through her dainty colour, like the deeper flush at the heart of a sulphur rose. Her lips were red, and kindly, and firm; and even then, at the first glance, I saw that light of mischief and mockery that danced away at the back of her great dark eyes. She took me then and there as though I had been her heritage, put out her hand and plucked me. She was, as I have said, in black, dressed in what seemed to me to be a wondrous fashion, with a black veil pushed up from her brow.

"Ah! Jack," said she, in a mincing English fashion, that she had learned at the boarding school. "No, no, we are rather old for that"—this because I in my awkward fashion was pushing my foolish brown face forward to kiss her, as I had done when I saw her last. "Just hurry up like a good fellow and give a shilling to the conductor, who has been exceedingly civil to me during the journey."

I flushed up red to the ears, for I had only a silver fourpenny piece in my pocket. Never had my lack of pence weighed so heavily upon me as just at that moment. But she read me at a glance, and there in an instant was a little moleskin purse with a silver clasp thrust into my hand. I paid the man, and would have given it back, but she still would have me keep it.

"You shall be my factor, Jack," said she, laughing. "Is this our carriage? How funny it looks! And where am I to sit?"

"On the sacking," said I.

"And how am I to get there?"

"Put your foot on the hub," said I. "I'll help you."

I sprang up and took her two little gloved hands in my own. As she came over the side her breath blew in my face, sweet and warm, and all that vagueness and unrest seemed in a moment to have been shredded away from my soul. I felt as if that instant had taken me out from myself, and made me one of the race. It took but the time of the flicking of the horse's tail, and yet something had happened, a barrier had gone down somewhere, and I was leading a wider and a wiser life. I felt it all in a flush, but shy and backward as I was, I could do nothing but flatten out the sacking for her. Her eyes were after the coach which was rattling away to Berwick, and suddenly she shook her handkerchief in the air.

"He took off his hat," said she. "I think he must have been an officer. He was very distinguished looking. Perhaps you noticed him—a gentleman on the outside, very handsome, with a brown overcoat."

I shook my head, with all my flush of joy changed to foolish resentment.

"Ah! well, I shall never see him again. Here are all the green braes and the brown winding road just the same as ever. And you, Jack, I don't see any great change in you either. I hope your manners are better than they used to be. You won't try to put any frogs down my back, will you?"

I crept all over when I thought of such a thing.

"We'll do all we can to make you happy at West Inch," said I, playing with the whip.

"I'm sure it's very kind of you to take a poor lonely girl in," said she.

"It's very kind of you to come, Cousin Edie," I stammered. "You'll find it very dull, I fear."

"I suppose it is a little quiet, Jack, eh? Not many men about, as I remember it."

"There is Major Elliott, up at Corriemuir. He comes down of an evening, a real brave old soldier who had a ball in his knee under Wellington."

"Ah, when I speak of men. Jack, I don't mean old folk with balls in their knees. I meant people of our own age that we could make friends of. By the way, that crabbed old doctor had a son, had he not?"

"Oh yes, that's Jim Horscroft, my best friend."

"Is he at home?"

"No. He'll be home soon. He's still at Edinburgh studying."

"Ah! then we'll keep each other company until he comes, Jack. And I'm very tired and I wish I was at West Inch."

I made old Souter Johnnie cover the ground as he has never done before or since, and in an hour she was seated at the supper table, where my mother had laid out not only butter, but a glass dish of gooseberry jam, which sparkled and looked fine in the candle-light. I could see that my parents were as overcome as I was at the difference in her, though not in the same way. My mother was so set back by the feather thing that she had round her neck that she called her Miss Calder instead of Edie, until my cousin in her pretty flighty way would lift her forefinger to her whenever she did it. After supper, when she had gone to bed, they could talk of nothing but her looks and her breeding.

"By the way, though," says my father, "it does not look as if she were heart-broke about my brother's death."

And then for the first time I remembered that she had never said a word about the matter since I had met her.

CHAPTER 3

The Shadow on the Waters

It was not very long before Cousin Edie was queen of West Inch, and we all her devoted subjects from my father down. She had money and to spare, though none of us knew how much. When my mother said that four shillings the week would cover all that she would cost, she fixed on seven shillings and sixpence of her own free will. The south room, which was the sunniest and had the honeysuckle round the window, was for her; and it was a marvel to see the things that she brought from Berwick to put into it. Twice a week she would drive over, and the cart would not do for her, for she hired a gig from Angus Whitehead, whose farm lay over the hill. And it was seldom that she went without bringing something back for one or other of us. It was a wooden pipe for my father, or a Shetland plaid for my mother, or a book for me, or a brass collar for Rob the collie. There was never a woman more free-handed.

But the best thing that she gave us was just her own presence. To me it changed the whole country-side, and the sun was brighter and the braes greener and the air sweeter from the day she came. Our lives were common no longer now that we spent them with such a one as she, and the old dull grey house was another place in my eyes since she had set her foot across the door-mat. It was not her face, though that was winsome enough, nor her form, though I never saw the lass that could match her; but it was her spirit, her queer mocking ways, her fresh new fashion of talk, her proud whisk of the dress and toss of the head, which made one feel like the ground beneath her feet, and then the quick challenge in her eye, and the kindly word that brought one up to her level again.

But never quite to her level either. To me she was always something above and beyond. I might brace myself and blame myself, and do what I would, but still I could not feel that the same blood ran in our veins, and that she was but a country lassie, as I was a country lad. The more I loved her the more frightened I was at her, and she could see the fright long before she knew the love. I was uneasy to be away from her, and yet when I was with her I was in a shiver all the time for fear my stumbling talk might weary her or give her offence. Had I known more of the ways of women I might have taken less pains.

"You're a deal changed from what you used to be, Jack," said she, looking at me sideways from under her dark lashes.

"You said not when first we met," says I.

"Ah! I was speaking of your looks then, and of your ways now. You used to be so rough to me, and so masterful, and would have your own way, like the little man that you were. I can see you now with your tousled brown hair and your mischievous eyes. And now you are so gentle and quiet and soft-spoken."

"One learns to behave," says I.

"Ah, but, Jack, I liked you so much better as you were!"

Well, when she said that I fairly stared at her, for I had thought that she could never have quite forgiven me for the way I used to carry on. That anyone out of a daft house could have liked it, was clean beyond my understanding. I thought of how when she was reading by the door I would go up on the moor with a hazel switch and fix little clay balls at the end of it, and sling them at her until I made her cry. And then I thought of how I caught an eel in the Corriemuir burn and chivvied her about with it, until she ran screaming under my mother's apron half mad with fright, and my father gave me one on the ear-hole with the porridge stick which knocked me and my eel under the kitchen dresser. And these were the things that she missed! Well, she must miss them, for my hand would wither before I could do them now. But for the first time I began to understand the queerness that lies in a woman, and that a man must not reason about one, but just watch and try to learn.

We found our level after a time, when she saw that she had just to do what she liked and how she liked, and that I was as much at her beck and call as old Rob was at mine. You'll think I was a fool to have had my head so turned, and maybe I was; but then you must think how little I was used to women, and how much we were thrown together. Besides she was a woman in a million, and I can tell you that it was a strong head that would not be turned by her.

Why, there was Major Elliott, a man that had buried three wives, and had twelve pitched battles to his name, Edie could have turned him round her finger like a damp rag—she, only new from the boarding school. I met him hobbling from West Inch the first time after she came, with pink in his cheeks and a shine in his eye that took ten years from him. He was cocking up his grey moustaches at either end and curling them into his eyes, and strutting out with his sound leg as proud as a piper. What she had said to him the Lord knows, but it was like old wine in his veins.

"I've been up to see you, laddie," said he, "but I must home again now. My visit has not been wasted, however, as I had an opportunity of seeing *la belle cousine.* A most charming and engaging young lady, laddie."

He had a formal stiff way of talking, and was fond of jerking in a bit of the French, for he had picked some up in the Peninsula. He would have gone on talking of Cousin Edie, but I saw the corner of a newspaper thrusting out of his pocket, and I knew that he had come over, as was his way, to give me some news, for we heard little enough at West Inch.

"What is fresh, Major?" I asked. He pulled the paper out with a flourish.

"The allies have won a great battle, my lad," says he. "I don't think Nap can stand up long against this. The Saxons have thrown him over, and he's been badly beat at Leipzig. Wellington is past the Pyrenees, and Graham's folk will be at Bayonne before long."

I chucked up my hat.

"Then the war will come to an end at last," I cried.

"Aye, and time too," said he, shaking his head gravely. "It's been a bloody business. But it is hardly worth while for me to say now what was in my mind about you."

"What was that?"

"Well, laddie, you are doing no good here, and now that my knee is getting more limber I was hoping that I might get on active service again. I wondered whether maybe you might like to do a little soldiering under me."

My heart jumped at the thought.

"Aye, would I!" I cried.

"But it'll be clear six months before I'll be fit to pass a board, and it's long odds that Boney will be under lock and key before that."

"And there's my mother," said I, "I doubt she'd never let me go."

"Ah! well, she'll never be asked to now," he answered, and hobbled on upon his way.

I sat down among the heather with my chin on my hand, turning the thing over in my mind, and watching him in his old brown clothes, with the end of a grey plaid flapping over his shoulder, as he picked his way up the swell of the hill. It was a poor life this, at West Inch, waiting to fill my father's shoes, with the same heath, and the same burn, and the same sheep, and the same grey house for ever before me. But over there, over the blue sea, ah! there was a life fit for a man. There was the Major, a man past his prime, wounded and spent, and yet planning to get to work again, whilst I, with all the strength of my youth, was wasting it upon these hillsides. A hot wave of shame flushed over me, and I sprang up all in a tingle to be off and playing a man's part in the world.

For two days I turned it over in my mind, and on the third there came something which first brought all my resolutions to a head, and then blew them all to nothing like a puff of smoke in the wind.

I had strolled out in 'the afternoon with Cousin Edie and Rob, until we found ourselves upon the brow of the slope which dips away down to the beach. It was late in the fall, and the links were all bronzed and faded; but the sun still shone warmly, and a south breeze came in little hot pants, rippling the broad blue sea with white curling lines. I pulled an armful of bracken to make a couch for Edie, and there she lay in her listless fashion, happy and contented; for of all folk that I have ever met, she had the most joy from warmth and light. I leaned on a tussock of grass, with Rob's head upon my knee, and there as we sat alone in peace in the wilderness, even there we saw suddenly thrown upon the waters in front of us the shadow of that great man over yonder, who had scrawled his name in red letters across the map of Europe. There was a ship coming up with the wind, a black sedate old merchant-man, bound for Leith as likely as not. Her yards were square and she was running with all sail set. On the other tack, coming from the north-east, were two great ugly lugger-like craft, with one high mast each, and a big square brown sail. A prettier sight one would not wish than to see the three craft dipping along upon so fair a day. But of a sudden there came a spurt of flame and a whirl of blue smoke from one lugger, then the same from the second, and a rap, rap, rap, from the ship. In a twinkling hell had elbowed out heaven, and there on the waters was hatred and savagery and the lust for blood.

We had sprung to our feet at the outburst, and Edie put her hand all in a tremble upon my arm.

"They are fighting, Jack!" she cried. "What are they? Who are they?"

My heart was thudding with the guns, and it was all that I could do to answer her for the catch of my breath.

"It's two French privateers, Edie," said I, "Chasse-marries, they call them, and yon's one of our merchant ships, and they'll take her as sure as death; for the Major says they've always got heavy guns, and are as full of men as an egg is full of meat. Why doesn't the fool make back for Tweedmouth bar?"

But not an inch of canvas did she lower, but floundered on in her stolid fashion, while a little black ball ran up to her peak, and the rare old flag streamed suddenly out from the halliard. Then again came the rap, rap, rap, of her little guns, and the boom, boom of the big carronades in the bows of the lugger.

An instant later the three ships met, and the merchant-man staggered on like a stag with two wolves hanging to its haunches. The three became but a dark blur amid the smoke, with the top spars thrusting out in a bristle, and from the heart of that cloud came the quick red flashes of flame, and such a devils' racket of big guns and small, cheering and screaming, as was to din in my head for many a week. For a stricken hour the hell-cloud moved slowly across the face of the water, and still with our hearts in our mouths we watched the flap of the flag, straining to see if it were yet there. And then suddenly, the ship, as proud and black and high as ever, shot on upon her way; and as the smoke cleared we saw one of the luggers squattering like a broken winged duck upon the water, and the other working hard to get the crew from her before she sank.

For all that hour I had lived for nothing but the fight. My cap had been whisked away by the wind, but I had never given it a thought. Now with my heart full I turned upon my Cousin Edie, and the sight of her took me back six years. There was the vacant staring eye and the parted lips, just as I had seen them in her girlhood, and her little hands were clenched until the knuckles gleamed like ivory.

"Ah, that captain!" said she, talking to the heath and the whin-bushes. "There is a man so strong, so resolute! What woman would not be proud of a man like that?"

"Aye, he did well!" I cried with enthusiasm.

She looked at me as if she had forgotten my existence.

"I would give a year of my life to meet such a man," said she. "But that is what living in the country means. One never sees anybody but just those who are fit for nothing better."

I do not know that she meant to hurt me, though she was never very backward at that; but whatever her intention, her words seemed to strike straight upon a naked nerve.

"Very well, Cousin Edie," I said, trying to speak calmly, "that puts the cap on it. I'll take the bounty in Berwick tonight."

"What, Jack! you be a soldier!"

"Yes, if you think that every man that bides in the country must be a coward."

"Oh, you'd look so handsome in a red coat, Jack, and it improves you vastly when you are in a temper. I wish your eyes would always flash like that, for it looks so nice and manly. But I am sure that you are joking about the soldiering."

"I'll let you see if I am joking."

Then and there I set off running over the moor, until I burst into the kitchen where my mother and father were sitting on either side of the ingle.

"Mother," I cried, "I'm off for a soldier!"

Had I said I was off for a burglar they could not have looked worse over it, for in those days among the decent canny country folks it was mostly the black sheep that were herded by the sergeant. But, my word, those same black sheep did their country some rare service too. My mother put up her mittens to her eyes, and my father looked as black as a peat hole.

"Hoots, Jock, you're daft," says he.

"Daft or no, I'm going."

"Then you'll have no blessing from me."

"Then I'll go without."

At this my mother gives a screech and throws her arms about my neck. I saw her hand, all hard and worn and knuckly with the work she had done for my up-bringing, and it pleaded with me as words could not have done. My heart was soft for her, but my will was as hard as a flint-edge. I put her back in her chair with a kiss, and then ran to my room to pack my bundle. It was already growing dark, and I had a long walk before me, so I thrust a few things together and hastened out. As I came through the side door someone touched my shoulder, and there was Edie in the gloaming.

"Silly boy," said she, "you are not really going."

"Am I not? You'll see."

"But your father does not wish it, nor your mother."

"I know that."

"Then why go?"

"You ought to know."

"Why, then?"

"Because you make me!"

"I don't want you to go, Jack."

"You said it. You said that the folk in the country were fit for nothing better. You always speak like that. You think no more of me than of those doos in the cot. You think I am nobody at all. I'll show you different."

All my troubles came out in hot little spurts of speech. She coloured up as I spoke, and looked at me in her queer half-mocking, half-petting fashion.

"Oh, I think so little of you as that?" said she. "And that is the reason why you are going away? Well then, Jack, will you stay if I am—if I am kind to you?"

We were face to face and close together, and in an instant the thing was done. My arms were round her, and I was kissing her, and kissing her, and kissing her, on her mouth, her cheeks, her eyes, and pressing her to my heart, and whispering to her that she was all, all, to me, and that I could not be without her. She said nothing, but it was long before she turned her face aside, and when she pushed me back it was not very hard.

"Why, you are quite your rude, old, impudent self!" said she, patting her hair with her two hands. "You have tossed me, Jack; I had no idea that you would be so forward!"

But all my fear of her was gone, and a love tenfold hotter than ever was boiling in my veins. I took her up again, and kissed her as if it were my right.

"You are my very own now!" I cried. "I shall not go to Berwick, but I'll stay and marry you."

But she laughed when I spoke of marriage.

"Silly boy! Silly boy!" said she, with her forefinger up; and then when I tried to lay hands on her again, she gave a little dainty curtsy, and was off into the house.

CHAPTER 4

The Choosing of Jim

And then there came those ten weeks which were like a dream, and are so now to look back upon. I would weary you were I to tell you what passed between us; but oh, how earnest and fateful and all-important it was at the time! Her waywardness; her ever-varying moods, now bright, now dark, like a meadow under drifting clouds; her causeless angers; her sudden repentances, each in turn filling me with joy or sorrow: these were my life, and all the rest was but emptiness. But ever deep down behind all my other feelings was a vague disquiet, a fear that I was like the man who set forth to lay hands upon the rainbow, and that the real Edie Calder, however near she might seem, was in truth for ever beyond my reach.

For she was so hard to understand, or, at least, she was so for a dull-witted country lad like me. For if I would talk to her of my real prospects, and how by taking in the whole of Corriemuir we might earn a hundred good pounds over the extra rent, and maybe be able to build out the parlour at West Inch, so as to make it fine for her when we married, she would pout her lips and droop her eyes, as though she scarce had patience to listen to me. But if I would let her build up dreams about what I might become, how I might find a paper which proved me to be the true heir of the laird, or how, without joining the army, which she would by no means hear of, I showed myself to be a great warrior until my name was in all folks' mouths, then she would be as blithe as the May. I would keep up the play as well as I could, but soon some luckless word would show that I was only plain Jock Calder of West Inch, and out would come her lip again in scorn of me. So we moved on, she in the air and I on the ground; and if the rift had not come in one way, it must in another.

It was after Christmas, but the winter had been mild, with just frost enough to make it safe walking over the peat bogs. One fresh morning Edie had been out early, and she came back to breakfast with a fleck of colour on her cheeks.

"Has your friend the doctor's son come home, Jack?" says she.

"I heard that it was expected."

"Ah! then it must have been him that I met on the muir."

"What! you met Jim Horscroft?"

"I am sure it must be he. A splendid-looking man—a hero, with curly black hair, a short, straight nose, and grey eyes. He had shoulders like a statue, and as to height, why, I suppose that your head, Jack, would come up to his scarf-pin."

"Up to his ear, Edie!" said I indignantly. "That is, if it was Jim. But tell me. Had he a brown wooden pipe stuck in the corner of his mouth?"

"Yes, he was smoking. He was dressed in grey, and he has a grand deep strong voice."

"Ho, ho! you spoke to him!" said I.

She coloured a little, as if she had said more than she meant.

"I was going where the ground was a little soft, and he warned me of it," she said.

"Ah! it must have been dear old Jim," said I. "He should have been a doctor years back, if his brains had been as strong as his arm. Why, heart alive, here is the very man himself!"

I had seen him through the kitchen window, and now I rushed out with my half-eaten bannock in my hand to greet him. He ran forward too, with his great hand out and his eyes shining.

"Ah! Jock," he cried, "it's good to see you again. There are no friends like the old ones."

Then suddenly he stuck in his speech, and stared with his mouth open over my shoulder. I turned, and there was Edie, with such a merry, roguish smile, standing in the door. How proud I felt of her, and of myself too, as I looked at her!

"This is my cousin, Miss Edie Calder, Jim," said I.

"Do you often take walks before breakfast, Mr. Horscroft?" she asked, still with that roguish smile.

"Yes," said he, staring at her with all his eyes.

"So do I, and generally over yonder," said she. "But you are not very hospitable to your friend, Jack. If you do not do the honours, I shall have to take your place for the credit of West Inch."

Well, in another minute we were in with the old folk, and Jim had his plate of porridge ladled out for him; but hardly a word would he speak, but sat with his spoon in his hand staring at Cousin Edie. She shot little twinkling glances across at him all the time, and it seemed to me that she was amused at his backwardness, and that she tried by what she said to give him heart.

"Jack was telling me that you were studying to be a doctor," said she. "But oh, how hard it must be, and how long it must take before one can gather so much learning as that!"

"It takes me long enough," Jim answered ruefully; "but I'll beat it yet."

"Ah! but you are brave. You are resolute. You fix your eyes on a point and you move on towards it, and nothing can stop you."

"Indeed, I've little to boast of," said he. "Many a one who began with me has put up his plate years ago, and here am I but a student still."

"That is your modesty, Mr. Horscroft. They say that the bravest are always humble. But then, when you have gained your end, what a glorious career—to carry healing in your hands, to raise up the suffering, to have for one's sole end the good of humanity!"

Honest Jim wriggled in his chair at this.

"I'm afraid I have no such very high motives, Miss Calder," said he. "It's to earn a living, and to take over my father's business, that I do it. If I carry healing in one hand, I have the other out for a crown-piece."

"How candid and truthful you are!" she cried; and so they went on, she decking him with every virtue, and twisting his words to make him play the part, in the way that I knew so well.

Before he was done I could see that his head was buzzing with her beauty and her kindly words. I thrilled with pride to think that he should think so well of my kin.

"Isn't she fine, Jim?" I could not help saying when we stood outside the door, he lighting his pipe before he set off home.

"Fine!" he cried; "I never saw her match!"

"We're going to be married," said I.

The pipe fell out of his mouth, and he stood staring at me. Then he picked it up and walked off without a word. I thought that he would likely come back, but he never did; and I saw him far off up the brae, with his chin on his chest.

But I was not to forget him, for Cousin Edie had a hundred questions to ask me about his boyhood, about his strength, about the women that he was likely to know; there was no satisfying her. And then again, later in the day, I heard of him, but in a less pleasant fashion.

It was my father who came home in the evening with his mouth full of poor Jim. He had been deadly drunk since midday, had been down to Westhouse Links to fight the gipsy champion, and it was not certain that the man would live through the night. My father had met Jim on the highroad, dour as a thunder-cloud, and with an insult in his eye for every man that passed him. "Guid sakes!" said the old man. "He'll make a fine practice for himsel', if breaking banes will do it."

Cousin Edie laughed at all this, and I laughed because she did; but I was not so sure that it was funny.

On the third day afterwards, I was going up Corriemuir by the sheep-track, when who should I see striding down but Jim himself. But he was a different man from the big, kindly fellow who had supped his porridge with us the other morning. He had no collar nor tie, his vest was open, his hair matted, and his face mottled, like a man who has drunk heavily overnight. He carried an ash stick, and he slashed at the whin-bushes on either side of the path.

"Why, Jim!" said I.

But he looked at me in the way that I had often seen at school when the devil was strong in him, and when he knew that he was in the wrong, and yet set his will to brazen it out. Not a word did he say, but he brushed past me on the narrow path and swaggered on, still brandishing his ash-plant and cutting at the bushes.

Ah well, I was not angry with him. I was sorry, very sorry, and that was all. Of course I was not so blind but that I could see how the matter stood. He was in love with Edie, and he could not bear to think that I should have her. Poor devil, how could he help it? Maybe I should have been the same. There was a time when I should have wondered that a girl could have turned a strong man's head like that, but I knew more about it now.

For a fortnight I saw nothing of Jim Horscroft, and then came the Thursday which was to change the whole current of my life.

I had woke early that day, and with a little thrill of joy which is a rare thing to feel when a man first opens his eyes. Edie had been kinder than usual the night before, and I had fallen asleep with the thought that maybe at last I had caught the rainbow, and that without any imaginings or make-believes she was learning to love plain, rough Jock Calder of West Inch. It was this thought, still at my heart, which had given me that little morning chirrup of joy. And then I remembered that if I hastened I might be in time for her, for it was her custom to go out with the sunrise.

But I was too late. When I came to her door it was half-open and the room empty. Well, thought I, at least I may meet her and have the homeward walk with her. From the top of Corriemuir hill you may see all the country round; so, catching up my stick, I swung off in that direction. It was bright, but cold, and the surf, I remember, was booming loudly, though there had been no wind in our parts for days. I zigzagged up the steep pathway, breathing in the thin, keen morning air, and humming a lilt as I went, until I came out, a little short of breath, among the whins upon the top. Looking down the long slope of the farther side, I saw Cousin Edie, as I had expected; and I saw Jim Horscroft walking by her side.

They were not far away, but too taken up with each other to see me. She was walking slowly, with the little petulant cock of her dainty head which I knew so well, casting her eyes away from him, and shooting out a word from time to time. He paced along beside her, looking down at her and bending his head in the eagerness of his talk. Then as he said something, she placed her hand with a caress upon his arm, and he, carried off his feet, plucked her up and kissed her again and again. At the sight I could neither cry out nor move, but stood, with a heart of lead and the face of a dead man, staring down at them. I saw her hand passed over his shoulder, and that his kisses were as welcome to her as ever mine had been.

Then he set her down again, and I found that this had been their parting; for, indeed, in another hundred paces they would have come in view of the upper windows of the house. She walked slowly away, with a wave back once or twice, and he stood looking after her. I waited until she was some way off, and then down I came, but so taken up was he, that I was within a hand's-touch of him before he whisked round upon me. He tried to smile as is eye met mine.

"Ah, Jock," says he, "early afoot!"

"I saw you!" I gasped; and my throat had turned so dry that I spoke like a man with a quinsy.

"Did you so?" said he, and gave a little whistle. "Well, on my life, Jock, I'm not sorry. I was thinking of coming up to West Inch this very day, and having it out with you. Maybe it's better as it is."

"You've been a fine friend!" said I.

"Well now, be reasonable, Jock," said he, sticking his hands into his pockets and rocking to and fro as he stood. "Let me show you how it stands. Look me in the eye, and you'll see that I don't lie. It's this Way. I had met Edi—Miss Calder that is— before I came that morning, and there were things which made me look upon her as free; and, thinking that, I let my mind dwell on her. Then you said she wasn't free, but was promised to you, and that was the worst knock I've had for a time. It clean put me off, and I made a fool of myself for some days, and it's a mercy I'm not in Berwick gaol. Then by chance I met her again—on my soul, Jock, it was chance for me—and when I spoke of you she laughed at the thought. It was cousin and cousin, she said; but as for her not being free, or you being more to her than a friend, it was fool's talk. So you see, Jock, I was not so much to blame, after all: the more so as she promised that she would let you see by her conduct that you were mistaken in thinking that you had any claim upon her. You must have noticed that she has hardly had a word for you for these last two weeks."

I laughed bitterly.

"It was only last night," said I, "that she told me that I was the only man in all this earth that she could ever bring herself to love."

Jim Horscroft put out a shaking hand and laid it on my shoulder, while he pushed his face forward to look into my eyes.

"Jock Calder," said he, "I never knew you tell a lie. You are not trying to score trick against trick, are you? Honest now, between man and man."

"It's God's truth," said I.

He stood looking at me, and his face had set like that of a man who is having a hard fight with himself. It was a long two minutes before he spoke.

"See here, Jock!" said he. "This woman is fooling us both. D'you hear, man? she's fooling us both! She loves you at West Inch, and she loves me on the braeside; and in her devil's heart she cares a whin-blossom for neither of us. Let's join hands, man, and send the hellfire hussy to the right-about!"

But this was too much. I could not curse her in my own heart, and still less could I stand by and hear another man do it; not though it was my oldest friend.

"Don't you call names!" I cried.

"Ach! you sicken me with your soft talk! I'll call her what she should be called!"

"Will you, though?" said I, lugging off my coat. "Look you here, Jim Horscroft, if you say another word against her, I'll lick it down your throat, if you were as big as Berwick Castle! Try me and see!"

He peeled off his coat down to the elbows, and then he slowly put it on again.

"Don't be such a fool, Jock!" said he. "Four stone and five inches is more than mortal man can give. Two old friends mustn't fall out over such a—well, there, I won't say it. Well, by the Lord, if she hasn't nerve for ten!"

I looked round, and there she was, not twenty yards from us, looking as cool and easy and placid as we were hot and fevered.

"I was nearly home," said she, "when I saw you two boys very busy talking, so I came all the way back to know what it was about."

Horscroft took a run forward and caught her by the wrist. She gave a little squeal at the sight of his face, but he pulled her towards where I was standing. "Now, Jock, we've had tomfoolery enough," said he. "Here she is. Shall we take her word as to which she likes? She can't trick us now that we're both together."

"I am willing," said I.

"And so am I. If she goes for you, I swear I'll never so much as turn an eye on her again. Will you do as much for me?"

"Yes, I will."

"Well then, look here, you! We're both honest men, and friends, and we tell each other no lies; and so we know your double ways. I know what you said last night. Jock knows what you said today. D'you see? Now then, fair and square! Here we are before you; once and have done. Which is it to be, Jock or me?"

You would have thought that the woman would have been overwhelmed with shame, but instead of that her eyes were shining with delight; and I dare wager that it was the proudest moment of her life. As she looked from one to the other of us, with the cold morning sun glittering on her face, I had never seen her look so lovely. Jim felt it also, I am sure; for he dropped her wrist, and the harsh lines were softened upon his face.

"Come, Edie! which is it to be?" he asked.

"Naughty boys, to fall out like this!" she cried. "Cousin Jack, you know how fond I am of you."

"Oh, then go to him!" said Horscroft.

"But I love nobody but Jim. There is nobody that I love like Jim."

She snuggled up to him, and laid her cheek against his breast.

"You see, Jock!" said he, looking over her shoulder.

I did see; and away I went for West Inch, another man from the time that I left it.

CHAPTER 5

The Man From the Sea

Well, I was never one to sit groaning over a cracked pot. If it could not be mended, then it is the part of a man to say no more of it. For weeks I had an aching heart; indeed, it is a little sore now, after all these years and a happy marriage, when I think of it. But I kept a brave face on me; and, above all, I did as I had promised that day on the hillside. I was as a brother to her, and no more: though there were times when I had to put a hard curb upon myself; for even now she would come to me with her coaxing ways, and with tales about how rough Jim was, and how happy she had been when I was kind to her; for it was in her blood to speak like that, and she could not help it.

But for the most part Jim and she were happy enough. It was all over the countryside that they were to be married when he had passed his degree, and he would come up to West Inch four nights a week to sit with us. My folk were pleased about it, and I tried to be pleased too.

Maybe at first there was a little coolness between him and me: there was not quite the old schoolboy trust between us. But then, when the first smart was passed, it seemed to me that he had acted openly, and that I had no just cause for complaint against him. So we were friendly, in a way; and as for her, he had forgotten all his anger, and would have kissed the print of her shoe in the mud. We used to take long rambles together, he and I; and it is about one of these that I now want to tell you.

We had passed over Bramston Heath and round the clump of firs which screens the house of Major Elliott from the sea wind.

It was spring now, and the year was a forward one, so that the trees were well leaved by the end of April. It was as warm as a summer day, and we were the more surprised when we saw a huge fire roaring upon the grass-plot before the Major's door. There was half a fir-tree in it, and the flames were spouting up as high as the bedroom windows. Jim and I stood staring, but we stared the more when out came the Major, with a great quart pot in his hand, and at his heels his old sister who kept house for him, and two of the maids, and all four began capering about round the fire. He was a douce, quiet man, as all the country knew, and here he was like old Nick at the carlin's dance, hobbling around and waving his drink above his head. We both set off running, and he waved the more when he saw us coming.

"Peace!" he roared. "Huzza, boys! Peace!"

And at that we both fell to dancing and shouting too; for it had been such a weary war as far back as we could remember, and the shadow had lain so long over us, that it was wondrous to feel that it was lifted. Indeed it was too much to believe, but the Major laughed our doubts to scorn.

"Aye, aye, it is true," he cried, stopping with his hand to his side. "The Allies have got Paris, Boney has thrown up the sponge, and his people are all swearing allegiance to Louis XVIII."

"And the Emperor?" I asked. "Will they spare him?"

"There's talk of sending him to Elba, where he'll be out of mischief's way. But his officers, there are some of them who will not get off so lightly. Deeds have been done during these last twenty years that have not been forgotten. There are a few old scores to be settled. But it's Peace! Peace!"

And away he went once more with his great tankard hopping round his bonfire.

Well, we stayed some time with the Major, and then away we went down to the beach, Jim and I, talking about this great news, and all that would come of it. He knew a little, and I knew less, but we pieced it all together and talked about how the prices would come down, how our brave fellows would return home, how the ships could go where they would in peace, and how we could pull all the coast beacons down, for there was no enemy now to fear. So we chatted as we walked along the clean, hard sand, and looked out at the old North Sea. How little did Jim know at that moment, as he strode along by my side so full of health and of spirits, that he had reached the extreme summit of his life, and that from that hour all would, in truth, be upon the downward slope!

There was a little haze out to sea; for it had been very misty in the early morning, though the sun had thinned it. As we looked seawards we suddenly saw the sail of a small boat break out through the fog, and come bobbing along towards the land. A single man was seated in the sheets, and she yawed about as she ran, as though he were of two minds whether to beach her or no. At last, determined it may be by our presence, he made straight for us, and her keel grated upon the shingle at our very feet. He dropped his sail, sprang out, and pulled her bows up on the beach.

"Great Britain, I believe?" said he, turning briskly round and facing us.

He was a man somewhat above middle height, but exceedingly thin. His eyes were piercing and set close together, a long sharp nose jutted out from between them, and beneath them was a bristle of brown moustache as wiry and stiff as a cat's whiskers. He was well dressed in a suit of brown with brass buttons, and he wore high boots which were all roughened and dulled by the sea water. His face and hands were so dark that he might have been a Spaniard, but as he raised his hat to us we saw that the upper part of his brow was quite white and that it was from without that he had his swarthiness. He looked from one to the other of us, and his grey eyes had something in them which I had never seen before. You could read the question; but there seemed to be a menace at the back of it, as if the answer were a right and not a favour.

"Great Britain?" he asked again, with a quick tap of his foot on the shingle.

"Yes," said I, while Jim burst out laughing.

"England? Scotland?"

"Scotland. But it's England past yonder trees."

"*Bon!* I know where I am now. I've been in a fog without a compass for nearly three days, and I didn't thought I was ever to see land again."

He spoke English glibly enough, but with some strange turn of speech from time to time.

"Where did you come from then?" asked Jim.

"I was in a ship that was wrecked," said he shortly. "What is the town down yonder?"

"It is Berwick."

"Ah! well, I must get stronger before I can go further."

He turned towards the boat, and as he did so he gave a lurch, and would have fallen had he not caught the prow. On this he seated himself and looked round with a face that was flushed, and two eyes that blazed like a wild beast's.

"*Voltigeurs de la Garde,*" he roared in a voice like a trumpet call, and then again "*Voltigeurs de la Garde!*"

He waved his hat above is head, and suddenly pitching forwards upon his face on the sand, he lay all huddled into a little brown heap.

Jim Horscroft and I stood and stared at each other. The coming of the man had been so strange, and his questions, and now this sudden turn. We took him by a shoulder each and turned him upon his back. There he lay with his jutting nose and his cat's whiskers, but his lips were bloodless, and his breath would scarce shake a feather.

"He's dying, Jim!" I cried.

"Aye, for want of food and water. There's not a drop or crumb in the boat. Maybe there's something in the bag."

He sprang and brought out a black leather bag, which with a large blue coat was the only thing in the boat. It was locked, but Jim had it open in an instant. It was half full of gold pieces.

Neither of us had ever seen so much before—no, nor a tenth part of it. There must have been hundreds of them, all bright new British sovereigns. Indeed, so taken up were we that we had forgotten all about their owner until a groan took our thoughts back to him. His lips were bluer than ever, and his jaw had dropped. I can see his open mouth now, with its row of white wolfish teeth.

"My God, he's off!" cried Jim. "Here, run to the burn. Jock, for a hatful of water. Quick, man, or he's gone! I'll loosen his things the while." Away I tore, and was back in a minute with as much water as would Stay in my Glengarry. Jim had pulled open the man's coat and shirt, and we doused the water over him, and forced some between his lips. It had a good effect; for after a gasp or two he sat up and rubbed his eyes slowly, like a man who is waking from a deep sleep. But neither Jim nor I were looking at his face now, for our eyes were fixed upon his uncovered chest.

There were two deep red puckers in it, one just below the collar bone, and the other about half-way down on the right side. The skin of his body was extremely white up to the brown line of his neck, and the angry crinkled spots looked the more vivid against it. From above I could see that there was a corresponding pucker in the back at one place, but not at the other. Inexperienced as I was, I could tell what that meant. Two bullets had pierced his chest; one had passed through it, and the other had remained inside.

But suddenly he staggered up to his feet, and pulled his shirt to, with a quick suspicious glance at us.

"What have I been doing?" he asked. "I've been off my head. Take no notice of anything I may have said. Have I been shouting?"

"You shouted just before you fell."

"What did I shout?"

I told him, though it bore little meaning to my mind. He looked sharply at us, and then he shrugged his shoulders.

"It's the words of a song," said he. "Well, the question is, What am I to do now? I didn't thought I was so weak. Where did you get the water?"

I pointed towards the burn, and he staggered off to the bank. There he lay down upon his face, and he drank until I thought he would never have done. His long skinny neck was outstretched like a horse's, and he made a loud supping noise with his lips. At last he got up with a long sigh, and wiped his moustache with his sleeve.

"That's better," said he. "Have you any food?"

I had crammed two bits of oat-cake into my pocket when I left home, and these he crushed into his mouth and swallowed. Then he squared his shoulders, puffed out his chest, and patted his ribs with the flat of his hands.

"I am sure that I owe you exceedingly well," said he. "You have been very kind to a stranger. But I see that you have had occasion to open my bag."

"We hoped that we might find wine or brandy there when you fainted."

"Ah! I have nothing there but just a little—how do you say it?—my savings. They are not much, but I must live quietly upon them until I find something to do. Now one could live quietly here, I should say. I could not have come upon a more peaceful place, without perhaps so much as a *gendarme* nearer than that town."

"You haven't told us yet who you are, where you come from, nor what you have been," said Jim bluntly.

The stranger looked him up and down with a critical eye:

"My word, but you would make a grenadier for a flank company," said he. "As to what you ask, I might take offence at it from other lips; but you have a right to know, since you have received me with so great courtesy. My name is Bonaventure de Lapp. I am a soldier and a wanderer by trade, and I have come from Dunkirk, as you may see printed upon the boat."

"I thought that you had been shipwrecked!" said I.

But he looked at me with the straight gaze of an honest man.

"That is right," said he, "but the ship went from Dunkirk, and this is one of her boats. The crew got away in the long boat, and she went down so quickly that I had no time to put anything into her. That was on Monday."

"And today's Thursday. You have been three days without bite or sup."

"It is too long," said he. "Twice before I have been for two days, but never quite so long as this. Well, I shall leave my boat here, and see whether I can get lodgings in any of these little grey houses upon the hillsides. Why is that great fire burning over yonder?"

"It is one of our neighbours who has served against the French. He is rejoicing because peace has been declared."

"Oh, you have a neighbour who has served then! I am glad; for I, too, have seen a little soldiering here and there."

He did not look glad, but he drew his brows down over his keen eyes.

"You are French, are you not?" I asked, as we all walked up the hill together, he with his black bag in his hand and his long blue cloak slung over his shoulder.

"Well, I am of Alsace," said he; "and, you know, they are more German than French. For myself, I have been in so many lands that I feel at home in all. I have been a great traveller; and where do you think that I might find a lodging?"

I can scarcely tell now, on looking back with the great gap of five-and-thirty years between, what impression this singular man had made upon me. I distrusted him, I think, and yet I was fascinated by him also; for there was something in his bearing, in his look, and his whole fashion of speech which was entirely unlike anything that I had ever seen. Jim Horscroft was a fine man, and Major Elliott was a brave one, but they both lacked something that this wanderer had. It was the quick alert look, the flash of the eye, the nameless distinction which is so hard to fix. And then we had saved him when he lay gasping upon the shingle, and one's heart always softens towards what one has once helped.

"If you will come with me," said I, "I have little doubt that I can find you a bed for a night or two, and by that time you will be better able to make your own arrangements."

He pulled off his hat, and bowed with all the grace imaginable. But Jim Horscroft pulled me by the sleeve, and led me aside.

"You're mad, Jock," he whispered. "The fellow's a common adventurer. What do you want to get mixed up with him for?"

But I was as obstinate a man as ever laced his boots, and if you jerked me back it was the finest way of sending me to the front.

"He's a stranger, and it's our part to look after him," said I.

"You'll be sorry for it," Said he.

210

"Maybe so."

"If you don't think of yourself, you might think of your cousin."

"Edie can take very good care of herself."

"Well, then, the devil take you, and you may do what you like!" he cried, in one of his sudden flushes of anger. Without a word of farewell to either of us, he turned off upon the track that led up towards his father's house. Bonaventure de Lapp smiled at me as we walked on together.

"I didn't thought he liked me very much," said he. "I can see very well that he has made a quarrel with you because you are taking me to your home. What does he think of me then? Does he think perhaps that I have stole the gold in my bag, or what is it that he fears?"

"Tut, I neither know nor care," said I. "No stranger shall pass our door without a crust and a bed."

With my head cocked and feeling as if I was doing something very fine, instead of being the most egregious fool south of Edinburgh, I marched on down the path with my new acquaintance at my elbow.

CHAPTER 6

A Wandering Eagle

My father seemed to be much of Jim Horscroft's opinion; for he was not over warm to this new guest and looked him up and down with a very questioning eye. He set a dish of vinegared herrings before him, however, and I noticed that he looked more askance than ever when my companion ate nine of them, for two were always our portion. When at last he had finished Bonaventure de Lapp's lids were drooping over his eyes, for I doubt that he had been sleepless as well as foodless for these three days. It was but a poor room to which I had led him, but he threw himself down upon the couch, wrapped his big blue cloak around him, and was asleep in an instant. He was a very high and strong snorer, and, as my room was next to his, I had reason to remember that we had a stranger within our gates.

When I came down in the morning, I found that he had been beforehand with me; for he was seated opposite my father at the window-table in the kitchen, their heads almost touching, and a little roll of gold pieces between them. As I came in my father looked up at me, and I saw a light of greed in his eyes such as I had never seen before. He caught up the money with an eager clutch and swept it into his pocket.

"Very good, mister," said he; "the room's yours, and you pay always on the third of the month."

"Ah! and here is my first friend," cried de Lapp, holding out his hand to me with a smile which was kindly enough, and yet had that touch of patronage which a man uses when he smiles to his dog. "I am myself again now, thanks to my excellent supper and good night's rest. Ah! it is hunger that takes the courage from a man. That most, and cold next."

"Aye, that's right," said my father; "I've been out on the moors in a snow-drift for six-and-thirty hours, and ken what it's like."

"I once saw three thousand men starve to death," remarked de Lapp, putting out his hands to the fire. "Day by day they got thinner and more like apes, and they did come down to the edge of the pontoons where we did keep them, and they howled with rage and pain. The first few days their howls went over the whole city, but after a week our sentries on the bank could not hear them, so weak they had fallen."

"And they died!" I exclaimed.

"They held out a very long time. Austrian Grenadiers they were, of the corps of Starowitz, fine stout men as big as your friend of yesterday; but when the town fell there were but four hundred alive, and a man could lift them three at a time as if they were little monkeys. It was a pity. Ah! my friend, you will do me the honours with *madame* and with *mademoiselle*."

It was my mother and Edie who had come into the kitchen. He had not seen them the night before, but now it was all I could do to keep my face as I watched him; for instead of our homely Scottish nod, he bent up his back like a louping trout, and slid his foot, and clapped his hand over his heart in the queerest way. My mother stared, for she thought he was making fun of her; but Cousin Edie fell into it in an instant, as though it had been a game, and away she went in a great curtsy until I thought she would have had to give it up, and sit down right there in the middle of the kitchen floor. But no, she up again as light as a piece of fluff, and we all drew up our stools and started on the scones and milk and porridge.

He had a wonderful way with women, that man. Now if I were to do it, or Jim Horscroft, it would look as if we were playing the fool, and the girls would have laughed at us; but with him it seemed to go with his style of face and fashion of speech, so that one came at last to look for it: for when he spoke to my mother or Cousin Edie—and he was never backward in speaking—it would always be with a bow and a look as if it would hardly be worth their while to listen to what he had to say, and when they answered he would put on a face as though every word they said was to be treasured up and remembered for ever. And yet, even while he humbled himself to a woman, there was always a proud sort of look at the back of his eye as if he meant to say that it was only to them that he was so meek, and that he could be stiff enough upon occasion. As to my mother, it was wonderful the way she softened to him, and in half-an-hour she had told him all about her uncle, who was a surgeon in Carlisle, and the highest of any upon her side of the house. She spoke to him about my brother Rob's death, which I had never heard her mention to a soul before, and he looked as if the tears were in his eyes over it—he, who had just told us how he had seen three thousand men starved to death! As to Edie, she did not say much, but she kept shooting little glances at our visitor, and once or twice he looked very hard at her.

When he had gone to his room after breakfast, my father pulled out eight golden pounds and laid them on the table. "What think ye of that, Martha?" said he.

"You've sold the twa black tups after all."

"No, but it's a month's pay for board and lodging from Jock's friend, and as much to come every four weeks."

But my mother shook her head when she heard it.

"Two pounds a week is over much," said she; "and it is not when the poor gentleman is in distress that we should put such a price on his bit food."

"Tut!" cried my father, "he can very well afford it, and he with a bag full of gold. Besides, it's his own proposing."

"No blessing will come from that money," said she.

"Why, woman, he's turned your head wi' his foreign ways of speech!" cried my father.

"Aye, and it would be a good thing if Scottish men had a little more of that kindly way," she said, and that was the first time in all my life that I had heard her answer him back.

He came down soon and asked me whether I would come

out with him. When we were in the sunshine he held out a little cross made of red stones, one of the bonniest things that ever I had set eyes upon.

"These are rubies," said he, "and I got it at Tudela, in Spain. There were two of them, but I gave the other to a Lithuanian girl. I pray that you will take this as a memory of your exceedingly kindness to me yesterday. It will fashion into a pin for your cravat."

I could but thank him for the present, which was of more value than anything I had ever owned in my life.

"I am off to the upper muir to count the lambs," said I; "maybe you would care to come up with me and see something of the country?"

He hesitated for a moment, and then he shook his head.

"I have some letters," he said, "which I ought to write as soon as possible. I think that I will stay at quiet this morning and get them written."

All forenoon I was wandering over the links, and you may imagine that my mind was turning all the time upon this strange man whom chance had drifted to our doors. Where did he gain that style of his, that manner of command, that haughty menacing glint of the eye? And his experiences to which he referred so lightly, how wonderful the life must have been which had put him in the way of them! He had been kind to us, and gracious of speech, but still I could not quite shake myself clear of the distrust with which I had regarded him. Perhaps, after all, Jim Horscroft had been right and I had been wrong about taking him to West Inch.

When I got back he looked as though he had been born and bred in the steading. He sat in the big wooden-armed inglechair, with the black cat on his knee. His arms were out, and he held a skein of worsted from hand to hand which my mother was busily rolling into a ball. Cousin Edie was sitting near, and I could see by her eyes that she had been crying.

"Hullo, Edie!" said I, "what's the trouble?"

"Ah! *mademoiselle*, like all good and true women, has a soft heart," said he. "I didn't thought it would have moved her, or

I should have been silent. I have been talking of the suffering of some troops of which I knew something when they were crossing the Guadarama mountains in the winter of 1808. Ah! yes, it was very bad, for they were fine men and fine horses. It is strange to see men blown by the wind over the precipices, but the ground was so slippery and there was nothing to which they could hold. So companies all linked arms, and they did better in that fashion; but one artilleryman's hand came off as I held it, for he had had the frost-bite for three days."

I stood staring with my mouth open.

"And the old Grenadiers, too, who were not so active as they used to be, they could not keep up; and yet if they lingered the peasants would catch them and crucify them to the barn doors with their feet up and a fire under their heads, which was a pity for these fine old soldiers. So when they could go no further, it was interesting to see what they would do; for they would sit down and say their prayers, sitting on an old saddle, or their knapsacks, maybe, and then take off their boots and their stockings, and lean their chin on the barrel of their musket. Then they would put their toe on the trigger, and *pouf!* it was all over, and there was no more marching for those fine old Grenadiers. Oh, it was very rough work up there on these Guadarama mountains!"

"And what army was this?" I asked.

"Oh, I have served in so many armies that I mix them up sometimes. Yes, I have seen much of war. Apropos I have seen your Scotchmen fight, and very stout *fantassins* they make, but I thought from them, that the folk over here all wore—how do you say it?—petticoats."

"Those are the kilts, and they wear them only in the Highlands."

"Ah! on the mountains. But there is a man out yonder. Maybe he is the one who your father said would carry my letters to the post."

"Yes, he is Farmer Whitehead's man. Shall I give them to him?"

"Well, he would be more careful of them if he had them from your hand."

He took them from his pocket and gave them over to me. I hurried out with them, and as I did so my eyes fell upon the address of the topmost one. It was written very large and clear: *A Son Majeste, Le Roi de Suede, Stockholm.*

I did not know very much French, but I had enough to make that out. What sort of eagle was this which had flown into our humble little nest?

CHAPTER 7

The Corriemuir Peel Tower

Well, it would weary me, and I am very sure that it would weary you also, if I were to attempt to tell you how life went with us after this man came under our roof, or the way in which he gradually came to win the affections of every one of us. With the women it was quick work enough; but soon he had thawed my father too, which was no such easy matter, and had gained Jim Horscroft's goodwill as well as my own. Indeed, we were but two great boys beside him, for he had been everywhere and seen everything; and of an evening he would chatter away in his limping English until he took us clean from the plain kitchen and the little farm steading, to plunge us into courts and camps and battlefields and all the wonders of the world. Horscroft had been sulky enough with him at first; but de Lapp, with his tact and his easy ways, soon drew him round, until he had quite won his heart, and Jim would sit with Cousin Edie's hand in his, and the two be quite lost in listening to all that he had to tell us. I will not tell you all this; but even now, after so long an interval, I can trace how, week by week and month by month, by this word and that deed, he moulded us all as he wished.

One of his first acts was to give my father the boat in which he had come, reserving only the right to have it back in case he should have need of it. The herring were down on the coast that autumn, and my uncle before he died had given us a fine set of nets, so the gift was worth many a pound to us. Sometimes de Lapp would go out in the boat alone, and I have seen him for a whole summer day rowing slowly along and stopping every half-dozen strokes to throw over a stone at the end of a string. I could not think what he was doing until he told me of his own freewill.

"I am fond of studying all that has to do with the military," said he, "and I never lose a chance. I was wondering if it would be a difficult matter for the commander of an army corps to throw his men ashore here."

"If the wind were not from the east," said I.

"Ah! quite so, if the wind were not from the east. Have you taken soundings here?"

"No."

"Your line of battleships would have to lie outside; but there is water enough for a forty-gun frigate right up within musket range. Cram your boats with tirailleurs, deploy them behind these sandhills, then back with the launches for more, and a stream of grape over their heads from the frigates. It could be done! it could be done!"

His moustaches bristled out more like a cat's than ever, and I could see by the flash of his eyes that he was carried away by his dream.

"You forget that our soldiers would be upon the beach," said I indignantly.

"*Ta, ta, ta!*" he cried. "Of course it takes two sides to make a battle. Let us see now; let us work it out. What could you get together? Shall we say twenty, thirty thousand. A few regiments of good troops: the rest, *pouf!*—conscripts, bourgeois with arms. How do you call them—volunteers?"

"Brave men!" I shouted.

"Oh yes, very brave men, but imbecile. Ah, *mon Dieu*, it is incredible how imbecile they would be! Not they alone, I mean, but all young troops. They are so afraid of being afraid that they would take no precaution. Ah, I have seen it! In Spain I have seen a battalion of conscripts attack a battery of ten pieces. Up they went, ah, so gallantly! and presently the hillside looked, from where I stood, like—how do you say it in English?—a raspberry tart. And where was our fine battalion of conscripts?

Then another battalion of young troops tried it, all together in a rush, shouting and yelling; but what will shouting do against a *mitraille* of grape? And there was our second battalion laid out on the hillside. And then the foot chasseurs of the Guard, old soldiers, were told to take the battery; and there was nothing fine about their advance—no column, no shouting, nobody killed— just a few scattered lines of tirailleurs and pelotons of support; but in ten minutes the guns were silenced, and the Spanish gunners cut to pieces. War must be learned, my young friend, just the same as the farming of sheep."

"Pooh!" said I, not to be out-crowed by a foreigner. "If we had thirty thousand men on the line of the hill yonder, you would come to be very glad that you had your boats behind you."

"On the line of the hill?" said he, with a flash of his eyes along the ridge. "Yes, if your man knew his business he would have his left about your house, his centre on Corriemuir, and his right over near the doctor's house, with his tirailleurs pushed out thickly in front. His horse, of course, would try to cut us up as we deployed on the beach. But once let us form, and we should soon know what to do. There's the weak point, there at the gap. I would sweep it with my guns, then roll in my cavalry, push the infantry on in grand columns, and that wing would find itself up in the air. Eh, Jack, where would your volunteers be?"

"Close at the heels of your hindmost man," said I; and we both burst out into the hearty laugh with which such discussions usually ended.

Sometimes when he talked I thought he was joking, and at other times it was not quite so easy to say. I well remember one evening that summer, when he was sitting in the kitchen with my father, Jim, and me, after the women had gone to bed, he began about Scotland and its relation to England.

"You used to have your own king and your own laws made at Edinburgh," said he. "Does it not fill you with rage and despair when you think that it all comes to you from London now?"

Jim took his pipe out of his mouth.

"It was we who put our king over the English; so if there's any rage, it should have been over yonder," said he.

This was clearly news to the stranger, and it silenced him for the moment.

"Well, but your laws are made down there, and surely that is not good," he said at last.

"No, it would be well to have a Parliament back in Edinburgh," said my father; "but I am kept so busy with the sheep that I have little enough time to think of such things."

"It is for fine young men like you two to think of it," said de Lapp. "When a country is injured, it is to its young men that it looks to avenge it."

"Aye! the English take too much upon themselves sometimes," said Jim.

"Well, if there are many of that way of thinking about, why should we not form them into battalions and march them upon London?" cried de Lapp.

"That would be a rare little picnic," said I, laughing. "And who would lead us?"

He jumped up, bowing, with his hand on his heart, in his queer fashion.

"If you will allow me to have the honour!" he cried; and then seeing that we were all laughing, he began to laugh also, but I am sure that there was really no thought of a joke in his mind.

I could never make out what his age could be, nor could Jim Horscroft either. Sometimes we thought that he was an oldish man that looked young, and at others that he was a youngish man who looked old. His brown, stiff, close-cropped hair needed no cropping at the top, where it thinned away to a shining curve. His skin too was intersected by a thousand fine wrinkles, lacing and interlacing, and was all burned, as I have already said, by the sun. Yet he was as lithe as a boy, and he was as tough as whalebone, walking all day over the hills or rowing on the sea without turning a hair. On the whole we thought that he might be about forty or forty-five, though it was hard to see how he could have seen so much of life in the time. But one day we got talking of ages, and then he surprised us.

I had been saying that I was just twenty, and Jim said that he was twenty-seven.

"Then I am the most old of the three," said de Lapp.

We laughed at this, for by our reckoning he might almost have been our father.

"But not by so much," said he, arching his brows. "I was nine-and-twenty in December."

And it was this even more than his talk which made us understand what an extraordinary life it must have been that he had led. He saw our astonishment, and laughed at it.

"I have lived! I have lived!" he cried. "I have spent my days and my nights. I led a company in a battle where five nations were engaged when I was but fourteen. I made a king turn pale at the words I whispered in his ear when I was twenty. I had a hand in remaking a kingdom and putting a fresh king upon a great throne the very year that I came of age. *Mon Dieu*, I have lived my life!"

That was the most that I ever heard him confess of his past life, and he only shook his head and laughed when we tried to get something more out of him. There were times when we thought that he was but a clever impostor; for what could a man of such influence and talents be loitering here in Berwickshire for? But one day there came an incident which showed us that he had indeed a history in the past.

You will remember that there was an old officer of the Peninsula who lived no great way from us, the same who danced round the bonfire with his sister and the two maids. He had gone up to London on some business about his pension and his wound money, and the chance of having some work given him, so that he did not come back until late in the autumn. One of the first days after his return he came down to see us, and there for the first time he clapped eyes upon de Lapp. Never in my life did I look upon so astonished a face, and he stared at our friend for a long minute without so much as a word. De Lapp looked back at him equally hard, but there was no recognition in his eyes.

"I do not know who you are, sir," he said at last; "but you look at me as if you had seen me before."

"So I have," answered the Major.

"Never to my knowledge."

"But I'll swear it!"

"Where then?"

"At the village of Astorga, in the year '8."

De Lapp started, and stared again at our neighbour.

"*Mon Dieu*, what a chance!" he cried. "And you were the English *parlementaire*? I remember you very well indeed, sir. Let me have a whisper in your ear."

He took him aside and talked very earnestly with him in French for a quarter of an hour, gesticulating with his hands, and explaining something, while the Major nodded his old grizzled head from time to time. At last they seemed to come to some agreement, and I heard the Major say "*Parole a'honneur*" several times, and afterwards "*Fortune de la guerre*," which I could very well understand, for they gave you a fine upbringing at Birt-whistle's. But after that I always noticed that the Major never used the same free fashion of speech that we did towards our lodger, but bowed when he addressed him, and treated him with a wonderful deal of respect. I asked the Major more than once what he knew about him, but he always put it off, and I could get no answer out of him.

Jim Horscroft was at home all that summer, but late in the autumn he went back to Edinburgh again for the winter session, and as he intended to work very hard and get his degree next spring if he could, he said that he would bide up there for the Christmas. So there was a great leave-taking between him and Cousin Edie; and he was to put up his plate and to marry her as soon as he had the right to practise. I never knew a man love a woman more fondly than he did her, and she liked him well enough in a way—for, indeed, in the whole of Scotland she would not find a finer looking man—but when it came to marriage, I think she winced a little at the thought that all her wonderful dreams should end in nothing more than in being the wife of a country surgeon. Still there was only me and Jim to choose out of, and she took the best of us.

Of course there was de Lapp also; but we always felt that he was of an altogether different class to us, and so he didn't count.

I was never very sure at that time whether Edie cared for him or not. When Jim was at home they took little notice of each other. After he was gone they were thrown more together, which was natural enough, as he had taken up so much of her time before. Once or twice she spoke to me about de Lapp as though she did not like him, and yet she was uneasy if he were not in in the evening; and there was no one so fond of his talk, or with so many questions to ask him, as she. She made him describe what queens wore, and what sort of carpets they walked on, and whether they had hairpins in their hair, and how many feathers they had in their hats, until it was a wonder to me how he could find an answer to it all. And yet an answer he always had; and was so ready and quick with his tongue, and so anxious to amuse her, that I wondered how it was that she did not like him better.

Well, the summer and the autumn and the best part of the winter passed away, and we were still all very happy together. We got well into the year 1815, and the great Emperor was still eating his heart out at Elba; and all the ambassadors were wrangling together at Vienna as to what they should do with the lion's skin, now that they had so fairly hunted him down. And we in our little corner of Europe went on with our petty peaceful business, looking after the sheep, attending the Berwick cattle fairs, and chatting at night round the blazing peat fire. We never thought that what all these high and mighty people were doing could have any bearing upon us; and as to war, why everybody was agreed that the great shadow was lifted from us for ever, and that, unless the Allies quarrelled among themselves, there would not be a shot fired in Europe for another fifty years.

There was one incident, however, that stands out very clearly in my memory. I think that it must have happened about the February of this year, and I will tell it to you before I go any further.

You know what the border peel castles are like, I have no doubt. They were just square heaps built every here and there along the line, so that the folk might have some place of protection against raiders and moss-troopers. When Percy and his men were over the Marches, then the people would drive some of their cattle into the yard of the tower, shut up the big gate, and light a fire in the brazier at the top, which would be answered by all the other Peel towers, until the lights would go twinkling up to the Lammermuir Hills, and so carry the news on to the Pentlands and to Edinburgh. But now, of course, all these old keeps were warped and crumbling, and made fine nesting places for the wild birds. Many a good egg have I had for my collection out of the Corriemuir Peel Tower.

One day I had been a very long walk, away over to leave a message at the Laidlaw Armstrongs, who live two miles on this side of Ayton. About five o'clock, just before the sun set, I found myself on the brae path with the gable end of West Inch peeping up in front of me and the old Peel tower lying on my left. I turned my eyes on the keep, for it looked so fine with the flush of the level sun beating full upon it and the blue sea stretching out behind; and as I stared, I suddenly saw the face of a man twinkle for a moment in one of the holes in the wall.

Well I stood and wondered over this, for what could anybody be doing in such a place now that it was too early for the nesting season? It was so queer that I was determined to come to the bottom of it; so, tired as I was, I turned my shoulder on home, and walked swiftly towards the tower. The grass stretches right up to the very base of the wall, and my feet made little noise until I reached the crumbling arch where the old gate used to be. I peeped through, and there was Bonaventure de Lapp standing inside the keep, and peeping out through the very hole at which I had seen his face. He was turned half away from me, and it was clear that he had not seen me at all, for he was staring with all his eyes over in the direction of West Inch. As I advanced my foot rattled the rubble that lay in the gateway, and he turned round with a start and faced me.

He was not a man whom you could put out of countenance, and his face changed no more than if he had been expecting me there for a twelvemonth; but there was something in his eyes which let me know that he would have paid a good price to have me back on the brae path again.

"Hullo!" said I, "what are you doing here?"

"I may ask you that," said he.

"I came up because I saw your face at the window."

"And I because, as you may well have observed, I have very much interest for all that has to do with the military, and, of course, castles are among them. You will excuse me for one moment, my dear Jack."

And he stepped out suddenly through the hole in the wall, so as to be out of my sight.

But I was very much too curious to excuse him so easily. I shifted my ground swiftly to see what it was that he was after. He was standing outside, and waving his hand frantically, as in a signal.

"What are you doing?" I cried; and then, running out to his side, I looked across the moors to see whom he was beckoning to.

"You go too far, sir," said he, angrily; "I didn't thought you would have gone so far. A gentleman has the freedom to act as he choose without your being the spy upon him. If we are to be friends, you must not interfere in my affairs."

"I don't like these secret doings," said I, "and my father would not like them either."

"Your father can speak for himself, and there is no secret," said he, curtly. "It is you with your imaginings that make a secret. *Ta, ta, ta!* I have no patience with such foolishness."

And without as much as a nod, he turned his back upon me, and started walking swiftly to West Inch.

Well, I followed him, and in the worst of tempers; for I had a feeling that there was some mischief in the wind, and yet I could not for the life of me think what it all meant. Again I found myself puzzling over the whole mystery of this man's coming, and of his long residence among us. And whom could he have expected to meet at the Peel Tower? Was the fellow a spy, and was it some brother spy who came to speak with him there? But that was absurd. What could there be to spy about in Berwickshire? And besides, Major Elliott knew all about him, and he would not show him such respect if there were anything amiss.

I had just got as far as this in my thoughts when I heard a cheery hail, and there was the Major himself coming down the hill from his house, with his big bulldog Bounder held in leash. This dog was a savage creature, and had caused more than one accident on the countryside; but the Major was very fond of it, and would never go out without it, though he kept it tied with a good thick thong of leather. Well, just as I was looking at the Major, waiting for him to come up, he stumbled with his lame leg over a branch of gorse, and in recovering himself he let go his hold of the leash, and in an instant there was the beast of a dog flying down the hillside in my direction.

I did not like it, I can tell you; for there was neither stick nor stone about, and I knew that the brute was dangerous. The Major was shrieking to it from behind, and I think that the creature thought that he was hallooing it on, so furiously did it rush. But I knew its name, and I thought that maybe that might give me the privileges of acquaintanceship; so as it came at me with bristling hair and its nose screwed back between its two red eyes, I cried out "Bounder! Bounder!" at the pitch of my lungs. It had its effect, for the beast passed me with a snarl, and flew along the path on the traces of Bonaventure de Lapp.

He turned at the shouting, and seemed to take in the whole thing at a glance; but he strolled along as slowly as ever. My heart was in my mouth for him, for the dog had never seen him before; and I ran as fast as my feet would carry me to drag it away from him. But somehow, as it bounded up and saw the twittering finger and thumb which de Lapp held out behind him, its fury died suddenly away, and we saw it wagging its thumb of a tail and clawing at his knee.

"Your dog then, Major?" said he, as its owner came hobbling up. "Ah, it is a fine beast—a fine, pretty thing!"

The Major was blowing hard, for he had covered the ground nearly as fast as I.

"I was afraid lest he might have hurt you," he panted.

"Ta, ta, ta!" cried de Lapp. "He is a pretty, gentle thing; I always love the dogs. But I am glad that I have met you, Major; for here is this young gentleman, to whom I owe very much, who has begun to think that I am a spy. Is it not so, Jack?"

I was so taken aback by his words that I could not lay my tongue to an answer, but coloured up and looked askance, like the awkward country lad that I was.

"You know me, Major," said de Lapp, "and I am sure that you will tell him that this could not be."

"No, no, Jack! Certainly not! certainly not!" cried the Major.

"Thank you," said de Lapp. "You know me, and you do me justice. And yourself, I hope that your knee is better, and that you will soon have your regiment given you."

"I am well enough," answered the Major; "but they will never give me a place unless there is war, and there will be no more war in my time."

"Oh, you think that!" said de Lapp with a smile. "Well, *nous verrons!* We shall see, my friend!"

He whisked off his hat, and turning briskly he walked off in the direction of West Inch. The Major stood looking after him with thoughtful eyes, and then asked me what it was that had made me think that he was a spy. When I told him he said nothing, but he shook his head, and looked like a man who was ill at ease in his mind.

CHAPTER 8

The Coming of the Cutter

I never felt quite the same to our lodger after that little business at the Peel Castle. It was always in my mind that he was holding a secret from me—indeed, that he was all a secret together, seeing that he always hung a veil over his past. And when by chance that veil was for an instant whisked away, we always caught just a glimpse of something bloody and violent and dreadful upon the other side. The very look of his body was terrible. I bathed with him once in the summer, and I saw then that he was haggled with wounds all over. Besides seven or eight scars and slashes, his ribs on one side were all twisted out of shape, and a part of one of his calves had been torn away. He laughed in his merry way when he saw my face of wonder.

"Cossacks! Cossacks!" said he, running his hand over his scars. "And the ribs were broke by an artillery tumbrel. It is very bad to have the guns pass over one. Now with cavalry it is nothing. A horse will pick its steps however fast it may go. I have been ridden over by fifteen hundred cuirassiers A and by the Russian hussars of Grodno, and I had no harm from that. But guns are very bad."

"And the calf?" I asked.

"*Pouf!* It is only a wolf bite," said he. "You would not think how I came by it! You will understand that my horse and I had been struck, the horse killed, and I with my ribs broken by the tumbrel. Well, it was cold—oh, bitter, bitter!—the ground like iron, and no one to help the wounded, so that they froze into such shapes as would make you smile. I too felt that I was freezing, so what did I do? I took my sword, and I opened my dead horse, so well as I could, and I made space in him for me to lie, with one little hole for my mouth. *Sapristi!* It was warm enough there. But there was not room for the entire of me, so my feet and part of my legs stuck out. Then in the night, when I slept, there came the wolves to eat the horse, and they had a little pinch of me also, as you can see; but after that I was on guard with my pistols, and they had no more of me. There I lived, very warm and nice, for ten days."

"Ten days!" I cried. "What did you eat?"

"Why, I ate the horse. It was what you call board and lodging to me. But of course I have sense to eat the legs, and live in the body. There were many dead about who had all their water bottles, so I had all I could wish. And on the eleventh day there came a patrol of light cavalry, and all was well."

It was by such chance chats as these—hardly worth repeating in themselves—that there came light upon himself and his past. But the day was coming when we should know all; and how it came I shall try now to tell you.

The winter had been a dreary one, but with March came the first signs of spring, and for a week on end we had sunshine and winds from the south. On the 7th Jim Horscroft was to come back from Edinburgh; for though the session ended with the 1st, his examination would take him a week. Edie and I were out walking on the sea beach on the 6th, and I could talk of nothing but my old friend—for, indeed, he was the only friend of my own age that I had at that time. Edie was very silent, which was a rare thing with her; but she listened smiling to all that I had to say.

"Poor old Jim!" said she once or twice under her breath. "Poor old Jim!"

"And if he has passed," said I, "why, then of course he will put up his plate and have his own house, and we shall be losing our Edie."

I tried to make a jest of it and to speak lightly, but the words still stuck in my throat.

"Poor old Jim!" said she again, and there were tears in her

eyes as she said it. "And poor old Jock!" she added, slipping her hand into mine as we walked. "You cared for me a little bit once also, didn't you, Jock? Oh, is not that a sweet little ship out yonder!"

It was a dainty cutter of about thirty tons, very swift by the rake of her masts and the lines of her bow. She was coming up from the south under jib, foresail, and mainsail; but even as we watched her all her white canvas shut suddenly in, like a kittiwake closing her wings, and we saw the splash of her anchor just under her bowsprit. She may have been rather less than a quarter of a mile from the shore—so near that I could see a tall man with a peaked cap, who stood at the quarter with a telescope to his eye, sweeping it backwards and forwards along the coast.

"What can they want here?" asked Edie.

"They are rich English from London," said I; for that was how we explained everything that was above our comprehension in the border counties. We stood for the best part of an hour watching the bonny craft, and then, as the sun was lying low on a cloudbank and there was a nip in the evening air, we turned back to West Inch.

As you come to the farmhouse from the front, you pass up a garden, with little enough in it, which leads out by a wicket-gate to the road; the same gate at which we stood on the night when the beacons were lit, the night that we saw Walter Scott ride past on his way to Edinburgh. On the right of this gate, on the garden side, was a bit of a rockery which was said to have been made by my father's mother many years before. She had fashioned it out of water-worn stones and sea shells, with mosses and ferns in the chinks. Well, as we came in through the gates my eyes fell upon this stone heap, and there was a letter stuck in a cleft stick upon the top of it. I took a step forward to see what it was, but Edie sprang in front of me, and plucking it off she thrust it into her pocket.

"That's for me," said she, laughing. But I stood looking at her with a face which drove the laugh from her lips.

"Who is it from, Edie?" I asked.

She pouted, but made no answer.

"Who is it from, woman?" I cried. "Is it possible that you have been as false to Jim as you were to me?"

"How rude you are, Jock!" she cried. "I do wish that you would mind your own business."

"There is only one person that it could be from," I cried. "It is from this man de Lapp!"

"And suppose that you are right, Jock?"

The coolness of the woman amazed and enraged me.

"You confess it!" I cried. "Have you, then, no shame left?"

"Why should I not receive letters from this gentleman?"

"Because it is infamous."

"And why?"

"Because he is a stranger."

"On the contrary," said she, "he is my husband!"

CHAPTER 9

The Doings at West Inch

I can remember that moment so well. I have heard from others that a great, sudden blow has dulled their senses. It was not so with me. On the contrary, I saw and heard and thought more clearly than I had ever done before. I can remember that my eyes caught a little knob of marble as broad as my palm, which was imbedded in one of the grey stones of the rockery, and I found time to admire its delicate mottling. And yet the look upon my face must have been strange, for Cousin Edie screamed, and leaving me she ran off to the house. I followed her and tapped at the window of her room, for I could see that she was there.

"Go away, Jock, go away!" she cried. "You are going to scold me! I won't be scolded! I won't open the window! Go away!"

But I continued to tap.

"I must have a word with you!"

"What is it, then?" she cried, raising the sash about three inches. "The moment you begin to scold I shall close it."

"Are you really married, Edie?"

"Yes, I am married."

"Who married you?"

"Father Brennan, at the Roman Catholic Chapel at Berwick."

"And you a Presbyterian?"

"He wished it to be in a Catholic Church."

"When was it?"

"On Wednesday week."

I remembered then that on that day she had driven over to Berwick, while de Lapp had been away on a long walk, as he said, among the hills.

"What about Jim?" I asked.

"Oh, Jim will forgive me!"

"You will break his heart and ruin his life."

"No, no; he will forgive me."

"He will murder de Lapp! Oh, Edie, how could you bring such disgrace and misery upon us?"

"Ah, now you are scolding!" she cried, and down came the window.

I waited some little time, and tapped, for I had much still to ask her; but she would return no answer, and I thought that I could hear her sobbing. At last I gave it up; and I was about to go into the house, for it was nearly dark now, when I heard the click of the garden gate. It was de Lapp himself.

But as he came up the path he seemed to me to be either mad or drunk. He danced as he walked, cracked his fingers in the air, and his eyes blazed like two will-o'-the-wisps. *"Voltigeurs!"* he shouted; *"Voltigeurs de la Garde!"* just as he had done when he was off his head; and then suddenly, *"En avant! en avant!"* and up he came, waving his walking-cane over his head. He stopped short when he saw me looking at him, and I daresay he felt a bit ashamed of himself.

"*Hola*, Jock!" he cried. "I didn't thought anybody was there. I am in what you call the high spirits tonight."

"So it seems!" said I, in my blunt fashion. "You may not feel so merry when my friend Jim Horscroft comes back to-morrow."

"Ah! he comes back to-morrow, does he? And why should I not feel merry?

"Because, if I know the man, he will kill you."

"Ta, ta, ta!" cried de Lapp. "I see that you know of our marriage. Edie has told you. Jim may do what he likes."

"You have given us a nice return for having taken you in."

"My good fellow," said he, "I have, as you say, given you a very nice return. I have taken Edie from a life which is unworthy of her, and I have connected you by marriage with a noble family. However, I have some letters which I must write tonight, and the rest we can talk over to-morrow, when your friend Jim is here to help us."

He stepped towards the door.

"And this was whom you were awaiting at the peel tower!" I cried, seeing light suddenly.

"Why, Jock, you are becoming quite sharp," said he, in a mocking tone; and an instant later I heard the door of his room close and the key turn in the lock.

I thought that I should see him no more that night; but a few minutes later he came into the kitchen, where I was sitting with the old folk.

"*Madame*," said he, bowing down with his hand over his heart, in his own queer fashion, "I have met with much kindness in your hands, and it shall always be in my heart. I didn't thought I could have been so happy in the quiet country as you have made me. You will accept this small souvenir; and you also, sir, you will take this little gift, which I have the honour to make to you."

He put two little paper packets down upon the table at their elbows, and then, with three more bows to my mother, he walked from the room.

Her present was a brooch, with a green stone set in the middle and a dozen little shining white ones all round it. We had never seen such things before, and did not know how to set a name to them; but they told us afterwards at Berwick that the big one was an emerald and the others were diamonds, and that they were worth much more than all the lambs we had that spring. My dear old mother has been gone now this many a year, but that bonny brooch sparkles at the neck of my eldest daughter when she goes out into company; and I never look at it that I do not see the keen eyes and the long thin nose and the cat's whiskers of our lodger at West Inch. As to my father, he had a fine gold watch with a double case; and a proud man was he as he sat with it in the palm of his hand, his ear stooping to hearken to the tick. I do not know which was best pleased, and they would talk of nothing but what de Lapp had given them.

"He's given you something more," said I at last.

"What then, Jock?" asked father.

"A husband for Cousin Edie," said I.

They thought I was daffing when I said that; but when they came to understand that it was the real truth, they were as proud and as pleased as if I had told them that she had married the laird. Indeed, poor Jim, with his hard drinking and his fighting, had not a very bright name on the country-side, and my mother had often said that no good could come of such a match. Now, de Lapp was, for all we knew, steady and quiet and well-to-do. And as to the secrecy of it, secret marriages were very common in Scotland at that time, when only a few words were needed to make man and wife, so nobody thought much of that. The old folk were as pleased, then, as if their rent had been lowered; but I was still sore at heart, for it seemed to me that my friend had been cruelly dealt with, and I knew well that he was not a man who would easily put up with it.

Chapter 10

The Return of the Shadow

I woke with a heavy heart the next morning, for I knew that Jim would be home before long, and that it would be a day of trouble. But how much trouble that day was to bring, or how far it would alter the lives of us, was more than I had ever thought in my darkest moments. But let me tell you it all, just in the order that it happened.

I had to get up early that morning; for it was just the first flush of the lambing, and my father and I were out on the moors as soon as it was fairly light. As I came out into the passage a wind struck upon my face, and there was the house door wide open, and the grey light drawing another door upon the inner wall. And when I looked again there was Edie's room open also, and de Lapp's too; and I saw in a flash what that giving of presents meant upon the evening before. It was a leave-taking, and they were gone.

My heart was bitter against Cousin Edie as I stood looking into her room. To think that for the sake of a newcomer she could leave us all without one kindly word, or as much as a hand-shake. And he, too! I had been afraid of what would happen when Jim met him; but now there seemed to be something cowardly in this avoidance of him. I was angry and hurt and sore, and I went out into the open without a word to my father, and climbed up on to the moors to cool my flushed face.

When I got up to Corriemuir I caught my last glimpse of Cousin Edie. The little cutter still lay where she had anchored, but a rowboat was pulling out to her from the shore. In the stern

I saw a flutter of red, and I knew that it came from her shawl. I watched the boat reach the yacht and the folk climb on to her deck. Then the anchor came up, the white wings spread once more, and away she dipped right out to sea. I still saw that little red spot on the deck, and de Lapp standing beside her. They could see me also, for I was outlined against the sky, and they both waved their hands for a long time, but gave it up at last when they found that I would give them no answer.

I stood with my arms folded, feeling as glum as ever I did in my life, until their cutter was only a square hickering patch of white among the mists of the morning. It was breakfast time and the porridge upon the table before I got back, but I had no heart for the food. The old folk had taken the matter coolly enough, though my mother had no word too hard for Edie; for the two had never had much love for each other, and less of late than ever.

"There's a letter here from him," said my father, pointing to a note folded up on the table; "it was in his room. Maybe you would read it to us." They had not even opened it; for, truth to tell, neither of the good folk were very clever at reading ink, though they could do well with a fine large print. It was addressed in big letters to "The good people of West Inch;" and this was the note, which lies before me all stained and faded as I write:

My Friends,

I didn't thought to have left you so suddenly, but the matter was in other hands than mine. Duty and honour have called me back to my old comrades. This you will doubtless understand before many days are past. I take your Edie with me as my wife; and it may be that in some more peaceful time you will see us again at West Inch. Meanwhile, accept the assurance of my affection, and believe me that I shall never forget the quiet months which I spent with you, at the time when my life would have been worth a week at the utmost had I been taken by the Allies. But the reason of this you may also learn some day. *Yours*
Bonaventure de Lissac
Colonel des Voltigeurs de la Garde
Aide-de-camp de S.M.I. L'Empereur Napoleon

I whistled when I came to those words written under his name; for though I had long made up my mind that our lodger could be none other than one of those wonderful soldiers of whom we had heard so much, who had forced their way into every capital of Europe, save only our own, still I had little thought that our roof covered Napoleon's own *aide-de-camp* and a colonel of his Guard.

"So," said I, "de Lissac is his name, and not de Lapp. Well, colonel or no, it is as well for him that he got away from here before Jim laid hands upon him. And time enough, too," I added, peeping out at the kitchen window, "for here is the man himself coming through the garden."

I ran to the door to meet him, feeling that I would have given a deal to have him back in Edinburgh again. He came running, waving a paper over his head; and I thought that maybe he had a note from Edie, and that it was all known to him. But as he came up I saw that it was a big, stiff, yellow paper which crackled as he waved it, and that his eyes were dancing with happiness.

"Hurrah, Jock!" he shouted. "Where is Edie? Where is Edie?"

"What is it, man?" I asked.

"Where is Edie?"

"What have you there?"

"It's my diploma, Jock. I can practise when I like. It's all right. I want to show it to Edie."

"The best you can do is to forget all about Edie," said I.

Never have I seen a man's face change as his did when I said those words.

"What! What d'ye mean, Jock Calder?" he stammered.

He let go his hold of the precious diploma as he spoke, and away it went over the hedge and across the moor, where it stuck flapping on a whin-bush; but he never so much as glanced at it. His eyes were bent upon me, and I saw the devil's spark glimmer up in the depths of them.

"She is not worthy of you," said I.

He gripped me by the shoulder.

"What have you done?" he whispered. "This is some of your hanky-panky! Where is she?"

"She's off with that Frenchman who lodged here."

I had been casting about in my mind how I could break it gently to him; but I was always backward in speech, and I could think of nothing better than this.

"Oh!" said he, and stood nodding his head and looking at me, though I knew very well that he could neither see me, nor the steading, nor anything else. So he stood for a minute or more, with his hands clenched and his head still nodding. Then he gave a gulp in his throat, and spoke in a queer dry, rasping voice.

"When was this?" said he.

"This morning."

"Were they married?"

"Yes."

He put his hand against the door-post to steady himself.

"Any message for me?"

"She said that you would forgive her."

"May God blast my soul on the day I do! Where have they gone to?"

"To France, I should judge."

"His name was de Lapp, I think?"

"His real name is de Lissac; and he is no less than a colonel in Boney's Guards."

"Ah! he would be in Paris, likely. That is well! That is well!"

"Hold up!" I shouted. "Father! Father! Bring the brandy!"

His knees had given way for an instant, but he was himself again before the old man came running with the bottle.

"Take it away!" said he.

"Have a soop, Mister Horscroft," cried my father, pressing it upon him. "It will give you fresh heart!"

He caught hold of the bottle and sent it flying over the garden hedge.

"It's very good for those who wish to forget," said he; "I am going to remember!"

"May God forgive you for sinfu' waste!" cried my father aloud.

"And for well-nigh braining an officer of his Majesty's infantry!" said old Major Elliott, putting his head over the hedge.

"I could have done with a nip after a morning's walk, but it is something new to have a whole bottle whizz past my ear. But what is amiss, that you all stand round like mutes at a burying?"

In a few words I told him our trouble, while Jim, with a grey face and his brows drawn down, stood leaning against the doorpost. The Major was as glum as we by the time I had finished, for he was fond both of Jim and of Edie.

"Tut, tut!" said he. "I feared something of the kind ever since that business of the peel tower. It's the way with the French. They can't leave the women alone. But, at least, de Lissac has married her, and that's a comfort. But it's no time now to think of our own little troubles, with all Europe in a roar again, and another twenty years' war before us, as like as not."

"What d'ye mean?" I asked.

"Why, man, Napoleon's back from Elba, his troops have flocked to him, and Louis has run for his life. The news was in Berwick this morning."

"Great Lord!" cried my father. "Then the weary business is all to do over again!"

"Aye, we thought we were out from the shadow, but it's still there. Wellington is ordered from Vienna to the Low Countries, and it is thought that the Emperor will break out first on that side. Well, it's a bad wind that blows nobody any good. I've just had news that I am to join the 71st as senior major."

I shook hands with our good neighbour on this, for I knew how it had lain upon his mind that he should be a cripple, with no part to play in the world.

"I am to join my regiment as soon as I can; and we shall be over yonder in a month, and in Paris, maybe, before another one is over."

"By the Lord, then, I'm with you, Major!" cried Jim Horscroft. "I'm not too proud to carry a musket, if you will put me in front of this Frenchman."

"My lad, I'd be proud to have you serve under me," said the Major. "And as to de Lissac, where the Emperor is he will be."

"You know the man," said I. "What can you tell us of him?"

"There is no better officer in the French army, and that is a

241

big word to say. They say that he would have been a marshal, but he preferred to stay at the Emperor's elbow. I met him two days before Corunna, when I was sent with a flag to speak about our wounded. He was with Soult then. I knew him again when I saw him."

"And I will know him again when I see him!" said Horscroft, with the old dour look on his face.

And then at that instant, as I stood there, it was suddenly driven home to me how poor and purposeless a life I should lead while this crippled friend of ours and the companion of my boyhood were away in the forefront of the storm. Quick as a flash my resolution was taken.

"I'll come with you too, Major," I cried.

"Jock! Jock!" said my father, wringing his hands.

Jim said nothing, but put his arm half round me and hugged me. The Major's eyes shone and he flourished his cane in the air.

"My word, but I shall have two good recruits at my heels," said he. "Well, there's no time to be lost, so you must both be ready for the evening coach."

And this was what a single day brought about; and yet years pass away so often without a change. Just think of the alteration in that four-and-twenty hours. De Lissac was gone. Edie was gone. Napoleon had escaped. War had broken out. Jim Horscroft had lost everything, and he and I were setting out to fight against the French. It was all like a dream, until I tramped off to the coach that evening, and looked back at the grey farm steading and at the two little dark figures: my mother with her face sunk in her Shetland shawl, and my father waving his drover's stick to hearten me upon my way.

CHAPTER 11

The Gathering of the Nations

And now I come to a bit of my story that clean takes my breath away as I think of it, and makes me wish that I had never taken the job of telling it in hand. For when I write I like things to come slow and orderly and in their turn, like sheep coming out of a paddock. So it was at West Inch. But now that we were drawn into a larger life, like wee bits of straw that float slowly down some lazy ditch, until they suddenly find themselves in the dash and swirl of a great river; then it is very hard for me with my simple words to keep pace with it all. But you can find the cause and reason of everything in the books about history, and so I shall just leave that alone and talk about what I saw with my own eyes and heard with my own ears.

The regiment to which our friend had been appointed was the 71st Highland Light Infantry, which wore the red coat and the trews, and had its depot in Glasgow town. There we went, all three, by coach: the Major in great spirits and full of stories about the Duke and the Peninsula, while Jim sat in the corner with his lips set and his arms folded, and I knew that he killed de Lissac three times an hour in his heart. I could tell it by the sudden glint of his eyes and grip of his hand. As to me, I did not know whether to be glad or sorry; for home is home, and it is a weary thing, however you may brazen it out, to feel that half Scotland is between you and your mother.

We were in Glasgow next day, and the Major took us down to the depot, where a soldier with three stripes on his arm and a fistful of ribbons from his cap, showed every tooth he had in his head at the sight of Jim, and walked three times round him to have the view of him, as if he had been Carlisle Castle. Then he came over to me and punched me in the ribs and felt my muscle, and was nigh as pleased as with Jim.

"These are the sort, Major, these are the sort," he kept saying. "With a thousand of these we could stand up to Boney's best."

"How do they run?" asked the Major.

"A poor show," said he, "but they may lick into shape. The best men have been drafted to America, and we are full of Militiamen and recruities."

"Tut, tut!" said the Major. "We'll have old soldiers and good ones against us. Come to me if you need any help, you two."

And so with a nod he left us, and we began to understand that a Major who is your officer is a very different person from a Major who happens to be your neighbour in the country.

Well, well, why should I trouble you with these things? I could wear out a good quill-pen just writing about what we did, Jim and I, at the depot in Glasgow; and how we came to know our officers and our comrades, and how they came to know us. Soon came the news that the folk of Vienna, who had been cutting up Europe as if it had been a jigget of mutton, had flown back, each to his own country, and that every man and horse in their armies had their faces towards France. We heard of great reviews and musterings in Paris too, and then that Wellington was in the Low Countries, and that on us and on the Prussians would fall the first blow. The Government was shipping men over to him as fast as they could, and every port along the east coast was choked with guns and horses and stores. On the third of June we had our marching orders also, and on the same night we took ship from Leith, reaching Ostend the night after. It was my first sight of a foreign land, and indeed most of my comrades were the same, for we were very young in the ranks. I can see the blue waters now, and the curling surf line, and the long yellow beach, and queer windmills twisting and turning—a thing that a man would not see from one end of Scotland to the other. It was a clean, well-kept town, but the folk were undersized, and there was neither ale nor oatmeal cakes to be bought amongst them.

From there we went on to a place called Bruges; and from there to Ghent, where we picked up with the 52nd and the 95th, which were the two regiments that we were brigaded with. It's a wonderful place for churches and stonework is Ghent, and indeed of all the towns we were in there was scarce one but had a finer kirk than any in Glasgow. From there we pushed on to Ath, which is a little village on a river, or a burn rather, called the Dender. There we were quartered—in tents mostly, for it was fine sunny weather—and the whole brigade set to work at its drill from morning till evening. General Adams was our chief, and Reynell was our colonel, and they were both fine old soldiers; but what put heart into us most was to think that we were under the Duke, for his name was like a bugle call. He was at Brussels with the bulk of the army, but we knew that we should see him quick enough if he were needed.

I had never seen so many English together, and indeed I had a kind of contempt for them, as folk always have if they live near a border. But the two regiments that were with us now were as good comrades as could be wished. The 52nd had a thousand men in the ranks, and there were many old soldiers of the Peninsula among them. They came from Oxfordshire for the most part. The 95th were a rifle regiment, and had dark green coats instead of red. It was strange to see them loading, for they would put the ball into a greasy rag and then hammer it down with a mallet, but they could fire both further and straighter than we. All that part of Belgium was covered with British troops at that time; for the Guards were over near Enghien, and there were cavalry regiments on the further side of us. You see, it was very necessary that Wellington should spread out all his force, for Boney was behind the screen of his fortresses, and of course we had no means of saying on what side he might pop out, except that he was pretty sure to come the way that we least expected him. On the one side he might get between us and the sea, and so cut us off from England; and on the other he might shove in between the Prussians and ourselves. But the Duke was as clever as he, for he had his horse and his light troops all round him, like a great spider's web, so that the moment a French foot stepped across the border he could close up all his men at the right place.

For myself, I was very happy at Ath, and I found the folk very kindly and homely. There was a farmer of the name of Bois, in whose fields we were quartered, and who was a real good friend to many of us. We built him a wooden barn among us in our spare time, and many a time I and Jeb Seaton, my rear-rank man, have hung out his washing, for the smell of the wet linen seemed to take us both straight home as nothing else could do. I have often wondered whether that good man and his wife are still living, though I think it hardly likely, for they were of a hale middle-age at the time. Jim would come with us too, sometimes, and would sit with us smoking in the big Flemish kitchen, but he was a different Jim now to the old one. He had always had a hard touch in him, but now his trouble seemed to have turned him to flint, and I never saw a smile upon his face, and seldom heard a word from his lips. His whole mind was set on revenging himself upon de Lissac for having taken Edie from him, and he would sit for hours with his chin upon his hands glaring and frowning, all wrapped in the one idea. This made him a bit of a butt among the men at first, and they laughed at him for it; but when they came to know him better they found that he was not a good man to laugh at, and then they dropped it.

We were early risers at that time, and the whole brigade was usually under arms at the flush of dawn. One morning—it was the sixteenth of June—we had just formed up, and General Adams had ridden up to give some order to Colonel Reynell within a musket-length of where I stood, when suddenly they both stood staring along the Brussels road. None of us dared move our heads, but every eye in the regiment whisked round, and there we saw an officer with the cockade of a general's *aide-de-camp* thundering down the road as hard as a great dapple-grey horse could carry him. He bent his face over its mane and flogged at its neck with the slack of the bridle, as though he rode for very life.

"Hullo, Reynell!" says the general. "This begins to look like business. What do you make of it?"

They both cantered their horses forward, and Adams tore open the dispatch which the messenger handed to him. The wrapper had not touched the ground before he turned, waving the letter over his head as if it had been a sabre.

"Dismiss!" he cried. "General parade and march in half-an-hour."

Then in an instant all was buzz and bustle, and the news on every lip. Napoleon had crossed the frontier the day before, had pushed the Prussians before him, and was already deep in the country to the east of us with a hundred and fifty thousand men. Away we scuttled to gather our things together and have our breakfast, and in an hour we had marched off and left Ath and the Dender behind us for ever. There was good need for haste, for the Prussians had sent no news to Wellington of what was doing, and though he had rushed from Brussels at the first whisper of it, like a good old mastiff from its kennel, it was hard to see how he could come up in time to help the Prussians.

It was a bright warm morning, and as the brigade tramped down the broad Belgian road the dust rolled up from it like the smoke of a battery. I tell you that we blessed the man that planted the poplars along the sides, for their shadow was better than drink to us. Over across the fields, both to the right and the left, were other roads, one quite close, and the other a mile or more from us. A column of infantry was marching down the near one, and it was a fair race between us, for we were each walking for all we were worth. There was such a wreath of dust round them that we could only see the gun-barrels and the bearskins breaking out here and there, with the head and shoulders of a mounted officer coming out above the cloud, and the flutter of the colours. It was a brigade of the Guards, but we could not tell which, for we had two of them with us in the campaign. On the far road there was also dust and to spare, but through it there flashed every now and then a long twinkle of brightness, like a hundred silver beads threaded in a line; and the breeze brought down such a snarling, clanging, clashing kind of music as I had never listened to. If I had been left to myself it would have been long before I knew what it was; but our corporals and sergeants were all old soldiers, and I had one trudging along with his halbert at my elbow, who was full of precept and advice.

"That's heavy horse," said he. "You see that double twinkle? That means they have helmet as well as cuirass. It's the Royals, or the Enniskillens, or the Household. You can hear their cymbals and kettles. The French heavies are too good for us. They have ten to our one, and good men too. You've got to shoot at their faces or else at their horses. Mind you that when you see them coming, or else you'll find a four-foot sword stuck through your liver to teach you better. Hark! Hark! Hark! There's the old music again!"

And as he spoke there came the low grumbling of a cannonade away somewhere to the east of us, deep and hoarse, like the roar of some blood-daubed beast that thrives on the lives of men. At the same instant there was a shouting of *"Heh! heh! heh!"* from behind, and somebody roared, "Let the guns get through!"

Looking back, I saw the rear companies split suddenly in two and hurl themselves down on either side into the ditch, while six cream-coloured horses, galloping two and two with their bellies to the ground, came thundering through the gap with a fine twelve-pound gun whirling and creaking behind them. Behind were another, and another, four-and-twenty in all, flying past us with such a din and clatter, the blue-coated men clinging on to the gun and the tumbrels, the drivers cursing and cracking their whips, the manes flying, the mops and buckets clanking, and the whole air filled with the heavy rumble and the jingling of chains. There was a roar from the ditches, and a shout from the gunners, and we saw a rolling grey cloud before us, with a score of busbies breaking through the shadow. Then we closed up again, while the growling ahead of us grew louder and deeper than ever.

"There's three batteries there," said the sergeant. "There's Bull's and Webber Smith's, but the other is new. There's some more on ahead of us, for here is the track of a nine-pounder, and the others were all twelves. Choose a twelve if you want to get hit; for a nine mashes you up, but a twelve snaps you like a carrot." And then he went on to tell about the dreadful wounds that he had seen, until my blood ran like iced water in my veins, and you might have rubbed all our faces in pipe clay and we should have been no whiter. "Aye, you'll look sicklier yet, when you get a hatful of grape into your tripes," said he.

And then, as I saw some of the old soldiers laughing, I began to understand that this man was trying to frighten us; so I began to laugh also, and the others as well, but it was not a very hearty laugh either.

The sun was almost above us when we stopped at a little place called Hal, where there is an old pump from which I drew and drank a shako full of water—and never did a mug of Scotch ale taste as sweet. More guns passed us here, and Vivian's Hussars, three regiments of them, smart men with bonny brown horses, a treat to the eye. The noise of the cannons was louder than ever now, and it tingled through my nerves just as it had done years before, when, with Edie by my side, I had seen the merchant-ship fight with the privateers. It was so loud now that it seemed to me that the battle must be going on just beyond the nearest wood, but my friend the sergeant knew better.

"It's twelve to fifteen mile off," said he. "You may be sure the general knows we are not wanted, or we should not be resting here at Hal."

What he said proved to be true, for a minute later down came the colonel with orders that we should pile arms and bivouac where we were; and there we stayed all day, while horse and foot and guns, English, Dutch, and Hanoverians, were streaming through. The devil's music went on till evening, sometimes rising into a roar, sometimes sinking into a grumble, until about eight o'clock in the evening it stopped altogether. We were eating our hearts out, as you may think, to know what it all meant, but we knew that what the Duke did would be for the best, so we just waited in patience.

Next day the brigade remained at Hal in the morning, but about mid-day came an orderly from the Duke, and we pushed on once more until we came to a little village called Braine something, and there we stopped; and time too, for a sudden thunderstorm broke over us, and a plump of rain that turned all the roads and the fields into bog and mire. We got into the barns at this village for shelter, and there we found two stragglers—one from a kilted regiment, and the other a man of the German Legion, who had a tale to tell that was as dreary as the weather.

Boney had thrashed the Prussians the day before, and our fellows had been sore put to it to hold their own against Ney, but had beaten him off at last. It seems an old stale story to you now, but you cannot think how we scrambled round those two men in the barn, and pushed and fought, just to catch a word of what they said, and how those who had heard were in turn mobbed by those who had not. We laughed and cheered and groaned all in turn as we heard how the 44th had received cavalry in line, how the Dutch-Belgians had fled, and how the Black Watch had taken the Lancers into their square, and then had killed them at their leisure. But the Lancers had had the laugh on their side when they crumpled up the 69th and carried off one of the colours. To wind it all up, the Duke was in retreat in order to keep in touch with the Prussians, and it was rumoured that he would take up his ground and fight a big battle just at the very place where we had been halted.

And soon we saw that this rumour was true; for the weather cleared towards evening, and we were all out on the ridge to see what we could see. It was such a bonny stretch of corn and grazing land, with the crops just half green and half yellow, and fine rye as high as a man's shoulder. A scene more full of peace you could not think of, and look where you would over the low curving corn-covered hills, you could see the little village steeples pricking up their spires among the poplars. But slashed right across this pretty picture was a long trail of marching men—some red, some green, some blue, some black—zigzagging over the plain and choking the roads, one end so close that we could shout to them, as they stacked their muskets on the ridge at our left, and the other end lost among the woods as far as we could see. And then on other roads we saw the teams of horses toiling and the dull gleam of the guns, and the men straining and swaying as they helped to turn the spokes in the deep, deep mud. As we stood there, regiment after regiment and brigade after brigade took position on the ridge, and ere the sun had set we lay in a line of over sixty thousand men, blocking Napoleon's way to Brussels. But the rain had come swishing down again, and we of the 71st rushed off to our barn once more, where we had better quarters than the greater part of our comrades, who lay stretched in the mud with the storm beating upon them until the first peep of day.

CHAPTER 12

The Shadow on the Land

It was still drizzling in the morning, with brown drifting clouds and a damp chilly wind. It was a queer thing for me as I opened my eyes to think that I should be in a battle that day, though none of us ever thought it would be such a one as it proved to be. We were up and ready, however, with the first light, and as we threw open the doors of our barn we heard the most lovely music that I had ever listened to playing somewhere in the distance. We all stood in clusters hearkening to it, it was so sweet and innocent and sad-like. But our sergeant laughed when he saw how it pleased us all.

"Them are the French bands," said he; "and if you come out here you'll see what some of you may not live to see again."

Out we went, the beautiful music still sounding in our ears, and stood on a rise just outside the barn. Down below at the bottom of the slope, about half a musket-shot from us, was a snug tiled farm with a hedge and a bit of an apple orchard. All round it a line of men in red coats and high fur hats were working like bees, knocking holes in the wall and barring up the doors.

"Them's the light companies of the Guards," said the sergeant. "They'll hold that farm while one of them can wag a finger. But look over yonder and you'll see the camp fires of the French."

We looked across the valley at the low ridge upon the further side, and saw a thousand little yellow points of flame with the dark smoke wreathing up in the heavy air. There was another farm-house on the further side of the valley, and as we looked we suddenly saw a little group of horsemen appear on a knoll beside it and stare across at us. There were a dozen Hussars behind, and in front five men, three with helmets, one with a long straight red feather in his hat, and the last with a low cap.

"By God!" cried the sergeant, "that's him! That's Boney, the one with the grey horse. Aye, I'll lay a month's pay on it."

I strained my eyes to see him, this man who had cast that great shadow over Europe, which darkened the nations for five-and-twenty years, and which had even fallen across our out-of-the-world little sheep-farm, and had dragged us all—myself, Edie, and Jim—out of the lives that our folk had lived before us. As far as I could see, he was a dumpy square-shouldered kind of man, and he held his double glasses to his eyes with his elbows spread very wide out on each side. I was still staring when I heard the catch of a man's breath by my side, and there was Jim with his eyes glowing like two coals, and his face thrust over my shoulder.

"That's he, Jock," he whispered.

"Yes, that's Boney," said I.

"No, no, it's he. This de Lapp or de Lissac, or whatever his devil's name is. It is he."

Then I saw him at once. It was the horseman with the high red feather in his hat. Even at that distance I could have sworn to the slope of his shoulders and the way he carried his head. I clapped my hands upon Jim's sleeve, for I could see that his blood was boiling at the sight of the man, and that he was ready for any madness. But at that moment Bonaparte seemed to lean over and say something to de Lissac, and the party wheeled and dashed away, while there came the bang of a gun and a white spray of smoke from a battery along the ridge. At the same instant the assembly was blown in our village, and we rushed for our arms and fell in. There was a burst of firing all along the line, and we thought that the battle had begun; but it came really from our fellows cleaning their pieces, for their priming was in some danger of being wet from the damp night.

From where we stood it was a sight now that was worth coming over the seas to see. On our own ridge was the chequer of red and blue stretching right away to a village over two miles from us. It was whispered from man to man in the ranks, however, that there was too much of the blue and too little of the red; for the Belgians had shown on the day before that their hearts were too soft for the work, and we had twenty thousand of them for comrades. Then, even our British troops were half made up of militiamen and recruits; for the pick of the old Peninsular regiments were on the ocean in transports, coming back from some fool's quarrel with our kinsfolk of America. But for all that we could see the bearskins of the Guards, two strong brigades of them, and the bonnets of the Highlanders, and the blue of the old German Legion, and the red lines of Pack's brigade, and Kempt's brigade and the green dotted rifle-men in front, and we knew that come what might these were men who would bide where they were placed, and that they had a man to lead them who would place them where they should bide.

Of the French we had seen little save the twinkle of their fires, and a few horsemen here and there upon the curves of the ridge; but as we stood and waited there came suddenly a grand blare from their bands, and their whole army came flooding over the low hill which had hid them, brigade after brigade and division after division, until the broad slope in its whole length and depth was blue with their uniforms and bright with the glint of their weapons. It seemed that they would never have done, still pouring over and pouring over, while our men leaned on their muskets and smoked their pipes looking down at this grand gathering and listening to what the old soldiers who had fought the French before had to say about them. Then when the infantry had formed in long deep masses their guns came whirling and bounding down the slope, and it was pretty to see how smartly they unlimbered and were ready for action. And then at a stately trot down came the cavalry, thirty regiments at the least, with plume and breastplate, twinkling sword and flut-tering lance, forming up at the flanks and rear, in long shifting, glimmering lines.

"Them's the chaps!" cried our old sergeant. "They're gluttons to fight, they are. And you see them regiments with the great high hats in the middle, a bit behind the farm? That's the Guard, twenty thousand of them, my sons, and all picked men—grey-headed devils that have done nothing but fight since they were as high as my gaiters. They've three men to our two, and two guns to our one, and, by God! they'll make you recruities wish you were back in Argyle Street before they have finished with you."

He was not a cheering man, our sergeant; but then he had been in every fight since Corunna, and had a medal with seven clasps upon his breast, so that he had a right to talk in his own fashion.

When the Frenchmen had all arranged themselves just out of cannon-shot we saw a small group of horsemen, all in a blaze with silver and scarlet and gold, ride swiftly between the divisions, and as they went a roar of cheering burst out from either side of them, and we could see arms outstretched to them and hands waving. An instant later the noise had died away, and the two armies stood facing each other in absolute deadly silence—a sight which often comes back to me in my dreams. Then, of a sudden, there was a lurch among the men just in front of us; a thin column wheeled off from the dense blue clump, and came swinging up towards the farm-house which lay below us. It had not taken fifty paces before a gun banged out from an English battery on our left, and the battle of Waterloo had begun.

It is not for me to try to tell you the story of that battle, and, indeed, I should have kept far enough away from such a thing had it not happened that our own fates, those of the three simple folk who came from the border country, were all just as much mixed up in it as those of any king or emperor of them all. To tell the honest truth, I have learned more about that battle from what I have read than from what I saw, for how much could I see with a comrade on either side, and a great white cloud-bank at the very end of my firelock? It was from books and the talk of others that I learned how the heavy cavalry charged, how they rode over the famous cuirassiers, and how they were cut to pieces before they could get back. From them, too, I learned all about the successive assaults, and how the Belgians fled, and how Pack and Kempt stood firm. But of my own knowledge I can only speak of what we saw during that long day in the rifts of the smoke and the lulls of the firing, and it is just of that that I will tell you.

We were on the right of the line and in reserve, for the Duke was afraid that Boney might work round on that side and get at him from behind; so our three regiments, with another British brigade and the Hanoverians, were placed there to be ready for anything. There were two brigades of light cavalry, too; but the French attack was all from the front, so it was late in the day before we were really wanted.

The English battery which fired the first gun was still banging away on our left, and a German one was hard at work upon our right, so that we were wrapped round with the smoke; but we were not so hidden as to screen us from a line of French guns opposite, for a score of round shot came piping through the air and plumped right into the heart of us. As I heard the scream of them past my ear my head went down like a diver, but our sergeant gave me a prod in the back with the handle of his halbert.

"Don't be so blasted polite," said he; "when you're hit, you can bow once and for all."

There was one of those balls that knocked five men into a bloody mash, and I saw it lying on the ground afterwards like a crimson football. Another went through the adjutant's horse with a plop like a stone in the mud, broke its back and left it lying like a burst gooseberry. Three more fell further to the right, and by the stir and cries we could tell that they had all told.

"Ah! James, you've lost a good mount," says Major Reed, just in front of me, looking down at the adjutant, whose boots and breeches were all running with blood.

"I gave a cool fifty for him in Glasgow," said the other. "Don't you think, major, that the men had better lie down now that the guns have got our range?"

"Tut!" said the other; "they are young, James, and it will do them good."

"They'll get enough of it before the day's done," grumbled the other; but at that moment Colonel Reynell saw that the Rifles and the 52nd were down on either side of us, so we had the order to stretch ourselves out too. Precious glad we were when we could hear the shot whining like hungry dogs within a few feet of our backs. Even now a thud and a splash every minute or so, with a yelp of pain and a drumming of boots upon the ground, told us that we were still losing heavily.

A thin rain was falling and the damp air held the smoke low, so that we could only catch glimpses of what was doing just in front of us, though the roar of the guns told us that the battle was general all along the lines. Four hundred of them were all crashing at once now, and the noise was enough to split the drum of your ear. Indeed, there was not one of us but had a singing in his head for many a long day afterwards. Just opposite us on the slope of the hill was a French gun, and we could see the men serving her quite plainly. They were small active men, with very tight breeches and high hats with great straight plumes sticking up from them; but they worked like sheep-shearers, ramming and sponging and training. There were fourteen when I saw them first, and only four left standing at the last, but they were working away just as hard as ever.

The farm that they called Hougoumont was down in front of us, and all the morning we could see that a terrible fight was going on there, for the walls and the windows and the orchard hedges were all flame and smoke, and there rose such shrieking and crying from it as I never heard before. It was half burned down, and shattered with balls, and ten thousand men were hammering at the gates; but four hundred guardsmen held it in the morning and two hundred held it in the evening, and no French foot was ever set within its threshold. But how they fought, those Frenchmen! Their lives were no more to them than the mud under their feet. There was one—I can see him now—a stoutish ruddy man on a crutch. He hobbled up alone in a lull of the firing to the side gate of Hougoumont and he beat upon it, screaming to his men to come after him. For five minutes he stood there, strolling about in front of the gun-barrels which spared him, but at last a Brunswick skirmisher in the orchard flicked out his brains with a rifle shot. And he was only one of many, for all day when they did not come in masses they came in twos and threes with as brave a face as if the whole army were at their heels.

So we lay all morning, looking down at the fight at Hougoumont; but soon the Duke saw that there was nothing to fear upon his right, and so he began to use us in another way.

The French had pushed their skirmishers past the farm, and they lay among the young corn in front of us popping at the gunners, so that three pieces out of six on our left were lying with their men strewed in the mud all round them. But the Duke had his eyes everywhere, and up he galloped at that moment—a thin, dark, wiry man with very bright eyes, a hooked nose, and big cockade on his cap. There were a dozen officers at his heels, all as merry as if it were a foxhunt, but of the dozen there was not one left in the evening.

"Warm work, Adams," said he as he rode up.

"Very warm, your grace," said our general.

"But we can outstay them at it, I think. Tut, tut, we cannot let skirmishers silence a battery! Just drive those fellows out of that, Adams."

Then first I knew what a devil's thrill runs through a man when he is given a bit of fighting to do. Up to now we had just lain and been killed, which is the weariest kind of work. Now it was our turn, and, my word, we were ready for it. Up we jumped, the whole brigade, in a four-deep line, and rushed at the cornfield as hard as we could tear. The skirmishers snapped at us as we came, and then away they bolted like corncrakes, their heads down, their backs rounded, and their muskets at the trail. Half of them got away; but we caught up the others, the officer first, for he was a very fat man who could not run fast. It gave me quite a turn when I saw Rob Stewart, on my right, stick his bayonet into the man's broad back and heard him howl like a damned soul. There was no quarter in that field, and it was butt or point for all of them. The men's blood was aflame, and little wonder, for these wasps had been stinging all morning without our being able so much as to see them.

And now, as we broke through the further edge of the cornfield, we got in front of the smoke, and there was the whole French army in position before us, with only two meadows and a narrow lane between us. We set up a yell as we saw them, and away we should have gone slap at them if we had been left to ourselves; for silly young soldiers never think that harm can come to them until it is there in their midst. But the Duke had cantered his horse beside us as we advanced, and now he roared something to the general, and the officers all rode in front of our line holding out their arms for us to stop. There was a blowing of bugles, a pushing and a shoving, with the sergeants cursing and digging us with their halberts; and in less time than it takes me to write it, there was the brigade in three neat little squares, all bristling with bayonets and in echelon, as they call it, so that each could fire across the face of the other.

It was the saving of us, as even so young a soldier as I was could very easily see; and we had none too much time either. There was a low rolling hill on our right flank, and from behind this there came a sound like nothing on this earth so much as the beat of the waves on the Berwick coast when the wind blows from the east. The earth was all shaking with that dull roaring sound, and the air was full of it.

"Steady, 71st! for God's sake, steady!" shrieked the voice of our colonel behind us; but in front was nothing but the green gentle slope of the grassland, all mottled with daisies and dandelions.

And then suddenly over the curve we saw eight hundred brass helmets rise up, all in a moment, each with a long tag of horsehair flying from its crest; and then eight hundred fierce brown faces all pushed forward, and glaring out from between the ears of as many horses. There was an instant of gleaming breastplates, waving swords, tossing manes, fierce red nostrils opening and shutting, and hoofs pawing the air before us; and then down came the line of muskets, and our bullets smacked up against their armour like the clatter of a hailstorm upon a window. I fired with the rest, and then rammed down another charge as fast as I could, staring out through the smoke in front of me, where I could see some long, thin thing which napped slowly backwards and forwards. A bugle sounded for us to cease firing, and a whiff of wind came to clear the curtain from in front of us, and then we could see what had happened.

I had expected to see half that regiment of horse lying on the ground; but whether it was that their breastplates had shielded them, or whether, being young and a little shaken at their coming, we had fired high, our volley had done no very great harm. About thirty horses lay about, three of them together within ten yards of me, the middle one right on its back with its four legs in the air, and it was one of these that I had seen flapping through the smoke. Then there were eight or ten dead men and about as many wounded, sitting dazed on the grass for the most part, though one was shouting *"Vive l'Empereur!"* at the top of his voice. Another fellow who had been shot in the thigh—a great black-moustached chap he was too—leaned his back against his dead horse and, picking up his carbine, fired as coolly as if he had been shooting for a prize, and hit Angus Myres, who was only two from me, right through the forehead. Then he out with his hand to get another carbine that lay near, but before he could reach it big Hodgson, who was the pivot man of the Grenadier company, ran out and passed his bayonet through his throat, which was a pity, for he seemed to be a very fine man.

At first I thought that the *cuirassiers* had run away in the smoke; but they were not men who did that very easily. Their horses had swerved at our volley, and they had raced past our square and taken the fire of the two other ones beyond. Then they broke through a hedge, and coming on a regiment of Hanoverians who were in line, they treated them as they would have treated us if we had not been so quick, and cut them to pieces in an instant. It was dreadful to see the big Germans running and screaming while the cuirassiers stood up in their stirrups to have a better sweep for their long, heavy swords, and cut and stabbed without mercy. I do not believe that a hundred men of that regiment were left alive; and the Frenchmen came back across our front, shouting at us and waving their weapons, which were crimson down to the hilts. This they did to draw our fire, but the colonel was too old a soldier; for we could have done little harm at the distance, and they would have been among us before we could reload.

These horsemen got behind the ridge on our right again, and we knew very well that if we opened up from the squares they would be down upon us in a twinkle. On the other hand, it was hard to bide as we were; for they had passed the word to a battery of twelve guns, which formed up a few hundred yards away from us, but out of our sight, sending their balls just over the brow and down into the midst of us, which is called a plunging fire. And one of their gunners ran up on to the top of the slope and stuck a handspike into the wet earth to give them a guide, under the very muzzles of the whole brigade, none of whom fired a shot at him, each leaving him to the other. Ensign Samson, who was the youngest subaltern in the regiment, ran out from the square and pulled down the hand-spike; but quick as a jack after a minnow, a lancer came flying over the ridge, and he made such a thrust from behind that not only his point but his pennon too came out between the second and third buttons of the lad's tunic. "Helen! Helen!" he shouted, and fell dead on his face, while the lancer, blown half to pieces with musket balls, toppled over beside him, still holding on to his weapon, so that they lay together with that dreadful bond still connecting them.

But when the battery opened there was no time for us to think of anything else. A square is a very good way of meeting a horseman, but there is no worse one of taking a cannon ball, as we soon learned when they began to cut red seams through us, until our ears were weary of the slosh and splash when hard iron met living flesh and blood. After ten minutes of it we moved our square a hundred paces to the right; but we left another square behind us, for a hundred and twenty men and seven officers showed where we had been standing. Then the guns found us out again, and we tried to open out into line; but in an instant the horsemen—lancers they were this time—were upon us from over the brae.

I tell you we were glad to hear the thud of their hoofs, for we knew that that must stop the cannon for a minute and give us a chance of hitting back. And we hit back pretty hard too that time, for we were cold and vicious and savage, and I for one felt that I cared no more for the horsemen than if they had been so many sheep on Corriemuir. One gets past being afraid or thinking of one's own skin after a while, and you just feel that you want to make some one pay for all you have gone through. We took our change out of the lancers that time; for they had no breastplates to shield them, and we cleared seventy of them out of their saddles at a volley. Maybe, if we could have seen seventy mothers weeping for their lads, we should not have felt so pleased over it; but then, men are just brutes when they are fighting, and have as much thought as two bull pups when they've got one another by the throttle.

Then the colonel did a wise stroke; for he reckoned that this would stave off the cavalry for five minutes, so he wheeled us into line, and got us back into a deeper hollow out of reach of the guns before they could open again. This gave us time to breathe, and we wanted it too, for the regiment had been melting away like an icicle in the sun. But bad as it was for us, it was a deal worse for some of the others. The whole of the Dutch Belgians were off by this time helter-skelter, fifteen thousand of them, and there were great gaps left in our line through which the French cavalry rode as pleased them best. Then the French guns had been too many and too good for ours, and our heavy horse had been cut to bits, so that things were none too merry with us. On the other hand, Hougoumont, a blood-soaked ruin, was still ours, and every British regiment was firm; though, to tell the honest truth, as a man is bound to do, there were a sprinkling of red coats among the blue ones who made for the rear. But these were lads and stragglers, the faint hearts that are found everywhere, and I say again that no regiment flinched. It was little we could see of the battle; but a man would be blind not to know that all the fields behind us were covered with flying men. But then, though we on the right wing knew nothing of it, the Prussians had begun to show, and Napoleon had set 20,000 of his men to face them, which made up for ours that had bolted, and left us much as we began. That was all dark to us, however; and there was a time, when the French horsemen had flooded in between us and the rest of the army, that we thought we were the only brigade left standing, and had set our teeth with the intention of selling our lives as dearly as we could.

At that time it was between four and five in the afternoon, and we had had nothing to eat, the most of us, since the night before, and were soaked with rain into the bargain. It had drizzled off and on all day, but for the last few hours we had not had a thought to spare either upon the weather or our hunger. Now we began to look round and tighten our waist-belts, and ask who was hit and who was spared. I was glad to see Jim, with his face all blackened with powder, standing on my right rear, leaning on his firelock. He saw me looking at him, and shouted out to know if I were hurt.

"All right, Jim," I answered.

"I fear I'm here on a wild-goose chase," said he gloomily, "but it's not over yet. By God, I'll have him, or he'll have me!"

He had brooded so much on his wrong, had poor Jim, that I really believe that it had turned his head; for he had a glare in his eyes as he spoke that was hardly human. He was always a man that took even a little thing to heart, and since Edie had left him I am sure that he was no longer his own master.

It was at this time of the fight that we saw two single fights, which they tell me were common enough in the battles of old, before men were trained in masses. As we lay in the hollow two horsemen came spurring along the ridge right in front of us, riding as hard as hoof could rattle. The first was an English dragoon, his face right down on his horse's mane, with a French cuirassier, an old, grey-headed fellow, thundering behind him, on a big black mare. Our chaps set up a hooting as they came flying on, for it seemed shame to see an Englishman run like that; but as they swept across our front we saw where the trouble lay. The dragoon had dropped his sword, and was unarmed, while the other was pressing him so close that he could not get a weapon. At last, stung maybe by our hooting, he made up his mind to chance it. His eye fell on a lance beside a dead Frenchman, so he swerved his horse to let the other pass, and hopping off cleverly enough, he gripped hold of it. But the other was too tricky for him, and was on him like a shot. The dragoon thrust up with the lance, but the other turned it, and sliced him through the shoulder-blade. It was all done in an instant, and the Frenchman cantering his horse up the brae, showing his teeth at us over his shoulder like a snarling dog.

That was one to them, but we scored one for us presently. They had pushed forward a skirmish line, whose fire was towards the batteries on our right and left rather than on us; but we sent out two companies of the 95th to keep them in check. It was strange to hear the crackling kind of noise that they made, for both sides were using the rifle. An officer stood among the French skirmishers—a tall, lean man with a mantle over his shoulders—and as our fellows came forward he ran out midway between the two parties and stood as a fencer would, with his sword up and his head back. I can see him now, with his lowered eyelids and the kind of sneer that he had upon his face. On this the subaltern of the Rifles, who was a fine well-grown lad, ran forward and drove full tilt at him with one of the queer crooked swords that the rifle-men carry. They came together like two rams—for each ran for the other—and down they tumbled at the shock, but the Frenchman was below. Our man broke his sword short off, and took the other's blade through his left arm; but he was the stronger man, and he managed to let the life out of his enemy with the jagged stump of his blade. I thought that the French skirmishers would have shot him down, but not a trigger was drawn, and he got back to his company with one sword through his arm and half of another in his hand.

CHAPTER 13

The End of the Storm

Of all the things that seem strange in that battle, now that I look back upon it, there is nothing that was queerer than the way in which it acted on my comrades; for some took it as though it had been their daily meat without question or change, and others pattered out prayers from the first gunfire to the last, and others again cursed and swore in a way that was creepy to listen to. There was one, my own left-hand man, Mike Threadingham, who kept telling about his maiden aunt, Sarah, and how she had left the money which had been promised to him to a home for the children of drowned sailors. Again and again he told me this story, and yet when the battle was over he took his oath that he had never opened his lips all day. As to me, I cannot say whether I spoke or not, but I know that my mind and my memory were clearer than I can ever remember them, and I was thinking all the time about the old folk at home, and about Cousin Edie with her saucy, dancing eyes, and de Lissac with his cat's whiskers, and all the doings at West Inch, which had ended by bringing us here on the plains of Belgium as a cockshot for two hundred and fifty cannons.

During all this time the roaring of those guns had been something dreadful to listen to, but now they suddenly died away, though it was like the lull in a thunderstorm when one feels that a worse crash is coming hard at the fringe of it. There was still a mighty noise on the distant wing, where the Prussians were pushing their way onwards, but that was two miles away. The other batteries, both French and English, were silent, and the smoke cleared so that the armies could see a little of each other. It was a dreary sight along our ridge, for there seemed to be just a few scattered knots of red and the lines of green where the German Legion stood, while the masses of the French appeared to be as thick as ever, though of course we knew that they must have lost many thousands in these attacks. We heard a great cheering and shouting from among them, and then suddenly all their batteries opened together with a roar which made the din of the earlier part seem nothing in comparison. It might well be twice as loud, for every battery was twice as near, being moved right up to point blank range, with huge masses of horse between and behind them to guard them from attack.

When that devil's roar burst upon our ears there was not a man, down to the drummer boys, who did not understand what it meant. It was Napoleon's last great effort to crush us. There were but two more hours of light, and if we could hold our own for those all would be well. Starved and weary and spent, we prayed that we might have strength to load and stab and fire while one of us stood upon his feet.

His cannon could do us no great hurt now, for we were on our faces, and in an instant we could turn into a huddle of bayonets if his horse came down again. But behind the thunder of the guns there rose a sharper, shriller noise, whirring and rattling, the wildest, jauntiest, most stirring kind of sound.

"It's the *pas-de-charge!*" cried an officer. "They mean business this time!"

And as he spoke we saw a strange thing. A Frenchman, dressed as an officer of hussars, came galloping towards us on a little bay horse. He was screeching *"Vive le roi! Vive le roi!"* at the pitch of his lungs, which was as much as to say that he was a deserter, since we were for the king and they for the emperor. As he passed us he roared out in English, "The Guard is coming! The Guard is coming!" and so vanished away to the rear like a leaf blown before a storm. At the same instant up there rode an *aide-de-camp*, with the reddest face that ever I saw upon mortal man.

"You must stop 'em, or we are done!" he cried to General Adams, so that all our company could hear him.

"How is it going?" asked the general.

"Two weak squadrons left out of six regiments of heavies," said he, and began to laugh like a man whose nerves are overstrung.

"Perhaps you would care to join in our advance? Pray consider yourself quite one of us," said the general, bowing and smiling as if he were asking him to a dish of tea.

"I shall have much pleasure," said the other, taking off his hat; and a moment afterwards our three regiments closed up, and the brigade advanced in four lines over the hollow where we had lain in square, and out beyond to the point whence we had seen the French army.

There was little of it to be seen now, only the red belching of the guns flashing quickly out of the cloudbank, and the black figures—stooping, straining, mopping, sponging—working like devils, and at devilish work. But through the cloud that rattle and whirr rose ever louder and louder, with a deep-mouthed shouting and the stamping of thousands of feet. Then there came a broad black blur through the haze, which darkened and hardened until we could see that it was a hundred men abreast, marching swiftly towards us, with high fur hats upon their heads and a gleam of brass work over their brows. And behind that hundred came another hundred, and behind that another, and on and on, coiling and writhing out of the cannon-smoke like a monstrous snake, until there seemed to be no end to the mighty column. In front ran a spray of skirmishers, and behind them the drummers, and up they all came together at a kind of tripping step, with the officers clustering thickly at the sides and waving their swords and cheering. There were a dozen mounted men too at their front, all shouting together, and one with his hat held aloft upon his sword point. I say again, that no men upon this earth could have fought more manfully than the French did upon that day.

It was wonderful to see them; for as they came onwards they got ahead of their own guns, so that they had no longer any help from them, while they got in front of the two batteries which had been on either side of us all day. Every gun had their range to a foot, and we saw long red lines scored right down the dark column as it advanced. So near were they, and so closely did they march, that every shot ploughed through ten files of them, and yet they closed up and came on with a swing and dash that was fine to see. Their head was turned straight for ourselves, while the 95th overlapped them on one side and the 52nd on the other.

I shall always think that if we had waited so the Guard would have broken us; for how could a four-deep line stand against such a column? But at that moment Colburne, the colonel of the 52nd, swung his right flank round so as to bring it on the side of the column, which brought the Frenchmen to a halt. Their front line was forty paces from us at the moment, and we had a good look at them. It was funny to me to remember that I had always thought of Frenchmen as small men; for there was not one of that first company who could not have picked me up as if I had been a child, and their great hats made them look taller yet. They were hard, wizened, wiry fellows too, with fierce puckered eyes and bristling moustaches, old soldiers who had fought and fought, week in, week out, for many a year. And then, as I stood with my finger upon the trigger waiting for the word to fire, my eye fell full upon the mounted officer with his hat upon his sword, and I saw that it was de Lissac.

I saw it, and Jim did too. I heard a shout, and saw him rush forward madly at the French column; and, as quick as thought, the whole brigade took their cue from him, officers and all, and flung themselves upon the Guard in front, while our comrades charged them on the flanks. We had been waiting for the order, and they all thought now that it had been given; but you may take my word for it, that Jim Horscroft was the real leader of the brigade when we charged the Old Guard.

God knows what happened during that mad five minutes. I remember putting my musket against a blue coat and pulling the trigger, and that the man could not fall because he was so wedged in the crowd; but I saw a horrid blotch upon the cloth, and a thin curl of smoke from it as if it had taken fire. Then I found myself thrown up against two big Frenchmen, and so squeezed together, the three of us, that we could not raise a weapon. One of them, a fellow with a very large nose, got his hand up to my throat, and I felt that I was a chicken in his grasp. *"Rendez-vous, coqin; rendez-vous!"* said he, and then suddenly doubled up with a scream, for someone had stabbed him in the bowels with a bayonet. There was very little firing after the first sputter; but there was the crash of butt against barrel, the short cries of stricken men, and the roaring of the officers. And then, suddenly, they began to give ground—slowly, sullenly, step by step, but still to give ground. Ah! it was worth all that we had gone through, the thrill of that moment, when we felt that they were going to break. There was one Frenchman before me, a sharp-faced, dark-eyed man, who was loading and firing as quietly as if he were at practice, dwelling upon his aim, and looking round first to try and pick off an officer. I remember that it struck me that to kill so cool a man as that would be a good service, and I rushed at him and drove my bayonet into him. He turned as I struck him and fired full into my face, and the bullet left a weal across my cheek which will mark me to my dying day. I tripped over him as he fell, and two others tumbling over me I was half smothered in the heap. When at last I struggled out, and cleared my eyes, which were half full of powder, I saw that the column had fairly broken, and was shredding into groups of men, who were either running for their lives or were fighting back to back in a vain attempt to check the brigade, which was still sweeping onwards. My face felt as if a red-hot iron had been laid across it; but I had the use of my limbs, so jumping over the litter of dead and mangled men, I scampered after my regiment, and fell in upon the right flank.

Old Major Elliott was there, limping along, for his horse had been shot, but none the worse in himself. He saw me come up, and nodded, but it was too busy a time for words. The brigade was still advancing, but the general rode in front of me with his chin upon his shoulder, looking back at the British position.

"There is no general advance," said he; "but I'm not going back."

"The Duke of Wellington has won a great victory," cried the

aide-de-camp, in a solemn voice; and then, his feelings getting the better of him, he added, "if the damned fool would only push on!"—which set us all laughing in the flank company.

But now anyone could see that the French army was breaking up. The columns and squadrons which had stood so squarely all day were now all ragged at the edges; and where there had been thick fringes of skirmishers in front, there were now a spray of stragglers in the rear. The Guard thinned out in front of us as we pushed on, and we found twelve guns looking us in the face, but we were over them in a moment; and I saw our youngest subaltern, next to him who had been killed by the lancer, scribbling great 71's with a lump of chalk upon them, like the schoolboy that he was. It was at that moment that we heard a roar of cheering behind us, and saw the whole British army flood over the crest of the ridge, and come pouring down upon the remains of their enemies. The guns, too, came bounding and rattling forward, and our light cavalry—as much as was left of it—kept pace with our brigade upon the right. There was no battle after that. The advance went on without a check, until our army stood lined upon the very ground which the French had held in the morning. Their guns were ours, their foot were a rabble spread over the face of the country, and their gallant cavalry alone was able to preserve some sort of order and to draw off unbroken from the field. Then at last, just as the night began to gather, our weary and starving men were able to let the Prussians take the job over, and to pile their arms upon the ground that they had won. That was as much as I saw or can tell you about the Battle of Waterloo, except that I ate a two-pound rye loaf for my supper that night, with as much salt meat as they would let me have, and a good pitcher of red wine, until I had to bore a new hole at the end of my belt, and then it fitted me as tight as a hoop to a barrel. After that I lay down in the straw where the rest of the company were sprawling, and in less than a minute I was in a dead sleep.

CHAPTER 14

The Tally of Death

Day was breaking, and the first grey light had just begun to steal through the long thin slits in the walls of our barn, when someone shook me hard by the shoulder, and up I jumped. I had the thought in my stupid, sleepy brain that the *cuirassiers* were upon us, and I gripped hold of a halbert that was leaning against the wall; but then, as I saw the long lines of sleepers, I remembered where I was. But I can tell you that I stared when I saw that it was none other than Major Elliott that had roused me up. His face was very grave, and behind him stood two sergeants, with long slips of paper and pencils in their hands.

"Wake up, laddie," said the Major, quite in his old easy fashion, as if we were back on Corriemuir again.

"Yes, Major?" I stammered.

"I want you to come with me. I feel that I owe something to you two lads, for it was I that took you from your homes. Jim Horscroft is missing."

I gave a start at that, for what with the rush and the hunger and the weariness I had never given a thought to my friend since the time that he had rushed at the French Guards with the whole regiment at his heels.

"I am going out now to take a tally of our losses," said the Major; "and if you cared to come with me, I should be very glad to have you."

So off we set, the Major, the two sergeants, and I; and oh! but it was a dreadful, dreadful sight!—so much so, that even now, after so many years, I had rather say as little of it as possible. It was bad to see in the heat of fight; but now in the cold morning, with no cheer or drum-tap or bugle blare, all the glory had gone out of it, and it was just one huge butcher's shop, where poor devils had been ripped and burst and smashed, as though we had tried to make a mock of God's image. There on the ground one could read every stage of yesterday's fight—the dead footmen that lay in squares and the fringe of dead horsemen that had charged them, and above on the slope the dead gunners, who lay round their broken piece. The Guards' column had left a streak right up the field like the trail of a snail, and at the head of it the blue coats were lying heaped upon the red ones where that fierce tug had been before they took their backward step.

And the very first thing that I saw when I got there was Jim himself. He was lying on the broad of his back, his face turned up towards the sky, and all the passion and the trouble seemed to have passed clean away from him, so that he looked just like the old Jim as I had seen him in his cot a hundred times when we were schoolmates together. I had given a cry of grief at the sight of him; but when I came to look upon his face, and to see how much happier he looked in death than I could ever have hoped to see him in life, it was hard to mourn for him. Two French bayonets had passed through his chest, and he had died in an instant, and without pain, if one could believe the smile upon his lips.

The Major and I were raising his head in the hope that some flutter of life might remain, when I heard a well-remembered voice at my side, and there was de Lissac leaning upon his elbow among a litter of dead guardsmen. He had a great blue coat muffled round him, and the hat with the high red plume was lying on the ground beside him. He was very pale, and had dark blotches under his eyes, but otherwise he was as he had ever been, with the keen, hungry nose, the wiry moustache, and the close-cropped head thinning away to baldness upon the top. His eyelids had always drooped, but now one could hardly see the glint of his eyes from beneath them.

"*Hola,* Jock!" he cried. "I didn't thought to have seen you here, and yet I might have known it, too, when I saw friend Jim."

"It is you that has brought all this trouble," said I.

"*Ta, ta, ta!*" he cried, in his old impatient fashion. "It is all arranged for us. When I was in Spain I learned to believe in Fate. It is Fate which has sent you here this morning."

"This man's blood lies at your door," said I, with my hand on poor Jim's shoulder.

"And mine on his, so we have paid our debts."

He flung open his mantle as he spoke, and I saw with horror that a great black lump of clotted blood was hanging out of his side.

"This is my thirteenth and last," said he, with a smile. "They say that thirteen is an unlucky number. Could you spare me a drink from your flask?"

The Major had some brandy and water. De Lissac supped it up eagerly. His eyes brightened, and a little fleck of colour came back in each of his haggard cheeks.

"It was Jim did this," said he. "I heard someone calling my name, and there he was with his gun against my tunic. Two of my men cut him down just as he fired. Well, well, Edie was worth it all! You will be in Paris in less than a month, Jock, and you will see her. You will find her at No. 11 of the Rue Miromesnil, which is near to the Madeleine. Break it very gently to her, Jock, for you cannot think how she loved me. Tell her that all I have are in the two black trunks, and that Antoine has the keys. You will not forget?"

"I will remember."

"And *madame*, your mother? I trust that you have left her very well. And *monsieur*, too, your father? Bear them my distinguished regards!"

Even now as death closed in upon him, he gave the old bow and wave as he sent his greetings to my mother.

"Surely," said I, "your wound may not be so serious as you think. I could bring the surgeon of our regiment to you."

"My dear Jock, I have not been giving and taking wounds this fifteen years without knowing when one has come home. But it is as well, for I know that all is ended for my little man, and I had rather go with my Voltigeurs than remain to be an exile and a beggar. Besides, it is quite certain that the Allies would have shot me, so I have saved myself from that humiliation."

"The Allies, sir," said the Major, with some heat, "would be guilty of no such barbarous action."

But de Lissac shook his head, with the same sad smile.

"You do not know, Major," said he. "Do you suppose that I should have fled to Scotland and changed my name if I had not more to fear than my comrades who remained in Paris? I was anxious to live, for I was sure that my little man would come back. Now I had rather die, for he will never lead an army again. But I have done things that could not be forgiven. It was I that led the party which took and shot the Duc d'Enghien. It was I—Ah, *mon Dieu!* Edie, Edie, *ma cherie!*"

He threw out both his hands, with all the fingers feeling and quivering in the air. Then he let them drop heavily in front of him, and his chin fell forward upon his chest. One of our sergeants laid him gently down, and the other stretched the big blue mantle over him; and so we left those two whom Fate had so strangely brought together, the Scotchman and the Frenchman, lying silently and peacefully within hand's touch of each other, upon the blood-soaked hillside near Hougoumont.

CHAPTER 15.

The End of It

And now I have very nearly come to the end of it all, and precious glad I shall be to find myself there; for I began this old memory with a light heart, thinking that it would give me some work for the long summer evenings, but as I went on I wakened a thousand sleeping sorrows and half-forgotten griefs, and now my soul is all as raw as the hide of an ill-sheared sheep. If I come safely out of it I will swear never to set pen to paper again, for it is so easy at first, like walking into a shelving stream, and then before you can look round you are off your feet and down in a hole, and can struggle out as best you may.

We buried Jim and de Lissac with four hundred and thirty-one others of the French Guards and our own Light Infantry in a single trench. Ah! if you could sow a brave man as you sow a seed, there should be a fine crop of heroes coming up there some day! Then we left that bloody battle-field behind us for ever, and with our brigade we marched on over the French border on our way to Paris.

I had always been brought up during all these years to look upon the French as very evil folk, and as we only heard of them in connection with fightings and slaughterings, by land and by sea, it was natural enough to think that they were vicious by nature and ill to meet with. But then, after all, they had only heard of us in the same fashion, and so, no doubt, they had just the same idea of us. But when we came to go through their country, and to see their bonny little steadings, and the douce quiet folk at work in the fields, and the women knitting by the roadside, and the old granny with a big white mutch smacking the baby to teach it manners, it was all so home-like that I could not think why it was that we had been hating and fearing these good people for so long. But I suppose that in truth it was really the man who was over them that we hated, and now that he was gone and his great shadow cleared from the land, all was brightness once more.

We jogged along happily enough through the loveliest country that ever I set my eyes on, until we came to the great city, where we thought that maybe there would be a battle, for there are so many folk in it that if only one in twenty comes out it would make a fine army. But by that time they had seen that it was a pity to spoil the whole country just for the sake of one man, and so they had told him that he must shift for himself in the future. The next we heard was that he had surrendered to the British, and that the gates of Paris were opened to us, which was very good news to me, for I could get along very well just on the one battle that I had had.

But there were plenty of folk in Paris now who loved Boney; and that was natural when you think of the glory that he had brought them, and how he had never asked his army to go where he would not go himself. They had stern enough faces for us, I can tell you, when we marched in, and we of Adams' brigade were the very first who set foot in the city. We passed over a bridge which they call Neuilly, which is easier to write than to say, and through a fine park—the Bois de Boulogne, and so into the Champs d'Elysees. There we bivouacked, and pretty soon the streets were so full of Prussians and English that it became more like a camp than a city.

The very first time that I could get away I went with Rob Stewart, of my company—for we were only allowed to go about in couples—to the Rue Miromesnil. Rob waited in the hall, and I was shown upstairs; and as I put my foot over the mat, there was Cousin Edie, just the same as ever, staring at me with those wild eyes of hers. For a moment she did not recognise me, but when she did she just took three steps forward and sprang at me, with her two arms round my neck.

"Oh, my dear old Jock," she cried, "how fine you look in a red coat!"

"Yes, I am a soldier now, Edie," said I, very stiffly; for as I looked at her pretty face, I seemed to see behind it that other face which had looked up to the morning sky on the Belgium battle-field.

"Fancy that!" she cried. "What are you, then, Jock? A general? A captain?"

"No, I am a private."

"What! Not one of the common people who carry guns?"

"Yes, I carry a gun."

"Oh, that is not nearly so interesting," said she. And she went back to the sofa from which she had risen. It was a wonderful room, all silk and velvet and shiny things, and I felt inclined to go back to give my boots another rub. As Edie sat down again, I saw that she was all in black, and so I knew that she had heard of de Lissac's death.

"I am glad to see that you know all," said I, for I am a clumsy hand at breaking things. "He said that you were to keep whatever was in the boxes, and that Antoine had the keys."

"Thank you, Jock, thank you," said she. "It was like your kindness to bring the message. I heard of it nearly a week ago. I was mad for the time—quite mad. I shall wear mourning all my days, although you can see what a fright it makes me look. Ah! I shall never get over it. I shall take the veil and die in a convent."

"If you please, *madame*," said a maid, looking in, "the Count de Beton wishes to see you."

"My dear Jock," said Edie, jumping up, "this is very important. I am sorry to cut our chat short, but I am sure that you will come to see me again, will you not, when I am less desolate? And would you mind going out by the side door instead of the main one? Thank you, you dear old Jock; you were always such a good boy, and did exactly what you were told."

And that was the last that I was ever to see of Cousin Edie. She stood in the sunlight with the old challenge in her eyes, and flash of her teeth; and so I shall always remember her, shining and unstable, like a drop of quicksilver. As I joined my comrade in the street below, I saw a grand carriage and pair at the door, and I knew that she had asked me to slip out so that her grand new friends might never know what common people she had been associated with in her childhood. She had never asked for Jim, nor for my father and mother who had been so kind to her. Well, it was just her way, and she could no more help it than a rabbit can help wagging its scut, and yet it made me heavy-hearted to think of it. Two months later I heard that she had married this same Count de Beton, and she died in child-bed a year or two later.

And as for us, our work was done, for the great shadow had been cleared away from Europe, and should no longer be thrown across the breadth of the lands, over peaceful farms and little villages, darkening the lives which should have been so happy. I came back to Corriemuir after I had bought my discharge, and there, when my father died, I took over the sheep-farm, and married Lucy Deane, of Berwick, and have brought up seven children, who are all taller than their father, and take mighty good care that he shall not forget it. But in the quiet, peaceful days that pass now, each as like the other as so many Scotch tups, I can hardly get the young folks to believe that even here we have had our romance, when Jim and I went a-wooing, and the man with the cat's whiskers came up from the sea.

Three Stories

A Foreign Office Romance
★
A Straggler of '15
★
The Slapping Sal

A Foreign Office Romance

There are many folk who knew Alphonse Lacour in his old age. From about the time of the Revolution of '48 until he died in the second year of the Crimean War he was always to be found in the same corner of the Café de Provence, at the end of the Rue St. Honoreé, coming down about nine in the evening, and going when he could find no one to talk with. It took some self-restraint to listen to the old diplomatist, for his stories were beyond all belief, and yet he was quick at detecting the shadow of a smile or the slightest little raising of the eyebrows. Then his huge, rounded back would straighten itself, his bull-dog chin would project, and his r's would burr like a kettle-drum. When he got as far as *"Ah, monsieur r-r-r-rit!"* or *"Vous ne me cr-r-r-royez pas donc!"* it was quite time to remember that you had a ticket for the opera.

There was his story of Talleyrand and the five oyster-shells, and there was his utterly absurd account of Napoleon's second visit to Ajaccio. Then there was that most circumstantial romance (which he never ventured upon until his second bottle had been uncorked) of the Emperor's escape from St. Helena—how he lived for a whole year in Philadelphia, while Count Herbert de Bertrand, who was his living image, personated him at Longwood. But of all his stories there was none which was more notorious than that of the Koran and the Foreign Office messenger. And yet when *Monsieur* Otto's memoirs were written it was found that there really was some foundation for old Lacour's incredible statement.

"You must know, *monsieur*," he would say, "that I left Egypt after Kleber's assassination. I would gladly have stayed on, for I was engaged in a translation of the Koran, and between ourselves I had thoughts at the time of embracing Mahometanism, for I was deeply struck by the wisdom of their views about marriage. They had made an incredible mistake, however, upon the subject of wine, and this was what the Mufti who attempted to convert me could never get over. Then when old Kleber died and Menou came to the top, I felt that it was time for me to go. It is not for me to speak of my own capacities, *monsieur*, but you will readily understand that the man does not care to be ridden by the mule. I carried my Koran and my papers to London, where *Monsieur* Otto had been sent by the first Consul to arrange a treaty of peace; for both nations were very weary of the war, which had already lasted ten years. Here I was most useful to *Monsieur* Otto on account of my knowledge of the English tongue, and also, if I may say so, on account of my natural capacity. They were happy days during which I lived in the Square of Bloomsbury. The climate of *monsieur*'s country is, it must be confessed, detestable. But then what would you have? Flowers grow best in the rain. One has but to point to *monsieur*'s fellow-country-women to prove it.

"Well, *Monsieur* Otto, our Ambassador, was kept terribly busy over that treaty, and all of his staff were worked to death. We had not Pitt to deal with, which was perhaps as well for us. He was a terrible man, that Pitt, and wherever half a dozen enemies of France were plotting together, there was his sharp-pointed nose right in the middle of them. The nation, however, had been thoughtful enough to put him out of office, and we had to do with *Monsieur* Addington. But Milord Hawkesbury was the Foreign Minister, and it was with him that we were obliged to do our bargaining.

"You can understand that it was no child's play. After ten years of war each nation had got hold of a great deal which had belonged to the other, or to the other's allies. What was to be given back? And what was to be kept? Is this island worth that peninsula? If we do this at Venice, will you do that at Sierra

Leone? If we give up Egypt to the Sultan, will you restore the Cape of Good Hope, which you have taken from our allies the Dutch? So we wrangled and wrestled; and I have seen *Monsieur* Otto come back to the Embassy so exhausted that his secretary and I had to help him from his carriage to his sofa. But at last things adjusted themselves, and the night came round when the treaty was to be finally signed.

"Now you must know that the one great card which we held, and which we played, played, played at every point of the game, was that we had Egypt. The English were very nervous about our being there. It gave us a foot on each end of the Mediterranean, you see. And they were not sure that that wonderful little Napoleon of ours might not make it the base of an advance against India. So whenever Lord Hawkesbury proposed to retain anything, we had only to reply, 'In that case, of course, we cannot consent to evacuate Egypt,' and in this way we quickly brought him to reason. It was by the help of Egypt that we gained terms which were remarkably favourable, and especially that we caused the English to consent to give up the Cape of Good Hope; we did not wish your people, *monsieur*, to have any foothold in South Africa, for history has taught us that the British foothold of one half-century is the British Empire of the next. It is not your army or your navy against which we have to guard, but it is your terrible younger son and your man in search of a career. When we French have a possession across the seas, we like to sit in Paris and to felicitate ourselves upon it. With you it is different. You take your wives and your children and you run away to see what kind of place this may be, and after that we might as well try to take that old Square of Bloomsbury away from you.

"Well, it was upon the first of October that the treaty was finally to be signed. In the morning I was congratulating *Monsieur* Otto upon the happy conclusion of his labours. He was a little pale shrimp of a man, very quick and nervous, and he was so delighted now at his own success that he could not sit still, but ran about the room chattering and laughing, while I sat on a cushion in the corner, as I had learned to do in the East. Suddenly, in came a messenger with a letter which had been forwarded from Paris. *Monsieur* Otto cast his eyes upon it, and then, without a word, his knees gave way, and he fell senseless upon the floor. I ran to him, as did the courier, and between us we carried him to the sofa. He might have been dead from his appearance, but I could still feel his heart thrilling beneath my palm.

"'What is this, then?' I asked.

"'I do not know,' answered the messenger. '*Monsieur* Tall-eyrand told me to hurry as never man hurried before, and to put this letter into the hands of *Monsieur* Otto. I was in Paris at midday yesterday.'

"I know that I am to blame, but I could not help glancing at the letter, picking it out of the senseless hand of *Monsieur* Otto. My God! the thunderbolt that it was! I did not faint, but I sat down beside my chief and I burst into tears. It was but a few words, but they told us that Egypt had been evacuated by our troops a month before. All our treaty was undone then, and the one consideration which had induced our enemies to give us good terms had vanished. In twelve hours it would not have mattered. But now the treaty was not yet signed. We should have to give up the Cape. We should have to let England have Malta. Now that Egypt was gone we had nothing to offer in exchange.

"But we are not so easily beaten, we Frenchmen. You English misjudge us when you think that because we show emotions which you conceal, that we are therefore of a weak and womanly nature. You cannot read your histories and believe that. *Monsieur* Otto recovered his sense presently, and we took counsel what we should do.

"'It is useless to go on, Alphonse,' said he. 'This Englishman will laugh at me when I ask him to sign.'

"'Courage!' I cried; and then a sudden thought coming into my head—'How do we know that the English will have news of this? Perhaps they may sign the treaty before they know of it.'

"*Monsieur* Otto sprang from the sofa and flung himself into my arms.

"'Alphonse,' he cried, 'you have saved me! Why should they know about it? Our news has come from Toulon, to Paris, and thence straight to London. Theirs will come by sea through the straits of Gibraltar. At this moment it is unlikely that any one in Paris knows of it, save only Talleyrand and the first Consul. If we keep our secret, we may still get our treaty signed.'

"Ah, *monsieur*, you can imagine the horrible uncertainty in which we spent the day. Never, never shall I forget those slow hours during which we sat together, starting at every distant shout, lest it should be the first sign of the rejoicing which this news would cause in London. *Monsieur* Otto passed from youth to age in a day. As for me, I find it easier to go out and meet danger than to wait for it. I set forth, therefore, toward evening. I wandered here, and wandered there. I was in the fencing-rooms of *Monsieur* Angelo, and in the *salon-de-boxe* of *Monsieur* Jackson, and in the club of Brooks, and in the lobby of the Chamber of Deputies, but nowhere did I hear any news. Still, it was possible that Milord Hawkesbury had received it himself just as we had. He lived in Harley Street, and there it was that the treaty was to be finally signed that night at eight. I entreated *Monsieur* Otto to drink two glasses of Burgundy before he went, for I feared lest his haggard face and trembling hands should rouse suspicion in the English minister.

"Well, we went round together in one of the Embassy's carriages, about half-past seven. *Monsieur* Otto went in alone; but presently, on excuse of getting his portfolio, he came out again, with his cheeks flushed with joy, to tell me that all was well.

"'He knows nothing,' he whispered. 'Ah, if the next half-hour were over!'

"'Give me a sign when it is settled,' said I.

"'For what reason?'

"'Because until then no messenger shall interrupt you. I give you my promise
—I, Alphonse Lacour.'

"He clasped my hand in both of his. 'I shall make an excuse to move one of the candles on to the table in the window,' said he, and hurried into the house, whilst I was left waiting beside the carriage.

"Well, if we could but secure ourselves from interruption for a single half-hour the day would be our own. I had hardly begun to form my plans when I saw the lights of a carriage coming swiftly from the direction of Oxford Street. Ah, if it should be the messenger! What could I do? I was prepared to kill him— yes, even to kill him, rather than at this last moment allow our work to be undone. Thousands die to make a glorious war. Why should not one die to make a glorious peace? What though they hurried me to the scaffold? I should have sacrificed myself for my country. I had a little curved Turkish knife strapped to my waist. My hand was on the hilt of it when the carriage which had alarmed me so rattled safely past me.

"But another might come. I must be prepared. Above all, I must not compromise the Embassy. I ordered our carriage to move on, and I engaged what you call a hackney coach. Then I spoke to the driver, and gave him a guinea. He understood that it was a special service.

"'You shall have another guinea if you do what you are told,' said I.

"'All right, master,' said he, turning his slow eyes upon me without a trace of excitement or curiosity.

"'If I enter your coach with another gentleman, you will drive up and down Harley Street and take no orders from any one but me. When I get out, you will carry the other gentleman to Watier's Club in Bruton Street.'

"'All right, master,' said he again.

"So I stood outside Milord Hawkesbury's house, and you can think how often my eyes went up to that window in the hope of seeing the candle twinkle in it. Five minutes passed, and another five. Oh, how slowly they crept along! It was a true October night, raw and cold, with a white fog crawling over the wet, shining cobblestones, and blurring the dim oil-lamps. I could not see fifty paces in either direction, but my ears were straining, straining, to catch the rattle of hoofs, or the rumble of wheels. It is not a cheering place, *monsieur*, that Street of Harley, even upon a sunny day. The houses are solid and very respectable over yonder, but there is nothing of the feminine about them. It is a city to be inhabited by males. But on that raw night, amid the damp and the fog, with the anxiety gnawing at my heart, it seemed the saddest, weariest spot in the whole wide world. I paced up and down, slapping my hands to keep them warm, and still straining my ears. And then suddenly out of the dull hum of the traffic down in Oxford Street I heard a sound detach itself, and grow louder and louder, and clearer and clearer with every instant, until two yellow lights came flashing through the fog, and a light cabriolet whirled up to the door of the Foreign Minister. It had not stopped before a young fellow sprang out of it and hurried to the steps, while the driver turned his horse and rattled off into the fog once more.

"Ah, it is in the moment of action that I am best, *monsieur*. You, who only see me when I am drinking my wine in the Café de Provence, cannot conceive the heights to which I rise. At that moment, when I knew that the fruits of a ten-years' war were at stake, I was magnificent. It was the last French campaign, and I the General and army in one.

"'Sir,' said I, touching him upon the arm, 'are you the messenger for Lord Hawkesbury?'

"'Yes,' said he.

"'I have been waiting for you half an hour,' said I. 'You are to follow me at once. He is with the French Ambassador.'

"I spoke with such assurance that he never hesitated for an instant. When he entered the hackney coach and I followed him in, my heart gave such a thrill of joy that I could hardly keep from shouting aloud. He was a poor little creature, this Foreign Office messenger, not much bigger than *Monsieur* Otto, and I-*monsieur* can see my hands now, and imagine what they were like when I was seven-and-twenty years of age.

"Well, now that I had him in my coach, the question was what I should do with him. I did not wish to hurt him if I could help it.

"'This is a pressing business,' said he. 'I have a despatch which I must deliver instantly.'

"Our coach had rattled down Harley Street, but now, in accordance with my instruction, it turned and began to go up again.

"'Hello?' he cried. 'What's this?'

"'What then?' I asked.

"'We are driving back. Where is Lord Hawkesbury?'

"'We shall see him presently.'

"'Let me out!' he shouted. 'There's some trickery in this. Coachman, stop the coach! Let me out, I say!'

"I dashed him back into his seat as he tried to turn the handle of the door. He roared for help. I clapped my palm across his mouth. He made his teeth meet though the side of it. I seized his own cravat and bound it over his lips. He still mumbled and gurgled, but the noise was covered by the rattle of our wheels. We were passing the minister's house, and there was no candle in the window.

"The messenger sat quiet for a little, and I could see the glint of his eyes as he stared at me through the gloom. He was partly stunned, I think, by the force with which I had hurled him into his seat. And also he was pondering, perhaps, what he should do next. Presently he got his mouth partly free from the cravat.

"'You can have my watch and my purse if you will let me go,' said he.

"'Sir,' said I, 'I am as honourable a man as you are yourself.'

"'Who are you, then?'

"'My name is of no importance.'

"'What do you want with me?'

"'It is a bet.'

"'A bet? What d'you mean? Do you understand that I am on the Government service, and that you will see the inside of a jail for this?'

"'That is the bet. That is the sport,' said I.

"'You may find it poor sport before you finish,' he cried. 'What is this insane bet of yours, then?'

"'I have bet,' I answered, 'that I will recite a chapter of the Koran to the first gentleman whom I should meet in the street.'

"I do not know what made me think of it, save that my translation was always running in my head. He clutched at the doorhandle, and again I had to hurl him back into his seat.

"'How long will it take?' he gasped.

"'It depends on the chapter,' I answered.

"'A short one, then, and let me go!'

"'But is it fair?' I argued. 'When I say a chapter I do not mean the shortest chapter, but rather one which should be of average length.'

"'Help! help! help!' he squealed, and I was compelled again to adjust his cravat.

"'A little patience,' said I, 'and it will soon be over. I should like to recite the chapter which would be of most interest to yourself. You will confess that I am trying to make things as pleasant as I can for you?'

"He slipped his mouth free again.

"'Quick, then, quick!' he groaned.

"'The Chapter of the Camel?' I suggested.

"'Yes, yes.'

"'Or that of the Fleet Stallion?'

"'Yes, yes. Only proceed!'

"We had passed the window and there was no candle. I settled down to recite the Chapter of the Stallion to him.

"Perhaps you do not know your Koran very well, *monsieur?* Well, I knew it by heart then, as I know it by heart now. The style is a little exasperating for any one who is in a hurry. But, then, what would you have? The people in the East are never in a hurry, and it was written for them. I repeated it all with the dignity and solemnity which a sacred book demands, and the young Englishman he wriggled and groaned.

"'When the horses, standing on three feet and placing the tip of their fourth foot upon the ground, were mustered in front of him in the evening, he said, "I have loved the love of earthly good above the remembrance of things on high, and have spent the time in viewing these horses. Bring the horses back to me." And when they were brought back he began to cut off their legs and———'

"It was at this moment that the young Englishman sprang at me. My God! how little can I remember of the next few minutes! He was a boxer, this shred of a man. He had been trained to strike. I tried to catch him by the hands. Pac, pac, he came upon my nose and upon my eye. I put down my head and thrust at him with it. Pac, he came from below. But, ah! I was too much for him. I hurled myself upon him, and he had no place where he could escape from my weight. He fell flat upon the cushions, and I seated myself upon him with such conviction that the wind flew from him as from a burst bellows.

"Then I searched to see what there was with which I could tie him. I drew the strings from my shoes, and with one I secured his wrists, and with another his ankles. Then I tied the cravat round his mouth again, so that he could only lie and glare at me. When I had done all this, and had stopped the bleeding of my own nose, I looked out of the coach, and ah, *monsieur*, the very first thing which caught my eyes was that candle, that dear little candle, glimmering in the window of the minister. Alone, with these two hands, I had retrieved the capitulation of an army and the loss of a province. Yes, *monsieur*, what Abercrombie and five thousand men had done upon the beach at Aboukir was undone by me, single-handed, in a hackney coach in Harley Street.

"Well, I had no time to lose, for at any moment *Monsieur* Otto might be down. I shouted to my driver, gave him his second guinea, and allowed him to proceed to Watier's. For myself, I sprang into our Embassy carriage, and a moment later the door of the minister opened. He had himself escorted *Monsieur* Otto downstairs, and now so deep was he in talk that he walked out bareheaded as far as the carriage. As he stood there by the open door, there came the rattle of wheels, and a man rushed down the pavement.

"'A despatch of great importance for Milord Hawkesbury!' he cried.

"I could see that it was not my messenger, but a second one. Milord Hawkesbury caught the paper from his hand and read it by the light of the carriage lamp.

His face, *monsieur*, was as white as this plate before he had finished.

"'*Monsieur* Otto,' he cried,' we have signed this treaty upon a false understanding. Egypt is in our hands.'

"'What!' cried *Monsieur* Otto. 'Impossible!'

"'It is certain. It fell to Abercrombie last month.'

"'In that case,' said *Monsieur* Otto, 'it is very fortunate that the treaty is signed.'

"'Very fortunate for you, sir,' cried Milord Hawkesbury, and he turned back to the house.

"Next day, *monsieur*, what they call the Bow Street runners were after me, but they could not run across salt water, and Alphonse Lacour was receiving the congratulations of *Monsieur* Talleyrand and the first Consul before ever his pursuers had got as far as Dover."

A Straggler of '15

It was a dull October morning, and heavy, rolling fog-wreaths lay low over the wet grey roofs of the Woolwich houses. Down in the long, brick-lined streets all was sodden and greasy and cheerless. From the high dark buildings of the arsenal came the whirr of many wheels, the thudding of weights, and the buzz and babble of human toil. Beyond, the dwellings of the workingmen, smoke-stained and unlovely, radiated away in a lessening perspective of narrowing road and dwindling wall.

There were few folk in the streets, for the toilers had all been absorbed since break of day by the huge smoke-spouting monster, which sucked in the manhood of the town, to belch it forth weary and work-stained every night. Little groups of children straggled to school, or loitered to peep through the single, front windows at the big, gilt-edged Bibles, balanced upon small, three-legged tables, which were their usual adornment. Stout women, with thick, red arms and dirty aprons, stood upon the whitened doorsteps, leaning upon their brooms, and shrieking their morning greetings across the road. One stouter, redder, and dirtier than the rest, had gathered a small knot of cronies around her and was talking energetically, with little shrill titters from her audience to punctuate her remarks.

"Old enough to know better!" she cried, in answer to an exclamation from one of the listeners. "If he hain't no sense now, I 'specs he won't learn much on this side o' Jordan. Why, 'ow old is he at all? Blessed if I could ever make out."

"Well, it ain't so hard to reckon," said a sharp-featured pale-faced woman with watery blue eyes. "He's been at the battle o' Waterloo, and has the pension and medal to prove it."

"That were a ter'ble long time agone," remarked a third. "It were afore I were born."

"It were fifteen year after the beginnin' of the century," cried a younger woman, who had stood leaning against the wall, with a smile of superior knowledge upon her face. "My Bill was a-saying so last Sabbath, when I spoke to him o' old Daddy Brewster, here."

"And suppose he spoke truth, Missus Simpson, 'ow long agone do that make it?"

"It's eighty-one now," said the original speaker, checking off the years upon her coarse red fingers, "and that were fifteen. Ten and ten, and ten, and ten, and ten—why, it's only sixty-and-six year, so he ain't so old after all."

"But he weren't a newborn babe at the battle, silly!" cried the young woman with a chuckle. "S'pose he were only twenty, then he couldn't be less than six-and-eighty now, at the lowest."

"Aye, he's that—every day of it," cried several.

"I've had 'bout enough of it," remarked the large woman gloomily. "Unless his young niece, or grandniece, or whatever she is, come today, I'm off, and he can find some one else to do his work. Your own 'ome first, says I."

"Ain't he quiet, then, Missus Simpson?" asked the youngest of the group.

"Listen to him now," she answered, with her hand half raised and her head turned slantwise towards the open door. From the upper floor there came a shuffling, sliding sound with a sharp tapping of a stick. "There he go back and forrards, doing what he call his sentry go. 'Arf the night through he's at that game, the silly old juggins. At six o'clock this very mornin' there he was beatin' with a stick at my door. 'Turn out, guard!' he cried, and a lot more jargon that I could make nothing of. Then what with his coughin' and 'awkin' and spittin', there ain't no gettin' a wink o' sleep. Hark to him now!"

"Missus Simpson, Missus Simpson!" cried a cracked and querulous voice from above.

"That's him!" she cried, nodding her head with an air of triumph. "He do go on somethin' scandalous. Yes, Mr. Brewster, sir."

"I want my morning ration, Missus Simpson."

"It's just ready, Mr. Brewster, sir."

"Blessed if he ain't like a baby cryin' for its pap," said the young woman.

"I feel as if I could shake his old bones up sometimes!" cried Mrs. Simpson viciously. "But who's for a 'arf of fourpenny?"

The whole company were about to shuffle off to the public house, when a young girl stepped across the road and touched the housekeeper timidly upon the arm. "I think that is No. 56 Arsenal View," she said. "Can you tell me if Mr. Brewster lives here?"

The housekeeper looked critically at the newcomer. She was a girl of about twenty, broad-faced and comely, with a turned-up nose and large, honest grey eyes. Her print dress, her straw hat, with its bunch of glaring poppies, and the bundle she carried, had all a smack of the country.

"You're Norah Brewster, I s'pose," said Mrs. Simpson, eyeing her up and down with no friendly gaze.

"Yes, I've come to look after my Granduncle Gregory."

"And a good job too," cried the housekeeper, with a toss of her head. "It's about time that some of his own folk took a turn at it, for I've had enough of it. There you are, young woman! In you go and make yourself at home. There's tea in the caddy and bacon on the dresser, and the old man will be about you if you don't fetch him his breakfast. I'll send for my things in the evenin'." With a nod she strolled off with her attendant gossips in the direction of the public house.

Thus left to her own devices, the country girl walked into the front room and took off her hat and jacket. It was a low-roofed apartment with a sputtering fire upon which a small brass kettle was singing cheerily. A stained cloth lay over half the table, with an empty brown teapot, a loaf of bread, and some coarse crockery. Norah Brewster looked rapidly about her, and in an instant took over her new duties. Ere five minutes had passed the tea was made, two slices of bacon were frizzling on the pan, the table was rearranged, the antimacassars straightened over the sombre brown furniture, and the whole room had taken a new air of comfort and neatness. This done she looked round curiously at the prints upon the walls. Over the fireplace, in a small, square case, a brown medal caught her eye, hanging from a strip of purple ribbon. Beneath was a slip of newspaper cutting. She stood on her tiptoes, with her fingers on the edge of the mantelpiece, and craned her neck up to see it, glancing down from time to time at the bacon which simmered and hissed beneath her. The cutting was yellow with age, and ran in this way:

On Tuesday an interesting ceremony was performed at the barracks of the Third Regiment of Guards, when, in the presence of the Prince Regent, Lord Hill, Lord Saltoun, and an assemblage which comprised beauty as well as valour, a special medal was presented to Corporal Gregory Brewster, of Captain Haldane's flank company, in recognition of his gallantry in the recent great battle in the Lowlands. It appears that on the ever-memorable 18th of June four companies of the Third Guards and of the Coldstreams, under the command of Colonels Maitland and Byng, held the important farmhouse of Hougoumont at the right of the British position. At a critical point of the action these troops found themselves short of powder. Seeing that Generals Foy and Jerome Buonaparte were again massing their infantry for an attack on the position, Colonel Byng dispatched Corporal Brewster to the rear to hasten up the reserve ammunition. Brewster came upon two powder tumbrels of the Nassau division, and succeeded, after menacing the drivers with his musket, in inducing them to convey their powder to Hougoumont. In his absence, however, the hedges surrounding the position had been set on fire by a howitzer battery of the French, and the passage of the carts full of powder became a most hazardous matter. The first tumbrel exploded, blowing the driver to fragments. Daunted by the fate of his comrade, the second driver turned his horses, but Corporal Brewster, springing upon his seat, hurled the man down, and urging the powder cart through the flames, succeeded in forcing his way to his companions. To this gallant deed may be directly attributed the success of the British arms, for without powder it would have been impossible to have held Hougoumont, and the Duke of Wellington had repeatedly declared that had Hougoumont fallen, as well as La Haye Sainte, he would have found it impossible to have held his ground. Long may the heroic Brewster live to treasure the medal which he has so bravely won, and to look back with pride to the day when, in the presence of his comrades, he received this tribute to his valour from the august hands of the first gentleman of the realm.

The reading of this old cutting increased in the girl's mind the veneration which she had always had for her warrior kinsman. From her infancy he had been her hero, and she remembered how her father used to speak of his courage and his strength, how he could strike down a bullock with a blow of his fist and carry a fat sheep under either arm. True, she had never seen him, but a rude painting at home which depicted a square-faced, clean shaven, stalwart man with a great bearskin cap, rose ever before her memory when she thought of him.

She was still gazing at the brown medal and wondering what the *"Dulce et decorum est"* might mean, which was inscribed upon the edge, when there came a sudden tapping and shuffling upon the stair, and there at the door was standing the very man who had been so often in her thoughts.

But could this indeed be he? Where was the martial air, the flashing eye, the warrior face which she had pictured? There, framed in the doorway, was a huge twisted old man, gaunt and puckered, with twitching hands and shuffling, purposeless feet. A cloud of fluffy white hair, a red-veined nose, two thick tufts of eyebrow and a pair of dimly questioning, watery blue eyes— these were what met her gaze. He leaned forward upon a stick, while his shoulders rose and fell with his crackling, rasping breathing.

"I want my morning rations," he crooned, as he stumped

forward to his chair. "The cold nips me without 'em. See to my fingers!" He held out his distorted hands, all blue at the tips, wrinkled and gnarled, with huge, projecting knuckles.

"It's nigh ready," answered the girl, gazing at him with wonder in her eyes. "Don't you know who I am, granduncle? I am Norah Brewster from Witham."

"Rum is warm," mumbled the old man, rocking to and fro in his chair, "and schnapps is warm, and there's 'eat in soup, but it's a dish o' tea for me. What did you say your name was?"

"Norah Brewster."

"You can speak out, lass. Seems to me folk's voices isn't as loud as they used."

"I'm Norah Brewster, uncle. I'm your grandniece come down from Essex way to live with you."

"You'll be brother Jarge's girl! Lor', to think o' little Jarge having a girl!" He chuckled hoarsely to himself, and the long, stringy sinews of his throat jerked and quivered.

"I am the daughter of your brother George's son," said she, as she turned the bacon.

"Lor, but little Jarge was a rare un!" he continued. "Eh, by Jimini, there was no chousing Jarge. He's got a bull pup o' mine that I gave him when I took the bounty. You've heard him speak of it, likely?"

"Why, grandpa George has been dead this twenty year," said she, pouring out the tea.

"Well, it was a bootiful pup—aye, a well-bred un, by Jimini! I'm cold for lack o' my rations. Rum is good, and so is schnapps, but I'd as lief have tea as either."

He breathed heavily while he devoured his food. "It's a middlin' goodish way you've come," said he at last. "Likely the stage left yesternight."

"The what, uncle?"

"The coach that brought you."

"Nay, I came by the mornin' train."

"Lor, now, think o' that! You ain't afeard o' those newfangled things! By Jimini, to think of you comin' by railroad like that! What's the world a-comin' to!"

297

There was silence for some minutes while Norah sat stirring her tea and glancing sideways at the bluish lips and champing jaws of her companion.

"You must have seen a deal o' life, uncle," said she. "It must seem a long, long time to you!"

"Not so very long neither. I'm ninety, come Candlemas; but it don't seem long since I took the bounty. And that battle, it might have been yesterday. Eh, but I get a power o' good from my rations!" He did indeed look less worn and colourless than when she first saw him. His face was flushed and his back more erect.

"Have you read that?" he asked, jerking his head towards the cutting.

"Yes, uncle, and I'm sure you must be proud of it."

"Ah, it was a great day for me! A great day! The Regent was there, and a fine body of a man too! 'The ridgment is proud of you,' says he. 'And I'm proud of the ridgment,' say I. 'A damned good answer too!' says he to Lord Hill, and they both bu'st out a-laughin'. But what be you a-peepin' out o' the window for?"

"Oh, uncle, here's a regiment of soldiers coming down the street with the band playing in front of them."

"A ridgment, eh? Where be my glasses? Lor, but I can hear the band, as plain as plain! Here's the pioneers an' the drum-major! What be their number, lass?" His eyes were shining and his bony yellow fingers, like the claws of some fierce old bird, dug into her shoulder.

"They don't seem to have no number, uncle. They've something wrote on their shoulders. Oxfordshire, I think it be."

"Ah, yes!" he growled. "I heard as they'd dropped the numbers and given them newfangled names. There they go, by Jimini! They're young mostly, but they hain't forgot how to march. They have the swing-aye, I'll say that for them. They've got the swing." He gazed after them until the last files had turned the corner and the measured tramp of their marching had died away in the distance.

He had just regained his chair when the door opened and a gentleman stepped in.

"Ah, Mr. Brewster! Better today?" he asked.

"Come in, doctor! Yes, I'm better. But there's a deal o' bubbling in my chest. It's all them toobes. If I could but cut the phlegm, I'd be right. Can't you give me something to cut the phlegm?"

The doctor, a grave-faced young man, put his fingers to the furrowed, blue-corded wrist.

"You must be careful," he said. "You must take no liberties." The thin tide of life seemed to thrill rather than to throb under his finger.

The old man chuckled.

"I've got brother Jarge's girl to look after me now. She'll see I don't break barracks or do what I hadn't ought to. Why, darn my skin, I knew something was amiss!

"With what?"

"Why, with them soldiers. You saw them pass, doctor—eh? They'd forgot their stocks. Not one on 'em had his stock on." He croaked and chuckled for a long time over his discovery. "It wouldn't ha' done for the Dook!" he muttered. "No, by Jimini! the Dook would ha' had a word there."

The doctor smiled. "Well, you are doing very well," said he. "I'll look in once a week or so, and see how you are." As Norah followed him to the door, he beckoned her outside.

"He is very weak," he whispered. "If you find him failing you must send for me."

"What ails him, doctor?"

"Ninety years ails him. His arteries are pipes of lime. His heart is shrunken and flabby. The man is worn out."

Norah stood watching the brisk figure of the young doctor, and pondering over these new responsibilities which had come upon her. When she turned a tall, brown-faced artilleryman, with the three gold chevrons of sergeant upon his arm, was standing, carbine in hand, at her elbow.

"Good-morning, miss," said he, raising one thick finger to his jaunty, yellow-banded cap. "I b'lieve there's an old gentleman lives here of the name of Brewster, who was engaged in the battle o' Waterloo?"

"It's my granduncle, sir," said Norah, casting down her eyes before the keen, critical gaze of the young soldier. "He is in the front parlour."

"Could I have a word with him, miss? I'll call again if it don't chance to be convenient."

"I am sure that he would be very glad to see you, sir. He's in here, if you'll step in. Uncle, here's a gentleman who wants to speak with you."

"Proud to see you, sir—proud and glad, sir," cried the sergeant, taking three steps forward into the room, and grounding his carbine while he raised his hand, palm forwards, in a salute. Norah stood by the door, with her mouth and eyes open, wondering if her granduncle had ever, in his prime, looked like this magnificent creature, and whether he, in his turn, would ever come to resemble her granduncle.

The old man blinked up at his visitor, and shook his head slowly.

"Sit ye down, sergeant," said he, pointing with his stick to a chair. "You're full young for the stripes. Lordy, it's easier to get three now than one in my day. Gunners were old soldiers then and the grey hairs came quicker than the three stripes."

"I am eight years' service, sir," cried the sergeant. "Macdonald is my name—Sergeant Macdonald, of H Battery, Southern Artillery Division. I have called as the spokesman of my mates at the gunner's barracks to say that we are proud to have you in the town, sir."

Old Brewster chuckled and rubbed his bony hands. "That were what the Regent said," he cried. "'The ridgment is proud of ye,' says he. 'And I am proud of the ridgment,' says I. 'And a damned good answer too,' says he, and he and Lord Hill bu'st out a-laughin'."

"The non-commissioned mess would be proud and honoured to see you, sir," said Sergeant Macdonald; "and if you could step as far you'll always find a pipe o' baccy and a glass o' grog a-waitin' you."

The old man laughed until he coughed. "Like to see me, would they? The dogs!" said he. "Well, well, when the warm weather comes again I'll maybe drop in. Too grand for a canteen, eh? Got your mess just the same as the orficers. What's the world a-comin' to at all!"

"You was in the line, sir, was you not?" asked the sergeant respectfully.

"The line?" cried the old man, with shrill scorn. "Never wore a shako in my life. I am a guardsman, I am. Served in the Third Guards—the same they call now the Scots Guards. Lordy, but they have all marched away—every man of them—from old Colonel Byng down to the drummer boys, and here am I a straggler—that's what I am, sergeant, a straggler! I'm here when I ought to be there. But it ain't my fault neither, for I'm ready to fall in when the word comes."

"We've all got to muster there," answered the sergeant. "Won't you try my baccy, sir?" handing over a sealskin pouch.

Old Brewster drew a blackened clay pipe from his pocket, and began to stuff the tobacco into the bowl. In an instant it slipped through his fingers, and was broken to pieces on the floor. His lip quivered, his nose puckered up, and he began crying with the long, helpless sobs of a child. "I've broke my pipe," he cried.

"Don't, uncle; oh, don't!" cried Norah, bending over him, and patting his white head as one soothes a baby. "It don't matter. We can easy get another."

"Don't you fret yourself, sir," said the sergeant. "'Ere's a wooden pipe with an amber mouth, if you'll do me the honour to accept it from me. I'd be real glad if you will take it."

"Jimini!" cried he, his smiles breaking in an instant through his tears. "It's a fine pipe. See to my new pipe, Norah. I lay that Jarge never had a pipe like that. You've got your firelock there, sergeant?"

"Yes, sir. I was on my way back from the butts when I looked in."

"Let me have the feel of it. Lordy, but it seems like old times to have one's hand on a musket. What's the manual, sergeant, eh? Cock your firelock—look to your priming—present your firelock—eh, sergeant? Oh, Jimini, I've broke your musket in halves!"

"That's all right, sir," cried the gunner laughing. "You pressed on the lever and opened the breech-piece. That's where we load 'em, you know."

"Load 'em at the wrong end! Well, well, to think o' that! And no ramrod neither! I've heard tell of it, but I never believed it afore. Ah! it won't come up to brown Bess. When there's work to be done, you mark my word and see if they don't come back to brown Bess."

"By the Lord, sir!" cried the sergeant hotly, "they need some change out in South Africa now. I see by this mornin's paper that the Government has knuckled under to these Boers. They're hot about it at the non-com. mess, I can tell you, sir."

"Eh—eh," croaked old Brewster. "By Jimini! it wouldn't ha' done for the Dook; the Dook would ha' had a word to say over that."

"Ah, that he would, sir!" cried the sergeant; "and God send us another like him. But I've wearied you enough for one sitting. I'll look in again, and I'll bring a comrade or two with me, if I may, for there isn't one but would be proud to have speech with you."

So, with another salute to the veteran and a gleam of white teeth at Norah, the big gunner withdrew, leaving a memory of blue cloth and of gold braid behind him. Many days had not passed, however, before he was back again, and during all the long winter he was a frequent visitor at Arsenal View. There came a time, at last, when it might be doubted to which of the two occupants his visits were directed, nor was it hard to say by which he was most anxiously awaited. He brought others with him; and soon, through all the lines, a pilgrimage to Daddy Brewster's came to be looked upon as the proper thing to do. Gunners and sappers, linesmen and dragoons, came bowing and bobbing into the little parlour, with clatter of side arms and clink of spurs, stretching their long legs across the patchwork rug, and hunting in the front of their tunics for the screw of tobacco or paper of snuff which they had brought as a sign of their esteem.

It was a deadly cold winter, with six weeks on end of snow

on the ground, and Norah had a hard task to keep the life in that time-worn body. There were times when his mind would leave him, and when, save an animal outcry when the hour of his meals came round, no word would fall from him. He was a white-haired child, with all a child's troubles and emotions. As the warm weather came once more, however, and the green buds peeped forth again upon the trees, the blood thawed in his veins, and he would even drag himself as far as the door to bask in the life-giving sunshine.

"It do hearten me up so," he said one morning, as he glowed in the hot May sun. "It's a job to keep back the flies, though. They get owdacious in this weather, and they do plague me cruel."

"I'll keep them off you, uncle," said Norah.

"Eh, but it's fine! This sunshine makes me think o' the glory to come. You might read me a bit o' the Bible, lass. I find it wonderful soothing."

"What part would you like, uncle?"

"Oh, them wars."

"The wars?"

"Aye, keep to the wars! Give me the Old Testament for choice. There's more taste to it, to my mind. When parson comes he wants to get off to something else; but it's Joshua or nothing with me. Them Israelites was good soldiers—good growed soldiers, all of 'em."

"But, uncle," pleaded Norah, "it's all peace in the next world."

"No, it ain't, gal."

"Oh, yes, uncle, surely!"

The old corporal knocked his stick irritably upon the ground. "I tell ye it ain't, gal. I asked parson."

"Well, what did he say?"

"He said there was to be a last fight. He even gave it a name, he did. The battle of Arm—Arm——"

"Armageddon."

"Aye, that's the name parson said. I 'specs the Third Guards'll be there. And the Dook—the Dook'll have a word to say."

303

An elderly, grey-whiskered gentleman had been walking down the street, glancing up at the numbers of the houses. Now as his eyes fell upon the old man, he came straight for him.

"Hullo!" said he; "perhaps you are Gregory Brewster?"

"My name, sir," answered the veteran.

"You are the same Brewster, as I understand, who is on the roll of the Scots Guards as having been present at the battle of Waterloo?"

"I am that man, sir, though we called it the Third Guards in those days. It was a fine ridgment, and they only need me to make up a full muster."

"Tut, tut! they'll have to wait years for that," said the gentleman heartily. "But I am the colonel of the Scots Guards, and I thought I would like to have a word with you."

Old Gregory Brewster was up in an instant, with his hand to his rabbit-skin cap. "God bless me!" he cried, "to think of it! to think of it!"

"Hadn't the gentleman better come in?" suggested the practical Norah from behind the door.

"Surely, sir, surely; walk in, sir, if I may be so bold." In his excitement he had forgotten his stick, and as he led the way into the parlour his knees tottered, and he threw out his hands. In an instant the colonel had caught him on one side and Norah on the other.

"Easy and steady," said the colonel, as he led him to his chair.

"Thank ye, sir; I was near gone that time. But, Lordy I why, I can scarce believe it. To think of me the corporal of the flank company and you the colonel of the battalion! How things come round, to be sure!"

"Why, we are very proud of you in London," said the colonel. "And so you are actually one of the men who held Hougoumont." He looked at the bony, trembling hands, with their huge, knotted knuckles, the stringy throat, and the heaving, rounded shoulders. Could this, indeed, be the last of that band of heroes? Then he glanced at the half-filled phials, the blue liniment bottles, the long-spouted kettle, and the sordid details of the sick room. "Better, surely, had he died under the blazing rafters of the Belgian farmhouse," thought the colonel.

"I hope that you are pretty comfortable and happy," he remarked after a pause.

"Thank ye, sir. I have a good deal o' trouble with my toobes—a deal o' trouble. You wouldn't think the job it is to cut the phlegm. And I need my rations. I gets cold without 'em. And the flies! I ain't strong enough to fight against them."

"How's the memory?" asked the colonel.

"Oh, there ain't nothing amiss there. Why, sir, I could give you the name of every man in Captain Haldane's flank company."

"And the battle—you remember it?"

"Why, I sees it all afore me every time I shuts my eyes. Lordy, sir, you wouldn't hardly believe how clear it is to me. There's our line from the paregoric bottle right along to the snuff box. D'ye see? Well, then, the pill box is for Hougoumont on the right—where we was—and Norah's thimble for La Haye Sainte. There it is, all right, sir; and here were our guns, and here behind the reserves and the Belgians. Ach, them Belgians!" He spat furiously into the fire. "Then here's the French, where my pipe lies; and over here, where I put my baccy pouch, was the Proosians a-comin' up on our left flank. Jimini, but it was a glad sight to see the smoke of their guns!"

"And what was it that struck you most now in connection with the whole affair?" asked the colonel.

"I lost three half-crowns over it, I did," crooned old Brewster. "I shouldn't wonder if I was never to get that money now. I lent 'em to Jabez Smith, my rear rank man, in Brussels. 'Only till payday, Grig,' says he. By Gosh! he was stuck by a lancer at Quatre Bras, and me with not so much as a slip o' paper to prove the debt! Them three half-crowns is as good as lost to me."

The colonel rose from his chair laughing. "The officers of the Guards want you to buy yourself some little trifle which may add to your comfort," he said. "It is not from me, so you need not thank me." He took up the old man's tobacco pouch and slipped a crisp banknote inside it.

"Thank ye kindly, sir. But there's one favour that I would like to ask you, colonel."

"Yes, my man."

"If I'm called, colonel, you won't grudge me a flag and a firing party? I'm not a civilian; I'm a guardsman—I'm the last of the old Third Guards."

"All right, my man, I'll see to it," said the colonel. "Good-bye; I hope to have nothing but good news from you."

"A kind gentleman, Norah," croaked old Brewster, as they saw him walk past the window; "but, Lordy, he ain't fit to hold the stirrup o' my Colonel Byng!"

It was on the very next day that the old corporal took a sudden change for the worse. Even the golden sunlight streaming through the window seemed unable to warm that withered frame. The doctor came and shook his head in silence. All day the man lay with only his puffing blue lips and the twitching of his scraggy neck to show that he still held the breath of life. Norah and Sergeant Macdonald had sat by him in the afternoon, but he had shown no consciousness of their presence. He lay peacefully, his eyes half closed, his hands under his cheek, as one who is very weary.

They had left him for an instant and were sitting in the front room, where Norah was preparing tea, when of a sudden they heard a shout that rang through the house. Loud and clear and swelling, it pealed in their ears—a voice full of strength and energy and fiery passion. "The Guards need powder!" it cried; and yet again, "The Guards need powder!"

The sergeant sprang from his chair and rushed in, followed by the trembling Norah. There was the old man standing up, his blue eyes sparkling, his white hair bristling, his whole figure towering and expanding, with eagle head and glance of fire. "The Guards need powder!" he thundered once again, "and, by God, they shall have it!" He threw up his long arms, and sank back with a groan into his chair. The sergeant stooped over him, and his face darkened.

"Oh, Archie, Archie," sobbed the frightened girl, "what do you think of him?"

The sergeant turned away. "I think," said he, "that the Third Guards have a full muster now."

The "Slapping Sal"

It was in the days when France's power was already broken upon the seas, and when more of her three-deckers lay rotting in the Medway than were to be found in Brest harbour. But her frigates and corvettes still scoured the ocean, closely followed ever by those of her rival. At the uttermost ends of the earth these dainty vessels, with sweet names of girls or of flowers, mangled and shattered each other for the honour of the four yards of bunting which flapped from the end of their gaffs.

It had blown hard in the night, but the wind had dropped with the dawning, and now the rising sun tinted the fringe of the storm-wrack as it dwindled into the west and glinted on the endless crests of the long, green waves. To north and south and west lay a skyline which was unbroken save by the spout of foam when two of the great Atlantic seas dashed each other into spray. To the east was a rocky island, jutting out into craggy points, with a few scattered clumps of palm trees and a pennant of mist streaming out from the bare, conical hill which capped it. A heavy surf beat upon the shore, and, at a safe distance from it, the British 32-gun frigate *Leda*, Captain A. P. Johnson, raised her black, glistening side upon the crest of a wave, or swooped down into an emerald valley, dipping away to the nor'ard under easy sail. On her snow-white quarter-deck stood a stiff little brown-faced man, who swept the horizon with his glass.

"Mr. Wharton!" he cried, with a voice like a rusty hinge.

A thin, knock-kneed officer shambled across the poop to him.

"Yes, sir."

"I've opened the sealed orders, Mr. Wharton."

A glimmer of curiosity shone upon the meagre features of the first lieutenant. The *Leda* had sailed with her consort, the *Dido*, from Antigua the week before, and the admiral's orders had been contained in a sealed envelope.

"We were to open them on reaching the deserted island of Sombriero, lying in north latitude eighteen, thirty-six, west longitude sixty-three, twenty-eight. Sombriero bore four miles to the north-east from our port-bow when the gale cleared, Mr. Wharton."

The lieutenant bowed stiffly. He and the captain had been bosom friends from childhood. They had gone to school together, joined the navy together, fought again and again together, and married into each other's families, but so long as their feet were on the poop the iron discipline of the service struck all that was human out of them and left only the superior and the subordinate. Captain Johnson took from his pocket a blue paper, which crackled as he unfolded it.

> The 32-gun frigates *Leda* and *Dido* (Captains A. P. Johnson and James Munro) are to cruise from the point at which these instructions are read to the mouth of the Caribbean Sea, in the hope of encountering the French frigate *La Gloire* (48), which has recently harassed our merchant ships in that quarter. H.M. frigates are also directed to hunt down the piratical craft known sometimes as the *Slapping Sal* and sometimes as the *Hairy Hudson*, which has plundered the British ships as per margin, inflicting barbarities upon their crews. She is a small brig, carrying ten light guns, with one twenty-four pound carronade forward. She was last seen upon the 23rd ult. to the north-east of the island of Sombriero.
>
> (Signed) *James Montgomery*
> Rear-Admiral, H.M.S. *Colossus*
> Antigua

"We appear to have lost our consort," said Captain Johnson, folding up his instructions and again sweeping the horizon with his glass. "She drew away after we reefed down. It would be a pity if we met this heavy Frenchman without the *Dido*, Mr. Wharton. Eh?"

The lieutenant twinkled and smiled.

"She has eighteen-pounders on the main and twelves on the poop, sir," said the captain. "She carries four hundred to our two hundred and thirty-one. Captain de Milon is the smartest man in the French service. Oh, Bobby boy, I'd give my hopes of my flag to rub my side up against her!" He turned on his heel, ashamed of his momentary lapse. "Mr. Wharton," said he, looking back sternly over his shoulder, "get those square sails shaken out and bear away a point more to the west."

"A brig on the port-bow," came a voice from the forecastle.

"A brig on the port-bow," said the lieutenant.

The captain sprang upon the bulwarks and held on by the mizzen-shrouds, a strange little figure with flying skirts and puckered eyes. The lean lieutenant craned his neck and whispered to Smeaton, the second, while officers and men came popping up from below and clustered along the weather-rail, shading their eyes with their hands—for the tropical sun was already clear of the palm trees. The strange brig lay at anchor in the throat of a curving estuary, and it was already obvious that she could not get out without passing under the guns of the frigate. A long, rocky point to the north of her held her in.

"Keep her as she goes, Mr. Wharton," said the captain. "Hardly worth while our clearing for action, Mr. Smeaton, but the men can stand by the guns in case she tries to pass us. Cast loose the bow-chasers and send the small-arm men to the forecastle."

A British crew went to its quarters in those days with the quiet serenity of men on their daily routine. In a few minutes, without fuss or sound, the sailors were knotted round their guns, the marines were drawn up and leaning on their muskets, and the frigate's bowsprit pointed straight for her little victim.

"Is it the *Slapping Sal*, sir?"

"I have no doubt of it, Mr. Wharton."

"They don't seem to like the look of us, sir. They've cut their cable and are clapping on sail."

It was evident that the brig meant struggling for her freedom. One little patch of canvas fluttered out above another, and her people could be seen working like madmen in the rigging. She made no attempt to pass her antagonist, but headed up the estuary. The captain rubbed his hands.

"She's making for shoal water, Mr. Wharton, and we shall have to cut her out, sir. She's a footy little brig, but I should have thought a fore-and-after would have been more handy."

"It was a mutiny, sir."

"Ah, indeed!"

"Yes, sir, I heard of it at Manila: a bad business, sir. Captain and two mates murdered. This Hudson, or Hairy Hudson as they call him, led the mutiny. He's a Londoner, sir, and a cruel villain as ever walked."

"His next walk will be to Execution Dock, Mr. Wharton. She seems heavily manned. I wish I could take twenty topmen out of her, but they would be enough to corrupt the crew of the ark, Mr. Wharton."

Both officers were looking through their glasses at the brig. Suddenly the lieutenant showed his teeth in a grin, while the captain flushed a deeper red.

"That's Hairy Hudson on the after-rail, sir."

"The low, impertinent blackguard! He'll play some other antics before we are done with him. Could you reach him with the long eighteen, Mr. Smeaton?"

"Another cable length will do it, sir."

The brig yawed as they spoke, and as she came round a spurt of smoke whiffed out from her quarter. It was a pure piece of bravado, for the gun could scarce carry halfway. Then with a jaunty swing the little ship came into the wind again, and shot round a fresh curve in the winding channel. "The water's shoaling rapidly, sir," repeated the second lieutenant.

"There's six fathoms by the chart."

"Four by the lead, sir."

"When we clear this point we shall see how we lie. Ha! I thought as much! Lay her to, Mr. Wharton. Now we have got her at our mercy!"

The frigate was quite out of sight of the sea now at the head of this river-like estuary. As she came round the curve the two shores were seen to converge at a point about a mile distant. In the angle, as near shore as she could get, the brig was lying with her broadside towards her pursuer and a wisp of black cloth streaming from her mizzen. The lean lieutenant, who had reappeared upon deck with a cutlass strapped to his side and two pistols rammed into his belt, peered curiously at the ensign.

"Is it the Jolly Rodger, sir?" he asked.

But the captain was furious.

"He may hang where his breeches are hanging before I have done with him!" said he. "What boats will you want, Mr. Wharton?"

"We should do it with the launch and the jolly-boat."

"Take four and make a clean job of it. Pipe away the crews at once, and I'll work her in and help you with the long eighteens."

With a rattle of ropes and a creaking of blocks the four boats splashed into the water. Their crews clustered thickly into them: bare-footed sailors, stolid marines, laughing middies, and in the sheets of each the senior officers with their stern schoolmaster faces. The captain, his elbows on the binnacle, still watched the distant brig. Her crew were tricing up the boarding-netting, dragging round the starboard guns, knocking new portholes for them, and making every preparation for a desperate resistance. In the thick of it all a huge man, bearded to the eyes, with a red nightcap upon his head, was straining and stooping and hauling. The captain watched him with a sour smile, and then snapping up his glass he turned upon his heel. For an instant he stood staring.

"Call back the boats!" he cried in his thin, creaking voice. "Clear away for action there! Cast loose those main-deck guns. Brace back the yards, Mr. Smeaton, and stand by to go about when she has weigh enough."

Round the curve of the estuary was coming a huge vessel. Her great yellow bowsprit and white-winged figure-head were jutting out from the cluster of palm trees, while high above them towered three immense masts with the tricolour flag floating superbly from the mizzen. Round she came, the deep-blue water creaming under her fore foot, until her long, curving, black side, her line of shining copper beneath and of snow-white hammocks above, and the thick clusters of men who peered over her bulwarks were all in full view. Her lower yards were slung, her ports triced up, and her guns run out all ready for action. Lying behind one of the promontories of the island, the lookout men of the *Gloire* upon the shore had seen the *cul de sac* into which the British frigate was headed, so that Captain de Milon had served the *Leda* as Captain Johnson had the *Slapping Sal*.

But the splendid discipline of the British service was at its best in such a crisis. The boats flew back; their crews clustered aboard; they were swung up at the davits and the fall-ropes made fast. Hammocks were brought up and stowed, bulkheads sent down, ports and magazines opened, the fires put out in the galley, and the drums beat to quarters. Swarms of men set the headsails and brought the frigate round, while the gun-crews threw off their jackets and shirts, tightened their belts, and ran out their eighteen-pounders, peering through the open portholes at the stately French man. The wind was very light. Hardly a ripple showed itself upon the clear blue water, but the sails blew gently out as the breeze came over the wooded banks. The Frenchman had gone about also, and both ships were now heading slowly for the sea under fore-and-aft canvas, the *Gloire* a hundred yards in advance. She luffed up to cross the *Leda's* bows, but the British ship came round also, and the two rippled slowly on in such a silence that the ringing of the ramrods as the French marines drove home their charges clanged quite loudly upon the ear.

"Not much sea-room, Mr. Wharton," remarked the captain.

"I have fought actions in less, sir."

"We must keep our distance and trust to our gunnery. She is very heavily manned, and if she got alongside we might find ourselves in trouble."

"I see the shakoes of soldiers aboard other."

"Two companies of light infantry from Martinique. Now we have her! Hard-a-port, and let her have it as we cross her stern!"

The keen eye of the little commander had seen the surface

ripple, which told of a passing breeze. He had used it to dart across the big Frenchman and to rake her with every gun as he passed. But, once past her, the *Leda* had to come back into the wind to keep out of shoal water. The manoeuvre brought her on to the starboard side of the Frenchman, and the trim little frigate seemed to heel right over under the crashing broadside which burst from the gaping ports. A moment later her topmen were swarming aloft to set her top-sails and royals, and she strove to cross the *Gloire's* bows and rake her again. The French captain, however, brought his frigate's head round, and the two rode side by side within easy pistol-shot, pouring broadsides into each other in one of those murderous duels which, could they all be recorded, would mottle our charts with blood.

In that heavy tropical air, with so faint a breeze, the smoke formed a thick bank round the two vessels, from which the topmasts only protruded. Neither could see anything of its enemy save the throbs of fire in the darkness, and the guns were sponged and trained and fired into a dense wall of vapour. On the poop and the forecastle the marines, in two little red lines, were pouring in their volleys, but neither they nor the seamen-gunners could see what effect their fire was having. Nor, indeed, could they tell how far they were suffering themselves, for, standing at a gun, one could but hazily see that upon the right and the left. But above the roar of the cannon came the sharper sound of the piping shot, the crashing of riven planks, and the occasional heavy thud as spar or block came hurtling on to the deck. The lieutenants paced up and down the line of guns, while Captain Johnson fanned the smoke away with his cocked-hat and peered eagerly out.

"This is rare, Bobby!" said he, as the lieutenant joined him. Then, suddenly restraining himself, "What have we lost, Mr. Wharton?"

"Our maintopsail yard and our gaff, sir."

"Where's the flag?"

"Gone overboard, sir."

"They'll think we've struck! Lash a boat's ensign on the starboard arm of the mizzen cross-jack-yard."

"Yes, sir."

A round-shot dashed the binnacle to pieces between them. A second knocked two marines into a bloody palpitating mash. For a moment the smoke rose, and the English captain saw that his adversary's heavier metal was producing a horrible effect. The *Leda* was a shattered wreck. Her deck was strewed with corpses. Several of her portholes were knocked into one, and one of her eighteen-pounder guns had been thrown right back on to her breech, and pointed straight up to the sky. The thin line of marines still loaded and fired, but half the guns were silent, and their crews were piled thickly round them.

"Stand by to repel boarders!" yelled the captain.

"Cutlasses, lads, cutlasses!" roared Wharton.

"Hold your volley till they touch!" cried the captain of marines.

The huge loom of the Frenchman was seen bursting through the smoke. Thick clusters of boarders hung upon her sides and shrouds. A final broad-side leapt from her ports, and the mainmast of the *Leda*, snapping short off a few feet above the deck, spun into the air and crashed down upon the port guns, killing ten men and putting the whole battery out of action. An instant later the two ships scraped together, and the starboard bower anchor of the *Gloire* caught the mizzen-chains of the *Leda* upon the port side. With a yell the black swarm of boarders steadied themselves for a spring.

But their feet were never to reach that blood-stained deck. From some where there came a well-aimed whiff of grape, and another, and another. The English marines and seamen, waiting with cutlass and musket behind the silent guns, saw with amazement the dark masses thinning and shredding away. At the same time the port broadside of the Frenchman burst into a roar.

"Clear away the wreck!" roared the captain. "What the devil are they firing at?"

"Get the guns clear!" panted the lieutenant. "We'll do them yet, boys!"

The wreckage was torn and hacked and splintered until first one gun and then another roared into action again. The Frenchman's anchor had been cut away, and the *Leda* had worked herself free from that fatal hug. But now, suddenly, there was a scurry up the shrouds of the *Gloire*, and a hundred Englishmen were shouting themselves hoarse: "They're running! They're running! They're running!"

And it was true. The Frenchman had ceased to fire, and was intent only upon clapping on every sail that he could carry. But that shouting hundred could not claim it all as their own. As the smoke cleared it was not difficult to see the reason. The ships had gained the mouth of the estuary during the fight, and there, about four miles out to sea, was the *Leda's* consort bearing down under full sail to the sound of the guns. Captain de Milon had done his part for one day, and presently the *Gloire* was drawing off swiftly to the north, while the *Dido* was bowling along at her skirts, rattling away with her bow-chasers, until a headland hid them both from view.

But the Leda lay sorely stricken, with her mainmast gone, her bulwarks shattered, her mizzen-topmast and gaff shot away, her sails like a beggar's rags, and a hundred of her crew dead and wounded. Close beside her a mass of wreckage floated upon the waves. It was the stern-post of a mangled vessel, and across it, in white letters on a black ground, was printed, "*The Slapping Sal.*"

"By the Lord! it was the brig that saved us!" cried Mr. Wharton. "Hudson brought her into action with the Frenchman, and was blown out of the water by a broadside!"

The little captain turned on his heel and paced up and down the deck. Already his crew were plugging the shot-holes, knotting and splicing and mending. When he came back, the lieutenant saw a softening of the stern lines about his eyes and mouth.

"Are they all gone?"

"Every man. They must have sunk with the wreck."

The two officers looked down at the sinister name, and at the stump of wreckage which floated in the discoloured water. Something black washed to and fro beside a splintered gaff and a tangle of halliards. It was the outrageous ensign, and near it a scarlet cap was floating.

"He was a villain, but he was a Briton!" said the captain at last. "He lived like a dog, but, by God, he died like a man!"

Sir Arthur Conan Doyle's Napoleonic Library

My Napoleonic Library

I am rather proud of my collection of Napoleonic military memoirs. There is a story told of an illiterate millionaire who gave a wholesale dealer an order for a copy of all books in any language treating of any aspect of Napoleon's career. He thought it would fill a case in his library. He was somewhat taken aback, however, when in a few weeks he received a message from the dealer that he had got 40,000 volumes, and awaited instructions as to whether he should send them on as an instalment, or wait for a complete set. The figures may not be exact, but at least they bring home the impossibility of exhausting the subject, and the danger of losing one's self for years in a huge labyrinth of reading, which may end by leaving no very definite impression upon your mind. But one might, perhaps, take a corner of it, as I have done here in the military memoirs, and there one might hope to get some finality.

Here is Marbot at this end—the first of all soldier books in the world. This is the complete three-volume French edition, with red and gold cover, smart and debonair like its author. Here he is in one frontispiece with his pleasant, round, boyish face, as a captain of his beloved Chasseurs. And here in the other is the grizzled old bull-dog as a full general, looking as full of fight as ever. It was a real blow to me when some one began to throw doubts upon the authenticity of Marbot's memoirs. Homer may be dissolved into a crowd of skin-clad bards. Even Shakespeare may be jostled in his throne of honour by plausible Baconians; but the human, the gallant, the inimitable Marbot! His book is that which gives us the best picture by far of the Napoleonic soldiers, and to me they are even more interesting than their great leader, though his must ever be the most singular figure in history. But those soldiers, with their huge shakoes, their hairy knapsacks, and their hearts of steel—what men they were! And what a latent power there must be in this French nation which could go on pouring out the blood of its sons for twenty-three years with hardly a pause!

It took all that time to work off the hot ferment which the Revolution had left in men's veins. And they were not exhausted, for the very last fight which the French fought was the finest of all. Proud as we are of our infantry at Waterloo, it was really with the French cavalry that the greenest laurels of that great epic rested. They got the better of our own cavalry, they took our guns again and again, they swept a large portion of our allies from the field, and finally they rode off unbroken, and as full of fight as ever. Read Gronow's *Memoirs*, that chatty little yellow volume yonder which brings all that age back to us more vividly than any more pretentious work, and you will find the chivalrous admiration which our officers expressed at the fine performance of the French horsemen.

It must be admitted that, looking back upon history, we have not always been good allies, nor yet generous co-partners in the battlefield. The first is the fault of our politics, where one party rejoices to break what the other has bound. The makers of the Treaty are staunch enough, as the Tories were under Pitt and Castlereagh, or the Whigs at the time of Queen Anne, but sooner or later the others must come in. At the end of the Marlborough wars we suddenly vamped up a peace and, left our allies in the lurch, on account of a change in domestic politics. We did the same with Frederick the Great, and would have done it in the Napoleonic days if Fox could have controlled the country. And as to our partners of the battlefield, how little we have ever said that is hearty as to the splendid staunchness of the Prussians at Waterloo. You have to read the Frenchman, Houssaye, to get a central view and to understand the part they played. Think of old Blucher, seventy years old, and ridden over by a regiment of charging cavalry the day before, yet swearing that he would come to Wellington if he had to be strapped to his horse. He nobly redeemed his promise.

The loss of the Prussians at Waterloo was not far short of our own. You would not know it, to read our historians. And then the abuse of our Belgian allies has been overdone. Some of them fought splendidly, and one brigade of infantry had a share in the critical instant when the battle was turned. This also you would not learn from British sources. Look at our Portuguese allies also! They trained into magnificent troops, and one of Wellington's earnest desires was to have ten thousand of them for his Waterloo campaign. It was a Portuguese who first topped the rampart of Badajos. They have never had their due credit, nor have the Spaniards either, for, though often defeated, it was their unconquerable pertinacity which played a great part in the struggle. No; I do not think that we are very amiable partners, but I suppose that all national history may be open to a similar charge.

It must be confessed that Marbot's details are occasionally a little hard to believe. Never in the pages of Lever has there been such a series of hairbreadth escapes and dare-devil exploits. Surely he stretched it a little sometimes. You may remember his adventure at Eylau—I think it was Eylau—how a cannon-ball, striking the top of his helmet, paralyzed him by the concussion of his spine; and how, on a Russian officer running forward to cut him down, his horse bit the man's face nearly off. This was the famous charger which savaged everything until Marbot, having bought it for next to nothing, cured it by thrusting a boiling leg of mutton into its mouth when it tried to bite him. It certainly does need a robust faith to get over these incidents. And yet, when one reflects upon the hundreds of battles and skirmishes which a Napoleonic officer must have endured—how they must have been the uninterrupted routine of his life from the first dark hair upon his lip to the first grey one upon his head, it is presumptuous to say what may or may not have been possible in such unparalleled careers. At any rate, be it fact or fiction—fact it is, in my opinion, with some artistic touching up of the high lights—there are few books which I could not spare from my shelves better than the memoirs of the gallant Marbot.

I dwell upon this particular book because it is the best; but take the whole line, and there is not one which is not full of interest. Marbot gives you the point of view of the officer. So does De Ségur and De Fezensac and Colonel Gonville, each in some different branch of the service. But some are from the pens of the men in the ranks, and they are even more graphic than the others. Here, for example, are the papers of good old Cogniet, who was a grenadier of the Guard, and could neither read nor write until after the great wars were over. A tougher soldier never went into battle. Here is Sergeant Bourgogne, also with his dreadful account of that nightmare campaign in Russia, and the gallant Chevillet, trumpeter of Chasseurs, with his matter-of-fact account of all that he saw, where the daily *combat* is sandwiched in betwixt the real business of the day, which was foraging for his frugal breakfast and supper. There is no better writing, and no easier reading, than the records of these men of action.

A Briton cannot help asking himself, as he realizes what men these were, what would have happened if 150,000 Cogniets and Bourgognes, with Marbots to lead them, and the great captain of all time in the prime of his vigour at their head, had made their landing in Kent? For months it was touch-and-go. A single naval slip which left the Channel clear would have been followed by an embarkation from Boulogne, which had been brought by constant practice to so incredibly fine a point that the last horse was aboard within two hours of the start. Any evening might have seen the whole host upon the Pevensey Flats. What then? We know what Humbert did with a handful of men in Ireland, and the story is not reassuring.

Conquest, of course, is unthinkable. The world in arms could not do that. But Napoleon never thought of the conquest of Britain. He has expressly disclaimed it. What he did contemplate was a gigantic raid in which he would do so much damage that for years to come England would be occupied at home in picking up the pieces, instead of having energy to spend abroad in thwarting his Continental plans.

Portsmouth, Plymouth, and Sheerness in flames, with London either levelled to the ground or ransomed at his own figure—that was a more feasible programme. Then, with the united fleets of conquered Europe at his back, enormous armies and an inexhaustible treasury, swollen with the ransom of Britain, he could turn to that conquest of America which would win back the old colonies of France and leave him master of the world. If the worst happened and he had met his Waterloo upon the South Downs, he would have done again what he did in Egypt and once more in Russia: hurried back to France in a swift vessel, and still had force enough to hold his own upon the Continent. It would, no doubt, have been a big stake to lay upon the table—150,000 of his best—but he could play again if he lost; while, if he won, he cleared the board. A fine game—if little Nelson had not stopped it, and with one blow fixed the edge of salt water as the limit of Napoleon's power.

There's the cast of a medal on the top of that cabinet which will bring it all close home to you. It is taken from the die of the medal which Napoleon had arranged to issue on the day that he reached London. It serves, at any rate, to show that his great muster was not a bluff, but that he really did mean serious business. On one side is his head. On the other France is engaged in strangling and throwing to earth a curious fish-tailed creature, which stands for perfidious Albion. *"Frappé à Londres"* is printed on one part of it, and *"La Descente dans Angleterre"* upon another. Struck to commemorate a conquest, it remains now as a souvenir of a fiasco. But it was a close call.

By the way, talking of Napoleon's flight from Egypt, did you ever see a curious little book called, if I remember right, *Intercepted Letters*? No; I have no copy upon this shelf, but a friend is more fortunate. It shows the almost incredible hatred which existed at the end of the eighteenth century between the two nations, descending even to the most petty personal annoyance. On this occasion the British Government intercepted a mailbag of letters coming from French officers in Egypt to their friends at home, and they either published them, or at least allowed them to be published, in the hope, no doubt, of causing domestic complications. Was ever a more despicable action? But who knows what other injuries had been inflicted to draw forth such a retaliation? I have myself seen a burned and mutilated British mail lying where De Wet had left it; but suppose the refinement of his vengeance had gone so far as to publish it, what a thunder-bolt it might have been!

As to the French officers, I have read their letters, though even after a century one had a feeling of guilt when one did so. But, on the whole, they are a credit to the writers, and give the impression of a noble and chivalrous set of men. Whether they were all addressed to the right people is another matter, and therein lay the poisoned sting of this most un-British affair. As to the monstrous things which were done upon the other side, remember the arrest of all the poor British tourists and commercials who chanced to be in France when the war was renewed in 1803. They had run over in all trust and confidence for a little outing and change of air. They certainly got it, for Napoleon's steel grip fell upon them, and they rejoined their families in 1814. He must have had a heart of adamant and a will of iron. Look at his conduct over the naval prisoners. The natural proceeding would have been to exchange them. For some reason he did not think it good policy to do so. All representations from the British Government were set aside, save in the case of the higher officers. Hence the miseries of the hulks and the dreadful prison barracks in England. Hence also the unhappy idlers of Verdun. What splendid loyalty there must have been in those humble Frenchmen which never allowed them for one instant to turn bitterly upon the author of all their great misfortunes. It is all brought vividly home by the description of their prisons given by Borrow in *Lavengro*. This is the passage—

> What a strange appearance had those mighty *casernes*, with their blank, blind walls, without windows or grating, and their slanting roofs, out of which, through orifices where the tiles had been removed, would be protruded dozens of grim heads, feasting their prison-sick

eyes on the wide expanse of country unfolded from their airy height. Ah! there was much misery in those *casernes*; and from those roofs, doubtless, many a wistful look was turned in the direction of lovely France. Much had the poor inmates to endure, and much to complain of, to the disgrace of England be it said—of England, in general so kind and bountiful. Rations of carrion meat, and bread from which I have seen the very hounds occasionally turn away, were unworthy entertainment even for the most ruffian enemy, when helpless and captive; and such, alas! was the fare in those *casernes*. And then, those visits, or rather ruthless inroads, called in the slang of the place 'straw-plait hunts,' when in pursuit of a contraband article, which the prisoners, in order to procure themselves a few of the necessaries and comforts of existence, were in the habit of making, red-coated battalions were marched into the prisons, who, with the bayonet's point, carried havoc and ruin into every poor convenience which ingenious wretchedness had been endeavouring to raise around it; and then the triumphant exit with the miserable booty, and worst of all, the accursed bonfire, on the barrack parade of the plait contraband, beneath the view of glaring eyeballs from those lofty roofs, amid the hurrahs of the troops frequently drowned in the curses poured down from above like a tempest-shower, or in the terrific war-whoop of '*Vive l'Empereur!*'

There is a little vignette of Napoleon's men in captivity. Here is another which is worth preserving of the bearing of his veterans when wounded on the field of battle. It is from Mercer's recollections of the Battle of Waterloo. Mercer had spent the day firing case into the French cavalry at ranges from fifty to two hundred yards, losing two-thirds of his own battery in the process. In the evening he had a look at some of his own grim handiwork.

I had satisfied my curiosity at Hougoumont, and was retracing my steps up the hill when my attention was called to a group of wounded Frenchmen by the calm, dignified, and soldier-like oration addressed by one of them to the rest. I cannot, like Livy, compose a fine harangue for my hero, and, of course, I could not retain the precise words, but the import of them was to exhort them to bear their sufferings with fortitude; not to repine, like women or children, at what every soldier should have made up his mind to suffer as the fortune of war, but above all, to remember that they were surrounded by Englishmen, before whom they ought to be doubly careful not to disgrace themselves by displaying such an unsoldier-like want of fortitude.

The speaker was sitting on the ground with his lance stuck upright beside him—an old veteran with thick bushy, grizzly beard, countenance like a lion—a lancer of the old guard, and no doubt had fought in many a field. One hand was flourished in the air as he spoke, the other, severed at the wrist, lay on the earth beside him; one ball (case-shot, probably) had entered his body, another had broken his leg. His suffering, after a night of exposure so mangled, must have been great; yet he betrayed it not. His bearing was that of a Roman, or perhaps an Indian warrior, and I could fancy him concluding appropriately his speech in the words of the Mexican king, 'And I too; am I on a bed of roses?'

What a load of moral responsibility upon one man! But his mind was insensible to moral responsibility. Surely if it had not been it must have been crushed beneath it. Now, if you want to understand the character of Napoleon—but surely I must take a fresh start before I launch on so portentous a subject as that.

But before I leave the military men let me, for the credit of my own country, after that infamous incident of the letters, indicate these six well-thumbed volumes of Napier's *History*. This is the story of the great Peninsular War, by one who fought through it himself, and in no history has a more chivalrous and manly account been given of one's enemy. Indeed, Napier seems to me to push it too far, for his admiration appears to extend not only to the gallant soldiers who opposed him, but to the character and to the ultimate aims of their leader. He was, in fact, a political follower of Charles James Fox, and his heart seems to have been with the enemy even at the moment when he led his men most desperately against them. In the verdict of history the action of those men who, in their honest zeal for freedom, inflamed somewhat by political strife, turned against their own country, when it was in truth the Champion of Freedom, and approved of a military despot of the most uncompromising kind, seems wildly foolish.

But if Napier's politics may seem strange, his soldiering was splendid, and his prose among the very best that I know. There are passages in that work—the one which describes the breach of Badajos, that of the charge of the Fusiliers at Albuera, and that of the French advance at Fuentes d'Onoro—which once read haunt the mind for ever. The book is a worthy monument of a great national epic. Alas! for the pregnant sentence with which it closes, "So ended the great war, and with it all memory of the services of the veterans." Was there ever a British war of which the same might not have been written?

The quotation which I have given from Mercer's book turns my thoughts in the direction of the British military reminiscences of that period, less numerous, less varied, and less central than the French, but full of character and interest all the same. I have found that if I am turned loose in a large library, after hesitating over covers for half an hour or so, it is usually a book of soldier memoirs which I take down. Man is never so interesting as when he is thoroughly in earnest, and no one is so earnest as he whose life is at stake upon the event. But of all types of soldier the best is the man who is keen upon his work, and yet has general culture which enables him to see that work in its due perspective, and to sympathize with the gentler aspirations of mankind. Such a man is Mercer, an ice-cool fighter, with a sense of discipline and decorum which prevented him from moving when a bombshell was fizzing between his feet, and yet a man of thoughtful and philosophic temperament, with a weakness for solitary musings, for children, and for flowers. He has written for all time the classic account of a great battle, seen from the point of view of a battery commander. Many others of Wellington's soldiers wrote their personal reminiscences. You can get them, as I have them there, in the pleasant abridgement of *Wellington's Men* (admirably edited by Dr. Fitchett)—Anton the Highlander, Harris the rifleman, and Kincaid of the same corps. It is a most singular fate which has made an Australian nonconformist clergyman the most sympathetic and eloquent reconstructor of those old heroes, but it is a noble example of that unity of the British race, which in fifty scattered lands still mourns or rejoices over the same historic record.

And just one word, before I close down this over-long and too discursive chatter, on the subject of yonder twin red volumes which flank the shelf. They are Maxwell's *History of Wellington*, and I do not think you will find a better or more readable one. The reader must ever feel towards the great soldier what his own immediate followers felt, respect rather than affection. One's failure to attain a more affectionate emotion is alleviated by the knowledge that it was the last thing which he invited or desired. "Don't be a damned fool, sir!" was his exhortation to the good citizen who had paid him a compliment. It was a curious, callous nature, brusque and limited. The hardest huntsman learns to love his hounds, but he showed no affection and a good deal of contempt for the men who had been his instruments. "They are the scum of the earth," said he. "All English soldiers are fellows who have enlisted for drink. That is the plain fact—they have all enlisted for drink." His general orders were full of undeserved reproaches at a time when the most lavish praise could hardly have met the real deserts of his army. When the wars were done he saw little, save in his official capacity, of his old comrades-in-arms. And yet, from major-general to drummer-boy, he was the man whom they would all have elected to serve under, had the work to be done once more. As one of them said, "The sight of his long nose was worth ten thousand men on a field of battle." They were themselves a leathery breed, and cared little for the gentler amenities so long as the French were well drubbed.

His mind, which was comprehensive and alert in warfare, was singularly limited in civil affairs. As a statesman he was so constant an example of devotion to duty, self-sacrifice, and high disinterested character, that the country was the better for his presence. But he fiercely opposed Catholic Emancipation, the Reform Bill, and everything upon which our modern life is founded. He could never be brought to see that a pyramid should stand on its base and not on its apex, and that the larger the pyramid, the broader should be the base. Even in military affairs he was averse from every change, and I know of no improvements which came from his initiative during all those years when his authority was supreme. The floggings which broke a man's spirit and self-respect, the leathern stock which hampered his movements, all the old traditional regime found a champion in him. On the other hand, he strongly opposed the introduction of the percussion cap as opposed to the flint and steel in the musket. Neither in war nor in politics did he rightly judge the future.

And yet in reading his letters and dispatches, one is surprised sometimes at the incisive thought and its vigorous expression. There is a passage in which he describes the way in which his soldiers would occasionally desert into some town which he was besieging. He writes:

> They knew that they must be taken, for when we lay our bloody hands upon a place we are sure to take it, sooner or later; but they liked being dry and under cover, and then that extraordinary caprice which always pervades the English character! Our deserters are very badly treated by the enemy; those who deserted in France were treated as the lowest of mortals, slaves and scavengers. Nothing but English caprice can account for it; just what makes our noblemen associate with stage-coach drivers, and become stage-coach drivers themselves.

After reading that passage, how often does the phrase "the extraordinary caprice which always pervades the English character" come back as one observes some fresh manifestation of it!

But let not my last note upon the great duke be a carping one. Rather let my final sentence be one which will remind you of his frugal and abstemious life, his carpetless floor and little camp bed, his precise courtesy which left no humblest letter unanswered, his courage which never flinched, his tenacity which never faltered, his sense of duty which made his life one long unselfish effort on behalf of what seemed to him to be the highest interest of the State. Go down and stand by the huge granite sarcophagus in the dim light of the crypt of St. Paul's, and in the hush of that austere spot, cast back your mind to the days when little England alone stood firm against the greatest soldier and the greatest army that the world has ever known. Then you feel what this dead man stood for, and you pray that we may still find such another amongst us when the clouds gather once again.

You see that the literature of Waterloo is well represented in my small military library. Of all books dealing with the personal view of the matter, I think that *Siborne's Letters*, which is a collection of the narratives of surviving officers made by Siborne in the year 1827, is the most interesting. Gronow's account is also very vivid and interesting. Of the strategical narratives, Houssaye's book is my favourite. Taken from the French point of view, it gets the actions of the allies in truer perspective than any English or German account can do; but there is a fascination about that great combat which makes every narrative that bears upon it of enthralling interest.

Wellington used to say that too much was made of it, and that one would imagine that the British Army had never fought a battle before. It was a characteristic speech, but it must be admitted that the British Army never had, as a matter of fact, for many centuries fought a battle which was finally decisive of a great European war. There lies the perennial interest of the incident, that it was the last act of that long-drawn drama, and that to the very fall of the curtain no man could tell how the play would end—"the nearest run thing that ever you saw"—that was the victor's description. It is a singular thing that during those twenty-five years of incessant fighting the material and methods of warfare made so little progress. So far as I know, there was no great change in either between 1789 and 1805. The breech-loader, heavy artillery, the ironclad, all great advances in the art of war, have been invented in time of peace. There are some improvements so obvious, and at the same time so valuable, that it is extraordinary that they were not adopted. Signalling, for example, whether by heliograph or by flag-waving, would have made an immense difference in the Napoleonic campaigns. The principle of the semaphore was well known, and Belgium, with its numerous windmills, would seem to be furnished with natural semaphores. Yet in the four days during which the campaign of Waterloo was fought, the whole scheme of military operations on both sides was again and again imperilled, and finally in the case of the French brought to utter ruin by lack of that intelligence which could so easily have been conveyed. June 18th was at intervals a sunshiny day—a four-inch glass mirror would have put Napoleon in communication with Gruchy, and the whole history of Europe might have been altered. Wellington himself suffered dreadfully from defective information which might have been easily supplied. The unexpected presence of the French army was first discovered at four in the morning of June 15. It was of enormous importance to get the news rapidly to Wellington at Brussels that he might instantly concentrate his scattered forces on the best line of resistance-—yet, through the folly of sending only a single messenger, this vital information did not reach him until three in the afternoon, the distance being thirty miles. Again, when Blücher was defeated at Ligny on the 16th, it was of enormous importance that Wellington should know at once the line of his retreat so as to prevent the French from driving a wedge between them. The single Prussian officer who was despatched with this information was wounded, and never reached his destination, and it was only next day that Wellington learned the Prussian plans. On what tiny things does History depend!

The contemplation of my fine little regiment of French military memoirs had brought me to the question of Napoleon himself, and you see that I have a very fair line dealing with him also. There is Scott's life, which is not entirely a success. His ink was too precious to be shed in such a venture. But here are the three volumes of the physician Bourrienne—that Bourrienne who knew him so well. Does any one ever know a man so well as his doctor? They are quite excellent and admirably translated. Meneval also—the patient Meneval—who wrote for untold hours to dictation at ordinary talking speed, and yet was expected to be legible and to make no mistakes. At least his master could not fairly criticize his legibility, for is it not on record that when Napoleon's holograph account of an engagement was laid before the President of the Senate, the worthy man thought that it was a drawn plan of the battle? Meneval survived his master and has left an excellent and intimate account of him. There is Constant's account, also written from that point of view in which it is proverbial that no man is a hero. But of all the vivid terrible pictures of Napoleon the most haunting is by a man who never saw him and whose book was not directly dealing with him. I mean Taine's account of him, in the first volume of *Les Origines de la France Contemporaine*. You can never forget it when once you have read it. He produces his effect in a wonderful, and to me a novel, way. He does not, for example, say in mere crude words that Napoleon had a more than medieval Italian cunning. He presents a succession of documents—gives a series of contemporary instances to prove it. Then, having got that fixed in your head by blow after blow, he passes on to another phase of his character, his cold-hearted amorousness, his power of work, his spoiled child wilfulness, or some other quality, and piles up his illustrations of that. Instead, for example, of saying that the Emperor had a marvellous memory for detail, we have the account of the head of Artillery laying the list of all the guns in France before his master, who looked over it and remarked, "Yes, but you have omitted two in a fort near Dieppe." So the man is gradually etched in with indelible ink. It is a wonderful figure of which you are conscious in the end, the figure of an archangel, but surely of an archangel of darkness.

We will, after Taine's method, take one fact and let it speak for itself. Napoleon left a legacy in a codicil to his will to a man who tried to assassinate Wellington. There is the medieval

Italian again! He was no more a Corsican than the Englishman born in India is a Hindu. Read the lives of the Borgias, the Sforzas, the Medicis, and of all the lustful, cruel, broad-minded, art-loving, talented despots of the little Italian States, including Genoa, from which the Buonapartes migrated. There at once you get the real descent of the man, with all the stigmata clear upon him—the outward calm, the inward passion, the layer of snow above the volcano, everything which characterized the old despots of his native land, the pupils of Machiavelli, but all raised to the dimensions of genius. You can whitewash him as you may, but you will never get a layer thick enough to cover the stain of that cold-blooded deliberate endorsement of his noble adversary's assassination.

Another book which gives an extraordinarily vivid picture of the man is this one—the Memoirs of Madame de Remusat. She was in daily contact with him at the Court, and she studied him with those quick critical eyes of a clever woman, the most unerring things in life when they are not blinded by love. If you have read those pages, you feel that you know him as if you had yourself seen and talked with him. His singular mixture of the small and the great, his huge sweep of imagination, his very limited knowledge, his intense egotism, his impatience of obstacles, his boorishness, his gross impertinence to women, his diabolical playing upon the weak side of every one with whom he came in contact—they make up among them one of the most striking of historical portraits.

Most of my books deal with the days of his greatness, but here, you see, is a three-volume account of those weary years at St. Helena. Who can help pitying the mewed eagle? And yet if you play the great game you must pay a stake. This was the same man who had a royal duke shot in a ditch because he was a danger to his throne. Was not he himself a danger to every throne in Europe? Why so harsh a retreat as St. Helena, you say? Remember that he had been put in a milder one before, that he had broken away from it, and that the lives of fifty thousand men had paid for the mistaken leniency. All this is forgotten now, and the pathetic picture of the modern Prometheus chained to his rock and devoured by the vultures of his own bitter thoughts, is the one impression which the world has retained. It is always so much easier to follow the emotions than the reason, especially where a cheap magnanimity and second-hand generosity are involved. But reason must still insist that Europe's treatment of Napoleon was not vindictive, and that Hudson Lowe was a man who tried to live up to the trust which had been committed to him by his country.

It was certainly not a post from which any one would hope for credit. If he were slack and easy-going all would be well. But there would be the chance of a second flight with its consequences. If he were strict and assiduous he would be assuredly represented as a petty tyrant. "I am glad when you are on outpost," said Lowe's general in some campaign, "for then I am sure of a sound rest." He was on outpost at St. Helena, and because he was true to his duties Europe (France included) had a sound rest. But he purchased it at the price of his own reputation. The greatest schemer in the world, having nothing else on which to vent his energies, turned them all to the task of vilifying his guardian. It was natural enough that he who had never known control should not brook it now. It is natural also that sentimentalists who have not thought of the details should take the Emperor's point of view. What is deplorable, however, is that our own people should be misled by one-sided accounts, and that they should throw to the wolves a man who was serving his country in a post of anxiety and danger, with such responsibility upon him as few could ever have endured. Let them remember Montholon's remark: "An angel from heaven would not have satisfied us." Let them recall also that Lowe with ample material never once troubled to state his own case. *"Je fais mon devoir et suis indifférent pour le reste,"* said he, in his interview with the Emperor. They were no idle words.

Apart from this particular epoch, French literature, which is so rich in all its branches, is richest of all in its memoirs. Whenever there was anything of interest going forward there was always some kindly gossip who knew all about it, and was ready to set it down for the benefit of posterity. Our own history has not nearly enough of these charming sidelights. Look at our sailors in the Napoleonic wars, for example. They played an epoch-making part. For nearly twenty years Freedom was a Refugee upon the seas. Had our navy been swept away, then all Europe would have been one organized despotism. At times everybody was against us, fighting against their own direct interests under the pressure of that terrible hand. We fought on the waters with the French, with the Spaniards, with the Danes, with the Russians, with the Turks, even with our American kinsmen. Middies grew into post-captains, and admirals into dotards during that prolonged struggle. And what have we in literature to show for it all? Marryat's novels, many of which are founded upon personal experience, Nelson's and Collingwood's letters, Lord Cochrane's biography—that is about all. I wish we had more of Collingwood, for he wielded a fine pen. Do you remember the sonorous opening of his Trafalgar message to his captains?—

The ever to be lamented death of Lord Viscount Nelson, Duke of Bronte, the Commander-in-Chief, who fell in the action of the 21st, in the arms of Victory, covered with glory, whose memory will be ever dear to the British Navy and the British Nation; whose zeal for the honour of his king and for the interests of his country will be ever held up as a shining example for a British seaman—leaves to me a duty to return thanks, etc., etc.

It was a worthy sentence to carry such a message, written too in a raging tempest, with sinking vessels all around him. But in the main it is a poor crop from such a soil. No doubt our sailors were too busy to do much writing, but none the less one wonders that among so many thousands there were not some to understand what a treasure their experiences would be to their descendants. I can call to mind the old three-deckers which used to rot in Portsmouth Harbour, and I have often thought, could they tell their tales, what a missing chapter in our literature they could supply. Agna faccum dunt digna feumsan heniscilit ad ero esed magniatum dolenisl ulput er am nonsed ero odolore con eum vel dunt dolore feugue

LEONAUR

ALSO FROM LEONAUR
AVAILABLE IN SOFTCOVER OR HARDCOVER WITH DUST JACKET

LIGHT BOB by *Robert Blakeney*—The experiences of a young officer in H.M 28th & 36th regiments of the British Infantry during the Peninsular Campaign of the Napoleonic Wars 1804 - 1814.

NAPOLEON'S RUSSIAN CAMPAIGN by *Philippe Henri de Segur*—The Invasion, Battles and Retreat by an Aide-de-Camp on the Emperor's Staff

SWORDS OF HONOUR by *Henry Newbolt & Stanley L. Wood*—The Careers of Six Outstanding Officers from the Napoleonic Wars, the Wars for India and the American Civil War. Illustrated.

HUSSAR IN WINTER by *Alexander Gordon*—A British Cavalry Officer during the retreat to Corunna in the Peninsular campaign of the Napoleonic Wars.

THE LIFE OF THE REAL BRIGADIER GERARD VOLUME 1 THE YOUNG HUSSAR 1782 - 1807 by *Jean-Baptiste De Marbot*—A French Cavalryman Of the Napoleonic Wars at Marengo, Austerlitz, Jena, Eylau & Friedland.

THE LIFE OF THE REAL BRIGADIER GERARD VOLUME 2 IMPERIAL AIDE-DE-CAMP 1807 - 1811 by *Jean-Baptiste De Marbot*—A French Cavalryman of the Napoleonic Wars at Saragossa, Landshut, Eckmuhl, Ratisbon, Aspern-Essling, Wagram, Busaco & Torres Vedras.

THE LIFE OF THE REAL BRIGADIER GERARD VOLUME 3 COLONEL OF CHASSEURS 1811 - 1815 by *Jean-Baptiste De Marbot*—A French Cavalryman in the retreat from Moscow, Lutzen, Bautzen, Katzbach, Leipzig, Hanau & Waterloo.

RIFLEMAN COSTELLO by *Edward Costello*—The adventures of a soldier of the 95th (Rifles) in the Peninsular & Waterloo Campaigns of the Napoleonic wars.

WITH THE LIGHT DIVISION by *John H. Cooke*—The Experiences of an Officer of the 43rd Light Infantry in the Peninsula and South of France During the Napoleonic Wars.

COLBORNE: A SINGULAR TALENT FOR WAR by *John Colborne*—The Napoleonic Wars Career of One of Wellington's Most Highly Valued Officers in Egypt, Holland, Italy, the Peninsula and at Waterloo.

A VOICE FROM WATERLOO by *Edward Cotton*—The Personal Experiences of a British Cavalryman Who Became a Battlefield Guide and Authority on the Campaign of 1815.

LEONAUR

ALSO FROM LEONAUR

AVAILABLE IN SOFTCOVER OR HARDCOVER WITH DUST JACKET

WELLINGTON AND THE PYRENEES CAMPAIGN VOLUME I: FROM VI-TORIA TO THE BIDASSOA *by F. C. Beatson*—The final phase of the campaign in the Iberian Peninsula.

WELLINGTON AND THE INVASION OF FRANCE VOLUME II: THE BIDAS-SOA TO THE BATTLE OF THE NIVELLE *by F. C. Beatson*—The second of Beatson's series on the fall of Revolutionary France published by Leonaur, the reader is once again taken into the centre of Wellington's strategic and tactical genius.

WELLINGTON AND THE FALL OF FRANCE VOLUME III: THE GAVES AND THE BATTLE OF ORTHEZ by *F. C. Beatson*—This final chapter of F. C. Beatson's brilliant trilogy shows the 'captain of the age' at his most inspired and makes all three books essential additions to any Peninsular War library.

NAVAL BATTLES OF THE NAPOLEONIC WARS *by W. H. Fitchett*—Cape St.Vincent, the Nile, Cadiz, Copenhagen, Trafalgar & Others

SERGEANT GUILLEMARD: THE MAN WHO SHOT NELSON? *by Robert Guillemard*—A Soldier of the Infantry of the French Army of Napoleon on Campaign Throughout Europe

WITH THE GUARDS ACROSS THE PYRENEES by *Robert Batty*—The Experiences of a British Officer of Wellington's Army During the Battles for the Fall of Napoleonic France, 1813.

A STAFF OFFICER IN THE PENINSULA *by E. W. Buckham*—An Officer of the British Staff Corps Cavalry During the Peninsula Campaign of the Napoleonic Wars

THE LEIPZIG CAMPAIGN: 1813—NAPOLEON AND THE "BATTLE OF THE NATIONS" *by F. N. Maude*—Colonel Maude's analysis of Napoleon's campaign of 1813.

BUGEAUD: A PACK WITH A BATON by *Thomas Robert Bugeaud*—The Early Campaigns of a Soldier of Napoleon's Army Who Would Become a Marshal of France.

TWO LEONAUR ORIGINALS

SERGEANT NICOL by *Daniel Nicol*—The Experiences of a Gordon Highlander During the Napoleonic Wars in Egypt, the Peninsula and France.

WATERLOO RECOLLECTIONS by *Frederick Llewellyn*—Rare First Hand Accounts, Letters, Reports and Retellings from the Campaign of 1815.